A HAUNTING ON THE HILL

BOOKS BY ELIZABETH HAND

CASS NEARY NOVELS

A
HAUNTING
ON THE
HILL

ELIZABETH HAND

MULHOLLAND BOOKS

Little, Brown and Company
New York Boston London

Copyright © 2023 by Elizabeth Hand, and Laurence Jackson Hyman for the children of Shirley Jackson

Mulholland Books / Little, Brown and Company
Hachette Book Group
1290 Avenue of the Americas, New York, NY 10104
mulhollandbooks.com

First Edition: October 2023

Mulholland Books is an imprint of Little, Brown and Company, a division of Hachette Book Group, Inc. The Mulholland Books name and logo are trademarks of Hachette Book Group, Inc.

The Hachette Speakers Bureau provides a wide range of authors for speaking events. To find out more, go to hachettespeakersbureau.com or email hachettespeakers @hbgusa.com.

Little, Brown and Company books may be purchased in bulk for business, educational, or promotional use. For information, please contact your local bookseller or the Hachette Book Group Special Markets Department at special.markets@hbgusa.com.

Interior book design by Marie Mundaca

ISBN 9780316527323
LCCN 2023935283

Printing 2, 2023

LSC-C

Printed in the United States of America

In memory of Peter Straub
Beloved friend and tireless guide through the dark

This workaday actuality of ours—with its bricks, its streets, its woods, its hills, its waters—may have queer and, possibly, terrifying holes in it.

—*Walter de la Mare*

A HAUNTING ON THE HILL

PROLOGUE

Most houses sleep, and nearly all of them dream: of conflagrations and celebrations, births and buckled floors; of children's footsteps and clapboards in need of repair, of ailing pets and peeling paint, wakes and weddings and windows that no longer keep out rain and snow but welcome them, furtively, when no one is home to notice.

Hill House neither sleeps nor dreams. Shrouded within its overgrown lawns and sprawling woodlands, the long shadows of mountains and ancient oaks, Hill House watches. Hill House waits.

CHAPTER 1

I left the rental just as the sun poked its head above the nearby mountains, and golden light filled the broad stretch of river that ran alongside the little town. Nisa was still curled up in bed, breathing deeply, her dark curls stuck to her cheek. I brushed them aside but she never stirred. Nisa slept like a child. Unlike me, she was never troubled by nightmares or insomnia. It would be another hour or two before she woke. Longer, maybe. Probably.

I kissed her cheek, breathing in her scent—lilac-and-freesia perfume mingled with my own imported Jasmin et Tabac, one of my few luxuries—and ran my hand along her bare shoulder. I was tempted to crawl back into bed beside her, but I also felt an odd restlessness, a nagging sense that there was somewhere I needed to be. There wasn't—we knew no one around here except for Theresa and Giorgio, and both would be at work in their home offices overlooking the river.

I kissed Nisa again: if she woke, I'd take it as a sign, and remain here. But she didn't wake.

I scrawled a note on a piece of paper—Nisa often forgot to turn her notifications off, she'd be grumpy all morning if a text woke her. Going for a drive, back with provisions. Love you.

I dressed quickly, propelled by an anticipation I couldn't explain. Being in a new place, perhaps, and out of New York City after such a long time.

The night before, we'd polished off a bottle of champagne in our rental, and that was after beers and celebratory shots of twelve-year-old Jura at the bar that Theresa had recommended as the best in this part of upstate. The rental had been Theresa's idea, too. She and her husband, Giorgio, had bought a second home here years ago, but during the pandemic, they'd forsaken their Queens apartment and moved permanently. Ever since, they'd been on me and Nisa and their other friends still in the city to do the same.

"Seriously, Hols, you will love it," Theresa had urged me the night before. "You should have done it years ago, you know that, right?"

"Right," Nisa retorted. She thought Theresa and Giorgio were going insane with boredom, which was likely true. They came down to the city at least once or twice a month, couch-surfing because even for them short-term rentals had become too expensive, and they'd sublet their own beautiful two-bedroom in Sunnyside. "And I should have had a father who left me a million dollars when his ultralight crashed last time he was out at Torrey Pines. Why didn't I *think* of that?"

Nisa smacked herself in the forehead. Theresa smiled ruefully, made a *touché* gesture, and ordered another round for all of us. She and her father had long been estranged. The inheritance was a surprise, and she liked to share her largesse.

Still, Theresa had a point. It *was* beautiful up here. The long winding journey along the river, the city's sprawl giving way first to outer exurbia—apple orchards, pastures repurposed as solar farms, and warehouses, all those not-yet-gentrified, sketchy-seeming river towns, poisoned by brownfields and decades of poverty. Nisa and I had passed a lot of For Sale by Owner signs, in front of houses that seemed too derelict to merit anything but a teardown. And you'd still have to remediate soil made toxic by runoff from mass agriculture and factories that had been shuttered half a century ago.

But after several hours, the long drive had rewarded us with jeweled villages like this one. Little towns long since colonized by self-styled art-ists and artisans who are really just people rich enough to flee the city and call themselves whatever they want. Craft brewers, textile designers, glass artists specializing in bespoke bongs and neti pots. Dog chiroprac-tors. Masons who would demolish a centuries-old fieldstone chimney, number each stone, and then rebuild it, piece by piece, in an adjoining room. People who distilled rare liqueurs from echinacea and comfrey, or made syrup out of white pine needles, or wove intricate rings and brooches from your own hair, charging what I earned as a teacher in a month. A very good month.

I tried not to think about that as I eased my old Camry along Main Street, craning my neck to see if the café was open yet. Nisa and I had chatted with the owner the day before—he was from Queens, too. He'd only been here for six months, but he told us that there were lines outside the café every morning when he arrived to unlock the door.

Apparently, he still kept city hours—it was six a.m., and the place was closed. But the parking lot at the Cup and Saucer, on the outskirts of town, was packed, pickups and SUVs sprawled across the cracked asphalt. I pulled in alongside a tractor-trailer rig and stepped inside, past three guys who stood by the door, talking.

"Morning," one said. He caught my gaze and held it long enough that I felt obligated to smile, though he hadn't.

I grabbed a to-go coffee, heavy on the half-and-half, glanced at the donuts on the counter. I decided to hold off and get some croissants at the café when I returned. They'd cost twice as much but Nisa didn't like donuts. Too bad, since these were homemade and the real deal, fried in lard.

I headed back to the car and for a few minutes sat, sipping my cof-fee as I debated what to do with my restless energy. I didn't want to return and wake Nisa, not without croissants and lattes. But in the past two days, we'd already combed through the village. I remembered that Theresa and Giorgio had also given us ample suggestions for other well-heeled towns nearby.

"Just don't bother with Hillsdale." Giorgio had flicked his fingers, as though Hillsdale were a mosquito buzzing by. "It's a dump."

Theresa had nodded. "There must be a problem with the water supply or something. That whole town's been depressed for as long as we've been coming here. You'd think they'd be happy to expand their tax base, but they really, really hate outsiders."

This seemed odd—that one small town would remain blighted, when surrounded by so many places that had benefited from the real estate boom. But it also suggested that Hillsdale might be someplace where Nisa and I could afford to buy a fixer-upper someday. I decided to do a quick bit of recon. If Hillsdale seemed interesting, we could both head out later to investigate. I finished my coffee, rolled down the window, and drove out of town. I didn't bother to check my phone for directions. Route 9K was the only real road here, and I was on it.

The air had the intoxicating bite of early autumn: goldenrod and dry sedge and the first fallen leaves, cut with the river's scent of fish and mud. With the road straight before me, my mind began to wander. Some people hate summer's end, but I always loved it, the same way I always loved the beginning of the school year as a kid.

That had changed once I started working at a private school in Queens, a job I fell into by chance nearly two decades ago and had never learned to love. I'd had no teaching degree, I wasn't certified, but you don't need that to teach at a private school. Not the one that employed me, anyhow. The pay wasn't great but it wasn't terrible, and the school covered half my health insurance. For years I'd told myself it was only temporary, I'd find theater work again soon.

That had never happened. If I ever complained, Nisa pointed out that I was lucky to have a job even marginally related to my interests. Who wants to employ an unsuccessful playwright? I taught English, and as time passed, I'd at least been able to incorporate plays for the eighth graders, starting with heavily stripped-down versions of Shakespeare—*Macbeth* and *A Midsummer Night's Dream, Twelfth Night,* even *Hamlet.*

The students read the scripts I adapted aloud in class, and sometimes performed them in the small gymnasium that doubled as an events space, for an audience of parents, siblings, and the few teaching colleagues I could guilt into attending, and filled with the overwhelming scents of Axe, Victoria's Secret cologne, and fruity lip gloss, like a Walgreens had exploded. It was all light-years away from what I'd set out to do with my life after I got a BFA in playwriting from a top drama school.

And yet those afternoons with the students did, sometimes, ease my despair. Running lines with them; watching them slowly gain confidence; witnessing the magic that never failed to take over, when they finally put on costumes and makeup and looked at themselves in amazement, realizing they had become someone, something, new and wonderful and strange. For those few hours, I could imagine that it wasn't too late. That I, too, might still be transformed.

Delighted parents, learning of my background, would ask why I didn't write something for the kids to perform. I always begged off, politely. I was terrified to see my work performed, even by kids. I knew this made me seem standoffish, and I never developed any real relationships among my fellow teachers. Instead, I kept up with a few close friends in the theater world. And while I hadn't had a play produced since everything blew up all those years ago, I continued to write. More recently, I'd even begun to apply for grants and fellowships.

I didn't tell Nisa. Instead, over the last few years I'd collected dozens of rejections in secret.

Part of this was superstition—I didn't want to jinx my possible success. Most of it had to do with the fact that Nisa's own career was taking off. She'd always had a small but intense following as a singer-songwriter. As the pandemic faded, she'd begun auditioning for acting jobs as well. No one had cast her yet, but she'd had some callbacks. Obviously I wanted my girlfriend to succeed. But I wanted to succeed, too.

And now, at last, it seemed like I had. In the early summer, I'd received a grant for a new play: the first sign of hope in decades, which made it seem like, at last, things really would be different. Ten thousand dollars, to be used however I wanted to further my work. I'd immediately arranged for a leave of absence from teaching for the fall semester. It wasn't enough money to quit my job (if only!), but it bought me a few months of freedom.

That summer was a wonderful time for me and Nisa, celebrating my good luck with our friends, culminating in this long weekend upstate and this beautiful drive. After all those years of teaching, autumn again felt like possibility—a chance to be someone else, not who I'd been just weeks earlier. A shift in attitude and wardrobe. New shoes; a new career. Being out of the city now, following the river north, made me feel like wonderful things were about to happen. Maybe it wasn't too late for me to dream, to imagine a life that could conceivably align with the one I'd anticipated, twenty years ago, before everything got derailed by Macy-Lee Barton's death.

CHAPTER 2

So here I was, driving aimlessly upstate in early September—too early for leaf-peeping season, too late for the summer people. Second-home owners were still in the city, recovering from Labor Day parties before their kids started school. As I headed toward Hillsdale, there wasn't much traffic. Pickups rushing out to job sites, a few electric vehicles with out-of-state plates.

The morning sun set the river ablaze, igniting the windows of raised ranches that had been turned into Craftsman homes, and a new Tudor-style mansion on a modest lot where the dirt still bore an outline of a double-wide trailer. Behind security gates, expensive subdivisions had sprung up on former farmland. I noticed a sign for a PYO orchard and thought I'd bring Nisa back later. Nisa loved pie.

I sped on, only slowing when the speed limit dropped. A crooked sign stuck out into the road like a hitchhiker's thumb.

ENTERING HILLSDALE

Immediately the road surface deteriorated into chunks of blacktop and frost heaves. A sign flapped in front of a burned-out gas station: UNLEADED .99. I passed a boarded-up dollar store, its vacant parking lot glittering with broken glass. You know your town has hit bottom when even the dollar store has closed.

Hillsdale had no sidewalks. One-story houses with cinder-block steps and bug-pocked siding slumped a few yards from the street, separated by patches of putty-colored grass. Children trudged by on their way to school, heads bowed over phones. At one corner, I rolled to a stop and honked at a skinny gray mutt sprawled in the middle of the road, gnawing its front paw. The dog remained where it was, not even looking up as I edged past.

Giorgio and Theresa were right: Hillsdale was a freaking dump. The thought of slipping back into bed beside Nisa with croissants grew more enticing. I looked in vain for a place to turn around without driving onto somebody's front yard.

But after the next block, things improved. I reached what passed for a downtown. No cross street, though here at least was a sidewalk. And shops, including some that seemed to still be in business. A diner and a real estate agent, a thrift shop, a dingy convenience store that sold lottery tickets and cigarettes.

At the end of the street, an old church missing its steeple stood on a corner. A sign was perched in front of it.

I ATE THIS CHURCH

—SATAN

I frowned, then realized a letter was missing. I HATE THIS CHURCH— SATAN.

I laughed. Nisa would like that. But then I again recalled Macy-Lee Barton, with her talk of ghosts and demon babies, and felt a pinch of unease. *I should get back,* I thought. It was inconceivable there was anything else in Hillsdale worth seeing. And I didn't need to fall back down that dark rabbit hole, not now.

Still, I didn't turn around. I felt light-headed—I should have grabbed one of those donuts at the Cup and Saucer after all—but also oddly unmoored, a compass needle wavering as it seeks north. I lifted my foot from the gas pedal and let the car drift for a few seconds, waiting to see where it took me.

Across from the church stood another gas station, modern pumps incongruous with its ramshackle office. Immediately past that, a dirt road veered off to the left. I glanced at my phone. It had been only half an hour since I'd left the Airbnb. Nina hadn't texted or called. She'd sleep for another hour and a half if I wasn't there to wake her.

I looked in the rearview mirror and saw no other cars. That stupid mutt hadn't moved. Ahead of me, Route 9K was empty, save where the breeze kicked up a dust devil or dead leaves. To the left, the dirt road wound steeply up through a stretch of birch trees, fallen yellow leaves covering its rough surface until it curved and was lost to sight.

What lay beyond? I looked for a street sign but saw nothing. My strange drifty feeling vanished as the anticipation I'd felt earlier returned, just as the sun broke through the trees so that the dirt road gleamed, gold and bronze. I glanced at the dash—plenty of gas—and turned off Route 9K.

CHAPTER 3

It was more a winding mountain trail than a proper road. Barely wide enough for a single vehicle, with ruts so narrow and deep they might have been made by horse-drawn carriages, not cars. Branches scraped my Camry, and I kept having to steer around large rocks exposed by flooding. Old-growth forest, unmaintained road—it didn't look like anyone lived up here.

But I was wrong. After a few miles, the road made a forty-five-degree turn, so unexpectedly that I nearly lost control of the car before I straightened out. After that, the road widened. To my right, the forest had been cleared, the ground graded and leveled. A single-wide mobile home sat surrounded by weedy undergrowth, dotted with clumps of hostas and goldenrod, purple asters, Queen Anne's lace. White birch trees reared protectively around a battered Subaru, and curls of their bark fetched up at the base of the trailer like old newspaper. Something darted out from beneath the Subaru—a cat, I thought.

I slowed, worried it might run across the road, and realized it wasn't a cat but an enormous rabbit. Much too big for a cottontail, bigger even than the white snowshoe hare I'd once glimpsed while skiing in Vermont. But it wasn't a snowshoe hare—it wasn't brown or white but glossy black, with ears long and pointed as garden shears, and copper-colored eyes. For a few seconds we gazed at each other, before it bounded into the trees. I'd started once more to drive, when I realized someone was watching me.

A woman stood in front of the trailer. I hadn't seen the door open—she must have come from out back. In her late fifties or early sixties, long ash-brown hair flecked with gray. Strongly built, with that weathered skin you get from a lifetime outdoors. She wore beat-up jeans and a too-big plaid flannel shirt beneath a dark blue hoodie.

I lifted a finger in a wave and smiled tentatively. The woman opened her mouth, too, only she was baring her teeth like a dog. She raised her hand, which held a knife with a long blade. Not a kitchen knife but a hunting knife. Without a sound, she began to run toward my car, her eyes wide with fury.

Shocked, I hit the gas and the car lurched forward. *What the hell?* I veered around another sharp curve, and for a terrifying moment thought I'd drive straight into the trees. But I sped on, the Camry heaving over rocks and potholes. In the rearview mirror, the clearing disappeared behind me, though not before I caught a last glimpse of the woman standing in the road, face contorted, shouting something I couldn't hear.

"Jesus," I whispered. The locals really *didn't* like outsiders.

A safe distance up the road, still shaken, I noticed movement in the bushes. I slowed the car again to peer out the side window. Another black hare crouched in the undergrowth. Or was it the same one I'd just seen? I couldn't be sure, but as I stared, the hare raised itself onto its hind legs. And then it kept rising. Its body extended, growing longer and longer and thinner and thinner, as though made of some substance other than flesh and fur and bone, until it seemed like it might snap like a piece of Silly Putty stretched too far. If it had stood beside me, the tips of its ears would have brushed my chin. It gazed back at me with unblinking eyes the color of a new penny, and then it sprang into the forest.

CHAPTER 4

When you're confronted with something deeply strange or obviously implausible in a book or movie or painting, you know it means something. It's a symbol, a clue. A warning.

But in real life, that's not necessarily how it works. I stared into the woods, trying to see where the animal had gone. Rabbit, hare: whatever it was, it had vanished. I took a deep breath. That unnatural stretching I'd seen, or thought I'd seen, had surely been a trick of light and shadow. Right now, everything seemed calm, the breeze stirring my hair as sunlight slanted down through the evergreens.

I glanced at my phone. I had one service bar, so that was good. No message from Nisa. It was still only forty-five minutes since I'd left her asleep in the Airbnb. Which seemed crazy, yet there it was: 6:47.

Still, I should head back. By the time I got to town, the café would be open. But there wasn't enough room here to turn the car, not without running into a tree. And I would have been leery of trying to back down an unfamiliar road, anyway. Not to mention that armed woman, standing guard below. No thanks. I opened my map app to see where the road led.

The app wouldn't load. After a minute, I began to drive, creeping along at five miles an hour while I stared at the screen in my hand. Finally I gave up and tossed the phone onto the passenger seat. I'd keep going, and hope the road continued down the other side of the mountain, or hill, or whatever this was.

I hadn't bothered to clock the odometer when I started up here, but I guessed I'd gone about five miles. It seemed farther. Everything about this morning had taken on a strange tone—distance, time, even the sunlight, which now looked more like sunset than sunrise, a continuous crimson flicker through the branches of centuries-old trees.

The entrance appeared so suddenly I nearly drove into it: a pair of massive wrought-iron gates, set into a stone wall. The wall was well maintained, its once-white paint faded to lichen gray and covered with grapevines. The orange berries of bittersweet glowed like embers against the stones. The gates were open, a length of heavy chain dangling from one side. As with the road, I saw no name. Dead leaves had pitched up at the base of the pillars—this autumn's leaves, not the black mulch from last year.

So maybe someone lived here? Maybe that's who the woman was, some kind of caretaker?

I scanned the surroundings for a No Trespassing sign, evidence of CCTV or other surveillance. Again, nothing. Which didn't mean the place wasn't being watched. If nothing else, that woman had seen me drive up here.

But she hadn't chased after me. And she didn't seem to have called the police, not yet, at any rate. I sat in the car for another minute, waiting to see if anyone might come down the drive.

What the hell, I thought, and drove on through the open gates.

CHAPTER 5

The driveway wound through stands of oaks and towering pines, interspersed with impenetrable thickets of rhododendrons. I didn't know rhododendrons could grow to this size—tall as a house, with gnarled trunks and knotted limbs like rats' tails. Once, I thought I glimpsed something pale in the shadow of the trees, a scrap of newspaper or a plastic bag or perhaps a face. But when I slowed, whatever it was melted into the leaves.

It all should have seemed ominous. Yet I felt a peculiar, almost perverse, exhilaration, the way I used to feel when I'd sit down at my laptop to write. *Something is going to happen. I am going to make something happen.*

I'd been climbing steadily since passing that woman's trailer. Now the treetops parted to reveal wide swathes of sky, no longer sunset-tinged but palest blue. I rolled down the window and inhaled the smell of dying leaves, crushed acorns, earth not yet frozen but cold enough to hold its secrets: secrets that might only be shared, come spring, with the right person.

Something is going to happen...

The echo of a woman's voice startled me. I glanced at my face in the rearview mirror. Nisa told me I talked in my sleep sometimes. Had I spoken aloud?

Of course not. I would have realized.

Besides, all writers talk to themselves. Especially playwrights. It's an occupational hazard. With all those voices in your head, you long to hear the words. For me, that was the most magical moment in theater—the first instant during a reading when an actor disappears and your character takes their place. That moment of transformation had always felt like ecstasy, like a ritual of transubstantiation.

"Or possession," my friend Stevie Liddell had retorted, when I'd tried to explain the sensation to him. "Like you're not giving any agency to the actor. Like it's some woo-woo thing that *you* make happen."

I thought that was rich, coming from someone who once mixed the husks of venomous caterpillars with belladonna in a ritual to ensure that a rival didn't get a part in a regional production of *Urinetown*. The weird thing was, it had worked, so I couldn't even lord it over him.

Still, I knew I hadn't spoken aloud as I drove through the rhododendron grove. I felt a flicker of disquiet. That word of Stevie's, "possession," had made me think again of Macy-Lee Barton. Nothing that had happened had been my fault, despite what some people believed. Occasionally, very late at night, I might feel otherwise, but sunlight and caffeine would dispel those dark thoughts. I kept my eyes on the road ahead of me, determined not to let anything puncture the ballooning joy I'd begun to feel, more and more powerfully, as I drove on.

It's the play, I thought, *it's my new play. Everything is different now. I'm finally getting another chance.*

CHAPTER 6

I'd come across *The Witch of Edmonton* the summer before the pandemic, during a weekend stay with friends in Putnam County. We'd spent the morning scouring tag sales and antique shops, thumbing through old books and magazines. By midafternoon my hands were ink-stained and coated with a layer of dust. We were ready to give up treasureless and head back home when we passed a driveway where several boxes of junk had been set out with a FREE sign.

"Stop!" I yelled.

"Those are tag sale rejects," my friend Lauren said. "Trust me, Holly, even you don't want them—it's just crap."

We stopped anyway. Lauren was right, it was all crap. Headless Barbies, plastic Christmas decorations, Ball mason jars missing their lids. One carton was filled with waterlogged textbooks and a box of floppy disks. I barely glanced at it, but then something caught my eye—a large sheaf of pages stapled together into a manuscript. I picked it up, the pages dry and yellowed but still intact.

THE WITCH OF EDMONTON
BY WILLIAM ROWLEY, THOMAS DEKKER, AND JOHN FORD

I'd thought it was someone's college paper, painstakingly written long ago on an old-fashioned typewriter. But as I flipped through, I realized it was the script for an early-seventeenth-century play. I looked again at the names on the first page. I didn't recognize the first two, but "John Ford" rang a bell—a Jacobean playwright best known for "'Tis Pity She's a Whore."

I loved witches, so I tucked the script into my bag, brought it back with me to the city, and read it a few nights later.

I wish I could say that *The Witch of Edmonton* was a lost gem, but I thought it was a mess. A misogynistic patchwork of Jacobean melodrama, unfunny rustics, thwarted romance, and a bigamist who murders one of his wives to collect a larger dowry from the other.

But yes, also a witch—an old, bad-tempered, one-eyed woman named Elizabeth Sawyer, who seeks to avenge herself on her heartless neighbors. She makes a deal with the Devil in the form of a black dog named Tomasin and wreaks havoc on the people who've been mistreating her. The Devil betrays her, of course, and she's executed for witchcraft, though her major crime, it seemed to me, was being old, unmarried, poor, and female.

When I finished reading the typescript, I turned on my computer and began to research the play.

CHAPTER 7

I'd assumed that *The Witch of Edmonton* was one of those unwieldy mashups of melodrama, potted history, and woefully outdated comedy that littered the early-seventeenth-century stage. I was surprised to find that Elizabeth Sawyer had been a real person, a woman accused of witchcraft in what is now part of North London. Her neighbor Agnes had owned a sow that died after eating a piece of Elizabeth's soap. Agnes accused Elizabeth of cursing the sow with "a washing-beetle," whatever that was. When Agnes died four days later, Elizabeth was blamed for that, too. More neighbors jumped in to blame Elizabeth for other things, until their suspicions of witchcraft were confirmed—they set her house on fire and Elizabeth arrived barely in time to put out the flames.

And to finde out who should bee the author of this mischiefe, an old ridiculous custome was vsed, which was to plucke the Thatch of her house, and to burne it, and it being so burnd, the author of such mischiefe should presently then come...

"It's like *Monty Python and the Holy Grail!*" I'd exclaimed to Stevie the next day on a video call. Witches were totally in Stevie's wheelhouse, along with psychotropic herbs, Victorian toy theaters, obscure Eastern European horror films, and social media accounts belonging to dead Hollywood starlets. "They found her guilty of witchcraft in 1621 and executed her, it doesn't say how."

"Burned at the stake, probably." Stevie sucked at his vape pen. "More of an audience. Keep going."

"So then this minister, Henry Goodcole, wrote a pamphlet about Elizabeth's story, as a warning for other witches."

"Right! Because otherwise, they would all be lining up to get burned at the stake."

"Yeah. Also, he added the Devil and a black dog."

"That's definitely gonna bring them out of the woodwork. I hope it was a talking dog?"

"You know it," I said, and Stevie clapped in delight. "So, after Elizabeth was killed, they write this play about her. Like we have true crime series now? Back then, there were broadsheets and murder ballads about all kinds of shit. Men murdering their wives and children, stories about witches. Who were mostly women accused of seducing someone else's husband, or—"

"Or causing a farmer's cows to go dry, or some other random shit," Stevie broke in. "Remember, I've seen *Witchfinder General* seven times. The M.O. is always to find an unmarried woman, blame her, and execute her."

"Bingo. Anyway, this play must've been a big success—Elizabeth Sawyer died in 1621, the play was produced two years after that, and eventually published in 1658, like thirty years later. No one ever went broke showing blood and guts and sex. Four hundred years later, we're still listening to podcasts about the same kinds of stuff."

I shook the script pages in front of my laptop screen so Stevie could see them. "Plus, it has a really catchy title," I added, taking a deep breath before I read it aloud.

"The Witch of Edmonton: A known True Story. Composed into a Tragi-Comedy by divers well esteemed Poets, William Rowley, Thomas Dekker, John Ford, &c. Acted by the Prince's Servants, often at the CockPit in Drury-Lane, once at Court, with singular Applause."

"Hmmm. 'Singular applause.'" Stevie tapped a finger against his chin. "That suggests a *very small audience,* Holly. No wonder we haven't heard about this play before."

"Eileen Atkins played Elizabeth in 2014, for the Royal Shakespeare Company," I offered. "She got great reviews. The play, not so much."

"Was the performance recorded?" I shook my head, and Stevie's face fell. "Bummer. So why are you so excited about this, Holly?"

I stared at the screen while Stevie took another hit of CBD. "I like witches," I said at last, and Stevie gave me a thumbs-up. "And there's this weird erotic tension between Elizabeth and Tomasin."

"He's the dog?"

"Yeah. Actually, he's the Devil, but he takes on the form of the black dog. He promises to do Elizabeth's bidding, take down her enemies and make her rich, et cetera, et cetera. But of course he betrays her and—"

"And she gets burned to a crisp! Holly, are you thinking of adapting this? I have to ask: what are the stakes?"

He cackled at his own joke, which I ignored. "Look, I'm just gonna take some more notes, okay, Stevie? I'll talk to you later."

But it did seem to me there was an opportunity here: what if I turned the story inside out and made Elizabeth triumphant? She and Tomasin could destroy their enemies and bring the other, barely sketched female characters into their fold. The real Elizabeth had died a horrible death centuries before: maybe I could give her a second life.

I'd spent nearly the next three years on the project, updating Elizabeth's story, braiding in contemporary details and events. The well of misogyny never runs dry. When lockdown ended, I'd had Stevie and a few other theater friends read it aloud, again and again in my apartment.

That was when Nisa had begun to add her voice, too. She was enthralled with the Child Ballads, the classic collection of ancient songs she loved as if they were all her own, especially the more gruesome murder ballads. Hearing us read my play, she'd convinced me that they'd be the perfect musical accompaniment.

"It's the same source material, really," she'd said, after we'd listened to yet another version of "Matty Groves."

"Too bad no one wrote a song about Elizabeth. Then we could work that in, too."

"*I'll* write her song! All those other murder ballads are in the public domain, I can just tweak them for the play."

I bit my tongue, noting that she'd said "*the* play" rather than "*your* play." But Nisa was right: they were perfect for Elizabeth's story. Which I had begun to think of as *my* story, and not just in the sense that I'd modernized it. Like me, Elizabeth Sawyer had been unfairly condemned by others. Like me, she was an older woman—I was barely forty, but in Elizabeth's time the average life expectancy was only forty-two. The fictional Elizabeth had made a pact with the Devil to secure her success, but I didn't need to go that far.

Instead, after several years of obsessive writing and revision on the work I now called *Witching Night,* I used it to apply for arts grants. There are never enough of those, especially for little-known playwrights, but that summer, something had clicked. I'd received a grant for ten thousand dollars. I cried reading the email. Not just for me, but for Elizabeth, too—who had come back to rescue me from the life I hadn't been meant to live.

After years of being in creative free fall, I had finally landed in a space where I might bring my vision, and Elizabeth Sawyer, back to life.

CHAPTER 8

Space—that was what I sensed now, driving up that road to nowhere, below a sky that seemed to promise some powerful, nearly inconceivable revelation. *Endless space. Endless possibility.* A strand of mist rose from the treetops, twisting into unreadable calligraphy before it disappeared. A bird's insistent cry hinted at something I couldn't quite comprehend. The world was sending me a message—one I felt just on the verge of understanding.

It's somewhere up here, I thought. *It's coming, I'll see it soon, I can almost see it now.*

In front of me the trees swayed, gold and crimson leaves rippling. I wondered how long ago this land had been cleared, if it had been in the same family since then? It was unusual not to glimpse old stone walls, cellar holes, or any other signs of human habitation. Someone had spent a ton of money to put a road here, yet I'd seen no residence apart from that mobile home.

As if sensing my thoughts, the next curve revealed ragged lawns shaded by immense old oaks and evergreens. Beside the road, one had been cut down long ago, leaving a stump choked with poison ivy, a riot of scarlet leaves and white berries. I drove cautiously on, conscious I was an interloper. The lawns appeared untended, but someone still might live here.

Indeed, from the trees a vast house finally emerged, with granite walls and not enough windows, and a porch that extended along its front and sides. I brought the car to a stop, peering up through the windshield. Not a house: a mansion. As I stared, it seemed to recede, then move closer, like waves overtaking a beach. I struggled to focus on its black walls.

But hadn't those walls been gray? Or no, white, an unearthly, glowing white? No, I recalled, that had been the poison ivy's berries. The house was gray, gray stone. Like the gateway had been. Right? I squeezed my eyes shut and opened them. Definitely gray. I glanced at the dashboard clock.

6:29

That was impossible. I'd checked the time before I started up the driveway, and it had been 6:47. I grabbed my phone and swiped at the screen.

6:29

I stared at the screen until the numerals changed—*6:30*—and checked the dashboard clock again.

6:30

I shook my head. I'd gotten the hour wrong, or misread it. That was actually good. I still had plenty of time to stop for croissants and lattes and get back to Nisa.

I stepped out of the car, lifting my head to gaze at the house, looming above me like a stone cloud. The building was completely hideous.

I loved it.

CHAPTER 9

In theater, you're occasionally confronted with set designs that don't work. Backdrops where the perspective is skewed, color choices that make you cringe, furniture that doesn't suit the setting. Perhaps the stage itself is off: a two-hander that calls for intimacy drowns beyond a huge proscenium, or a full-cast musical suffocates within a black box. Often, something just doesn't feel right—the theater was poorly constructed, the sight lines are terrible, the stage is raked so steeply that actors stumble.

Yet now and then, the space itself feels *wrong*. I've known actors and crew who refuse to perform in certain places. I once asked an AD why she'd dropped out of a modern production of *Lysistrata* at a new theater repurposed from a London brewery.

"It just felt bad." She shivered at the memory. "It was a bad place. You just knew something awful would happen there."

"And did anything happen?"

She laughed awkwardly. "Not onstage. The reviews were really good. Great, in fact. But the audiences never came. It was like people sensed there was something wrong. The owners and investors lost everything. I was glad I left when I did."

I had never experienced anything like that—until now. Just looking at the gray house made me feel both exhilarated and queasy, like wearing a pair of VR goggles that haven't been adjusted correctly. The overall design was Victorian Gothic—three stories, with deep gables and carved stone buttresses, elaborate parapet balconies, stained-glass windows, an extensive veranda. I counted eight chimneys, both brick and fieldstone. Someone had sunk a bundle into building it, that was for sure.

I couldn't put a finger on what was wrong. Was the design itself flawed? Not quite Gothic enough? Or maybe they'd cut corners when it was built, making the end result not what was originally intended.

But for the most part, it seemed to have been relatively well maintained. One chimney was missing a few bricks. Cracks webbed an upper window. At the right front corner rose a granite tower, its base wood-shingled, which had begun to pull away from the main structure. Someone had repaired it with a series of rebars, binding it to the front of the house like a severed arm that had been sutured back in place.

Still, I found its facade weirdly compelling. It's *jolie laide,* I told myself, like one of those actors whose unconventional features shouldn't conspire to beauty but somehow do. This house wasn't beautiful, but I'd seen worse.

The chill wind bit at my neck, so I grabbed my jacket from the car, pulled it on. Then I walked to the front steps. Dead leaves covered the stairs in a foot-high drift. Someone had raked the gated entrance, but no one had been up here for a while.

I found my footing and went to the front door: tall and solid oak, with a cast-iron knocker in its center. The knocker was shaped like a man's face, his mouth unsmiling, suspicious of visitors. When I tried to turn the knob, it didn't budge. I glanced back to see if anyone had followed me but saw only my old car, looking dejected in the mansion's shadow.

I wandered along the veranda, its rails mottled with mildew, floorboards bearing the skeletal imprints of long-dead leaves. Someone had stubbed out a cigarette butt. Considering how desiccated it was, that could have been a year ago.

I stopped to peer through grimy windows into darkened rooms. One held a piano. In another, dingy flowered sheets covered a couple of armchairs. Paintings hung on the walls, but it was too dim for me to see what they depicted. A room with dark green walls contained a pool table and smaller ones for bridge. The dining room held a long table and chairs for a dozen people.

At the back of the house, my snooping revealed a large, modernized kitchen, with an old wood-burning Glenwood stove still in one corner. Turning to gaze over the veranda rail, I had a spectacular view of the distant mountains in their early-autumn glory.

I felt a sudden pang, a yearning for something I hadn't known I wanted. What would it be like to live here—all this space and privacy, after decades of crappy apartments? I could have my pick of rooms to use as an office. Nisa and I could drink our morning coffee on one of those upstairs balconies. In the late afternoons, we'd sit out on this veranda, kicking back with a bottle of wine to watch the sun go down. I could even work outside. The weather would stay fine until the end of October. I could see myself in a sweater and fingerless gloves, dragging out a table for my laptop.

There wouldn't just be plenty of room for Nisa and me. Stevie and Amanda Greer could come here as well. Alongside Nisa, they were the other two performers I'd decided to cast in my play. We could rehearse and hone the script to a fine sheen. Where better to launch *Witching Night* than a vast old empty house in the countryside?

Excited, I continued on until I was once more at the front of the building, and gazed at the dilapidated tower. My initial revulsion—that feeling that the house held some subcutaneous wrongness, like cancerous cells manifesting in the body years before detection—had disappeared.

I pushed the hair from my eyes, thinking. I had the grant money, and I'd already taken the semester off from teaching. Nisa could go on hiatus from her day job at the café. She'd balk at having to postpone some of her singing gigs, but it would only be for a few weeks. Stevie mostly couch-surfed anyway. And legendary Amanda Greer, who had only recently agreed to be my leading lady, would love the grand surroundings.

Luck had brought me here, I decided, luck or fate or some other impulse I couldn't name. A few hours ago, I couldn't even have imagined a place like this. Now I could think of nothing else.

CHAPTER 10

I wandered to the front door, trudging through dead leaves. The knocker looked like Stevie, I realized. Stevie's narrow face and wide eyes, Stevie's mouth.

I took several photos to send to him and Nisa. The veranda's ceiling blocked the thin light filtering through the trees, so I was surprised to see that the pictures were all overlit. I shot a few more from a different angle, but every time it was the same. The knocker's cast-iron face glowed white, making it difficult to pick out any details.

I edited the best photo, adding shadows and contrast, so you could tell that it looked like Stevie, kind of. Yet whenever I tried to save the edits, the photo reverted to the original. Frustrated, I returned to the car, got inside, and texted the photo to Nisa.

On my way. Look who I found

The wind had kicked up, though the sky remained a cloudless, searing blue. As I eased the car down the driveway, my phone pinged: Nisa.

> Where are you??? what is that a
> picture of! I'm starving

I'm bringing croissants!
And coffee

> They'll be sold out

Not this early.

> They sell out by 10

Yeah but it's only—

I glanced at the time. 10:17.

What the hell? I checked the dashboard clock: 10:17.

Last time I'd looked, it had been 6:30. Was the clock broken?

But why would both my phone and the car clock show the same wrong time? It was impossible that more than three hours had passed—I'd left the Airbnb around six.

The phone pinged again.

> Whatever just come back I'm
> starved

Sorry, lost track!
See you soon, love you

I looked into the rearview mirror as I drove off. Sunlight now flooded the veranda and upper stories, turning the windows to gold. Only the front door remained in twilight, the knocker now a black smear, its face lost to shadow.

CHAPTER 11

Nisa perched on the rental's back deck, laptop on her knees and a mug of coffee in one hand.

"Sorry, babe." I pulled the other chair alongside her and sat. "I swear, my phone said six thirty, then you texted and it was, like, three hours later."

"Three hours and forty-five minutes." Nisa sighed. "Whatever."

I handed her the bag with the croissants and raised a large to-go cup. "I got you a latte."

"I'm all set. You have it." Nisa opened the paper bag and inhaled. "Okay, you're forgiven." She removed an almond croissant and took a bite. "Oh my god, these are so much better than anything back in the city. Why is that?"

"No idea. Listen, I need to tell you what I found..."

I recounted my long drive—through Hillsdale, up the dirt road, past the creepy woman in the trailer, my discovery of the empty mansion at the hill's summit.

"I don't think it's abandoned." I paused to take a gulp of the latte. "It's in decent shape, and there's still furniture inside. It doesn't look like anyone lives there, but someone's definitely keeping it up."

"Did you go in?"

"No. I tried all the doors, but everything was locked."

"What about the windows?"

I smiled. "You can do that. What do you think? Do you want to check it out?"

"With Crazy Trailer Lady waiting there with an ax? Nope."

"It was a knife. And she wasn't around when I drove back. Her car was gone, she must've headed to work."

"Yeah, well, no thanks. I'm good. I thought *we* were going to work?" Nisa pointed at her laptop. "I've been writing new lyrics for 'Allison Grose,' listen—"

She reached for the laptop, but I stopped her. "This *is* work. This house...I'm thinking we could rent it."

"Rent it?" Nisa frowned. "You said it's a mansion."

"It is. I'm not talking about a year—maybe just a few weeks. Or one week. Or I dunno, a long weekend. Now, before the holidays, before the bad weather comes. It would be quiet, we could all work on the show. You and me, Stevie, Amanda. Maybe a few other people. Like a residency, only we'd know everyone."

"Except Amanda, who we haven't actually met. Who actually has a career."

"Amanda hasn't had a major role in twelve years. You *know* this show could be fantastic. I've made it almost perfect—"

Nisa's eyes narrowed. "*You've* made it perfect?"

"We've both made it," I said quickly, and grabbed her hand. "It's so much better with your music, Nis—"

"And my voice."

"And your voice. Everything you do just makes what I've done so much better. I'm so lucky. *We're* so lucky. Come on, baby," I urged, drawing her closer to me. "You just have to see this place, then you'll get it."

"You're asking everyone to, what? Drop everything and move here?"

"Just for a week or two. You and Stevie can take off work, and I'll ask Amanda if she can, too. I'll *beg* Amanda."

"Do you even know if it's available to rent?"

"No. That's what I thought we could do now. There's a real estate place in Hillsdale. We can drop by and see."

"How would we pay for it?"

"My grant money. It's a legit expense. If it costs too much, we don't do it. But if it's a few grand for two weeks, or even one week, I can swing it."

Nisa had finished her croissant and was now absently twisting a finger through her curls. "That grant money's supposed to be for you to work on the play."

"This *is* working on the play." I scooted closer, taking her hand to still it. "In the long term, it would save time. And money. Bookwise, it's so close to being ready for a public reading. That's a requirement of my grant—I have to do a staged reading within a year."

"But do you even have a director?"

"I've talked to Imani Nelson, she's definitely interested."

"Imani Nelson. Okay, that would be amazing. But how are you going to afford all this?"

"That's what the grant is for, Nisa," I said, aggravated. "And don't say anything about Imani to anyone else, because there's a chance she won't be able to do it. But I told Amanda she definitely would, which is why Amanda is going to sign on."

"Oooh! Naughty Holly." Nisa drew her lips across my fingertips, glancing behind us toward the door that opened onto the bedroom. I smiled but shook my head.

"Later, baby. I need to think this through. If we had a solid week of rehearsals here, we could go back to the city and find a venue for the public reading. Imani said that space on Broome Street might be available—remember? It had really good acoustics. This would give us a chance to polish everything in time to show it off. Show *you* off," I added. "Imani says she knows a couple of people she could put me in touch with, investors for a backers' audition. She loved the script, and even if she can't come up now, she could jump in when we're back in the city and help get everything lined up for the reading."

"Really?" Nisa's eyes widened.

"Really." I handed her my phone. "Here. Look at the pictures."

Nisa scrolled through them, marveling. "Wow, it's huge. Do you know how many bedrooms?"

"No, but there has to be room for at least four of us, right? And whatever's wrong with it, at least it's not in Queens, across from a twenty-four-hour 7-Eleven and a fire station."

Nisa enlarged a photo. "This is weird. What is that?"

"A door knocker."

"I mean, what is that face? It looks familiar."

"I thought it looked like Stevie."

Nisa scrutinized it, then laughed. "You're right! It does, kind of."

I took the phone back, leaned over to press my forehead to hers. "So what do you think? Want to go to Hillsdale and check out that real estate agent? Probably nothing will happen, probably the place isn't available. But it's something to do."

"Something to do besides work." Nisa gazed longingly at her laptop, then shrugged. "But sure. I've always wanted to stay in an empty mansion."

"Who doesn't?" I said, and kissed her.

CHAPTER 12

Nisa loved murder ballads the way some people love show tunes. Instead of belting out "Let It Go" at parties, she'd sing "Child Owlet" or, in a rare nod to the twentieth century, "Cell Block Tango." After suggesting we incorporate murder ballads into my play, she'd also come up with a character who'd perform them. And of course she intended to take on that role, when the time came.

I hadn't argued. Nisa was a brilliant performer—I'd first fallen in love with her because of her voice. Yet it was still *my* play: a play with music, not a proper musical. When I submitted *Witching Night* for the grant, I'd left out her lyrics, a fact we'd argued about ever since. At the time, they'd felt ancillary to me, the same way the snippets of original text had become subsidiary to what I'd added.

I had at least mentioned I'd be using murder ballads in the actual production, and I knew from my acceptance letter that the jurors had been intrigued. But I had received the grant, not Nisa. By the time we were ready to mount the show, I figured, we'd sort it out. She'd get credit for her contributions and, I hoped, she'd get cast in the role I'd created for her. She was happy enough now to ride shotgun while we drove down Hillsdale's main drag.

"Are you sure there's a real estate agent here?" Nisa stared out her window. "It looks like one of those towns in Nebraska where they pay people to live."

"Maybe they do. Maybe they'll pay us to live in an empty mansion."

A single car was parked in front of the real estate office, a vintage-looking black Mercedes. "Well, somebody's doing okay," said Nisa as I parked alongside it. "Maybe we're too late for cheap rent. Maybe Hillsdale is alive with the sound of money."

"Probably they make their sales from places closer to the river. Everything around here looks derelict."

"That's what I mean," retorted Nisa. "Fixer-uppers—a few years ago you could've bought any house in Sullivan County for less than a hundred grand. Now everything costs a million."

"I seriously doubt there's a single house in Hillsdale that costs a million." I grabbed my bag and stepped out of the car. "Not even this mansion."

The office was in a small Carpenter Gothic house, by far the nicest I'd seen in Hillsdale. White paint, green gingerbread trim, with terra-cotta pots of hot-pink geraniums on the porch. A sign hung above the steps—AINSLEY ROWAN REAL ESTATE. I walked to the door, opened it, and peered inside, Nisa behind me.

"Hi!" A middle-aged white woman looked up from her laptop and smiled. "Can I help you?"

"Yes, maybe." I glanced around the room. Painted wicker furniture, more geraniums, a coffee table stacked with real estate brochures and shelter magazines. Filmy white curtains at the windows, a worn blue-and-white-striped rug, random art prints on the walls. Everything very tidy, but I recognized the signs of decorating on the cheap. Shabby chic teetering on the edge of just plain shabby.

"I'm Ainsley Rowan." The woman's voice was deep, slightly husky. "Come on in."

Nisa and I entered as Ainsley glided toward us. She seemed out of sync with the make-do furnishings and the town itself, an urban boho marooned in the gray desolation of Hillsdale. Petite and slim, she wore black leather jeggings, chunky red ankle boots, and a flowy white silk blouse, accented by silver bracelets and rings. Tarnished-silver hair was cut sleek against her skull, showcasing high cheekbones and close-set very pale gray eyes winged with heavy eyeliner. Her fingernails were square-cut and painted a lunar white. I caught a glimpse of a tiny tattoo above one breast, a symbol like an upside-down peace sign.

It should have added up to a ridiculous look, especially in a town like this, especially on someone her age. She must have been in her late fifties, perhaps older. But Ainsley Rowan didn't look ridiculous. She appeared powerful and confident and somewhat intimidating, despite being a good four inches shorter than me, and I'm five-five on a good day.

"Holly Sherwin," I said.

Nisa stepped alongside me. "Nisa Macari."

"Would you like some coffee? Or tea?" Ainsley gestured at a small kitchen. "I think there's some pomegranate juice or ruby grapefruit juice. Something red, anyway."

I shook my head. "No thanks."

"I'd love some pomegranate juice," said Nisa.

"Great! Sit wherever you want, I'll be right back."

We settled on a wicker love seat beside the coffee table. Nisa's phone pinged, she read a text and laughed, had started to show it to me when Ainsley returned.

"Here." She handed Nisa a small glass half-full of red liquid and settled into a chair across from us. "I know it looks like cabernet but honest, it's pomegranate juice. So, are you visiting from the city? Or do you live here?"

"We're visiting for a few days. We got an Airbnb in Takamac Falls."

I fell silent, unsure what the protocol was. I'd never visited a real estate agent before—all my city rentals had been sublets, most of them illegal.

"This is really good." Nisa drained the pomegranate juice, her lips stained dark red, and set the glass on the table. "Holly went for a drive this morning, she saw a place around here she was interested in."

"Really?" Ainsley looked taken aback, like this was the first time she'd heard of such a thing. Maybe it was. "What property was that?"

"Up there." I pointed out the window, to the dirt road behind the gas station. "That big mansion?"

Ainsley's expression changed, from surprise to disappointment. "You mean Hill House."

"I guess. It was the only place up there, except for a mobile home."

"I'm sorry," Ainsley said brusquely. "I know the house, and it's not for sale. There are a couple of sweet properties in the valley on the other side of that hill. You probably won't have seen them, you have to follow Route 9K for another few miles. There's a lovely old farm, thirteen acres, needs some TLC but that's why the price is—"

"Thanks, but I'm interested in that place. Hill House."

"Right. Like I said, it's not—"

I laughed. "I'm not in the market for a mansion. We'd just like to rent it."

"*She'd* like to rent it," said Nisa. She gave Ainsley a flirtatious look. "I haven't even seen it yet."

Ainsley took a deep breath. "Yes, well—"

"Does someone even live there?" I broke in. "It looks empty. I didn't go in, just peeked through the windows. It seems like it's being kept up, so I thought maybe it was available as a rental. Like an event space or something like that."

Ainsley pursed her lips as she regarded me appraisingly—I could practically see dollar signs flashing across her narrowed eyes. "What were you thinking of?"

"A couple of weeks."

"You're talking next summer."

"I'm talking now. Like next month, October. Even end of this month, if that was possible." I smiled, hoping I didn't come off as a pushy flatlander.

"Hm." Ainsley leaned back in her chair. "Usually people want it for the summer."

"So it *is* available as a rental."

"Not really. It's been on the market forever. There's always some interest—people drive up that road, usually because they take a wrong turn. No one who lives here goes up that way. But it's expensive. And it's not comfortable. Even in summer it can be chilly, and in addition to the rent, you'd have to pay for housekeeping. Someone comes in once a week, they have to stay all day to get everything done. That's one reason the whole place hasn't collapsed."

"What are the others?" Nisa smiled disarmingly.

Ainsley didn't take the bait. "It has to be plowed out in winter," she continued, "so even if you're there in summer, the cost is prorated to cover that, and other maintenance."

"It sounds like a pretty sweet deal for whoever owns it," said Nisa.

"It's a mixed bag."

"So who does own it?" I asked. "Someone in the city?"

"No." Ainsley reached into a pocket to withdraw a vape pen, turned her head to take a puff, exhaling a cloud of vapor that smelled of crushed ferns and phlox. "Hill House belongs to me."

CHAPTER 13

I stared at Ainsley with renewed interest. "Do you live there?"

"God, no. You've seen it. What would I do with eleven thousand square feet? I live here. And I know people dump on Hillsdale, but it's actually not bad," Ainsley continued, twisting a silver ring inset with a piece of amber the size of an acorn. "You have to drive to Takamac for groceries, but you've made that trip so you know it's not far. And real estate here in Hillsdale is cheaper. Much, much cheaper."

Her hand dropped from the amber ring. She gazed at me as though deciding whether I could be trusted. "Hill House belonged to my late husband, Jez Sanderson," she said, almost reluctantly. "He inherited it from his father. Honestly, there's been a lot of drama with Hill House—a lot of lawsuits. Even after they were settled, there were always issues with other people claiming they had title to it."

She slipped the vape pen back into her pocket. "Jez really wanted to sell. We were living in the city then and we hardly ever came up here—there's no train and the drive was too long, that's what we thought. Even before the pandemic, people would head up to this area for the weekend and I'd think, four hours for two days? Now they've all just moved here full time, so it's not an issue.

"Anyway," she went on, "seventeen years ago, Jez finally found a buyer, but right before the sale went through, Jez died. Cardiac arrest. Boom."

Ainsley clapped her hands so loudly that Nisa and I jumped. "It was a long time ago," she went on, "and I still can't believe he's gone. But after he died, the house sale fell through. In those days, I never bothered putting it back on the market. Now I wish I had."

She glanced at her amber ring and shrugged. "Jez worked on Wall Street so he left me well-off—not enough to keep living in New York, but plenty for living somewhere else. In the city I'd dabbled in real estate, so I got my license and moved up here. Like I said, it's a lot cheaper. But not if I stayed in Hill House—a place that big is exhausting if you're actually living in it. I pay Melissa Libby to come in and do housekeeping once a week. Her husband, Tru, keeps up with minor repairs and plows it out in winter."

"But isn't that expensive?" Nisa exclaimed, then shot her an apologetic smile. "I mean, if you're not even living in it."

"I'll be honest—I don't go up there unless I have to."

"Why not?"

"Let's say I'm not a fan of its architecture. The house still has most of the original details, and they're not to my taste. So, Holly and Nisa..."

She cocked her head to stare at us quizzically. With her heavily made-up eyes, she resembled a middle-aged sphinx. "Do you both work from home?"

"I'm a playwright. Nisa's a singer-songwriter. But we both have day jobs."

"Good to have a steady income." Ainsley's tone again grew terse. "Look, I'm sure you know this, but real estate has gone through the roof. Even in Hillsdale, the housing market has gotten really tight. There's no inventory, no—"

"I just received an arts grant for a play I've written. That's why we're here. Well, one reason—we also just wanted to get out of town for a few days. But I'm looking for a space where I can workshop with a few people—

you know, rehearse and put on the final touches. It's a very sizable grant," I added, annoyed that she was dismissing me.

"Hm." Ainsley tapped her amber ring. Her appraising look grew even more calculating. "Wouldn't you rather be in the city for that?"

"The rentals are insane."

"Tell me about it." The shrewd expression vanished as Ainsley gave us a selling smile. "What's your play about?"

"Witches."

"Witches?"

I reached into my bag for the print-on-demand copy of *The Witch of Edmonton* that I'd bought, a slightly improved version from the stapled typescript I'd found in Putnam County. I held it up so she could see the cover, a Victorian painting of gleeful-looking naked women on broomsticks.

"It's an obscure play," I explained, "and I've basically used it as a jumping-off point. My play's about control and coercion, how women, especially older women, are gaslighted and punished for—well, everything."

"Not exactly breaking news," said Ainsley.

"I'm doing the music," said Nisa. "Have you seen *Hadestown*? Or *Once on This Island*? That's what we're aiming for. Amanda Greer's the lead."

I shot Nisa a warning glance—too much information. But Ainsley appeared intrigued.

"Amanda Greer?" she asked. "I thought she'd retired. After..."

"No, she's still working." I dropped *The Witch of Edmonton* back into my bag. "She's read my play and she's excited about it. A lot of people are," I added. I didn't care if I sounded defensive. I was suddenly, strangely desperate for it all to happen, just as I'd pictured.

"Well," said Ainsley. "It seems like an interesting project." She almost sounded like she might mean it.

"It is," I agreed. "Could we take a look inside the house?"

Ainsley sat and stared at her amber ring. "I don't see why not," she announced, and again clapped her hands. "Give me a sec to find the keys."

She went upstairs, boot heels echoing on the steps. Nisa turned to me. "Did you see that ring? And..." She swooped her fingers along the outer edges of her eyes, mimicking wings. "That makeup! I love her."

"Shhh." I pressed a finger against Nisa's mouth. "I thought you didn't want to move upstate?"

"That was before I knew the Grand High Witch would be our landlady."

Ainsley clattered back downstairs, jingling the keys in her hand as she headed for the door. "Do you want to go in my car?"

"I'll just take mine," I said.

"I'll ride shotgun with Ainsley," said Nisa, standing to hurry after the real estate agent. "See you up there."

CHAPTER 14

I drove behind Ainsley, past the church that Satan ate and up the six miles of rough road to Hill House. She drove fast enough that several times I lost sight of her. Wasn't she worried about her suspension? I felt an unreasonable pang of fear, that somehow Ainsley had spirited Nisa away into the forest, never to be seen again.

Still, the Mercedes always hove back into view. I passed the mobile home—the Subaru was still gone. I'd have to ask Ainsley about her, too.

I reached the gate and continued up the drive until I saw Ainsley's car in front of Hill House. I parked behind it and hopped out. The house's front door was open, and I heard voices from inside.

As I hurried up the steps, something moved across the veranda. Another black hare? I froze, and it, too, halted. The noon sun turned the translucent skin of its ears coral as it spun to stare at me, its eyes ringed with black and its pupils enormous, more like an owl's than a hare's.

I tried not to move, holding my breath. The hare rose on its powerful back legs to face me head-on. My wonder turned to horror as, very slowly, it smiled, its mouth opening onto a row of square teeth stained red.

"Holly! What are you doing, come in!"

I turned. Nisa stood in the open doorway, waving at me impatiently. My throat had closed up so I couldn't speak. Instead, I pointed at the hare, trying to warn her away from it. But Nisa only gave me a blank look, and when I glanced back, the hare was gone.

CHAPTER 15

Y ou okay?" Nisa took my arm and pulled me inside. "What were you looking at?"

I stared out at the empty porch, bewildered. "Nothing," I finally said.

Ainsley had joined us again, waving a hand in front of her face. "Phew! It's a bit musty, sorry. No one's lived here since last year. Melissa comes in to clean, but…"

She gestured at the vast empty hall that surrounded us, its paneled walls and hardwood floors gleaming dully. Dust motes swarmed around us like gnats, and I caught a whiff of lemon furniture polish and the underlying odor of dead mouse.

"…she can't keep up with it," Ainsley finished. "No one can. Here, I'll show you around."

I followed her, trying to shake off the memory of the hare. Nisa held my hand and looked at me in concern. "Holly? Did something happen?"

I smiled wanly, trying to summon the excitement I'd felt in Ainsley's office. "I just thought I saw something outside. Too much to hope it was a Roomba?" I felt relieved when she laughed.

Ainsley strode to the center of the hall. A grand stairway led to the second floor, the kind of staircase I'd only ever seen in movies, or in the lobbies of hotels I could never afford.

"The best bedrooms are up there," she said, pointing to the second-floor landing. "The Rose Room and the Yellow Room are probably the nicest. But I'll show you down here first."

Stepping past the staircase, she opened a door onto a narrow corridor, beckoning Nisa and me to follow. Bare wooden floors, walls devoid of paintings or other ornamentation, a number of closed doors. No windows, and no electric lamps or sconces that I could see. Light only leaked in from a single door that had been left ajar.

I've never felt claustrophobic, not even when caving once with friends in Virginia. But this hallway made my stomach churn with anxiety. The wood floor felt spongy, as if covered with rotting carpet.

And the walls, too, seemed oddly porous—the paneling gave beneath my touch, like a too-soft mattress. I paused to press my palm against the wall, testing for damp. It felt solid, slightly warm to the touch.

"It's hot," I said to Nisa, who shrugged.

"That's good, right? It means the heat is working. Check this out."

She pushed open the door that had been left ajar and stepped into a large room, its walls a faded dark green, its tall windows hung with filmy curtains. The air smelled like an expensive cigar bar—tobacco smoke, whiskey, chalk dust. A rolled-up carpet was pushed against one wall, where a wooden rack held pool cues. Pale green light filtered through the curtains, so that we seemed to stand at the bottom of a swimming pool.

"Billiards room," said Ainsley as she joined us. "I sold the pool table, though it broke my heart to do it. Mahogany and the original felt, it was well over a hundred years old, with the original slate top—it weighed a ton. And all the original ivory billiard balls..."

She sighed. "I sold lots of beautiful things."

She walked to a window and pulled aside the curtain, revealing a glimpse of green lawn and blue sky.

"There were some beautiful statues, too. Carrara marble. The man who built Hill House commissioned them from Hamo Thornycroft in the 1880s—worth a fortune. About a decade ago, a couple from New York leased the house…They had to leave after just a few weeks. But the husband had fallen in love with the statues. He really wanted them for their new estate in Westchester. I almost couldn't bear to sell them, but…"

She opened her cupped hands, releasing an invisible butterfly. "You know how it goes. But it seems the house agreed with me. One of the movers he hired was badly injured—a statue slipped off the dolly and crushed his leg."

"That's horrible." I shuddered, looking around.

"I know."

Nisa stepped from one window to the next, the pale curtains drifting around her. She reached to touch one, and her hand seemed to disappear within the gauzy fabric. Frowning, she turned to Ainsley.

"Why are the curtains moving? The windows are all shut."

"It's an old house," replied Ainsley. "It breathes." She opened another door. "This was the music room."

Nisa followed her. I stayed where I was, confused. That morning on the veranda, I'd looked through the windows and seen a room with a pool table, small tables for bridge, paintings on the wall. This had been the same room, I was sure of it.

"Holly? You coming?" Nisa touched my arm.

"Yeah, sorry. Just—"

"It's really great, isn't it?" Nisa excitedly led me through the empty music room, then a short passage to another, very large room, the first to have any furniture in it. "So much space!"

She sounded giddy, and I smiled. "That's for sure."

"How many of you will there be?" Ainsley settled into an old wing chair, pointing at the much newer couch beside it. "Please, sit."

"Not that many." I moved aside a pillow to make room for Nisa beside me. "Me, Nisa. Stevie Liddell—I've worked with him before, he's going to do sound design. He and Nisa will read various roles as they're developed. Like I said, we're still in the early stages. Then there will be one or two other actors."

"Amanda Greer?"

"It'll depend on her availability, but I have a good feeling. Especially now."

I sank deeper into the couch. It looked like a recent addition, as did the chairs and glass-topped coffee table arranged in front of a huge fireplace. Faux midcentury modern pieces, probably from a catalog store, but still more expensive than anything I'd ever owned.

Same with the artwork on the walls, aggressively retro prints that nodded at Italian Futurism but made my eyes hurt. It all appeared out of place in the long, dark-paneled room, like a bunch of drunk teenagers lolling around while their parents were gone for the weekend. Only Ainsley's old wing chair seemed to belong, with its frayed upholstery and carved wooden arms.

"A different couple brought all these with them, a year before the pandemic," Ainsley explained, noticing my interest. "The upstairs beds, too. Which are super comfortable—so much better than what was there before. Some of the original furniture's stored in the attic. The rest I sold, or Jez's father did." She stroked the wing chair's arms fondly. "But I kept this. I keep planning to bring it to my house, but I think it wants to be here."

"How come no one ever stays?" asked Nisa.

"Various reasons. The house is just too huge—that's a big one. There was a family here in the late eighties, but..." She hesitated. "It didn't work out for them. People think they want to live in a mansion, but there's a reason all those old English country homes had cooks and maids and valets and gardeners. It's not just the upkeep. A place like this..."

She leaned back in the chair, its sides seeming to hold her protectively, and gazed at the ceiling high above us. "It's lonely. Without other people—it's like living in an empty hotel."

"'All work and no play make Jack a dull boy,'" I said, and Nisa laughed. "Does the house get lonely, too?"

Ainsley's mouth twisted—not in amusement, I thought. "Or they miss the city," she continued, as if I hadn't spoken. "A lot of people moved upstate during the pandemic, but not all of them could hack it. And Hill House..."

"Is it haunted?" asked Nisa.

Ainsley turned to her. "Haunted? No one has ever seen a ghost here, if that's what you mean. I would say that it's troubled, though Jez used to say it's demented."

"'Demented'?" Nisa started to giggle, then quickly covered her mouth at Ainsley's expression. "Sorry! I never heard someone say that about a house. Maybe in a movie but not in real life."

"Is this real life?" Ainsley stared at each of us, so keenly I thought she must be joking. But then I recalled how she'd looked moments ago—contemptuous but also angry.

Composing myself, I stared back at her and replied, "You tell me."

CHAPTER 16

"Every old house has a history," Ainsley said, her sharp features even more sphinxlike. "Hill House plays to people's expectations. Usually they think it's going to make them happy. A beautiful old mansion! Views for days! Et cetera, et cetera. Then they move here and they're just bored and miserable.

"But maybe you won't have that problem, Holly." She fixed her dark gaze on me. "You have a project, you'll have friends with you. If you decide to take on the rental."

She pushed herself from the wing chair, seeming reluctant to leave it. "I'll show you the rest. This is the conservatory."

I followed her through another passage into an expansive space like a human-scaled birdhouse, only with glass walls and ceiling. Even on this cool autumn day the air was warm and humid. It smelled of rotting vegetation, though there were no plants in sight, only oddly shaped century-old wicker furniture and big ceramic pots that looked like funerary urns but must have once held ferns or palms. The windows were filmed with algae that gave the room an underwater cast.

Ainsley stooped to right a footstool that had been overturned. As she straightened, a thin high voice rang out, an eerie echo that seemed to come from somewhere deep within the house.

Ainsley cried out, lifting her hand in front of her face. But even as I jumped, the voice resolved into words.

"If all those young maids were like hares on the mountain..."

"It's Nisa." I whirled to look at Ainsley—her face had gone white. "It's just her singing, she does this all the time."

Ainsley shook her head, and I noticed that the hand she'd kept raised protectively was the one with the amber ring. "She should stay with us," she said, and I heard the effort it took to keep her voice steady. "Tell her to come back."

"Nisa!" I yelled, walking to one of the doors leading into the corridor. "Nis, we're over here, come on..."

Moments later Nisa ran breathlessly into the conservatory, cheeks pinked and her dark eyes shimmering with excitement. "Did you hear that? The acoustics here are brilliant, I—"

"Let's keep going." Ainsley cut her off. "Dining room and kitchen are this way."

She walked briskly from the conservatory. Nisa looked at me curiously. "Did something happen?"

"No. We were just startled, that's all. Especially Ainsley."

"That's because she's never been exposed to the supernatural power of my voice before," Nisa said, sidling up to me and whispering in my ear. "She doesn't know what I can do with it."

I leaned in to kiss her, enveloped by the smell of freesia, her mouth tasting of pomegranate. "I do," I murmured. "Your song...Did you see it? When I first got here and you came out to the porch to meet me?"

"See what?"

"A hare, a big black hare."

She stared at me blankly. "Like a rabbit? No. How come?"

"Then why were you singing that song?"

"I don't know. It just came into my head. It's one of the songs we're using in the show, I guess I'd been thinking about it. Why?"

"I saw one earlier, too, by the trailer, and again when I first got here. But I hadn't told you about it, and——"

Ainsley's voice came from another room, calling us to join her. "And it's just weird, that's all," I finished.

I stared at Nisa, who only shrugged. "We better go," she said.

As she started for the door, I stepped alongside her, put my arm around her shoulder, and drew her to me. "Don't disappear like that, okay?"

She glanced at me, puzzled and a bit amused. "It's just a coincidence, Holly." But I wasn't really sure that was true.

CHAPTER 17

I'd met Nisa after I'd heard her singing at a tiny club's open mic. The theme that night was Midwinter. Stevie was supposed to join me—it was one of his favorite venues, a place where his neo-pagan and musical theater friends all came to hang out and perform. In classic Stevie fashion, he blew me off at the last minute, not (for once) because of a hookup, but because the French bulldog he was caring for had eaten a box of Vosges chocolates.

"I'm at urgent care—thank god we made it, the vet said she almost died. But you'll have fun, I'll call you tomorrow."

I'd joined the line outside the club's door—it was busy for a cold February night. I'd been here once before, with Stevie, and knew the drill. A lot of people in vaguely Mardi Gras–ish costume, a lot of people who'd been drinking before they arrived. A lot of buzzy chatter about auditions and hookups and who was rumored to be performing that night.

Before I knew her as Nisa, she was a dark young woman with deep-set eyes and a wicked grin, who took the stage to sing "The Bitter Withy," one of the few old ballads in which a man gets punished for wrongdoing.

She began playfully:

"As it befell on a bright holiday
When hail from the sky did fall,
Our sweet young Savior asked his mother
If he might go play ball."

I recognized the song—Stevie had made me listen to it at his annual Christmas dinner. When three rich young lords refuse to play ball with our sweet young Savior—a poor maid's child—does he turn the other cheek? He doth not.

With righteous anger, the young singer rose to her full height:

"He made him a bridge of the beams of the sun,
And over the water run he,
The rich young lords chased after him
And drowned they were all three."

Then, softening, she told of how the three grief-stricken young mothers confront Mary, the Savior's mother. To Mary's credit, she puts her son across her knee and gives him three lashes with a willow wand, whereupon he jumps up and curses the willow tree.

The crowded room erupted into cheers and laughter as, grinning, the singer stepped away from the mic and returned to her seat.

I watched her, intrigued—she was light-years beyond the other people who'd taken the stage before her.

"Nisa, get back up here," the emcee shouted, gesturing for more applause.

Nisa: that had been one of the names bandied about while I was waiting in line outside. I took another sip of my wine as the singer bounded back across the room for an encore. She stood in front of the microphone, tilting her head to catch the beam of a single follow spot. She closed her eyes and began again to sing: a small figure in a burgundy dress that hugged her curves, her round face dewed with sweat. She had no accompaniment; her voice was a pure soprano with a raspy edge, a razor blade slicing through thick velvet.

"If all those young maids sang like blackbirds
and thrushes
How many young men would go beating the bushes?

If all those young maids were like ducks on the water
How many young men would disrobe and dive under?"

I didn't know the song, but everyone else seemed to. Unlike the previous one, which had been jaunty and quick, this one unfolded slowly, almost mournfully.

I listened, enthralled as, gradually, the song's tone changed—not the tune but the words, and the way that the singer made them come alive, as though awakening something that might have better been left sleeping. The room filled with a susurrus of whispered and half-sung words that formed an eerie counterpoint, voices twining around the singer's in a harmony I found unsettling.

"If all those young men were sheep in the meadow
How many young maids would be burning the tallow?"

Someone began to slap their palms on a table. Others joined in, palms striking softly at first, then more forcefully. The girl's voice grew louder, too, louder than I would have thought possible for such a small figure. Her eyes were wide open now, and she stared at the ceiling, watching something unseen. I looked up but saw only the follow spot, and strings of tinsel dangling from a line of fairy lights.

"If all those young men were rushes a-growing
How many young maids would take scythes and go mowing?"

The thrum of feet pounding the floor joined the measured beat of hands. I heard faint murmurs, words behind the words that were being sung. My mouth was dry; I wanted to stand and leave but I was afraid—not embarrassed, but honestly afraid of what might happen if I tried to go.

"If all those young boys were hares on the mountain
How many young girls would get guns and go hunting?"

Abruptly the woman lowered her head to gaze out into the small crowd. Her eyes seemed unfocused as she repeated the last verse, her voice rising. I heard a sound like wings or footsteps behind the ceiling. And then everyone began to sing along, belting out words as my heartbeat kept time.

"If all those young boys were hares on the mountain
How many young girls would get guns and go hunting?"

The song reached a crescendo. The singer lifted her hands and all fell silent. I felt like I had been caught up in an avalanche, swept down a mountainside until I fetched up here, trying to figure out exactly what I'd just witnessed.

"Thank you!" the woman said, breathless. She appeared off-balance, like she'd had too much to drink. She stepped back, so that the spotlight illuminated only a patch of stage and she stood in shadow. Her dark eyes scanned the room urgently, and I glanced around, trying to see who she was looking for. When I turned back, I saw that she was watching me.

Before I could smile or acknowledge her, she'd already hopped off the stage. I expected her to be immediately surrounded by friends or fans. But while people reached from their chairs to touch her arm or give her a quick embrace, she continued on alone, until she stood by herself at the end of the bar. Another performer took the stage, a guy with a mandolin who started playing "Master of Puppets." I slipped from my chair and joined her.

"That was amazing," I said. "Can I buy you a drink? I'm Holly."

"Sure." She hit me with that wicked grin, crooking a finger at the bartender. "Can I please have a Moscow mule?"

"Same," I said.

It was February 2020. The next night, I made her dinner at my place in Queens. We finished off two bottles of Prosecco I'd bought at the bodega downstairs and stayed up all night talking. I learned she was steeped in music: her paternal grandfather came from St. Vincent, and he'd played with Lord Melody. His son, Nisa's father, had married into a famous clan of folk singers and musicians from Northern England. Her parents had divorced, her mother marrying a music industry lawyer and moving to LA, where Nisa lived until she was eighteen, at which point she'd decamped to New York to try to make it as a singer.

She'd managed to eke out a living on the margins, waiting tables, doing temp work, working for a food delivery service, as she'd built up a small but loyal following over the years. She told me that she loved French movies, especially anything with Juliette Binoche, Caribbean food in Flatbush, and trying to hit every open mic night in the city.

Sometime near dawn, we went to bed for the first time. She stayed over the next night, too, and pretty much never left.

CHAPTER 18

Nisa and I walked from Hill House's conservatory into a short passage, dim and smelling of dust and lemon wood polish. "Are you having second thoughts?" she asked me.

"No. I'm still processing my first thoughts. What about you?"

"I kind of love it. At first I thought you were batshit crazy." She laughed. "But now I can see you working here—you, me, Stevie, Amanda. Imani, if she actually comes. It really could be great. And the acoustics are incredible—I was singing to myself and you heard me all the way back there!"

"Where were you?"

"No idea. I just wandered out one door and down a hallway. I saw another room and I walked in. A little tiny room, a closet maybe? Though it was in a weird place for a closet. But the acoustics! Like Ainsley said, this house plays to people's strengths."

"That's not what she said."

But Nisa had already stepped from the corridor. "Come on, she's waiting."

"There you are." Ainsley appeared relieved to see us. "Thought I'd lost you. This is the dining room..."

The space was large and gloomy, with a long oak table, a sideboard, and a dozen mismatched chairs. A painting of a dying stag hung above a fireplace heaped with ash. The ashes gave the room a dank smell and also left a gray film over the furniture. I ran a finger along the oak table.

"I thought you said someone comes in to clean once a week?"

"She does." Ainsley walked to the fireplace and reached up inside it, tugging at something. A dull thump sounded, and she stepped away. "It's the damper, I think. It won't stay shut. Melissa sweeps out the ashes every time she comes, but they just keep sifting down."

"From where?" asked Nisa.

"We don't know. It's an old house, with so many chimneys, and some of the flues connect. I've never been able to keep track of them."

"There's eight." I smiled, trying not to look like a know-it-all. "I counted when I first came here."

"Oh, there are a lot more than that," Ainsley said vaguely. "I know because I've paid to have them cleaned. Now, this is the kitchen, here."

We followed her into the kitchen—the most comfortable part of the house so far. The walls were painted a sunny yellow, and expensive cookware filled the shelves. In addition to the old woodstove I'd seen from outside, there was a convection oven and high-end fridge, both shiny and almost new.

I opened the refrigerator to admire its pristine shelves. "Let me guess—another short-term tenant."

Ainsley nodded. "The same ones who left that furniture in the living room." She patted the convection oven fondly.

Nisa had wandered over to examine a set of Le Creuset pots and pans, the kind manufactured in France, not the cheaper American versions. "Somebody likes to cook."

"Tru. Melissa's husband. He went to CIA, he was a line cook at Longleat and doing really well. That place where you could only get a reservation by sending in a postcard with your phone number? Soup made from wild mushroom froth and nettles, that sort of thing. He made great money before everything shut down."

"Do he and Melissa stay over sometimes? Is that why he keeps his equipment here?"

"Never. They won't stay overnight. That same couple hired him to come in a few days a week to cook. The cookware was theirs; they left it all behind. Melissa won't let him bring it back to their place."

"Why not?"

Ainsley wrinkled her nose, and I couldn't tell if that was because of Nisa's question, a bad memory, or something else.

"Would he cook for us?" Nisa asked. I tried to catch her eye, warning her against too many questions, but she ignored me.

"Maybe. I know they could use the money. Tru's been out of permanent work for years now, except for what he does for me at Hill House, plowing and minor repairs. He felt like he was going places at Longleat, but…"

Ainsley shook her head. "Longleat closed, and he can't find another job like that around here. It's taken a toll on him. On both of them. On all of us. I always think it will change." She turned to me, the expression on her pale face now utterly defeated. "It never, ever does."

CHAPTER 19

Nisa murmured sympathetically. She stepped alongside Ainsley, fixed her with a sweet smile, and gently touched her arm. I knew that smile—the same one Nisa used to disarm audiences before launching into a version of "Nature Boy" that left them shivering.

"You said the house was demented," she said. "Why is that?"

Ainsley turned her amber ring, as though adjusting an old-fashioned radio dial. "I said that my late husband thought it was demented," she replied. "Not me."

"But why?"

"People project their own expectations onto it. Old houses can be noisy. They settle. The beams and walls expand and contract with the weather. Raccoons get into the attic; there are mice and flying squirrels and critters everywhere. House shrews, voles. That's country life. If you live here, you get used to it."

"What about that woman in the trailer?" I prodded. "The one on the way up here."

"Evadne? What about her?"

"When I drove up this morning, she charged after my car. With a knife."

Ainsley laughed—somewhat bitterly, I thought. "Did she really? That's Evadne. Evadne Morris. She won't bother you. She's a retired social worker—she used to run the domestic abuse shelter in Ashton. I've known her forever. We protested the Gulf War together, that's how long it's been. I sold her the land where her house is. I didn't want to, but..." She sighed. "Baby needs snowshoes."

"She looked like she wanted to attack me. *With a knife,*" I repeated, in case Ainsley hadn't registered that.

"She's very protective of her space. Working with domestic abuse victims will do that. And hunting season starts in a few weeks—she's a bow hunter, she field dresses her kills. Probably she'd been cleaning her gear. But Evadne's not a bad neighbor. Sometimes she acts like she owns this place—not Hill House, the land around it. I don't mind. She keeps an eye out."

"Are those rabbits hers? I saw a black rabbit by the trailer, and another one here before I came inside. It was huge. It—" I fell silent, recalling the animal's disturbingly human grin.

"I wouldn't know about that," said Ainsley.

Somehow, I knew that she was lying.

CHAPTER 20

Ainsley's phone pinged. She looked at it and groaned. "Oh god, I totally forgot! I have a showing in Ashton and they're waiting for me right now. I'm so sorry, I have to go."

She switched off the kitchen light and raced back to the main hall.

"What do you mean?" I took off after her, only dimly aware of Nisa behind me, and caught up with Ainsley on the veranda. "We haven't seen the rest of the house!"

"I know—I'm really sorry, but I've got clients waiting—"

"I'm a client, too," I retorted. "Can we finish looking around and lock up when we're done? Or meet you back here later?"

"No." Ainsley's tone was curt. "If you're really interested, I might be able to schedule some time tomorrow."

"I'll take it." The words came out so quickly that for a second I wasn't certain I was the one who'd spoken them. "For two weeks— could you draw up a contract for that? Say from the first till the middle of October. If I could get in before the end of this month, that would be great. If you'd be willing to prorate the extra days."

Again, Ainsley twisted her ring, the amber gleaming like an animal's tawny eye. Her expression grew avid, until she finally let her hands drop, and the amber eye winked out. "If you're certain you want to do this, yes. I'll need references, but I'll get a contract going and call you when it's ready to sign."

She locked the front door and hurried down the steps. She was already backing her car out, so I remained where I was, watching as the wind sent dead leaves flying after the Mercedes.

"Holly?" Nisa touched my cheek. "Are you sure you want to do this?"

"I'm sure I want to do *something*." My voice shook, misplaced fury and also an odd desperation.

"Why are you so pissed off? It's just a house. And today is the first time I've even heard you mention renting a place to work on the play."

I pulled away from her. "When will we ever have another chance to stay somewhere like this, with enough room to really be alone? When will I ever have another chance to work without being interrupted?" I saw Nisa flinch, but I didn't stop. "And Amanda and Imani will love it, right? It makes me look like I'm the real deal, like for once in my fucking life I know what I'm doing."

"You *do* know what you're doing," Nisa began, then stopped. "Holly?"

I took a step back, chastened. Nisa was right—today was the first time I'd given any serious thought to renting a place for us to work. Why was I so angry? "Jesus. Listen, I'm so sorry. I was—I don't know what I was. I guess I'm just wound up."

I held out my hand, and was relieved when she took it. "You'll have your own space, too," I said. "All those bedrooms upstairs. And we haven't even explored the rest of the first floor."

We walked down the steps, pausing to gaze up at the dilapidated tower. Its gray shingles appeared much darker than they had earlier, stained by rain. But the sky above us shone blue as early morning, and the cool autumn breeze brought the sweet smell of phlox still blooming among the weeds.

Nisa stared at the tower and shook her head. "We can never let Amanda up there, you know."

I tugged up my hood against the wind. "Yeah," I said, and we headed to the car. "I know."

CHAPTER 21

Late that afternoon, Nisa and I went to Ainsley's office to look over the contract. The security deposit was a kicker, but I'd get that back at the end of October. The real financial issue was the weekly cleaning fee.

"Melissa comes in once a week, no matter what," Ainsley said when I tried to negotiate. "And there's going to be a whole group of you, right?"

"Only four or five. But we're all adults, it's not like—"

"I'm sorry, but that's the deal. People here really need the work, especially with winter coming. And Melissa is a good friend. I also need to factor in the price of insurance. There are all kinds of hidden costs you don't know about unless you're a homeowner. I'd rather you didn't use any of the fireplaces—I haven't kept up with cleaning them all, and it's a fire risk."

There were also a number of clauses holding Ainsley free of any liability due to unforeseen causes, including loss of life, sight, hearing, and many other unpleasant events.

"Is that normal?" Nisa pointed to a line. "'Psychological trauma'?"

"In this state, you have to disclose to buyers if any tenant has ever considered the house to be haunted."

"But we're not buying," said Nisa. "And you said it's not haunted."

Ainsley set a pen beside the sheaf of pages on her desk. "I'm just taking precautions."

I took a deep breath. "In for a penny, right?" I signed and dated everything, leaned back in my chair. I felt fizzy-headed, like I'd stood up too fast, but I was sitting down.

"And what about Tru Libby cooking for us?" Nisa blurted out to Ainsley, then looked at me apologetically. "I mean, it would save all of us time and energy, right, Holly? You're the only one who cooks. It would take the pressure off you—off all of us. Like at a residency, we could just concentrate on working."

I thought about it. Nisa hated cooking. Stevie did things with seitan that, had they been inflicted on an innocent piece of fish or chicken, might constitute animal cruelty. I liked to cook, but not for days on end. And we couldn't ask Amanda Greer to prepare our meals.

I turned to Ainsley. "What do you think? Would he charge an arm and a leg?"

Ainsley's expression was unreadable. "Maybe an arm," she said. "I think whatever he charged would seem extremely reasonable to people used to paying city prices. Would you want Melissa to come in more often, to clean up?"

I stared at the contract, adding up the rent and various fees.

Nisa took my hand. "I shouldn't have said anything. We can all pitch in with meals, Holly, if that's what you want. The others won't mind—Stevie won't, for sure. And Amanda, I'm sure she won't either."

Amanda. Could I honestly ask Amanda Greer to pitch in with cooking and cleaning? What if she hated my chicken with olives and lemon? Did she even eat chicken?

I ran a finger across Nisa's knuckles. "No," I said. "It's a good idea. I want us to focus on work. I just need to budget for it. And probably I can write it off my taxes. So yes, Ainsley, if you don't mind, ask Tru and Melissa if they'd be open to the idea."

Ainsley nodded. "I'll talk to Melissa and sound her out, see if I can get a number for you."

She jumped to her feet, handing me my copy of the contract. "I don't see any problem with you coming a few days early, if you want to get settled before the others arrive." She seemed immediately more at ease now that the contract was signed, almost ebullient. "I'll let you know as soon as I can what I hear from Melissa."

Ainsley walked us outside to my car. I slid into the passenger seat and rolled down the window. For a few seconds I imagined Hill House and its tangled lawns, the rushing stream and the big black hare: everything transformed by the hours away into a bright image, like a page from a children's picture book. I felt a sudden desire to be there now with Nisa, to hole up in one of the bedrooms and never emerge.

When I looked up, I saw Nisa still standing in front of Ainsley's office. She gazed up at the promontory that rose high above us, hiding the view of Hill House. After a moment, she closed her eyes and began to sing.

"I feared I'd never have a home—
An outcast, hated and reviled
Until you found me, dear Tomasin,
And by your craft my enemies beguiled…"

I listened raptly, as did Ainsley. Nisa fell silent and spread her arms. Ainsley applauded on cue, and Nisa beamed.

"That's one of the songs I'm working on for the play," she explained.

"What a gorgeous voice!" Ainsley stared at her in delight, then at me. "Aren't you lucky that your girlfriend's your composer? Enjoy the rest of your stay—I'll be in touch."

"We will!" Nisa replied. She got into the car beside me, her face rosy with pleasure. "This will be good luck, Holly, I can feel it."

"I do, too," I said, meaning it, and started to drive back to our rental.

CHAPTER 22

The next several weeks went quickly, as Nisa and I prepared for the time ahead. I wished I'd taken more photos of Hill House to show to Stevie and Amanda Greer. Imani had bowed out—her daughter had college visits scheduled during the period we'd be there—but she'd assured me she was on board with directing the public reading once we all returned to the city.

The few overexposed photos I had weren't worth sharing, though I found myself gazing at them when no one else was around, feeling a faint jolt every time I did, as though I'd been sneaking a look at Nisa's phone. But mostly I was busy packing, and making sure Stevie didn't do something impulsive, like invite some guy he'd met on Grindr to come along.

I also had to make arrangements with Amanda. Who, it turned out, didn't want to tell her agent she was taking the job.

"It's two weeks out of town, without a producer attached—she'll tell me not to waste my time," she said when we spoke one afternoon. "No offense. But I really do like the script, and I'm sure we can come to an agreement..."

The agreement was considerably more than I'd anticipated, but probably less than what I'd have to shell out if I went through Amanda's agent and Equity. I went over my bank balance, totting up what I'd already paid out for Hill House, for Amanda Greer, for Melissa and Tru Libby (who had indeed agreed to cook), not to mention gas and food. Whenever I felt anxious at how quickly my grant money was disappearing, I'd scroll again through my blurry photos of Hill House and envision myself on the veranda with Nisa, a bottle of champagne between us as we watched the sun slide down the October sky.

And at last, we were headed back to Hillsdale, the day before Amanda was scheduled to arrive. Stevie came with Nisa and me, scrunched in the back seat along with our pillows, backpacks, and the oversized duffel bag that contained his laptop, microphone, and other recording equipment. Also his arsenal of vape pens, both tobacco and cannabis; a prescription bottle of alprazolam that had Stevie's name on it, though the various pills, mostly but not limited to sedatives, had in fact been pilfered from numerous friends and relatives.

"It stays with me, you know that," Stevie said when I'd raised an eyebrow at the duffel, currently flopped over his lap like an enormous green-and-white-striped slug. "If I put it in the trunk there'll be no room for Nisa's case of wine, or her guitar, or her books, or her extremely special coffee hand-roasted by cloistered nuns..."

"Oh my god," moaned Nisa. "How many weeks of this, Holly? And it's not nuns, it's Trappist monks."

Stevie and I burst out laughing. "Good to know," I said.

It was a beautiful morning. We'd left before dawn, and hit the Taconic at sunrise. The autumn leaves were just past peak, scarlet and blaze orange and luminous yellow. It was so early there were few other cars on the parkway. I glanced at Nisa. "Are you excited?"

"*So* excited," Stevie replied before Nisa could open her mouth. "You said this house is haunted, did you ever find out what the deal is?"

"Not haunted. Ainsley told us that—"

"Because I did." Stevie opened his window to take a hit from a vape pen, exhaling rose-scented mist. "The woman whose husband built the place was killed when her carriage ran into a tree. That was in 1880. Then another woman was killed about sixty years ago when her car ran into the same tree. Same thing happened again with another woman in the eighties. They finally cut the tree down."

"That doesn't sound haunted," I said. "It sounds like bad driveway design. I saw the stump—that tree must've been huge, I don't know how you couldn't see it."

"It was on a forum about haunted houses." Stevie adjusted his glasses in a professorial way, as though he were lecturing on DNA splicing rather than a Reddit thread. "They think maybe one of them killed herself. And there was something about a kid who might have poisoned his family when they were living there. No, not his family," he said, musing. "Someone visiting them. But that was a lot later, in the eighties, maybe."

"Wow." Nisa slid down in her seat. "That's crazy. Did you google it?"

"Of course I did."

"And…"

"And nothing. It was before the Internet, and Hillsdale's in the middle of nowhere. A couple mentions of a small-town tragedy, and Hillsdale got name-checked in some old article about all those Satanic preschool cases. Also, one on Satanic D&D players. Otherwise the only thing I saw was that one post on Reddit."

Nisa shot me a triumphant look. "I told you there were ghosts! Ainsley was lying."

"Nobody said they saw a ghost," Stevie said mournfully. "Just, you know, that Hill House has bad vibes. Also, bad cell reception."

"Haunted houses never have cell reception." Nisa turned to face Stevie. "That's how you know they're haunted."

Stevie laughed with more enthusiasm than her remark warranted. She leaned into the back seat to take his hand. "I'm so glad you're here," she said.

"Me too," he replied.

Stevie and I had met right out of school, at a shoestring theater that operated out of a former massage parlor on Broome Street. *Pay to Look,* a trio of short plays I'd written, had run there for a weekend. Stevie was the sound guy. Each play was based on a peep show. *Diableries* was inspired by an 1840 Parisian lithograph, and *The Murder of Maria Martin in the Red Barn* by a peep show from 1894 England; *Pay to Look* was based on my own fleeting experience as an Internet sex worker to put myself through my final year of college.

Pay to Look was only performed that one weekend, but Stevie behaved as though we'd been signed to a West End run. His sound design was exquisite: eerie captures of voices, distant rumblings of thunder, screams that became the cries of seagulls. I was surprised he knew about nineteenth-century peep shows, but it turned out Stevie was obsessed with Victorian toy theaters, which dovetailed with my own taste for Grand Guignol. He had an odd collection and would sometimes bring some of his cardboard models to our rehearsals.

"Don't you just wish you could disappear inside it?" he'd asked me once, reluctantly folding up a portrayal of *The True Story of Bluebeard.*

"I wouldn't fit. And you sure wouldn't."

We'd been so close back then, though never romantically involved. Stevie slept with both men and women, whereas I hadn't touched a guy sexually since I was in high school. We'd get high and wonder why we couldn't fall in love with each other, and not narcissistic children's book editors and actresses (me), and a series of bodybuilders, usually lawyers, prone to steroid-induced rages (Stevie).

"Is love dysphoria a thing?" he'd wondered aloud one night as we lay on his couch, limbs entwined and so stoned I couldn't feel my tongue. "Because I think that's what I have."

"It'll happen, baby," I'd reassured him.

But it never really had.

"Did you bring any of your creepy theaters?" I asked, hoping to shift his attention from Nisa.

"I did!" Stevie let go of Nisa's hand, stretching his long legs so his feet bumped the opposite side of the car. "*Bluebeard,* an original Jacobsen I found on eBay—Danish, it was *so* expensive but it's beautiful. The sets are all from a Moorish castle. I swear you could live in it. If you were, like, two inches tall."

"Oh my god, you are such a geek, Stevie." Nisa batted at him playfully.

"You'll thank me when you hear what I've done for your show. *Our* show," he corrected himself, catching a glimpse of my face in the rear-view mirror. "Holly's show."

"Our show," Nisa repeated, and stuck in her earbuds.

CHAPTER 23

It had been months since Nisa and Stevie had hooked up. Holly never knew, of course, and Nisa intended to keep it that way. Yet when she'd just touched his hand, she'd felt that familiar shock of recognition—intense desire and longing, not just to be with him but to protect him. Tall as he was, he always reminded her of an overgrown kid, with his tortoiseshell glasses and long brown hair falling into his face. With Stevie, it was easy to feel young, the way she had when she'd first started singing at open mics and seen the wonder in people's eyes. Who wouldn't want to feel like that all the time? That was why she loved him.

Holly never let her forget that they had adult worries and responsibilities—rent, health insurance, trying to save enough money so they weren't constantly living meager paycheck to meager paycheck. Nisa had hoped the grant would change that, and now it seemed like it had. She hadn't seen Holly so happy and relaxed in years, maybe since they'd first met. It made Nisa feel safe, like she could at last let her guard down and do what she did best—sing.

Yet Holly was so hypercompetitive about Nisa's contributions to the play. She knew how much better *Witching Night* was with Nisa involved but hadn't yet let anyone else hear Nisa sing, or even read the lyrics she'd adapted from old murder ballads. Nisa had grown up with those songs, steeped in their charged beauty and terror, in the legacy of violence that haunted women and children. She loved that tragedy could be transformed into works of uncanny, unsettling beauty, passed down for hundreds of years. People think that old ballads are about love, but really, they're about blood.

She stared out the window at the autumn trees, an old sign for the Chief Taghkanic Diner, the turnoff for Queechy Lake. She glanced at the time. Another two hours, and they should be back at Hill House. She recalled how her voice had sounded in that vast empty space, like a captive songbird finally loosed to soar up and disappear into the shadows, until only its echo remained. Now she hummed softly, too low for Holly to hear.

"Oh, Lamkin was a mason fine
As ever built with stone
He built Lord Wearie's castle
But payment he got none..."

The song was "Lamkin," one of the most gruesome of the Child Ballads and perfect for the play. If Nisa had been alone in the car with Stevie, they'd have rolled the windows down so she could belt it out.

"And O, it was a ghastly sight
When Lord Wearie came he home
And gazed upon his wife and child
Both bleeding on the stones..."

Holly loved watching Nisa perform onstage, but she got annoyed when Nisa auditioned for plays—musicals and, more often, straight plays. Jealousy, Nisa thought—Holly didn't like to think that Nisa could succeed where Holly hadn't.

And Holly got embarrassed when Nisa broke into song when they were walking outside, or at a party. She didn't understand how Nisa needed that release. Like sex, or being able to laugh until you cried, two things that Stevie was really good at.

Nisa glanced at him in the back seat, his eyes tightly closed and his lanky form twisted into a shape that Nisa yearned to untangle. *Oh, Stevie,* she thought, and then turned to clasp Holly's hand on the wheel.

"Love you," she murmured, and Holly smiled.

"You, too." Holly gave her a squeeze.

Nisa looked out the window, yawning. She'd only been on this route once before, when she and Holly came up to visit Giorgio and Theresa and discovered Hill House, but already the world outside felt both familiar and unknown, shimmering with some secret meaning. She reminded herself of the way Holly tasted, the way Holly looked at her when she sang up on stage. Nisa felt a shiver of delight at the thought of the days that lay ahead: she would wrap her supple voice around all those old ballads, squeezing them to see what came out, twisting the words until they become something unrecognizable, something you might hear in the dark.

CHAPTER 24

I drove in silence, torn between annoyance and relief that Nisa and Stevie had both fallen asleep, or were at least quiet. I wouldn't have to keep listening to their laughter over jokes I never seemed to be in on. Beside me, Nisa's heavy breath smelled of the spearmint weed gummy she'd eaten before we left. I glanced into the rearview mirror to see Stevie hugging his duffel, one leg scrunched into the wheel well, the other bent almost double and still grazing the door. Ouch.

Stevie was six foot four, lanky and stoop-shouldered. It was a joke that his name was Stevie Liddell, when he'd spent his life folding himself into spaces too small for him. A child star who played the Artful Dodger in a Caldbeck Playhouse revival of *Oliver!,* he was very public about the fact that he'd been groomed and sexually abused by one of the cast.

"Not by Fagin. Or Bill Sykes," he confided one night. "That would at least have been, you know, *Dickensian*. But he was this random guy in the chorus. He was just an ordinary pedophile."

"Didn't you tell anyone?"

"No. I was eleven, he was nineteen. I was excited to have this older kid as a friend. He died right after I got out of high school. He was in the MFA program at Yale and he went through a guardrail, doing ninety on the Merritt. I still feel a surge of happiness every time I drive past New Haven."

When Stevie's voice changed, he went from a cocky pipsqueak onstage to a beanpole middle schooler who was constantly tripping over untied shoelaces and furniture that seemed to move as he approached it. Eyeglasses helped, but by high school he was spending most of his time on his computer, creating music and DJing for parties. He did tech for school plays and community theater, and at first skipped college in favor of traveling cross-country to perform at music festivals.

By the time we met in school, he was intermittently working in theater again, doing sound. He favored flannel shirts and Carhartts before they became fashionable, and frequented neo-pagan shops like Hecate Rising.

That was another thing we had in common—witches. One reason I taught *Macbeth* to my students was that I'd fallen in love with Shakespeare when I was the same age, watching the three Weird Sisters stand over a plastic cauldron filled with dry ice, their faces painted with eldritch symbols I knew represented secrets far darker than anything ordinary thirteen-year-olds should know.

I pulled the car into Hillsdale shortly before noon. Ainsley had gone away for the weekend, but she'd left Hill House's keys under a flower pot outside her office. Nisa and Stevie woke up as I parked, hopping from the car to stretch.

"We're almost there!" Nisa sang. She hugged me as I returned to the car, key in hand. "Aren't you excited?"

"I am," I said, grinning. And I was.

CHAPTER 25

The six-mile drive up the winding road passed more quickly this time. I steeled myself for the sight of Evadne Morris as Stevie peered out the back window.

"Is that her trailer? The crazy lady with an ax?"

"Evadne, her name's Evadne. And it wasn't an ax, it was a knife. And Ainsley said she's nice."

"A knife doesn't sound very nice."

"Ainsley did not say she's nice," countered Nisa. "Ainsley said she's territorial and acts like she owns Hill House. She's a retired social worker."

Stevie gazed at Evadne's yard, still aflame with goldenrod and late-blooming tiger lilies. "I thought she'd be sitting on the porch with a shotgun in her lap," he said, disappointed.

"No porch," pointed out Nisa.

"Whoa—slow down, Holly..."

I tapped the brake, turning to see what Stevie pointed at.

"Those rocks." He stabbed at the window with a finger. "It's a stone circle—see? It goes all the way around the trailer. And there's a witch ball, too." His voice rose, triumphant. "She's a witch."

I let the car roll to a stop. He was right about the stone circle—how had I missed that before? The plants had hidden it, I realized. Now that the clumps of hostas and ferns had died back, you could see the rocks nestled within them. Most were knee high, a few almost four feet tall.

They formed a circle—more of an oval—encompassing the trailer and pretty much the entire yard, including the vegetable garden. A clothesline stretched above the dying tomato plants. Flattened aluminum cans dangled from it, along with animal bones and skulls, the jawbones of what might have been deer. There was some kind of scarecrow, too, made of branches and rags tied together to suggest a skeletal shape, with too many limbs and no head.

At one end of the stone circle, a ceramic pedestal held a silvery mirror ball streaked red and blue where it reflected maple leaves and sky.

"A gazing ball." Nisa smiled. "I love those."

Stevie shook his head. "It's called a witch ball. My grandmother's from Salem, everyone has one. They use them for scrying. And protection."

"She's not taking any chances." Nisa pointed at the skulls. "And—oh! Holly, look!"

An immense black rabbit had emerged from a ring of yellowing ferns. It hesitated, then leapt a good six feet to land beside the witch ball, raising itself on its hind legs to stare at us with coppery eyes. Stevie whistled.

"Is that a rabbit? It's as big as a couch!"

Nisa unrolled her window to take a photo. "Don't!" I hit the gas, and Nisa slammed back against her seat.

"What is wrong with you?" she exclaimed, fumbling for her dropped phone.

"It's her house! Someone lives there, you can't just stop and take pictures of her yard. A stranger, she——"

"Are you crazy? Stevie's entire Instagram feed is pictures of strangers crying on the L train."

"I only did that for a week," Stevie protested. "I felt bad so I deleted the account."

"Whatever." Nisa sighed as she scrolled through her phone. "You can't just tell someone they—oh."

She fell silent, staring at the screen while I fumed. Why had I thought I could survive five hours in the car with Nisa and Stevie, let alone two weeks in the middle of nowhere?

In only a few more minutes we reached the gate. Someone had cleared away the piles of fallen leaves and removed the decaying ivy. The realization that somebody else had been here, tidying the place up, made me feel better.

"They're expecting us," I said as we headed up the driveway.

"Who?" demanded Stevie.

"I don't know." I glanced at Nisa. She still hadn't said a word, just stared intently at her phone, using her fingers to enlarge, then shrink the image on the screen. "Everything okay?"

She held the phone out to me, and I stopped the car to look at it.

In the photo she'd just taken, there was no evidence of the rabbit, though I knew it had been there. We had all seen it.

Rather than the hare, a person stood beside the gazing ball. One hand resting upon its smooth reflective surface, the other hand raised, palm out, as she stared at the camera. A dark-haired woman in a blue hoodie. The photo had been enlarged so that I could see the deep grooves beside her mouth and her eyes, such a pale blue they seemed to have no iris, just a black fleck of pupil.

Evadne Morris.

CHAPTER 26

I handed the phone back to Nisa and continued to drive.

"Didn't you see?" Nisa demanded. "Holly!"

"See what?" asked Stevie, and Nisa passed the phone to him. "What am I looking at?"

"Her. Evadne."

"What happened to the rabbit?"

"You tell me."

Stevie returned the phone to Nisa. "That picture is messed up. She wasn't even outside. And I can't get service up here. Or, well, I can, but then every time it loads, everything freezes and turns red."

"Red?" asked Nisa.

He took out his phone, holding it up so we could see the screen, murky red streaked with brown and black. Nisa frowned. "Did you drop it?"

"No. It started back by that church. I think Satan ate my phone."

I steered past the large tree stump, careful not to draw Stevie's attention to it, and up the last curve to where Hill House waited.

"Shit," I muttered. My heart sank. "People are already here."

Two vehicles were parked in the circular drive. An old white pickup, its back loaded with cleaning supplies and a blaze-orange vest, and a Morris Minor, poison-apple green, with New York plates that read *THSPIAN.*

Amanda Greer had shown up a day early.

Nisa made a face. "Oh jeez. She beat us."

"Who? Oh!" Stevie stared at the Morris Minor and exploded into laughter. "'Thespian'? Are you kidding me?"

"Shut up," I ordered, and put my car in park. "If you screw this up, Stevie—"

"Oh please. You know I won't. But seriously, who has that license plate?" He opened his door and scrambled out, long legs and arms unfolding like a children's toy. "As long as she didn't take my room."

"Or ours," said Nisa. None of us had ever been upstairs, but we'd already claimed the two bedrooms that Ainsley had said were the nicest: Nisa and I in the Rose Room, Stevie in the Yellow Room next door.

We unpacked the car and stood for a minute in silence, taking in our surroundings. Up here, the glorious late-summer weather had already passed. The shift in altitude left Hill House more exposed to the elements, and most of the leaves were gone from the trees. They'd been raked in piles across the lawn, brown heaps that resembled grave mounds. But the goldenrod still was in bloom, and yellowing cattails nodded along the banks of the stream at wood's edge.

"Well." I took a deep breath and hefted my bags. "Ready?"

Nisa and I started for the steps, but Stevie held back. "Did you even check this place out?" he asked, staring at the upper story. "On TripAdvisor or something? It doesn't feel safe to me."

I knew that tone and that look. Stevie was super sensitive to anyone or anything he perceived as a threat. I chalked it up to what had happened to him in *Oliver!* Hanging out at occult boutiques probably didn't help, either. I used to tease him about it, when he'd warn me about events or people that he claimed weren't safe.

Yet he was often right. He'd told Nisa and me not to attend that party at the Brooklyn pop-up where a fire killed seven people. He'd insisted his brother get an MRI for his migraines, which revealed he had a small tumor—benign, as it turned out. Another time, Stevie told his then-boyfriend to take the New London ferry to Greenpoint for Thanksgiving, rather than 495. The boyfriend ignored him and was killed in a pileup when a tractor-trailer jackknifed in a snow squall.

Of course, usually Stevie got wound up because we chose a Nepalese restaurant for dinner over his favorite Cuban. Still, I'd learned to pay attention when he gave me that look.

Which he was doing now. "No. It's a private rental. It looks safe to me."

"Obviously not the tower," said Nisa.

Stevie clutched the heavy duffel to his chest like a personal flotation device. He gazed at the third-floor windows, dark despite the noon sun.

"Stevie." I touched his shoulder, and he began to fall backward. Nisa lunged for him as I grabbed his arm.

"What the fuck, Holly?" he said, straightening.

"You were zoning out! Are you okay?"

"I'm fine!"

"You didn't look fine." I glanced up at Hill House. "What's not safe?"

"Nothing. Everything is fine."

He grinned, lips parting so I saw his teeth, threaded with red. He'd bitten his lip when he'd lost his balance. I thought of the hare that had reared onto its hind legs to smile at me.

"I'm fine, Holly," he repeated, and headed up the steps. "You're right, everything is fine."

CHAPTER 27

Inside the main hall, thin sunlight filtered through the half-opened doorway and the windows. A strong scent of lemon polish and Murphy Oil Soap hung in the air, proof that Melissa Libby had been hard at work, but that foul underlying odor remained. Maybe there wasn't a dead mouse beneath the floorboards but something bigger, like a squirrel or raccoon?

I stopped and set down my bags, unsure what to do next. I saw no sign of Amanda or anyone else. Stevie was surveying the hall, but Nisa remained by the front door. She threw her head back, taking in the movie-ready stairway and minstrel gallery near the tower, and started to sing.

> *"She turned herself into a hare,*
> *To run about yon hill,*
> *And he became a quick greyhound*
> *And boldly he did follow..."*

She drew a breath, her voice echoing from the beams high above us.

"I'd rather I were dead and gone
And my body laid in grave——"

"Stop." Stevie put his hand over her mouth. Nisa pushed him away angrily as he said, "You're creeping me out."

"I wanted to test the acoustics."

"Not the right time, Nis. Read the room," he said, and gestured at me. "We just got here."

"I heard someone," I broke in, hurrying to the door near the stairway. "In the kitchen, maybe?"

The door opened onto the dim passage. I ran my hands along the walls, vainly searching for a light switch before I resorted to my phone's flashlight. It cast a dull beam as the others followed, Stevie right behind me, then Nisa, who complained, "Why didn't we just go the other way?"

"Come on, Nis," I said. "It's an adventure."

But it didn't feel like an adventure. Even with the phone's light, the corridor was so dark that I had to keep one hand pressed against the wall to find my way. The foul smell from the hall was stronger here—it filled my nostrils until I nearly gagged, then abruptly dissipated. I felt Stevie's fingers on my neck, steering me forward, then stroking my hair as he whispered, *Here,* or maybe *Hair.*

After a few seconds, the shadows diminished, as though someone had turned up a lamp. I could see where the cramped passage ended, a bright rectangle with blurred shapes moving within it, like fish in an aquarium. Nineties music played—jarringly, "Jump Around." We stumbled into the kitchen, blinking at the sunlight.

"You found us!" a woman exclaimed. She looked about my age, late thirties, and wore a do-rag around her dark hair, eyelids shimmering with silver and blue makeup. Women in Hillsdale really did seem to go all out. "Amanda's here, but I thought you weren't coming till tomorrow."

"No," I said, relieved to have escaped the passage but frustrated to feel so off-balance. "We were always coming today—Amanda wasn't supposed to come till tomorrow."

The woman laughed. "Well, she's here now. I'm Melissa." She stuck out her hand—silver nail polish, and I was surprised to see a silver ring like Ainsley's, with a chunk of amber big enough I could tell something was embedded in it, a tiny insect or petal. "Tru ran into town for oat milk, I guess that's what she puts in her coffee. Amanda. Did you find your rooms okay?"

"We barely found our way here," said Stevie.

We introduced ourselves as Melissa picked up her phone and switched it off. The music stopped. "Sorry about that. For some reason that one song keeps coming up on my playlist, it drives me nuts. But let's get your stuff and I'll show you your bedrooms. You've been here before, right?"

"Not the second floor," I said, as we followed her through a door that opened directly back onto the main hall.

Nisa looked at me. "How'd we miss that shortcut?"

"Maybe she brought the door with her," Stevie cut in.

We retrieved our belongings and straggled upstairs after Melissa. Nisa had only the bag with her clothes—she'd left her musical gear and wine in the car for later. She bounded up the steps, leaving Stevie and me to trudge with our own stuff. I gazed at the landing above us, its dark paneling and high ceiling lost in shadow, and my trepidation gave way to excitement.

This would be our home for the next two weeks. *Witching Night* would come to life here, my words and Nisa's songs, with Amanda Greer as Elizabeth Sawyer and Stevie as Tomasin, the black devil dog. Stevie would record our rehearsals, then work his peculiar magic on his laptop, looping and distorting everything, until our own voices became unrecognizable. We'd use that track as part of the live performance, too.

I felt a pang, recalling my earlier annoyance. Stevie was my oldest friend. He'd turned down a lucrative DJ gig to be here, money he couldn't really afford to lose. I paused to wait for him.

"Thanks," he said, adjusting his duffel. "This sucker's heavy."

"Thank you for coming. It means a lot to me. And Nisa, too."

"How could I miss this? "

We climbed the last few steps side by side. As we neared the landing, I paused to look back. The individual stair treads held dark impressions, left by generations of feet passing up and down.

Yet Ainsley had told me that few people had ever lived here. Except for those who had spent their lives at Hill House long ago, the mansion had been mostly empty for decades. There would have been servants, I supposed, and the occasional guest. Maybe someone had tracked in paint or blacktop, a stain Melissa couldn't erase?

I turned to Stevie, still waiting for me on the landing. "You okay, Holly?"

I nodded and joined him. "Had to catch my breath. Hey, what was it you said when we were walking to the kitchen?" He appeared bemused. "You were playing with my hair, I couldn't hear what you said."

He shook his head. "Maybe it was Nisa? I didn't touch your hair."

CHAPTER 28

Nisa and Melissa were waiting in the hallway, Nisa looking royally pissed off.

"Amanda took our room," she announced. She didn't bother to keep her voice down. "Even after Melissa told her it was our room, she totally ignored her!"

"I'm so sorry," said Melissa. Nervously, she loosened her do-rag, immediately reknotting it around her head. "I just thought you'd changed your minds about the sleeping arrangements."

She stared down a long hall that ran the length of the house, a number of closed doors on either side. I sighed. "Look, it doesn't matter. We can just—"

"It does too matter, Holly," Nisa said angrily. "You're the reason we're here, you should have first choice."

"What, are you twelve?" Stevie snapped. "You two can have my room—it's right next to that one, right?"

He turned to Melissa, who nodded. Stevie said, "Great. Now if you can just show me where the inferior bedrooms are, I'll unload my stuff and get settled."

Melissa accompanied us down the hall. The first door on our right was cracked, giving me a glimpse of a large suitcase on the floor and a window opened onto the October afternoon. Amanda's room.

Melissa halted. "How about this one, Stevie? The people who were here last, they were going to paint all the bedrooms. This was the only one they actually did."

Melissa opened the door. I winced, as did Nisa. Stevie's face tightened, but he just edged past Melissa into the room. "Great. This'll be fine."

"It's the same size as the others," Melissa said. "It's just..."

She gave us a helpless look. Because the room was just...awful. Pale lavender paint had been applied without first removing the wallpaper beneath, so that the surface had bubbled and buckled. The plaster ceiling had a large medallion in the center—a stylized sun, I thought, then saw it was a face, only flattened like it had been smashed in a car wreck. Its eyes resembled two holes poked in soft dough and its smile seemed menacing, almost a silent scream.

A newish, Scandi-style bed was pushed against the back wall, flanked by matching nightstands, Anglepoise lamps, and a striped rag rug. A too-big bureau had been jammed awkwardly against another wall like an afterthought. The decor aimed at bright and airy but had the opposite effect. The room felt dingy and cluttered. In spots the wallpaper had peeled away, revealing an older layer of wall covering, a mottled purple paisley that looked like dead jellyfish. It smelled utterly neglected, which seemed odd for a room that had been painted only a year before.

"It's just...so *cozy*." Stevie finished Melissa's sentence. "It's like the room in a Bergman movie where the maid lives. The one who ends up sleeping with her employer, who then kills her and takes on her identity."

"That's a different movie," said Nisa.

"It's actually like five different movies. Bergman, Argento, Hitchcock, De Palma, I forget who else. Whatever." He threw his duffel onto the bed. "I don't care. Thank you, Melissa. It's a lovely room and I'm sure I'll be very comfortable. If not, I can just move, right?"

"Of course," Melissa said quickly. I couldn't tell if she was relieved or apprehensive. Both, I decided. "I'll let you get settled. Holly and Nisa, you're next."

We walked down the hall to where Melissa had opened a door on the opposite side. Like Stevie's, this room had been redecorated, portions of the dark wainscoting painted pale yellow. Remnants of wallpaper clung to the corners and the original pattern bled through, garlands of orange flowers darkened to rust. The wainscoting's original wood stain showed through the yellow paint here and there like muddy handprints.

"Is that mold?" Nisa gingerly touched the wall.

"No." Melissa remained in the doorway. "They left before they did a second coat. Tru keeps saying he'll finish it, but..." She shrugged. "I don't think anything's really been done here since it was built. Things get started, but nothing's ever finished."

"Aren't all old houses like that?" I asked, hoping to lighten the mood. "That's what I always hear."

Melissa shook her head. "All old houses are definitely not like this one. Ainsley hasn't been able to get someone to finish a job here for thirty years. Before the pandemic, it was tough to get anyone to come. Now it's impossible."

"But you're here. And Tru."

"We're here because we need the work," she retorted angrily. "Tru can't find another cooking job, so he's helping Ross Littlefield deliver firewood and fills in at the gas station on weekends. He did catering off and on for summer people from the city but they all left after Labor Day.

"One of them stiffed him," she went on, staring pointedly at me. "We're barely getting by. I had clients in Ashton, but with the price of gas, that's too far to drive. And no one will hire me if I raise my rates. Thank god for Ainsley. She's keeping us afloat. Barely."

I grew hot. Did Melissa think I was some rich city person, acting like a diva because I didn't get the bedroom we'd been promised? I wanted to snap back with the truth, that this was an unimaginable luxury for all of us. Well, maybe not Amanda, but certainly for me and Nisa and Stevie. I started to argue but felt Nisa's light touch on my shoulder, as she looked sympathetically to Melissa.

"It sounds like you're the one keeping this place afloat," she said, and smiled.

Melissa didn't smile back. She remained in the doorway, arms crossed, and tilted her head toward the bedroom. "So, what do you think? Is this okay with both of you? It's right next to Amanda's—the two rooms are identical. Not the furniture but everything else. There's a shared bathroom, but Amanda didn't seem to have a problem with that. If you change your minds, you can always move into one of the other rooms. Let me know and I'll put on clean sheets."

"That won't be necessary," Nisa said. "This looks fine. Thank you so much, Melissa."

"Yes, thank you," I said, and Melissa gave me a grudging nod.

I took a step into the room along with Nisa. We'd known about the shared bath—another reason we wanted Stevie next to us, and not Amanda Greer. I saw the effort it took for Nisa to bite her tongue as she surveyed the space, taking in a sleigh bed, bird's-eye maple armoire, a worn green velvet armchair, and Persian carpet in shades of mustard and celadon. On the wall, an etching of an English country house, where a tiny figure pushed an old-fashioned lawn roller through the formal garden.

The antiques all appeared disgruntled and out of place, well-heeled guests marooned in a crappy budget motel. Tentatively, Nisa sat on the bed. The mattress didn't give an inch. She grimaced. "It feels like pavement."

"It'll be fine." I turned to Melissa. "Thank you very much. I appreciate everything you've done."

"*We* appreciate it." Nisa got to her feet and walked over to Melissa. "From what Ainsley says, Hill House has quite the history."

Melissa ignored her comment. "You should be able to find everything you need in the kitchen," she said. "I left some granola in the pantry, along with coffee and tea. Tru left your dinner for tonight in the fridge with instructions for heating it. There's lasagna for tomorrow night. I got you some cold cuts and salad fixings. Probably we'll be by tomorrow morning, but if there's anything else you need, just text me or leave a list. If he gets a work call, I'll drop off what I can."

"I hope we get to meet him, too," I said. "Maybe you can have dinner with us one night?"

She shook her head. "We don't ever come here after dark."

"Never?"

"Never," she repeated emphatically. "So don't ask." She tucked a strand of hair behind her ear. "I'll finish up a few things downstairs, and then I'm taking off."

Nisa and I thanked her yet again, stepping into the hall. The door to the room next to ours was now closed. "Is she really in there?" Nisa asked Melissa.

"Oh yeah. She's here all right." Melissa shot me a look I couldn't unpack. "You have a good night."

We returned to our bedroom. Nisa walked to the window and pulled back the sickly yellow-gray curtains. "Ugh, this house!"

She tied the curtains back and cracked the window—the room was stuffy, heat wafting up from a brass floor register.

"It's not that bad," I said, opening the armoire to put away my clothes. "And if we don't like this room, we can just move to another. We can move in with Amanda."

"I still don't believe she's here. She could have sent a body double. A replicant. She might have used a 3D printer to duplicate herself. Wouldn't the real Amanda have come out and given us a chance to express our undying gratitude for her taking the role?"

I laughed, as Nisa put a finger to her lips and tiptoed to the bathroom door. She got down on all fours to peer through the crack beneath. And screamed.

CHAPTER 29

Amanda was pleased to arrive before the other actors. Why should she wait an extra day? She was eager to get down to work. Plus, she didn't like the idea of them being there without her, gossiping and perhaps even cutting lines without Amanda present to put in her two cents.

Holly Sherwin had given her the real estate agent's contact info, so Amanda called Ainsley Rowan and arranged to meet her at Hill House. Holly had pitched it as a mansion: it felt more like a gargantuan folly, one of those smaller, faux-Gothic buildings that rich English people stuck somewhere on the grounds of their stately homes. Amanda'd once had a small part in a forgotten Merchant Ivory movie filmed at an estate in Kent, where the folly was a stone and crumbling concrete grotto, complete with real bats and slimy green walls.

Hill House wasn't quite so revolting, Amanda thought as she waited for Ainsley to unlock the front door. The exterior design was terrible, all those windows and doors aligned to suggest a deranged face. She wondered if the architect had some vendetta against the owner.

But there was no mold that she could see, and as she followed Ainsley inside, she was relieved to note that it didn't smell particularly musty.

The light was dim, despite the numerous windows, but Amanda had no problem with that—much more flattering to a woman of uncertain years.

"Holly has you in the Yellow Room," Ainsley announced as they walked upstairs, Amanda lugging her bag. "This one—"

Ainsley opened the door and Amanda glanced inside. Yuck. "What about this one?" she asked, turning the knob of the door beside it.

"That's the Rose Room, she and Nisa are—"

"It's perfect." Amanda walked in, turning to look at the blush-pink walls, the large window overlooking the veranda and leaf-covered lawns. Peach-colored curtains patterned with mottled carnations that had an unpleasantly meaty appearance, matching bedspread and pillows. A much better color than yellow. Well, marginally better. "Thank you!" she exclaimed brightly, and closed the door before Ainsley could argue.

Sun streamed through the window—here, she wanted bright light, the better to put on her makeup and fix her hair. One needed to keep up appearances in the hinterlands, a lesson she'd learned doing summer stock as a girl. You never knew who you might run into, even in a cultural wasteland, and you never knew who might prove useful.

Holly Sherwin was a case in point. Amanda remembered meeting her decades ago at Lilith Fair—a fifteen-year-old girl, overwhelmed by the performance she'd just seen and fumbling for words. The starstruck part wasn't unusual. Amanda's appearance in a tent, in front of an audience of seventeen mostly older women, was. She'd been reduced to jobs like this ever since the accident with Jason Pratt. Rebecca, her agent, used to advise against her taking them.

"Your star will shine again, Amanda. Take a year or two off, people will forget."

But Amanda couldn't afford to take time off—Rebecca of all people should know that.

And she didn't want to take time off. Being away from performing felt like an endless sick day. Not the good kind, where she'd lain in bed and watched *Grand Hotel* and *To Be or Not to Be* on TV, but the kind where you feel muddy-headed and leaden. Music had echoed from one of the small stages nearby—she'd been consigned to some obscure outer ring of the fairground, along with debut folk singers and some dreadlocked young women who juggled phallus-shaped pins that they set on fire. The remote location was an unexpected blessing. At least she wasn't drowned out by the main stage acts.

There were only two characters in *The Stronger*. Madame X had the speaking role—a forty-five-minute monologue delivered to a woman known as Madame Y, who never uttered a word. It had been Amanda's showpiece for years. People argued over whether it was a masterpiece of feminism or misogyny. Amanda liked to play it both ways—some nights women stormed from the house in a fury, other nights men did.

And this was an Equity gig. It paid scale. And it got her out of the house. She could have sleepwalked through the role. But her old habits of discipline and body memory took over. She burrowed into the part, ferreting out the darkest bits of the script in hopes that somebody in one of those folding chairs would feel their skin crawl.

> **Mme X:** Do you actually think I'd want to shoot you?
> Seriously? Good lord, I can't believe you thought
> that! I mean, it wouldn't surprise me, because of the
> way our paths crossed. I know you'll never forget
> that. But you know, I was the innocent one.

During those forty-five minutes, Amanda kept the teenage girl in her sights, casting subtle glances her way, once laughing and staring at her outright, like they shared a joke. She saw how breaking the fourth wall unnerved the girl. A performance is a temporary sanctuary: dismantling its architecture, even slightly, can shatter a sensitive audience member.

Afterward, the girl found her in the back of the tent, chugging water from a liter bottle, her wig on a folding chair along with her car keys. A scruffy teenager with mouse-brown hair and unmemorable features, except for her hazel eyes, which were so wide when she introduced her-self that Amanda wondered if she was on drugs.

"That was—that was fucking amazing," the girl stammered. "I mean, you were—you were so great."

Amanda finished what was left in the water bottle, wiped her mouth with a tissue, removing her crimson lipstick, and smiled. She knew that without the lipstick and wig she looked decades younger. She was only forty, though to this girl, she must have seemed ancient.

"Aren't you a sweetheart." She cocked her head, smiled again, dazzlingly, and laughed. "What's your name?"

"Holly. Holly Sherwin."

"Holly Sherwin."

She took the girl's face in her hands and kissed her on the lips. "Thank you, Holly Sherwin."

Amanda's memory was part of her toolkit, though it had taken a moment to recognize Holly Sherwin's name when it'd appeared in her email three months before.

Dear Amanda Greer,

Forgive me writing out of the blue like this. I'm a playwright who saw you perform in *The Stronger* at Lilith Fair in 1996, an experience that shook me to the core and cemented my desire to have a career in theater…

Amanda sighed. She knew the drill from countless letters, emails, phone messages over the last thirty years. *Never forgot your Lady Macbeth at Westport Playhouse…Medea was one of the most arresting performances I've ever seen…always wondered what happened to you…wanted to see if you might be interested in a new project…*

Often, she was interested. Indie films, off-off-off-Broadway plays, obscure theater festivals in the Midwest, better-known ones in New England. The occasional offer to perform in Europe or the UK, which she always jumped on. None of the work paid well, and some of it she did gratis, just to keep her name out there. In the right ways—because of that unfortunate event with Jason while rehearsing *Medea,* too many people remembered Amanda Greer for the wrong reason.

But as she read Holly's script, the role of Elizabeth Sawyer did sound intriguing. A one-eyed old woman who sells her soul to the Devil to take revenge on her tormentors? Amanda could relate. The real-life Elizabeth was executed as a witch, but in Holly's précis, Elizabeth triumphs. Amanda could see it as a comeback role. Probably not a huge amount of exposure, but these days, you never knew. The right influencer—another stage-smitten teenager, perhaps—and Amanda might see a moderate stage success.

Imagine that. She wrote a quick reply to Holly Sherwin, saying yes, thank you very much, she would definitely be interested in further discussion.

And now she was at Hill House, ready to begin rehearsals. She unpacked quickly, tossing a few cozy paperback mysteries and half a dozen scarves and blouses onto the comfy-looking armchair and dumping her other things into dresser drawers. She told herself she'd hang her clothes up later, though she knew that wouldn't happen. They were only here for two weeks. Besides, what was the point? Easier to find everything if it was in plain sight. The exception was her cosmetics cases, which she set carefully on top of the dresser.

An old silvered mirror hung on the wall behind it, and she stopped to gaze at her reflection as she always did, whenever she had the chance. Some people called it vanity, which Amanda found offensive. Though what was wrong with vanity, anyway? When young women took a million selfies, they called it empowerment. Amanda touched up her lipstick and concealer, smiling at the face in the mirror.

A haggard creature leered back, with wispy black hair failing to hide a high forehead, blotched eyeliner, and a red gash for a mouth. Amanda's momentary alarm quickly changed to irritation. She turned and adjusted the curtains—she was wrong about the sunlight, it made her look as though she was sitting beneath a hundred-watt bulb.

Maybe she should reconsider taking the Yellow Room, before the others arrived.

CHAPTER 30

I lunged for the bathroom door and yanked it open. An older woman crouched on the floor, her posture mirroring Nisa's.

"I'm so sorry," Nisa gasped, as she and the woman both scrambled to their feet.

"What were you doing?" I demanded.

"The same thing she was." The woman jabbed a finger in Nisa's direction. "Spying."

"I wasn't spying! I—"

"Amanda Greer." The woman dropped her hand. Her smile immediately catapulted me back to when I was a starstruck teenager in Doc Martens and an old flannel shirt, meeting her in a grubby tent. "I was just checking to see if anyone was in the next room. Now I know."

The three of us stared at each other, and Nisa burst out laughing. "Right—now you know. I'm Nisa Macari. Of course I know who *you* are."

Amanda lowered her gaze. "Aren't you kind."

"I'm Holly," I said. "I am so glad you're here, I can't tell you..."

Amanda grasped my outstretched hand with both of hers and squeezed it, hard—very hard—the way people used to at after-work gatherings where everyone was trying to figure out who had gotten an end-of-the-year bonus and who had not.

"I'm so pleased to meet you in person." Amanda released my hand. "This project, it's the most exciting thing I've seen in ages. And Nisa, you're the remarkable singer, aren't you?"

She turned her sharp gaze on Nisa, who flushed. "Yes! Singer-songwriter, I'll be adapting old English ballads——"

"Folk music." Amanda nodded discreetly, as if acknowledging that she and Nisa shared membership in an arcane society, or some twelve-step program Nisa had somehow kept secret from me. "I love folk music."

"It's not really folk music," Nisa started, but Amanda had already walked past her into our bedroom. She halted, scrutinizing bed, bureau, armchair, then stepped to the window, where she gazed outside.

"I like the yellow," she said abruptly. She turned and directed her unsettling stare at me. "But it's not my color. Washes me out. It suits you, though."

I murmured thanks. I never wear yellow. Amanda was sizing me up, so I did the same. Her dark hair was untamed as ever, though not as thick. I was sure it was dyed. She was well into her sixties, but I saw no trace of gray. Her face was mostly unlined—a few well-placed stabs of Botox would have helped with that.

Her features had always been well-suited for the stage. Large midnight-blue eyes, arching black brows filled in with a few strokes of eyebrow pencil. A wide expressive mouth, high forehead. A flattened nose with a small bump in it—she'd broken it during a childhood fall, a detail she'd shared on an old episode of *The Dick Cavett Show* I'd viewed on YouTube.

Not a beautiful face, but a powerful one. Like Maria Callas's, or Jeanne Moreau's, designed to command attention from the last rows in the balcony. Movies didn't treat it as kindly as the stage. Lingering close-ups allowed you to detect a slight asymmetry. One eye was fractionally larger than the other, and from the wrong angle, her strong chin could dominate her face.

Yet she could convey immense vulnerability. The night before we drove to Hill House, I made Nisa watch Amanda Greer playing Amanda Wingfield in a Hartford Stage production of *The Glass Menagerie,* recorded for Connecticut Public Television. I lingered on her expression when her fragile daughter Laura first opens the door and sees Jim, the gentleman caller, glance from her to her mother, then swiftly back outside, calculating how quickly he can escape.

During those seconds, we witnessed an entire life collapse upon itself, burying Amanda Wingfield's hope for her child as swiftly and silently as someone tossing a flower into an open grave. Amanda Greer does it without a single motion, without even blinking (a feat in itself). I've watched that clip dozens of times and cried during every single one.

"Holly?" I started, and saw Nisa observing me curiously. "You okay?"

"Yeah, sure."

"Come see my room," Amanda ordered us.

We walked through the bathroom, which still had its original fittings—big claw-foot tub, subway tile floor, pedestal sink. There were plenty of towels, and the toilet had been updated sometime in the twenty-first century.

"Oh, isn't this lovely," exclaimed Nisa as we entered the bedroom, her voice falsely bright. The room was a mess—clothes and cosmetics bags and paperbacks, a beach towel. Did Amanda think she was staying at a resort hotel? The room was identical to ours, though the walls had been painted an ugly pink, again without removing the blotched wallpaper beneath. The effect was of a fading bruise.

Amanda let loose a practiced peal of laughter. "Oh please—it's revolting! But I like it. It will help me get into character, right? This whole place—you could do a site-specific performance of *Witching Night* at Hill House. It would be perfect."

"Maybe. Right now I just want to get it onstage where people will see it. Your Elizabeth will definitely make that happen."

"Along with Nisa's music," Amanda said grandly, even though she hadn't yet heard a note. Nisa blushed as Amanda gave me an enigmatic smile. She walked to the bed, picked up a linen jacket, and hung it in the closet.

"She has a closet," said Nisa quietly.

"We have one too. It's stuck behind the wardrobe."

"I'm starved." Amanda shut the closet door, which immediately began to creep open again. "I eat early—what do you think about five o'clock?"

I looked outside. The sky had darkened to lichen-gray, with a dull orange glow in the west, and the wind sent the last leaves spinning from the trees. "Sure," I replied. "Why don't we meet downstairs around four thirty? We'll let Stevie know."

CHAPTER 31

Stevie had unpacked when they first arrived. First of all, he'd removed the toy theater from its archival cardboard sleeve and set it up on top of the dresser. He pinched the cardboard cut-outs between his fingers, gingerly sliding the various pieces into their proper slots. The elaborate front of the proscenium, with its red-and-orange columns and scarlet pediment; the cardboard curtains, a deeper red to suggest velvet, with painted golden tassels; the different bits of scenery—cardboard trees and housefronts, a topiary bird. Behind it all, the even more elaborately painted main stage set: Bluebeard's lowering gray castle; a forest of dark trees; white-capped mountains in the distance.

Last of all he slotted in the figures of Bluebeard, the corpses of his murdered wives, and the cowering form of the wife who used the golden key to open the forbidden cellar. The antique cardboard emitted a very faint scent of tuberose and smoke, residue of some earlier owner.

When he'd finished slotting them all in place he stood back to admire the miniature theater, in all its gilt and painted glory. He liked to envision himself living in that imaginary space—not with

Bluebeard, maybe, but inhabiting that tiny secondary world nestled within this one. It comforted him, the way that his friends found comfort in gaming or social media.

He opened the dresser to put away his clothes—a few sweaters, heavy wool socks, jeans and khakis. Stevie adhered to a philosophy inspired by a cartoon he'd seen at an older lover's house long ago, depicting a man at his prayers and the caption *I don't ask for much, but what I have should be of very good quality.*

The affair hadn't panned out. Very little in Stevie's life had, not his career or his relationships or his living situations. For some years now—decades, he'd recently been chagrined to realize—he'd subsisted mostly by couch-surfing, house-sitting, pet-sitting, and housecleaning, along with the occasional stint as a live-in lover.

I'm a sparkler, he wrote in his Grindr profile. *I burn fast and hot. I scorch your fingers if you try to hold on to me and then I'm cold.* Some people thought this was funny, a few even thought it was sexy, but only his closest friends, like Holly, knew it was true. He'd held on to a tiny rent-stabilized place in Chelsea that he'd sublet to the same tenant for seventeen years. When things got tough, she'd leave for a weekend or a month and Stevie would stabilize himself. His occasional gig at Hecate Rising, designing micro-doses for Wiccans and neo-pagans, along with occasional sound design work, kept him sane. Mostly.

Stevie sighed and took a deep cleansing breath through his nose, wishing it were cocaine. *That* would clear his head. He'd been looking forward to this for weeks, but now that he was finally here, he felt anxious as well as exhilarated. He hadn't performed in several years, and then it had been a Zoom production of *A Christmas Carol,* with Stevie cast as Marley's ghost. He'd wanted to play Bob Cratchit but the director couldn't be convinced.

"You *look* like Marley's ghost, Stevie!" Her tone suggested he should take this as a compliment, but he didn't see how that was even possible.

Tomasin, the devil dog, was a definite improvement. And he couldn't deny that he was excited that Nisa was on board, too. There was no way he'd sleep with her again, not with Holly here, not when they were working together. Those days were long gone, along with his cocaine habit and compulsive Grindr hookups.

Now he yearned for a different kind of oblivion: not to be absorbed by a person or drug, but by the darkness he'd known since he was a boy backstage in a shadowy dressing room, privy to a world he should never have known then, and one he now knew he'd never escape.

When he'd first read Holly's script and seen what she did with Tomasin, he recognized himself in the black dog, a creature seduced by a great evil, who then goes on to seduce others. Stevie had never committed anything close to the horrors he'd undergone as a child, but he'd been guilty of things that still woke him from a deep sleep. Voices in his head, images he couldn't erase no matter how much he drank or smoked.

When he was very young, acting had been joyful. Now the best he could hope for was catharsis, and the chance to disappear, even if it was just for a few hours during a rehearsal, or when he was behind his laptop, creating a soundscape that would inexorably draw others into it.

He was here, now, to do all those things. Grateful to Holly for giving him the opportunity; grateful that Nisa was here, for the spark her presence still ignited in him. He exhaled, counting to eight, stood and shook out his hands. He turned to give his room a once-over.

It was a nice room, he thought. The Violet Room. Okay, not nice, but passable. Poufy Laura Ashley curtains, matching bedcovers—incredibly dated, but they smelled clean. It was chilly but he liked sleeping in a cold room.

He'd started for the door when he saw something on the floor beneath the dresser. One of his new washable wool socks. He distinctly remembered folding them all before he put them neatly in the top drawer, remembered running a finger across the tidy rows, like a musician testing the keys of a newly tuned piano. He liked his things to be orderly. Nisa accused him of being OCD but it kept him from feeling anxious, especially in an unfamiliar place. How could the sock have fallen? He stooped, peering at the sock curled up against the wall.

"How'd you get down there?"

He knelt in front of the dresser but still couldn't reach the sock, so he stood and pulled the heavy piece of furniture toward him. He retrieved the sock, began to push the dresser back into place, and stopped.

A wooden baseboard ran around the room, half-covered by ragged strips of violet-patterned wallpaper. In moving the dresser, he'd revealed a section where the baseboard had been removed. A small panel had been inserted there, about six inches high and almost as wide.

Not a panel—a tiny wooden door, painted spruce-green and with a brass knob the size of a thumbtack head. Stevie stared at it, astonished. He wiped away the dust and cobwebs that clung to the door, pinched the minute knob between his finger and thumb, and pulled. It didn't move. He tugged at it again. Still nothing.

Frowning, he dug his fingernail into the hairline space above the door, felt flakes of grit and plaster adhere to his fingertip. He'd need a knife or some other tool to clean away the grime.

For a minute he sat there, staring at what he'd discovered. A strange exultation filled him, excitement and a thrill of apprehension, like when he'd meet someone for quick sex at a club, or sit behind his sound board on opening night, waiting to hear whether the audience applauded.

He wouldn't tell anyone about what he'd found. He didn't know why but he felt with absolute certainty that he had to keep it secret. For its own protection. Holly would want to incorporate it into her play as a motif or symbol. Nisa would use it in one of her songs.

And Amanda...

He grimaced, imagining Amanda Greer on her hands and knees, clawing at the tiny door: the miniature knob coming off in her fingers and the whole construction reduced to crumbs of plaster and splintered wood. No no no no no.

He got to his feet, sock in hand, shoved the dresser back against the wall protectively, shut off the light, and went to join the others for dinner.

CHAPTER 32

Thank god Holly Sherwin had cleaned up a bit since she was a teenager, Amanda thought as she headed downstairs for dinner. Lost
most of her puppy fat, cut her hair and dyed it blond. She didn't look as
pretty as the photo on her website, but who did?

But her girlfriend, Nisa—she assumed they were partners, why
share that horrible room otherwise?—she was beautiful, slight, dark,
her hair close-cropped, her eyes a deep brown that appeared gold
when they caught the light. Amanda had watched a few online videos
of her performing. Nisa Macari was the real deal—incredible range,
though Amanda liked her original songs best.

As for Holly's play, it seemed to be a vehicle for Nisa's music, and
a potential star turn for whoever played the witch. Possibly the part of
the black dog, too. Amanda would have to watch for that. You never
wanted to share the stage with an animal or child or puppet.

But Amanda as the witch would command the stage: it would be
her sacred space. Actors rarely talked about being possessed by a character during a performance—it's all technique, discipline, practice,
blah blah blah, not to mention eating disorders, plastic surgery, addic-
tion, narcissism, and the occasional bit of sociopathy. Amanda knew

all about it, she'd gone to Juilliard and studied with Stella Adler, done her share of classics and also crap.

Often, the audience couldn't even tell if there was a star, or former star, or almost-star, onstage. But she knew: she'd witnessed how something else takes over when a great actor performs. A pedestrian sentence becomes poetry. Words that didn't make sense on the page sound like an incantation. It made sense, really—theaters began as sacred spaces. Probably the first actors were participating in some ritual sacrifice. There was undeniably ancient power there. How else to account for the fact that people were still producing Euripides?

Actors didn't like hearing Amanda spout this sort of thing, and directors really hated it. When Amanda mentioned it to the guy who'd directed *Medea,* a hotshot who'd previously worked with Peter Sellars (not the funny one, the other one), he'd stared at her like she'd spat on his office floor.

Holly and her girlfriend were in the kitchen when she arrived downstairs, also the young man who'd ridden up with them. Stevie Somebody. Amanda's friend Jeremy had told her about him—they knew each other from the downtown club scene. He'd been in *Oliver!* as a boy, there was some nasty story there.

Liddell, that was it. Like the girl who inspired *Alice in Wonderland.* He must have been a sweet-faced little boy. Even now he looked like he subsisted on fresh air and goodwill. Amanda took a moment to prepare herself in the hall—smoothing her hair, squaring her shoulders—and then poked her head around the corner of the entry. "Oooh, is this where the party is?"

"Amanda! Yes, come in, you can help us schlep everything out to the table."

Holly handed her a platter as Stevie bounded up, a fistful of silverware in each hand. "Amanda Greer, we have a friend in common..."

And just like that, they all seemed to know each other and were settled around the dining table. Which was huge and could have sat twenty, but everyone dragged a chair to the end closest to the kitchen, where

Holly had propped the door open. The dining room was gloomy, the only light an old standing lamp with a vaguely sinister Art Nouveau look, like that Aubrey Beardsley drawing she'd immediately regretted looking at in the Tate.

Within minutes, its bulb was flickering, and so she exclaimed, "Are we having a séance?"

Nisa had laughed and Holly had looked a bit nervous, but Stevie jumped up and returned to the kitchen, where he found some candles in heavy silver holders. He lit them and carried them back to the dining table, where they cast long shadows that crept toward the corners of the room. It was still too dark, so Amanda opened the door to the hall, too.

"My god, it's pitch-black out there!" She'd fallen once in her own house not long ago—granted, after polishing off a bottle of pinot grigio, but it could happen to anybody. "Did someone think to leave a light on?"

"I'm not sure we even know where the switches are," Nisa mused. "Did you see them, Hols?"

Holly frowned. "No, but—"

"We'll be fine," Stevie reassured her. "I'll walk you to your room and make sure you're safe."

"Thank you," she said stiffly. Did he think she was his grandmother? "I'm sure I'll be fine."

The dinner was excellent, a casserole Tru had already prepared, along with fresh-baked bread and a green salad. There was even apple cobbler for dessert. Amanda was relieved to see that Holly had carried down several bottles of Rhône for dinner. Amanda had brought wine to Hill House as well, along with two bottles of an eighteen-year-old single malt, all of which remained in her room for the nonce. Nisa took a number of pictures for her social media feeds. Amanda made a point of lifting her chin and tilting her head so her good side showed.

"Hashtag Hill House?" Nisa asked, finger poised above her screen.

"How about *Witching Night*?" countered Holly.

"Whatever."

Nisa tapped at the phone. Amanda wished she could see the photos first, to make sure she didn't look like the dog's breakfast, but it turned out she didn't need to worry.

"No signal," Nisa announced in aggravation. "I thought Ainsley said we could get service up here."

Holly corrected her. "Ainsley said we could get intermittent service. It's better upstairs, but she said we should stay out of the big room at the end of the hall. It's not safe. Like the tower, I guess. Structural problems."

"That's just an excuse," said Stevie. "If it's not the site of an ax murder, it's structural problems. What it really means is, the house is haunted."

"It is *not* haunted." Holly looked annoyed. "Even Ainsley said it wasn't. People have to disclose that before they rent it."

"Before they sell it," said Nisa. "In this rental market, you can get away with not disclosing anything."

"I've always wanted to see a real haunted house." Amanda smiled. She'd invite Nisa to walk with her in the morning, and offhandedly suggest adding her own name to the hashtag. "It will make for a good story when we're promoting the play."

Holly pushed aside her wineglass. "Can't wait for that conversation." She stood, went into the kitchen, and returned with a glass of water.

"It's okay," Nisa said soothingly, and rubbed her girlfriend's neck. "Thank you, Holly, for having us all here."

Amanda reached across the table for the bottle. She refilled her glass. "*Slainte,* Holly," she said.

"*Slainte,*" everyone chimed in, and they all clinked glasses except for Stevie.

Nisa sighed. "Come on, Stevie."

"What?" demanded Amanda.

"He won't toast," said Nisa. "He—"

"I'll toast," Stevie broke in. "I just won't clink."

"Why not?"

"My Polish grandfather said it's bad luck. It rousts bad spirits."

"'Rousts'?" Amanda downed her wine, holding out her empty glass to Nisa. "Who are you, Robin Hood? Well, here's to Holly, anyway. Clink."

She tipped her glass toward Stevie, spilling red wine on the table-cloth. "Sorry," she said, but made no move to clean it up.

Holly started to her feet but Nisa pulled her back into her chair. "Leave it."

"But it will stain."

"It's already stained. Look."

Nisa pointed to a large liver-colored blotch in the center of the table-cloth. Amanda saw a smaller, darker stain near her own plate. She hadn't noticed it till now. Had she done that? She didn't think so. She touched the smaller stain and withdrew her finger. A smudge like the residue of a spoiled plum covered her fingertip. She hastily wiped it on the tablecloth, hoping no one had seen it.

"What's on the docket for tomorrow, Hols?" Nisa asked.

"Our first read-through, how does ten sound? Nisa, you might want to share a couple of your songs."

"Wonderful!" exclaimed Amanda, and saw Holly's mouth tighten.

Stevie nodded. "Sounds good."

"I thought I'd take a walk beforehand and go over my lines," said Amanda. On the tablecloth, the plum-colored stain had spread. She pushed her plate to cover it, stood, and moved to a chair on the other side of the table, where there was more light. "If anyone wants to join me."

"I'd be up for that," said Stevie. "Maybe."

They all fell quiet, sipping their wine or prodding at the remains of dessert. Stevie seemed to be stewing about something—her comment about Robin Hood? *Toughen up, kid,* she thought, and poured herself more wine.

"Ainsley said Hill House isn't haunted," he said. "Which I think is sort of unfair. What's the point of a place like this without ghosts?"

"She's wrong."

Amanda set down her glass and made a slow, sweeping gesture, the one she'd used as Prospera at the end of that Chicago production of *The Tempest*. The *Tribune* review said she'd seemed more Norma Desmond than sorceress, but Amanda had taken that as a compliment. "*We're the* ones haunting it," she proclaimed. "Actors, we channel the spirits. What do you think acting is? Bringing the dead to life."

"Characters in a play aren't dead," said Holly. "They're fictional."

"But they aren't alive, either, are they? Not until we summon them." Amanda had given this speech before, addressing college acting classes or community theater fund-raisers. Only there nobody interrupted her. "We memorize words, arrange objects in a ritual space, wear special clothing. Then, after weeks or months of preparation we're transformed. We're possessed. *Something else enters us.*"

She hissed the last few words, looking from Holly to Nisa to Stevie. A candle flame flickered, and she was gratified to see Stevie's enthralled expression as she continued.

"If you've opened yourself to it—if the words are under your skin so you can feel them moving when you move—you become a vessel. All those figures brought back to life, over and over again across the centuries—Clytemnestra and Hamlet, Doogie Howser and Prior Walter, Alexander Hamilton, and of course your Elizabeth Sawyer…"

She turned to Holly beside her. "*Elizabeth Sawyer,*" she repeated. "We're bringing her back to life, you and I…"

She let her voice fade into the dim room and inclined her head demurely, waiting for the applause that usually came at this point.

"What is that?" cried Stevie.

She looked up to see him staring—not at her, at the tablecloth.

And not just Stevie: all of them, gaping as Amanda glanced down to see the stain spreading across the white cloth, the color of red wine or beet juice.

But not blood, she thought, pushing her chair back as she stumbled to her feet, *not blood, how could it be blood?*

CHAPTER 33

I grabbed Amanda as she staggered from the table. She tried furiously to shake me off while Nisa and Stevie watched, confused. She'd had a lot to drink, more than the rest of us, though she didn't seem that drunk. She wasn't slurring her words, and her face wasn't flushed. It had turned paper white.

From embarrassment, I assumed—all that schtick about acting and possession, the knowing glances and deliberate pauses for an appreciative laugh. Some actors do it all the time, they're incapable of holding a conversation. Stevie calls it Death by Monologue. Right now, I was terrified that we might be witnessing an actual death.

"Amanda! Amanda, are you okay?"

Was she having a seizure? I'd seen the stain creeping across the table—wine, I'd thought, but there was so much of it. I thought she'd just spilled a bit of wine, but it looked more like blood. Maybe she'd dropped her glass and cut herself?

I looked at her hands, her exposed wrists and forearms. No blood that I could see.

Amanda took a deep breath and murmured, "I'm fine." Her body relaxed, and I loosened my hold on her. "Really, I'm fine, just—too much wine, I'm not used to drinking."

"Of course," I said. I stepped away, making sure she was steady on her feet. "Do you want to sit down? Somewhere else, I mean?"

"No thank you." She took another deep breath and straightened, extending her spine like a dancer at the barre, exhaled and closed her eyes. When she opened them, she gave me a thin smile. "I think I'll go to bed."

"Of course." It wasn't yet eight o'clock but felt hours later. "I'll go up with you."

"I'll go," said Stevie. "I'm a man of my word."

He extended his hand with exaggerated gallantry. Amanda hesitated, then took it.

"Seriously, I'm fine. But thank you." She turned to stare at the tablecloth. "What the hell is that? I only spilled a drop of wine!"

"I think it's some kind of polish or stain from the wood underneath," Nisa said. "I've seen it on old furniture that's refurbished. In damp weather, sometimes the old varnish comes through. My mom buys stuff at tag sales, cleans it up, and resells it in her shop," she explained to Amanda. "And looky here—"

She slipped into the kitchen and, when she came back, handed Stevie a large flashlight. "I found this in the pantry. There's a whole bunch of them, maybe we should each take one? "

Stevie took the flashlight and turned it on. "Okay, campers, I'll see you later."

He escorted Amanda from the room. Moments later I heard their footsteps moving slowly up the stairs.

CHAPTER 34

Stevie kept a gentle hold on Amanda's arm as he accompanied her along the steps. She seemed fine. Not drunk, really: more subdued.

He didn't blame her. He was way too familiar with the kind of embarrassment that swiftly becomes something more unsettling: the sensation of another self taking over before he came to his senses and booted it out. For him these days, it usually happened with sex, rather than drinking or drugs. With Amanda, it seemed like booze was the culprit. He'd try to keep an eye on her, make sure she drank plenty of water and didn't attempt these dark stairs on her own at night.

"Holly says you have ideas for the scene where Tomasin takes care of Elizabeth's enemies," she remarked. "The one where he turns them into beetles and eats them."

An odd choice for casual conversation. Then again, it was an odd play. Stevie nodded. "That's right. Deathwatch beetles. You find them in old houses like this, they make a very particular sound from behind the walls and ceilings. I'm hoping I'll be able to record them. Hey, be careful!"

He grabbed her as she reached the landing and, for an instant, lost her balance. "We don't need any more on-set accidents," he said with a grin. Then his face fell. "Shit, I'm sorry, I didn't mean——"

She'd stared at him frostily. When they reached her room, he opened the door, hand extended to assist her, but she pushed him aside.

"Thank you." She switched on her room's overhead light and closed the door without another word.

Stevie stood in the hallway, mortified. What an asshole thing to say, what was wrong with him? But then the whole evening had felt off-kilter.

She's stressed about what we must think of her, he mused, and continued down the hall. Not surprising when you considered what had happened with Jason Pratt. No one had mentioned it until he did just now, though of course they all knew.

But that had been a long time ago. Just as likely, Amanda regretted going on about actors and possession, the kind of woo-woo stuff Stevie and his neo-pagan friends loved to discuss long into the night.

And then she'd knocked over her wineglass. Knocked over an entire bottle, more like. He hoped the tablecloth wasn't some family heirloom.

He walked down the hall, half hoping Nisa and Holly would arrive. He wasn't quite ready to turn in. But they were taking their time, so he went into his bedroom. He hadn't remembered leaving the light on, but he was glad that he had. No stumbling around in the dark—he could hear Nisa and Holly still downstairs, bumping into furniture, a loud thump as though a chair had been overturned. His room was chilly, so he undressed quickly and got into bed, tugging the covers around him.

He opened his phone to check for messages, tossed it aside in disgust. The reception here was crap. He took a deep breath. It was fine, he honestly didn't care. He could always go into Hillsdale and find someplace with service. Ainsley's office, or there might be a café. He was too tired to read, so he rolled onto his side, reached to turn off the bedside lamp. He stopped when his gaze lit upon the dresser.

The little green door!

The mere thought of it filled him with an unexpected surge of gleeful anticipation: an emotion close to arousal, but, oddly, even more intense.

Who had put it here? And where did it lead? The paint had looked brighter than what he'd seen elsewhere in Hill House, and the brass knob had shone as though just polished. Maybe this had been a child's bedroom, and the door concealed a place where they could hide their toys? It was too small for a crawl space.

He was tempted to go look at it again, but that would mean moving aside the dresser. Which might arouse someone's attention, Nisa for one.

He felt an irrational, powerful urge to keep the door a secret. It was meant for him, even if it hid nothing but dust and mouse droppings. He'd find a way to discreetly ask Melissa about it, next time he saw her. He pulled the blankets over his head, and within minutes was asleep.

CHAPTER 35

Well, that was exciting," Nisa said after Stevie and Amanda went upstairs. She looped her arm around my shoulder and kissed me on the mouth. "You handled it very well."

I slipped my hand under her shirt. "Early bedtime, I know what we can do with that."

"Go grab another flashlight. I'll take care of that tablecloth."

After the shadowy dining room, the kitchen's bright overhead light made my eyes sting. Nisa put the leftovers in the fridge. Melissa had told us to leave the dishes in the sink, but I quickly rinsed and stacked them, calmed by the routine and the kitchen itself. The Glenwood stove and slate sinks testified to its age, but the convection oven, microwave, and coffee maker made it feel upscale, almost luxurious.

I took another flashlight and turned to where Nisa stood at the sink, filling it again. "I'm just going to leave it overnight," she said as she kneaded the soiled fabric. "God, this water is like ice. The whole thing is stained. I don't think it's going to come out."

Shuddering, she withdrew her hands and wiped them on her jeans. "Let's go. You have the flashlight?"

We stepped into the hall. Nisa switched off the kitchen light, and I froze.

I've never experienced darkness like that. Not a color or sensation but a void in which I dissolved, like a sand castle at high tide. I couldn't feel the flashlight in my hand, couldn't move or breathe. For a few seconds I couldn't even remember where I was, or who, or what. I was conscious of myself as nothing but a pinprick of being, consumed by an incoherent darkness.

"Give me that!"

Something folded around my fingers. Nisa's hand. She took the flashlight from me, turned it on, and swept it up to my face as I shielded my eyes.

"Holly? You okay, baby?"

I nodded, unable to speak. Finally I stammered, "I—I don't know what happened. I think the air in here is bad, maybe there's radon in the basement or something."

"You can't smell radon. You're just exhausted—I'm exhausted, and I haven't done half of what you have, getting everything organized to come here. Plus all that wine," she went on, leading me to and up the stairs. "And Norma Desmond there, ranting about Clytemnestra and Doogie Howser. Doogie Howser!"

She began to laugh uncontrollably, and I covered her mouth with my hand. "She'll hear you!"

"She's already asleep. See?"

We'd reached the top of the stairway. Nisa pointed to Amanda's bedroom door. No light showed beneath it. It hadn't been more than five minutes since Stevie had brought her upstairs—she must have passed out immediately. We listened and heard nothing, and Nisa led me to our own room.

I turned on the bedside lamps, while Nisa undressed and went into the bathroom. I sat on the bed, my inexplicable terror gone. Nisa was right: I felt bone-tired and slightly drunk.

Amanda's behavior at dinner had thrown me for a loop. I'd read the tabloid stories about her, but that had been eighteen years ago. Her work since then had been less flashy but still strong, and I'd assumed the event was what she'd said it was, a terrible accident.

"Your turn," Nisa said, emerging from the bathroom.

I brushed my teeth and washed up, then stood at the door into Amanda's room, listening until I heard a soft drone.

"She's definitely asleep." I closed the bathroom door behind me and undressed, pulled on a T-shirt, and slid into bed beside Nisa.

"Good thing you're the one in charge here," she said. "Between me and Stevie and Amanda, you're gonna have your hands full."

I laughed and took her in my arms. The flannel sheets smelled of lavender and were already warm from Nisa's body. We kissed, her mouth warm, too, and her hands.

"I held them under the hot water for like, five minutes," she said. "I swear, I couldn't feel them, they were so cold. Downstairs, in the dark? I was so cold, I couldn't feel anything."

"I can take care of that," I said, and turned off the lamp.

CHAPTER 36

Usually after sex I fall asleep immediately. Nisa's the one who gets energized and stays up, listening to murder podcasts or scrawling song lyrics in a notebook while she watches some inscrutable Jacques Rivette movie on the Criterion Channel.

Tonight, though, Nisa dozed off within minutes, her dark curls like scribbled ink against her forehead. I leaned over to kiss her, lay back on my pillow, and gazed at the windows, searching for a hint of starlight. There was only night, the rustling of tree limbs, and Nisa's soft breathing.

I don't know how long I was awake. Hours, maybe, though I didn't look at my phone. The worst thing you can do if you can't sleep is obsessively check the time. The enveloping dread I felt downstairs returned, the sense that I'd dissolved and only this speck of consciousness remained. I closed my eyes, then immediately opened them, to determine if I could see anything.

I couldn't. I saw nothing, not the windows or the walls or Nisa beside me. The darkness was like a liquid I couldn't feel or taste or smell, but which somehow coated my eyes or was absorbed by them. I tried to lift my hand to my face but the effort was too much.

Exhaustion pinned me to the bed, as I drifted between wakefulness and a bone-deep yearning for oblivion.

I don't know when the voices started. I grew aware of them only gradually, the way you wake to an alarm that's been set too low.

There was no mistaking the sound—not wind in the leaves or rain, or Amanda snoring in the next room, but a very soft murmuring. Words, though I couldn't understand them. There were two voices, one deeper than the other. Not a man's voice but an unctuous burbling, like water being sucked down a clogged drain.

The other voice was quieter but even more repellent, at once throaty and sibilant. Sometimes it grew so soft I almost couldn't hear it, and I found myself struggling to do so even though the noise was horrible. Now and then one or the other would make a sound like coughing or choking but I knew it was neither. It was laughter.

Occasionally the horrible nonsense cohered into a sound that did have meaning—my name. The gurgling grew more insistent, insinuating, almost accusatory. I couldn't move, and soon a great weight began to press against my chest, grew heavier and heavier until I couldn't breathe. I'd read about this happening in nightmares—witches and night hags riding victims while they slept.

But I wasn't asleep. I curled one hand into a fist, and dug my nails into the fleshy part of my palm, until I felt the skin break and blood ooze beneath my fingertip. Yet the accompanying pain was numbed, like I'd been given anesthesia.

The weight on my chest grew stronger as the voices burbled on, like a steady drip of noxious water from the eaves, gutters clogged with rotting leaves and the soft pulp of small birds that had been trapped there. The smell of decay filled my nostrils as I tried to summon the strength to shout and wake Nisa—yet that would draw their attention.

Gradually the voices receded. The odor of decay diminished, replaced by the smell of mildew and my own acrid sweat. I pulled the bedcovers around me, my skin chilled and head throbbing. *Maybe I'm sick,* I thought, *maybe this* was *all a fever dream.*

At last I must have slept. When I woke, Nisa stood in front of the window, curtains drawn back to let sunlight stream into the room.

"Morning, sleepyhead." She glanced back at me and smiled. "I slept like a log. What about you?"

I sat up groggily, glanced around the room. The sun highlighted every bulge in the painted-over yellow wallpaper, every hair-thin crack in the exposed wall beneath. I pulled my hands from under the covers, suddenly afraid again, but my palms were pale, unblemished. I looked back at Nisa, who'd gone back to gazing outside. "Okay, I guess. Weird dreams. What are you looking at?"

"That kid—" She pointed. "He just keeps staring at the house."

"Maybe because you're staring at him." I rolled out of bed and stepped to the window. "Where is he?"

"There at the edge of the woods—oops, no. He ran off—he must've seen us."

"Should we be worried?"

"Nah, he was just a kid. A teenager. Maybe he belongs to Evadne."

She turned to nuzzle me, casting a suggestive look in the direction of the bed.

"I really need coffee," I said. "And we have to get to work."

"Mmm."

She buried her face in my neck as I looked over my shoulder. A shadow moved where the birch trees swayed in the wind. I tried to get a better look, but saw nothing else.

CHAPTER 37

Amanda woke early, with no trace of a hangover. She knew the others thought she'd been royally drunk the night before, but she'd only had half a bottle of wine.

Well, maybe a bit more, she'd lost count—hadn't they been celebrating? Young people now were such puritans. *Dost thou think, because thou art virtuous, there shall be no more cakes and ale?*

And she never drank in the morning, unless she was in bed with someone, ideally in a foreign city. That hadn't occurred in such a long time that she sometimes wondered if it had ever truly happened, or if she was conflating real life with a scene in a movie she'd appeared in.

It was a shame about that tablecloth but honestly, who used white linen tablecloths these days? White was just asking for trouble. Red absorbed or hid a variety of sins. Wine, spaghetti sauce, blood.

She'd slept soundly, waking once or twice to hear Holly and Nisa murmuring in their room. It must have been two or three a.m., much too late for sleepover chatter between adults. That kind of low sniggering laugh mean girls always had, though one of them almost sounded like a man. Stevie might have snuck in, the three of them gossiping about Amanda while she slept. Old hag, typecast as Elizabeth Sawyer! Amanda had been tempted to rap on their door or text them—I CAN HEAR YOU—but fell asleep before she could.

Now she got out of bed, listened at the door to the shared bathroom before tiptoeing in. She washed up and put on her makeup, just enough to strike the balance between looking like she wasn't wearing any makeup and making it clear to the world that she still cared, she hadn't given up, that this was the face she'd been born with, minus peels every few months and the occasional Botox.

When she finished, she returned to her room and dressed, then locked the door between her bedroom and the bathroom. She didn't want them snooping around. They wouldn't dare sneak in from the hall but it would be easy from the bathroom. Little slinky sneaks, stirring things up. *Love gilds the scene, and women guide the plot.* She pulled on her walking shoes, grabbed her jacket, and left.

Outside her room, she paused. Something scrabbled behind the wainscoting, tiny claws scratching at the plaster and lath. Not so tiny, actually—could be a rat. The noise faded as whatever it was scurried off. She'd wait to mention it at dinner. Rats! That would cause some excitement.

Downstairs, no one else was awake. The deserted stairway and main hall had an expectant air, like a theater on opening night. She gazed around at the main hall's polished woodwork, the worn but expensive carpeting that still bore the marks of a vacuum cleaner in its nap. It seemed like a lot of effort to go through, to maintain a place this old and customarily vacant.

Ainsley said Hill House isn't haunted, Stevie had said last night.

Yet surely haunting was just a matter of perspective and perception. *I've only to pick up a newspaper to glimpse ghosts gliding between the lines.* Bats heard things that humans couldn't. If she had a bat's ears, she might be able to hear what was really going on around her. She knew that others thought she was a bit crazy—batty!

But Shakespeare knew that words were also spells, designed to intoxicate and enthrall the senses. Amanda had spent hours alone at her isolated house, listening to the night speak, getting to know its creatures. Training herself to hear the cries of bats, supposedly too high-pitched for humans to detect, but she could. House shrews were so blind and deaf that she could crouch beside them and they wouldn't move. They relied on their sense of smell. Amanda could bring her face to within an inch of their tiny snouts and poppyseed eyes, until she smelled the odor of the shrews themselves, like a spent match. Sulfurous. *That souls of animals infuse themselves / Into the trunks of men.*

Possibly Amanda herself would have been burned as a witch.

She peered into the kitchen, wrinkling her nose at the sight of the wadded-up tablecloth in the sink, like something from a crime scene. That stain would never come out. She should have just stuffed it in a trash bag. She'd do it now but the others would notice and probably complain.

She walked over to the counter and inspected the coffee machine, filters and a bag of coffee set out for whoever rose first to prepare. She'd leave it for someone else. Stevie, he seemed like the needy sort who'd do things so people would like him.

She stepped back into the hall. Were those voices? She cocked her head, listening, felt a sudden draft at her neck. Was someone else awake? She glanced upstairs but didn't see anyone. The voices had fallen silent.

The hall seemed darker than it had minutes ago, the walls closer and the ceiling lower, though that was just the light, or lack of it. The house had been horribly designed, if indeed it had been designed and not just constructed piecemeal, its corridors and doors and rooms like the aimless tunnels made by worms in the dirt.

Even worse was the thought that it had been designed this way on purpose. The ugly moldings and dark wainscoting, the ceiling height that changed in the corridors—in some spots, high above her head, in others so low she could graze it with her fingertips. She did that once. The ceiling felt moist and slightly yielding, and she snatched her hand back in disgust.

She shivered, zipping up her jacket, and hurried out the front door. The cold air stung her cheeks as she raced down the steps, momentarily blinded by sunlight and blue sky.

CHAPTER 38

Amanda headed down the drive, past three cars—hers, Holly's, and an unfamiliar white pickup. Maybe that woman who was the housekeeper, Melissa, or her husband? They must have come in the back door.

She decided she'd walk in the woods. If she took the road, she'd run the risk of having Melissa drive past on her way back to town. Amanda didn't feel like making small talk if Melissa stopped to greet her, and, based on her attitude yesterday, Melissa wasn't going to answer the one question Amanda really wanted to know: *Why don't you and your husband stay here after dark?*

And there was also the risk that Amanda might run into that other woman, the one the others had described, with the knife and the mobile home. People were so condescending about mobile homes; Amanda would have thought Holly and her friends would be more tolerant. Or at least mindful that a double-wide probably went for three or four hundred K in the current market.

Still, Amanda didn't want to antagonize the locals. She knew from her own small town that creatives like herself had to do a delicate dance to stay in the good graces of those who cleaned their houses, plowed their driveways, repaired their cars, delivered their firewood. Amanda sometimes hired people from a few towns over, just to avoid the awkwardness of dealing with people she had absolutely nothing in common with. Rude mechanicals, like in Shakespeare.

She walked until she saw a break in the trees and what looked like a path, clambered over a pile of rocks that might once have been a wall, and wandered into the forest. Crows shouted after her as she kicked at drifts of brown leaves, lifting her face to the sun. The air had the winey tang of late autumn. Goldenrod stalks nodded in the wind, flowers faded to brown.

After about ten minutes, she stopped to look back. She thought she'd come a good distance, but she clearly saw Hill House through a thin curtain of dying leaves and bare branches, so close it seemed to loom above her. The upper windows caught the light in a way that gave its facade a wide-eyed, deranged appearance. Amanda once worked with a younger actress who had that same look; she used to hear her crying into the pay phone during rehearsal breaks. Amanda was tempted to whisper "Grow up!" but the girl turned in a great performance, so score another point for the Method.

It is evil, Amanda thought, staring up at Hill House. *You can't fool me, I have magic eyes and I see you. I played Medea, and Clytemnestra—the fall of another house, the House of Atreus! So there.*

She turned, nearly lost her balance as she was buffeted by a sudden gust, not cold like the autumn morning but hot with the carious reek of rotting gums and tongue.

I see you too, it whispered.

CHAPTER 39

Stevie lay in bed, listening to the quiet house around him. No footfalls, no sound of running water, no voices. He stared at the ceiling, tracking spidery cracks in the plaster, the wobbly line where violet-patterned wallpaper had begun to curl away, then let his gaze drop to the wall opposite his bed. The door was hidden behind the dresser but he knew it was there. His secret.

But had he really seen it? Seized by sudden panic, he jumped up and went to the dresser, crouched to slide his hand behind it.

And yes, the door was still there, he hadn't imagined it. He recalled how it had felt, the smooth planed wood and the minute brass knob. He thought of grasping the knob and turning it, pulling the little door open. He could do that now, it would take half a minute to move the dresser and open the door and...

He squeezed his eyes shut. Better to postpone the pleasure. Like sex: let the anticipation build. Plus, if he explored it now, Nisa or Holly or Amanda might knock at his door, asking him to join them for breakfast. There'd be plenty of time later. He could wait till after everyone else had gone to bed. If he found nothing, it would be a funny story to tell them tomorrow morning. If he *did* find something...

He straightened, dressed, made his bed, and left the room. Holly and Nisa's door was shut. Amanda's too. He padded on down the dim stairway, the gloom belying the sunlight he'd seen through his window. The main hall seemed even bigger than it had yesterday, probably because there were no people in it.

And there seemed to be more doors than he recalled. The old music room, the billiards room, dining room, kitchen; and now he noticed two other doors, between the game room and dining room. He hadn't investigated that side of the house—as far as he knew, none of them had. In all he counted a dozen doors, all closed, and three—no, four corridors, leading who knows where.

He stood, musing. How many people had lived here since Hill House was built? Not many, based on Holly's account of what Ainsley had told her. Had they spent much time in the billiards room or conservatory or library?

And what about children? Didn't people back then have a million kids? Nisa had said there'd been a family here in the 1980s, another bit of info gleaned from Ainsley. Stevie turned in place and tried to imagine kids running up and down the stairs, shooting pool in the room down the hall, playing hide-and-seek in those mysterious halls and dimly lit rooms. This was exactly the kind of house he'd daydreamed about as a kid, huge and rambling and just waiting to be explored.

Yet Hill House pushed back against all that. Standing alone in the main hall, he felt it—like a hand shoved hard against his face, making it impossible for him to breathe, to see or call out for help…

Gasping, he stumbled backward, bumping into the stairway's newel post. He looked around but of course he was alone. He cocked his head—maybe the others were awake by now? He heard nothing from upstairs, though after a moment there came a low *clink* from the direction of the kitchen. Someone making coffee, or doing last night's dishes.

But he didn't smell coffee, so he remained where he was, feet sinking into the Persian rug that covered the floor. Its once-bright flowers had darkened to dingy purple and rust, and it was full of holes left by moths or mice. Near the front door, a large section of the carpet was stained. It was body-sized but didn't resemble a body, just a formless blotch. Mold? Or a leak?

He looked up to see a crack in the ceiling high above him. The crack ran from the chandelier to the wall where the tower was attached, which showed signs of a shoddy repair job—plywood panels, a seam of gray caulking like an exposed intestine. A padlock was attached to the door that opened onto the tower. Stevie walked over and gave it a tug. Locked, of course.

He turned and continued to the kitchen, halting at the open door. A man stood staring into the sink. When he heard Stevie he looked up, scowling.

"Oh, hey." Stevie lifted his hand in greeting and walked into the room. "I didn't know anyone else was—"

"What the fuck is this?" The man reached into the sink and held up the soiled tablecloth. He looked angry, and scared.

"Uh, yeah, sorry about that," Stevie stammered. "Someone spilled some wine at dinner. We figured we'd just clean it properly in the morning."

The man shot him a disgusted look. "I don't give a—"

"Tru."

Someone pushed past Stevie—Melissa. Yesterday, she'd been wearing sparkly eye makeup and a bright do-rag. A little much, but Stevie assumed she'd been making an effort to greet the newcomers. She wasn't wearing any makeup now.

She hurried to the sink. "Let me handle it, Tru."

Her husband shoved it at her. The sopping fabric filled her arms as she shrank from him, and he glared. He was almost as tall as Stevie but rangy, with deep lines scored beside his mouth, and hands covered with scars and calluses, a flattened pad where the tip of one finger had been sliced off.

Stevie looked away. Melissa had darted off to open a door to the veranda, sodden tablecloth clutched to her breast. Gazing at her wet clothes, the water pooling at her feet, Stevie felt weak with shame. She lifted her head to stare at him, then raced out the door.

Stevie hesitated, glancing over to see that Tru was now in the pantry, angrily shoving aside cookware. Stevie turned and slipped outside after Melissa. She'd moved to the back of the house, where she stood examining the tablecloth.

"Hey," he called softly, not wanting to take her by surprise. She looked up, her face blotchy and heavy-eyed, as though she'd underslept. "I'm Stevie."

"I remember." She gave him a wan smile, and he walked over to join her. "Did you get some breakfast?"

"Not yet. But dinner last night was fabulous. Your husband's a great cook."

"Mmm." She swiped a strand of hair from her eyes. The do-rag was gone, and he clearly saw the bruise it had been meant to hide. Was she deliberately not wearing it now? Trying to signal that something was wrong?

Melissa clocked his concern. "I bashed my head in the pantry a few days ago," she explained. "This place—every time I have to work here, I bump against something. Once I almost slipped and fell down those stairs in the hall—I grabbed the rail just in time, I would have broken my neck otherwise. Tru hates me coming here. He knows what people think."

Stevie felt his face grow hot. "I didn't—"

"I hate it, too." She began to fold the sopping tablecloth, fuming. "This fucking place. Hill House. Ainsley shouldn't rent it out."

"Holly said she needs the money to keep it up."

"Better if it just fell down," Melissa snapped. "It's not safe."

He raised an eyebrow, waiting for her to continue, but she'd turned her attention back to the tablecloth, pressing it against the veranda rail to squeeze out excess water. Which, Stevie noted in alarm, was still pink, despite having soaked overnight.

"God, I'm so sorry about that mess!" As he reached for the tablecloth, Melissa batted away his hand.

"Just leave it," she ordered.

"But that has to be some kind of antique, right?" She nodded, holding up a damp corner so he could see the monogram embroidered there: *HC*. Stevie winced. "Look, we can pay for it, or replace it, or—"

She straightened to stare at him. Without the glittery eye makeup, her deep-set eyes seemed alarmingly acute and a bit contemptuous: the eyes of a person accustomed to dealing with simpletons from away. "The tablecloth doesn't matter, Stevie. Once it's dry, we'll burn it."

"Burn it?"

"Won't be the first time."

"No wonder Ainsley needs to rent the place out." He'd meant it as a joke, but Melissa wasn't amused.

"She doesn't need to," she retorted. "She chooses to. That's why Evadne and I keep an eye on it."

"Evadne? The lady in the trailer?"

"My aunt. The two of them go way back. They're constantly arguing, they're like sisters. But Ainsley renting out Hill House is one thing they will never agree on, and..."

"And you're with your aunt?"

"Yeah. But Ainsley writes my checks." She lowered her head— self-conscious, maybe. "Still, this way, I can help Evadne. That's why she lives up here."

"To watch the house?"

She nodded. "You're here for a week?"

"Two. Holly—she's the one who organized everything, this is a really big deal for her. And, I mean, it seems okay—"

He leaned against the rail, staring at the sunlight falling through bare tree limbs, the bright blue sky overhead. "It's actually really beautiful, after being in the city for so long."

"That's what everyone thinks. All I can say is, be careful. Try to stick together at night."

"And don't go in the basement."

Again, Stevie hoped for a smile. He didn't get it, just a look that mingled anger, resignation, and perhaps pity. Embarrassed, he let his gaze drop to the silver ring she wore, the amber stone catching the sun so it glowed against her hands and chipped nail polish. "Your ring. Is it by the same person who did Ainsley's?"

"Yes. Evadne made it."

"Evadne?" he echoed in surprise.

Behind him, the door opened. He turned to see Tru, wiping his hands on a dish towel. "Missy, you want to give me a hand with the boiler? I need to change the filter."

"Yeah, I'll be right there."

Tru stepped back inside as Melissa hurriedly gathered the tablecloth. "I'll help him with that before we drive back home. So if you think of anything you want from town, find me and let me know. I'll drop by later with some food for tomorrow. We're supposed to get bad weather."

"Really?"

"Really." She stepped past him, holding the tablecloth at arm's length, and headed for the door. "Be careful," she called without looking back.

The kitchen door closed behind her, and Stevie stared at the trail she'd left in her wake: a sluice of water that was no longer pink but deep crimson, extending across the veranda floor.

CHAPTER 40

I left Nisa in the shower, singing one of the ballads she'd been rewriting for *Witching Night*.

> *"Last night I served the Devil's dog,*
> *And gently laid him down,*
> *And all the thanks I've gotten this night*
> *Is to be burned in London town..."*

The original, "Mary Hamilton," was a grim tale of rape, infanticide, and a woman's execution by hanging. Nisa's version ended with Elizabeth Sawyer turning the tables on her tormentors, and on Tomasin the demon dog as well. Her voice rang after me as I walked downstairs. If Amanda Greer wasn't awake earlier, she would be now.

Stevie sat alone in the kitchen, a mug of coffee in his hand. I greeted him, filled my own mug, and leaned against the counter. "How'd you sleep?" I asked.

"Okay, I guess." Stevie gestured at a basket of muffins on the counter. He seemed agitated, but he knew better than to engage me before I'd had my morning coffee. "Melissa and her husband dropped them off."

"Oh yeah?" I sidled over to get a muffin. "What's the husband like?"

"He definitely seems to have an attitude toward people like us."

"Meaning?"

"Meaning people from the city. Interlopers, flatlanders, gentrifiers— whatever you want to call us. He was really pissed off about the table-cloth. Melissa told me it was some kind of heirloom, she showed me the monogram."

"I don't blame him. Not a great first impression. But I still don't see how that much wine got spilled."

"I don't think it was wine, Holly."

I snorted. "What the hell do you think it was, Stevie? Blood?"

He jumped from his chair, stood, and opened the door to the veranda. "Look," he said, pointing.

I walked over to the door and glanced out, to where a damp trail led to the veranda rail, ten feet away. "What am I looking at, Stevie?"

"That!" He gestured furiously, then turned. His face grew pale. "Shit. It's—it's—it didn't look like that a minute ago."

"What did it look like? What *is* it?"

"She was wringing out the tablecloth. It was red—like, really red, like—"

I stepped beside him and ran the toe of my shoe through the trickle of water. "It's just wet, Stevie," I said. "See?" I stooped and touched my finger to the damp spot, held it up. "No blood. Nada."

"But—"

I quickly went back inside, irritated and also disconcerted. What-ever he'd seen or imagined, his reaction—his white face and obvious concern—had been real. Real enough that I gulped my coffee to keep my mouth from growing dry.

"What did Melissa say about it?" I asked in a matter-of-fact tone as I refilled my mug. "The tablecloth?"

"Nothing," he admitted. "Just that this sort of thing has happened before."

"Right. That's why white tablecloths are a really bad idea in rentals."

"But she seemed upset by something. Her husband...there's something off about him."

"'Off'?"

"I think maybe he's abusive or something."

I shook my head. Stevie was so hypervigilant about abuse that, while couch-surfing a few years ago, he'd called 911 when he overheard his neighbors watching *Big Little Lies*. "You don't know her—you don't know either of them. None of us do."

"Yeah, but—"

I held my hand up to silence him. "Stevie. Just stop."

He stared at me, mouth open to argue, but finally nodded. "Yeah, okay. But the tablecloth—"

"Stevie! We were all there! Amanda spilled some wine, that's all."

"I was here with Melissa just fifteen minutes ago, Holly, and that tablecloth looked like a body had been wrapped in it. I mean, it was ruined. I know, I know—"

Now he raised a hand to keep me from interrupting. "It was maybe half a glass. I saw her knock it over. And I'm just telling you: I saw this, too. A few minutes ago, that entire tablecloth was red, and so was the veranda outside the kitchen. I think it freaked Melissa out, and her husband." He took a sip of coffee and stared at his mug, troubled. "They won't stay overnight here. Melissa and Tru."

"I know, she told us that yesterday."

"Just now, Melissa told me that it's not safe. We should be careful."

"Careful how?"

"She didn't say. Just, be careful. A warning. Evadne is her aunt, did you know that?" I blinked, trying to hide my surprise, and gave a noncommittal shrug as he continued. "Melissa said that she and Evadne keep an eye on Hill House. Because it's not safe."

"You just said that, Stevie."

He looked at me, head tilted. "How did you sleep, Holly?"

"Fine," I said. "I had weird dreams."

"Weird how?"

If Stevie hadn't brought up the tablecloth and the gruesome suggestion of blood, I might have confided in him about the voices I'd heard. Or the boy Nisa had told me about, staring at our window. But if I mentioned them now, Stevie would go off on some grisly tangent.

Or, worse, tell Nisa about what he'd seen on the veranda. *Imagined he'd seen,* I thought. I sipped more coffee to steady myself.

"Nothing," I said. "I never sleep well the first night in a strange place, that's all."

"But it is strange, right? I mean, it's not just me—there's something about this house, it—"

"It's an old house, Stevie, that's all." I shook my head, trying to convince myself that I believed this. "Even before I signed the rental contract, Ainsley told me that people project their own expectations on old houses like this—they hear air in the pipes or mice or raccoons, and they think a place is haunted."

"I didn't say it was haunted," he said. "I said the tablecloth looked like evidence from a freaking crime scene. So maybe you shouldn't be so quick to diss the idea that possibly there is something going on here."

"Jesus, Stevie! We only arrived yesterday!" I looked at him pleadingly. "I just want us all to focus on my play, okay? We've got this place for two weeks! I want to get everything out of it that we can."

"Your play?" Stevie's eyes narrowed. For a few seconds he resembled the cast-iron knocker on the front door. "What about Nisa? Credit where it's due, Holly."

I pushed aside my mug and left my muffin half-eaten on its plate. "I'm going to take a walk," I said. "I'll see you at ten, okay?"

CHAPTER 41

Amanda pulled her coat tight around her and began to walk back toward the road, thrashing through tangled underbrush, past fallen branches and piles of rocks. She tried to force away the memory of that foul wind and its ominous whisper.

I see you too.

She could glimpse Hill House through the mature trees that edged the top of the driveway. From this angle, the upstairs windows seemed to watch her sideways, like one of those creepy paintings where the eyes appear to move. Hill House had the worst feng shui of anyplace she'd ever stayed. No wonder it was empty.

Though it's not empty, she thought. *We're there.*

She lifted her chin defiantly. She wouldn't give it the satisfaction of knowing it had frightened her. She wasn't going to let herself be gaslighted by an old ugly house.

She took a deep breath of the cold morning air, grounding herself, then started to run her lines, speaking them aloud. She knew them so well already she could recite them in her sleep. She knew most of Stevie Liddell's part, too. Stevie had been a professional actor but he looked hard done by. Drugs, alcohol, sex with strangers—not that there was anything wrong with those things, but she knew how they could wreak havoc on your memory. She didn't trust him to be off-book at this point, so she was ready to feed him his lines if needed.

"What manner of dog are you, that you can take whatever form you desire? Can you enter the shape of a woman, too?"

She raised her husky voice an octave to respond as Tomasin—she'd heard echoes of Stevie's boyhood soprano when he spoke, and so she reached for that.

"Of course! Any coarse shape will blind human eyes like yours—cat, dog, hare, ferret, frog, toad."

"Lice? Fleas? Deer ticks?"

"Absolutely. You mortals are never far from evil—tell a lie and I guarantee you, the Devil hears it. Whatever hand you play, he bets against it. The house always wins."

Damn, the dog really did have the best lines.

She lifted her head at the sound of a car starting up, one of the vehicles parked up at Hill House. Probably the white pickup, the housekeeper and her husband. Amanda was only a few yards from the road now, she could see it clearly through a scrim of branches and birch trees. The engine revved, and the sound grew louder as the vehicle backed up and then charged down the driveway.

Amanda flinched at the rattle of gravel thrown up by its wheels, brakes squealing as the vehicle barreled closer. If the driver lost control, it would come right at her.

"Slow down!" she yelled.

And whoever was driving *had* lost control. The engine shrieked and she smelled burning rubber as the car—it was a car, she spotted it through the trees—careered around the curve. She turned to run, crying out as her foot caught on a tree root and she fell, hitting the ground full force.

Her head pounded as she lay there, winded and stunned by the sudden silence. Gingerly she extracted her foot from the twisted root. Her knuckles stung where she'd scraped them, but otherwise, she seemed fine. She pulled herself up, setting a hand on a tree to steady herself, and peered out warily.

Everything had gone still, save for a crow clacking in the woods. Cautiously, she picked her way to the road.

It was empty.

And there were no new tire tracks in the dirt. Just her own footprints where she'd gone into the woods.

She took a deep breath and paced uphill toward Hill House, retracing her steps, and stopped. Holly's car was there, parked alongside her own, and the white pickup. Amanda stared at them dumbfounded.

She turned and walked downhill again, scanning the ground. That car had been so close! Surely it had left tracks, some sign as it raced past? She halted when she reached an enormous tree stump, shrouded with poison ivy. Had she noticed it before? She could easily imagine someone taking that curve too fast and slamming right into the stump.

Amanda checked the time. Nearly an hour had passed, which seemed impossible. But there it was—almost ten. She gave the road ahead a last leery look, turned, and strode toward Hill House for the first read-through.

CHAPTER 42

Before she showered, Nisa had knocked at the bathroom door to Amanda's room, to make sure she wasn't there.

"Amanda?"

Nope—it was locked. She ran the water in the shower and stepped inside, let the heat wash away her anxiety. Holly had been talking in her sleep last night. Nisa knew she was totally wound up about being here: excitement and also anxiety.

Still, it had been creepy. At first, Nisa had thought someone else was in the room with them. But what they were saying didn't make any sense, just nonsense sounds, besides which she knew there weren't two other people there. She'd nudged Holly, who rolled over and began to breathe heavily, then reached under her pillow for her earplugs, in case Holly started up again. If she did, Nisa'd slept through it.

The memory creeped her out. She forced it aside, brought her attention back to the morning light, the day ahead. For the first time, people other than Holly would have the chance to hear everything that Nisa had been working on for the last two years. Well, in person. Of course, she'd performed some of the songs at open mics and a showcase in Red Hook, and posted them online, where her various feeds had been growing slowly but steadily. Holly had forbidden her from saying anything outright about *Witching Night,* but people seemed to like her hints that there was something big to come.

Nisa suspected that Holly's ban came from fear—she was worried that Nisa's songs would outshine her text. Stevie had privately agreed with Nisa, a few weeks ago, when she'd shared recordings of "Black Dog" and "In the Earth," her version of the old standard "In the Pines."

"That's creepy as fuck," he'd said.

"Good." Nisa laughed. "My work here is done."

"Where does that come in the show?"

"After Elizabeth's destroyed her enemies, but before she casts the spell that helps her escape."

"Does Elizabeth sing it?" Stevie asked, and shook his head. "Because I don't think Amanda could pull it off."

"No. But I could."

"Yikes. We're going to need a trigger warning for that one."

Nisa had kissed him, delighted. "I sure hope so. But they'll love it, right?"

"They will if they can fall asleep afterward. Brr," he'd said, and shivered.

Now she stood in the shower and did her vocal exercises, letting the steam and hot water open her throat. Holly had shown her a YouTube clip of Amanda doing a passable version of "The Ladies Who Lunch." Nisa had taken her cues from that, coming up with a few snippets throughout the show that Amanda should be able to manage. She'd also written a song for Stevie as Tomasin, stealing lines from the original play. *I'll have a witch, I love a witch...*

But most of the songs she'd written for herself. Nisa knew they were good. More than good, another reason Holly was so edgy. When people saw *Witching Night,* they'd be impressed by Amanda Greer's comeback. But they wouldn't be able to forget Nisa Macari.

She'd spent so long working toward something like this. Sweating in the subway as she went to that open mic burlesque at Coney Island every summer weekend for three years, in addition to all the other auditions she dragged herself to, again and again. Other than playing Cosette in *Les Mis* in Williamstown one year, nothing bigger had ever panned out.

"You're too much yourself," a casting agent had told her, when she'd failed yet again to nail a role, a minor character in a direct-to-streaming slasher movie being shot in Bushwick. "You need to inhabit the characters, Nisa. Think of them like a house you're supposed to live in, not demolish."

The words had stung, even as Nisa knew they were true. She wanted to shine through the characters she played, or desperately wanted to play; break them open so that people could see—hear—not just what she could do, but what she *was*. Holly was older, and even in the relatively short time they'd been together, Nisa had seen how the constant hustle for work and recognition had left her with nothing but sharp edges and urgent ambition, neither of which jibed well with Holly's actual job as a private-school teacher.

Nisa didn't want to wait that long for success. Like Holly. Like Stevie. Like Amanda. She wanted to grab it and swallow it whole, right now.

She stepped from the shower. Before she grabbed her towel, she pulled the curtain across the bathroom window. It seemed unlikely that the teenage boy she'd seen earlier was a Peeping Tom, but you never knew. Giorgio had warned them that Hillsdale was sketchy.

She dried off and slipped into a vintage dress with a tight bodice and flowing skirt, all in a sumptuous knit, black and gold. Outside the sun shone fitfully, but that disgusting, peeling wallpaper absorbed the light. It felt like a classroom on a rainy afternoon, gloomy and dull.

She returned to the bathroom, combed out her wet hair, and dabbed her face with lilac-scented moisturizer. When she was finished, she knocked again at Amanda's room.

"Amanda? You there?"

No answer. And the handle was still locked. Venturing out into the hall, Nisa tried the other door, which opened easily. She stepped lightly inside.

Amanda's clothes were strewn everywhere. She'd brought two large suitcases, one of them still half-full of blouses and sweatpants, skirts and dresses. Nice clothes, kind of actress-y—a burnt-velvet shift, a black cashmere sweater, clumpy but expensive shoes. Nothing that would fit Nisa; Amanda was twice her size.

She did like Amanda's lipstick, which she'd left on the windowsill, amid a trove of high-end cosmetics, serums, and those facial masques that make you look like Jason Voorhees. Nisa picked up a lipstick and opened it, reddish-black in a long gold tube. The name made her laugh—Hemogoblin.

She put some on, just the tiniest smidge. Older women shouldn't wear dark lipstick, anyway, it aged them. She smiled at herself in the mirror, carefully recapped the tube, and replaced the lipstick on the windowsill. Amanda had expensive perfume, too, in a little bottle. Nisa liked light scents: freesia, pear. This was wisteria, which Nisa thought smelled like carrion. No temptation there.

She left Amanda's room and went downstairs to get some breakfast. She wondered if Amanda would notice she was wearing her lipstick.

CHAPTER 43

I stormed away from the kitchen, furious at Stevie but also at myself, for letting him spook me like this. I'd spent so much time trying to rebuild my confidence, letting go of the guilt I'd carried in the years since Macy-Lee's death. Finally allowing myself to write again, to share my work without fear of rejection. Without fear, period.

Yet now all that seemed like it might unravel. I'd assumed that getting away from the city with my friends would be inspiring, but being sequestered at Hill House seemed to have given the others an excuse to behave badly.

Two of them, anyway: Stevie indulging in the kind of superstitious, New Age-y crap he had never outgrown; Amanda Greer getting drunk and trashing a tablecloth. Only Nisa seemed imperturbable as ever. Give her an audience, or the promise of one, and she was self-possessed as an Abyssinian cat.

Which also got under my skin. After Stevie's outburst, I couldn't shake my own unease about being here. I had an hour before our first read-through: I needed to get out. I got my coat from the cloakroom downstairs and went to take a walk.

Immediately I wished I'd brought gloves, and a scarf—I hadn't expected it to be so cold. The wind had a bite to it, but the chill helped clear my head. I wandered down the driveway, hands in my pockets and my collar pulled up around my neck. A few clouds scudded high above, gradually overtaking the blue sky, and the smell of balsam fir vied with that of autumn leaves and crushed acorns.

I sensed a shift in the air, and shivered. Not just the cold but a clammy, underlying sense of dread, of wrongness.

Unbidden, the face of Macy-Lee Barton came to me. I didn't like to dwell on it, but she'd looked a bit like Nisa, dark-haired and dark-eyed. And while Nisa's stillness suggested self-assurance, Macy-Lee's had seemed almost premonitory, and ominous.

Macy-Lee didn't sing, though her speaking voice carried the Appalachian twang I associated with old-timers like Ralph Stanley. It had been a cold voice, I thought at the time, especially for someone so young, her tone bleak as she recounted what had happened to her—what she claimed had happened to her. Her voice didn't hold the undercurrent of anticipation or pleasure I was accustomed to hearing when someone told a ghost story. She'd sounded numb.

I seldom thought of Macy-Lee: she was a dark door I knew better than to open. But something about this remote place, the thick trees and the sky that seemed intent upon hiding behind them, brought her back to me. As though she'd been waiting for me to leave the city; as though she'd been waiting for me to be alone.

Almost twenty years earlier, just out of school, I'd been a promising young playwright, one of the 30 Under 30—and I was way under thirty, barely twenty-one when I wrote my first play, set in an isolated, unnamed backwoods town. I was old enough to know what I was doing, just not old enough to understand the repercussions of telling someone else's story, the tale Macy-Lee had recounted to me one drunken night, about how she'd once seen a ghost.

I had been working at a camp in the Blue Ridge Mountains. She'd been a local. We'd hooked up for an hour after a party, and then she'd stuck around, drinking and talking.

"I laid with a haint, you know." She'd announced this as calmly as though remarking on a passing car. "A ghost."

I laughed, but she'd continued to stare into the dying campfire, her dark eyes capturing the flames like fireflies. "What kind of ghost?" I asked.

"A real good-looking one. I didn't know he was a ghost—I thought he'd just wandered into the woods like me. You know, looking for a place to..." She mimed toking on a joint. "I was pretty stoned and he was easy on the eyes. It was dark, but not that dark."

I found myself scooching closer to her, captivated. "What'd he look like?"

"Kinda tall and slick-faced—real smooth skin, like a polished rock. But peaked—you know, pale. It was weird 'cause usually, I'd feel chancy, meeting someone like that in the middle of the woods. But he was just so—convincing."

She shivered with remembered pleasure. "So we did it, right there in the trees. That was the first time I ever came with a man. Only he wasn't a man, so I guess I still haven't done that."

She gave a weird fluting laugh that made me recoil slightly. "How'd you know he was a ghost?"

She leaned over to lay her hand on my thigh, and I jumped. "Because he was on top of me, and when he moved away he turned to fog. *Sssss—*"

Hissing, she moved her other hand through the smoke from the campfire. "Like that. Gone. I would've thought I dreamed it, only nine months later I dropped a baby in the woods. Never gained weight, never lost my monthlies, but I tell you, I hadn't felt right, and one night when I was out near the same place I doubled over. Laying on the ground, I nearly passed out."

Her eyes grew huge as she pointed to the patch of ground between us, dusted with ashes and embers gone black and cold. "Finally, I got it out of me—this slimy gray thing, cold as ice but...pulsing. And instead of an umbilical cord, all these tiny wriggly fingers were wrapped around a kind of face. Only it had no eyes or nose—it was just a jelly blob with a mouth, and this ropy string attached."

Her hand on my leg tightened as she stared at me. "It was the umbilical cord, and that thing bit it right through."

Her jaws snapped together so loudly that I jumped. "Damn straight," she said, nodding. "Then it slithered off like a snake. Gone, bang! You know I ran outta there so fast I passed myself on the way. Thought maybe I dreamed it, same as before.

"But then I went there the next day with my dog Rex. He snuffed through the ferns for like five minutes before he began to dig, and you know what he found?"

I shook my head, speechless.

"*Teeth*," she spat. "Tiny baby teeth, only sharp enough to bleed you. See?"

She thrust her hand at me and I saw the lines scored there, deep enough you could have slipped a maple seed's wing inside each one.

"That's crazy." I laughed shakily and took another swig from the bottle of bourbon we'd been sharing.

"It's true." She stared at me with huge black eyes. "It fucking happened."

"Sorry," I said, and finished the bourbon.

I left a few minutes later and never saw her again. But I used her story as the inspiration for my first play, *Knell/Nell.*

Somehow, after it took off at the Louisville New Play Festival, Macy-Lee had heard about the show. Somehow, she found my email address and sent me a message, accusing me of plagiarism and demanding I pay her ten thousand dollars, which of course I didn't have. Somehow, Macy-Lee got some Blue Ridge journalist to listen to her story—she still insisted it was true—and somehow an article in an obscure local newspaper appeared, painting me as a villain. Exploiting someone with a mental illness; stealing another woman's story and presenting it as my own work.

And *Knell/Nell was* my own work, the best thing I'd written until now. I'd spent a single night with Macy-Lee. I hadn't known she was mentally ill. Of course I hadn't believed her ghost story, and I had no reason to believe that she did, either. But before I had a chance to respond to the accusations, with an apology or explanation, Macy-Lee Barton had killed herself.

Thinking about Macy-Lee chilled me even more than the cold morning did: I hunched deeper into my coat, walking faster to warm myself. I'd always felt deep sorrow and guilt and shame. Yet I'd never regretted writing *Knell/Nell*. My long creative silence had been fueled by fear, that I wouldn't be able to write something as good as that one play—and also a subdued grief. For Macy-Lee, and also for myself, the young artist who'd been so vulnerable, poised for a flight that never came.

It was the pressure of being here, I thought. I'd hoped—assumed— that being at Hill House would restore my confidence, bring my work to the next level. Instead, I felt anxious and on edge, envisioning Macy-Lee staring at me, her black eyes sparking in the firelight, as something mewled and crawled toward us from the shadows.

"Ugh," I said aloud. "Go away, go away."

I glanced behind me. I'd been so caught up with my thoughts that I'd lost track of how far I'd come. Hill House had disappeared from sight. The road looked so deserted that it was hard to believe a huge mansion lurked somewhere behind. To either side of me, leafless birch trees moved in the wind, branches rattling where they touched.

I looked at my phone. I had to be back in half an hour. Time to turn around.

I'd only gone a hundred feet or so when a slash of yellow caught my eye. A clearing, deeper into the woods on the left and nearly hidden by the surrounding forest. When I stepped closer through the trees, I saw that the ground was covered with pale-gold leaves. They looked striking, like scattered coins against the otherwise barren earth and stark black trunks. I took a few photos, hoping to show Nisa when I got back. Maybe I'd use them to post about *Witching Night* on my sorely underutilized social media.

But the light wasn't right, the bright carpet of leaves overshadowed by a passing cloud. I stepped deeper into the woods to get a better shot.

By the time I'd reached the clearing, the sun had disappeared completely, the leaves dull and waxy once again. The passing clouds now looked more like the beginning of a front that stretched to the horizon. I took a few photos anyway. I could always edit them later.

Turning around, I looked up toward Hill House, though the building itself was still lost to view. About midway, however, I spotted a pale column protruding from the ground. I thought it was a larger birch, variegated white and gray.

Yet the longer I gazed at it, the harder it was to bring it into focus. Could it be a deer? I moved a few steps closer, careful where I set my feet, and stopped.

The column wasn't stationary; it moved, flickering in and out of focus like a strip of film in an old-fashioned projector. I froze so I wouldn't alarm whatever creature this was, or draw attention to myself if it was a predator. There must be coyotes here, and bobcats. Maybe even bears.

Its outline was blurred, though, and too tall. Some atmospheric anomaly, then? A plume of mist, or smoke rising from a nearly extinguished campfire? I thought once more of Macy-Lee. Had this been how she felt, in the woods that night? As I began to edge backward, the blurred shape grew clearer.

Not a deer or birch or mist, but a person. Tall, wearing light-colored clothes.

And spinning, spinning in one place, the way a child does to make herself dizzy. Although their arms weren't outspread the way a child's would be, but pressed against their sides. Their pace was measured, practiced, but still too fast for me to make out any features.

I crouched behind a tree, angling my head so I could still watch. I kept expecting the person to stop, or slow, or even to spin more quickly, but they continued to turn in one place, a relentless rotation that grew more horrible the longer I watched. What were they doing? The sheer mindlessness sickened me.

Squinting, I tried to determine what, or who, it was. For a fraction of a second, the vague form cohered into a face: no details save for two gaping holes. Eyes? I felt a sick fear that she—it—might somehow spin toward me, reaching out to touch my exposed skin.

My mouth went dry. I had to leave. Whoever this was, whatever it was, it felt wrong. I backed away and, when I had nearly reached the road, I turned and bolted, my blood pounding in my ears. I couldn't hear my own footsteps.

But someone could. A faint sound came from the woods, the snap of a broken twig. Instinctively I looked back. The figure continued to turn as it had before, though now splintered light fell on it, as the sun flashed through the clouds. For a split second I clearly saw a face staring at me.

Macy-Lee?

Then I took off running.

CHAPTER 44

Amanda had started up the steps to Hill House, still disturbed by the speeding car. She debated whether to tell the others. They already were looking at her sideways because she'd spilled a few drops of wine, but honest to god, who cared about that? She'd pay to replace the god-damn tablecloth, she'd just have to be careful that Ainsley didn't make some ridiculous claim that it was a valuable antique.

Actually, she wouldn't mention the tablecloth. Or the car, she decided. She reached the veranda and was heading for the door when she heard footsteps. She turned to see Holly racing up the drive. Her face was red from exertion, her eyes wild.

What's she running from? Amanda wondered. She peered past Holly but the road was empty. Holly lifted her head, saw Amanda, and immediately slowed down. Amanda waited for her to reach the house. "Are you all right?"

Holly nodded as she joined her on the veranda. "I'm fine," she replied breathlessly.

"Are you sure?" Holly didn't exactly look fine—had the speeding car returned? "Do you want some water?"

Holly forced a smile. "No, really, I'm good. I just—I was walking in the woods and I got spooked."

Amanda waited for her to go on, but Holly only shrugged. She pushed open the heavy front door, holding it for Amanda to walk inside. "Too much time in my own head," she sighed. "I'm too much of a city girl, I guess."

"It takes a little time to adjust, doesn't it? We're not used to all this luxury."

"I'm not sure it's that luxurious. I was hoping for more Downton Abbey." Holly pointed sheepishly at a large stain in the moth-eaten carpet, and nodded toward the padlocked tower, the buckled plywood that had been used in a half-assed repair. "Maybe formerly luxurious."

Amanda laughed, but Holly's expression grew serious. "No, really," she said. "I wanted this time to be…special. For all of us, but mostly for you. It means so much to me that you're here, Amanda. I know it's a job, but—thank you. I honestly couldn't imagine doing this play without you as Elizabeth."

Amanda stared at her, touched. "Well, thank you, Holly. It's a wonderful part—for me, for anyone. I always wished the three Weird Sisters had gotten their own play."

"Right?" Holly smiled. "Maybe that'll be the sequel."

"Are we still on for the read-through?"

"Absolutely. I'm just going to get my laptop and notes from the room. I'll see you there in a few, okay?"

Amanda waited a minute or two, pleased by Holly's words, and curious to see if the mysterious car made a reappearance. It didn't, so she headed upstairs to her own room. She found her copy of the script. She'd printed it out before she came here. Some young actors, maybe all of them, liked to read from their devices, but Amanda loved the feel of the pages in her hands.

Excitement stirred in her as she looked through them, her own dialogue highlighted in yellow. Holly had mentioned the public reading with

Imani Nelson, once they were all back in the city. Amanda had never worked with her, but she'd been impressed by her production of *Aunt Anansi*—Nelson was one of the relatively few directors, all women, whose work spotlighted older female actors. Initially, Amanda had been disappointed when Nelson had to bow out of the Hill House run-through, but now she was relieved. More time not just to rehearse but to polish this like glass; more opportunity for Amanda to make sure that Elizabeth Sawyer remained the play's beating heart, rather than Tomasin, or Nisa's unnamed Greek chorus of one.

It would definitely be a wild ride to share the stage with those two. Especially Stevie. Amanda had appeared in Albee's *The Goat, or Who Is Sylvia?* playing a woman whose husband fell in love with a goat. In *Witching Night,* Amanda's character became enamored of a dog. A brilliant piece of casting on Holly's part—you could actually imagine kissing a dog, if it looked like Stevie.

"'I am parched with madness and the ill wishes of evil men,'" Amanda recited as she walked to the bureau. She set the script beside her cosmetics bag and checked herself in the mirror. "'I need an innocent's blood to moisten your sweet lips! Kiss me, dear Tomasin, stand on your hind legs and kiss away the wrinkles on my brow.'"

She frowned at that last line. A little too on the nose, she thought, relaxing her face so her own wrinkles receded. She picked up her lipstick and opened it, twisting the gold cylinder. She gasped.

The top of the lipstick had been bitten off. She could clearly see the imprints of tiny teeth—a rat? A mouse? Too small for a person for sure, and who would bite off a lipstick? A child, maybe, but there were no children here. Shuddering, she twisted the lipstick back into the case, replaced the cap, and threw it into the wastebasket.

Ugh.

She had another lipstick, a lighter color—frosted peach. She examined it thoroughly before applying it, slipped the tube into her pocket, and perched on the edge of her bed, script in her lap.

Refocus.

She was off-book, for the most part. She'd done background research into the real Elizabeth Sawyer, the woman who'd been burned alive. But Amanda needed to focus on *her* Elizabeth, the one who lived to see her accusers and tormentors turned into beetles by Tomasin, who then gobbled them up.

"That sounds rather disgusting," she'd confided to Holly when they first spoke on the phone, after Amanda had read the script.

"It'll all be suggested in the sound design," Holly had reassured her. "Stevie's already working on it. He's a genius with that kind of stuff."

He better be, Amanda thought now, recalling Stevie's blunder when he made that stupid joke about the accident.

She got up and began to collect a few of the things she'd thrown onto chairs and the nightstand when she first arrived here. She'd intended to put them away last night, but then Stevie had ambushed her and made her think of Jason Pratt, the absolute last thing she wanted to brood about before bed. *We don't need any more on-set accidents.* They sure didn't need any here at Hill House—the whole place was an OSHA nightmare. An Equity rep would take one look at this venue and shut it down.

She still had a few minutes before she needed to meet the others downstairs. She folded up several scarves and slipped them into a drawer, shook out her burnt-velvet shift and hung it in the closet, then paused.

Jason Pratt. She'd hoped that nobody here would mention him, that they'd be too young to remember. But Stevie, for one, knew about it. Actors were such goddamn gossips.

She'd never had any intention of jumping. She wasn't afraid of heights, for one, and didn't killing yourself somehow mean facing your fear, or overcoming it, or giving in to it, or something? Amanda couldn't remember. Back then, it had been such a long time since she'd thought about that sort of thing. But she hadn't been afraid of the catwalk.

And she hadn't been thinking about suicide, she'd been thinking about the opposite. Well, not the opposite—what *was* the opposite of suicide?

She'd been angry. Enraged. A good emotion to channel if you were playing Medea, which she was, in a new translation with Jason Pratt playing Jason. The newspapers had fun with that: Jason as Jason! Like they needed to come up with some hook to write about him. If the tabloids had known sooner that the two of them were sleeping together, the play would have gotten better *Page Six* coverage.

But soon, Jason Pratt had already moved on, just like that other Jason. What a dick. To this day, Amanda couldn't get over how stupid she'd been, falling for him so quickly. But then he'd fallen for her, ha ha ha.

Okay, it wasn't funny. She wasn't heartless. Not totally heartless, anyway. But he'd been asking for it, really, treating her that way. The same way that Elizabeth Sawyer's tormentors treated her. *I am shunned and hated like a disease, scorned by all who fear my very touch upon their hands. If only I had some power, good or evil, by which I might be revenged upon these men...*

She'd been on the upper part of a catwalk—part of the set, designed to represent a tower in the palace at Corinth, where Jason betrays Medea. This was in the 1980s, during the first wave of turntable sets with gears you could hear in the gods, the era when you'd leave a show humming the scenery.

There were constant malfunctions during the rehearsals. Several catwalk ladders had been designed to swing away, their billowing draperies of black cloth representing the roil of emotions that would overcome Medea.

Only often, the swinging ladders didn't swing. They'd stick, or lurch, or shudder as though someone unseen clambered down, or up. And more things went wrong. Props disappeared. A bank of lights went out, plunging the set into darkness. The tech crew and engineers couldn't figure out what was wrong. Someone made a surreptitious call to an Equity rep, who threatened to halt the show. There was talk of a curse, like the Scottish play, of Medea working her malign enchantments. Amanda heard sniggering jokes from the crew and cast, but also genuine discomposure. Actors are superstitious.

"I swear it's a poltergeist," Jason said during one run-through.

Amanda waited a beat, then dropped the prop knife she was holding, which made everyone jump. She laughed, and they all did, too.

Once she and Jason had been stuck on that damn catwalk for two hours. That was before she'd seen him screwing a theater usher behind the fire curtain. A real class act.

Jason was the one terrified of heights, not Amanda. Their catwalk scene was short, but the director had refused to cut it, and Jason never stopped moaning. During that equipment malfunction, Amanda seriously thought he might pass out. She'd spent those two hours trying to distract him, trying to get him to shut his eyes, breathe deeply, put himself into the other Jason's head—*he* wasn't afraid of heights! Think of all his adventures with the Argonauts. He was supposed to be a Method actor, for chrissakes.

The accident occurred during yet another tech rehearsal, a week before press previews. Amanda was up on the catwalk, leaning way over the railing—it was low, to give the audience good sight lines. She wasn't thinking about jumping but she was considering what a long fall it would be, twenty feet. There should have been mats there, like the kind they have in the circus for acrobats, but you couldn't have actors stumbling over mats, that would have been a hazard in itself.

So: no mats, just the hard stage floor. From up here she could see the strips of tape set out for everyone's marks, a pencil that had dropped from someone's pocket. Probably Tory, the ASM.

Amanda was late on her line. Not late, she was deep into Medea's head, brooding about how Jason had betrayed her, thinking about how that usher was probably some NYU student not old enough to drink. She heard Jason come up behind her, hit his mark and stop, the metal grid vibrating under his heavy tread. He waited for her speech:

I should just kill myself—why not? I sacrificed my entire life for Jason, everything! I betrayed my father and killed my own brother, made myself an exile and bore Jason two sons, all for love of him.

And now he's abandoned me for that stupid girl! He'll marry the Princess of Corinth, leaving me and our children to be humiliated and to die alone.

Only Amanda stayed mute. She hadn't forgotten her lines: she was trying out a different approach to them, a Pinter pause. She heard Jason whisper Medea's lines, trying to help her out—*"I should just kill myself"*—heard Tory in the wings below echo the same words, her tone more urgent.

"Amanda?" Jason asked in a low voice. "You okay?"

He stepped closer. He sounded scared, like he actually thought Amanda would jump and kill herself over an asshole like him. He leaned forward, she could smell his breath, cigarette smoke, the beer he'd had with lunch, she could smell his cologne. He reached for her, started to grab her and pull her back—

—not in the script, Jason!—

And she backed away, panting as she struck at him—hard, everyone always underestimated how strong she was—as she cried out Medea's next line.

"Why not?"

Jason toppled forward. His arms flailed as he tried to grab the rail but she was in the way, blocking him though of course she hadn't meant to, she was holding on for dear life herself as he plunged over, his belly grazing the rail and his arms stretched wide, greeting the audience though there was no audience, no applause, only Tory screaming and the other actors racing onto the stage as Amanda stood there and stared at the man lying below, his blood fanning across the boards.

Betrayal twists love into blazing hatred, an evil that destroys even those helpless ones we love best.

She blinked, and found herself clutching the windowsill of her bedroom at Hill House. Hadn't she been in front of the closet, hanging up her velvet shift? She glanced over her shoulder, saw the closet door shut and her script pages scattered across the bed.

But she'd left the script on the dresser—she was sure of it. She was careless with her clothes, but with a script? Never, not since she'd been a very young actor on her way to an audition and left the script for *Hay Fever* on the A train.

She looked at her phone—almost ten! She gathered the script pages, sorting them as she headed for the door. A scrap of paper dropped out, and she caught it, not part of the script but something torn from a magazine. Not torn, she realized as she paused to stare at it, but cut with scissors. A man's face, vaguely familiar from some ad campaign dating back thirty or forty years.

Strange. She looked around uneasily, but her concern over being late won out. She tossed the scrap into the wastebasket with the discarded lipstick and hurried downstairs.

CHAPTER 45

I'd left Amanda to go up to our bedroom and catch my breath, relieved that Nisa wasn't there to see how shaken I was. What the hell had I seen in the forest? Not a person, surely? That glimpse of a face could have been anything—dead leaves in the crook of a tree, or even a bird or piece of discarded clothing.

But even as I fought to convince myself that I'd only imagined it, I knew I'd witnessed something real; something inexplicable. Perhaps this was Macy-Lee's vengeance: after all my years of discounting her terrible story as just that—a story—I'd let down my guard and allowed her to burrow back into my brain, dragging her ghost infant behind her.

I pushed away the ghastly image, went into the bathroom, and splashed cold water onto my face. I needed to compose myself before joining the others. Actors are like dogs, you can't let them smell your fear. Uncertainty is okay, self-doubt is okay, but I couldn't afford to indulge in either. I only had this fleeting window of time at Hill House to get everything right.

So far, everything seemed—well, not exactly wrong, but off-balance. I was reluctant to admit it, but Ainsley had been right. It was very easy to project my anxieties, conscious or not, onto the house.

If Nisa knew I was rattled, she'd use it to her advantage. They all would. That was what actors did with a work in progress—angle for more lines.

Or, in Nisa's case, new songs. At home, I'd been able to laugh it off—make a joke about Nisa hovering on social media, clocking how a new song was received. She had an unwavering belief in her own talent that I'd always found admirable, and sometimes envied.

Now I found myself thinking about the way she and Stevie had exchanged glances in the car yesterday and at dinner last night. The way she'd brought her songs up, again and again. She could never keep silent. To Nisa, any quiet moment was a void waiting to be filled.

I dried my face and stared out the bathroom window, but my anxiety wouldn't seep away. Turning to leave, I cast a last glance down at the lawn with its dead wildflowers and weeds. A dark shape moved in a stand of tall grass. As I stared, the stalks parted so I could see a black hare crouched against the ground. Far too small to be the spinning figure I'd watched in the woods—yet as I gazed at it, I felt a sense of recognition, almost a sound, a faint rustling as though I crouched there alongside it, the smell of bracken in my nostrils and long grass tickling my chin.

But I wasn't lying among the dry goldenrod: I was here, standing beside the window, gazing down. The hare's long ears twitched, and even though I hadn't moved, had hardly dared to breathe, it reared onto its hind legs, head raised so that it stared at me with russet eyes, its mouth parted in what, in a human, would be a mocking smile.

CHAPTER 46

Not real, not real, I thought, and stumbled from the bathroom. I snatched up my laptop and the folder with my notes, refusing to glance out the bedroom window to see if the black hare remained in the grass, and ran downstairs.

We gathered in the living room. I'd thought it would be the coziest spot—the one that most seemed to belong to the current century, other than the kitchen. Nisa immediately curled up in the old wing chair—she had a cat's instinct for occupying the most comfortable perch in any space. Stevie and I took the couch. Amanda settled in one of the remaining chairs, looking disgruntled. As the lead, I suppose, she'd expected to get the best seat.

"That looks cozy!" She shot Nisa a bright, false smile.

Nisa smiled back. "It is!"

They all had paper copies of the script. Amanda had one that she said she'd printed out a few weeks ago. Since then I'd emailed her changes, cutting some of her dialogue, but she claimed not to have received them.

The clear early morning had given way to more unsettled weather. Wind lashed at the trees. The blue sky had darkened as rain spattered down, and the windowpanes seemed streaked with watery ink. The cold seeped through them, making me feel like I wore wet clothes and not a flannel shirt and sweater. Amanda took some photos of everyone, Nisa smiling, Stevie pretending to look serious.

Me actually looking serious—I was eager to get started. Stevie had tried to start a fire in the fireplace, despite my protestations.

"Ainsley said we shouldn't start a fire."

"Ainsley said she *preferred* we didn't start a fire," Nisa corrected me. "Go for it, Stevie, this place is freezing."

I couldn't argue with that. But while the birch logs crackled brightly at first, the flames soon died. The logs smoldered, too dispirited to burn.

"Did you open the damper?" Melissa emerged from the hallway, wrinkling her nose at the smoke. She slipped on a fireplace glove, reached in to grasp at the damper. "There, now it's open. It just doesn't draw well. You need to—"

Before she could finish, Tru appeared in the doorway, pulling on his coat. "I'm leaving now. Unless you want to walk, let's go."

He glanced at the fireplace, then me, his disdain obvious. I stared back at him, refusing to be intimidated. "Thanks for all your help with meals."

"You're paying for it."

"Look, I'm sorry about the tablecloth," I said. "I'll be happy to—"

Ignoring me, he gave Melissa a peremptory look and stalked off. "Don't worry about the tablecloth," she said when he was out of earshot.

"Were you able to get the stain out?" asked Stevie.

"No. It won't ever come out—I told you, we'll burn it. I'll try to check in with you later, there's lasagna in the fridge, and there should be enough leftovers to get you through tomorrow if we can't get back."

Amanda raised an eyebrow. "A nor'easter," Melissa explained. "We might have a storm tonight. I have to go, sorry."

She hurried out as the rest of us stared at each other. "Thank god this place isn't creepy at all," Nisa said, and laughed.

"I think he hurts her," said Stevie. He sat on the couch beside me, his long legs and arms tucked around him, trying to make himself small enough to fit into the awkward space.

Again, Nisa laughed. Stevie turned to her, shocked. "I'm sorry!" She clapped a hand to her mouth. "It's just, you're always imagining the worst. Her husband's out of work and he resents having to come here to make money," she continued. "That's obvious. It doesn't mean he hurts her."

"She has a bruise on her head, that's why she wears a do-rag. She even said she bumped into a door——"

"Stevie." Nisa gave him a warning look. "Remember what we talked about after you called 911 that time? Stop jumping to conclusions. Maybe she just likes her do-rag."

"Her ring's like Ainsley's," I said. "Did you notice? Silver and amber."

"Evadne made it," Stevie replied. He seemed put out that Nisa had shut him down so quickly. "She's Melissa's aunt—Melissa told me."

"Right," Nisa broke in. "And Ainsley told us that Evadne used to work with victims of domestic abuse. So it's highly unlikely she wouldn't intervene if she thought something was going on with her own niece."

"Yes, but——"

Amanda leaned forward, holding up her sheaf of pages. "Perhaps we could run lines," she said evenly. "Break the spell."

"Great idea." I settled my laptop on my knees. Stevie did the same—I'd asked him to record all the read-throughs. I looked at Nisa. "Ready, baby?"

For an opener, Nisa had adapted a fourteenth-century ballad called "The Devil's Nine Questions," a series of riddles posed by a figure who was either a wicked knight or elf or the Devil, depending on the song variant. He intends to rape or kill (or both) the maiden who can't answer correctly.

Nisa had changed the maiden to an old woman—Elizabeth Sawyer, the witch, who counters the Devil's questions.

"What is sharper than a thorn?
What is louder than a horn?

Hunger is sharper than a thorn
And fear is louder than a horn…"

Nisa sang the Devil's lines in a low, insinuating near-whisper, her pure soprano twisting the words into something unearthly and foreboding, a barely contained rage that might erupt. I'd heard her perform the original ballad before, but still, the hairs on my neck stood up. Amanda's replies as Elizabeth sounded thin and unconvincing, more spoken than sung. Yet that worked in her favor: her Elizabeth was out of her element, vulnerable.

"What is deeper than the sky?
And what is worse than a woman's lies?

The grave is deeper than the sky
And you yourself are the King of Lies…"

Amanda's voice rose strongly as she recited her last line——she'd obviously been working on her singing. She sat up straight in her chair, as Nisa drew a deep breath and sang the final verse, triumphant, though this victory was meant to be Elizabeth's and not the Devil's. Only later would he come to her as the black dog, Tomasin.

"The moment that the fiend she named
Away he flew in a burst of flame…"

Nisa's voice filled the room like water fills a crystal tumbler. For an instant the shadows withdrew from the windows, allowing hazy light to show through the glass. I felt myself relax: the play was working. Better than that——it was casting its own spell, one we each had a hand in. *It's not just going to be okay, it's going to be great,* I thought. Smiling, I glanced at Nisa, then Amanda, waiting for her to speak her next line.

"Some call me witch, and through their hatred they've taught me how to be one..."

From there, it just got better and better. Often at a first read-through, actors give cursory performances—you can't even really call them performances, it's more like they're starting to find their way through the words and story and characters.

Now, however, everyone seemed almost uncannily immersed. Nisa's songs aching to be heard, like she'd just uncovered them in some dusty alcove filled with ancient scraps of sheet music. Stevie as the demon dog Tomasin projecting a skin-crawling combination of sensuality and threat. Even without makeup or costume, he somehow made me see the supple canine muscles flexing beneath his human skin, his eyeteeth seeming to grow longer when he smiled and touched Amanda's cheek.

"Come, do not fear me, dear Elizabeth. I love you too much
To want to hurt or frighten you.
If I seem terrible, that's only toward those who hate me, and you.
I know that your love for me is unfeigned. I've seen how your tormentors
hurt you, and my pity has drawn me to your side.
I'm here because of my love for you, to aid you in revenging yourself
Against your foes..."

As for Amanda—she combined the middle-aged Elizabeth's hurt and fear with a young woman's first sexual hunger and desire. I watched her in astonishment, even as she gazed transfixed at Stevie, who was uttering Tomasin's diabolical bargain:

"Command me to destroy anyone who has hurt you, sweet Elizabeth:
I will do this faster than you can draw breath, on condition
That you give your body and soul to me..."

Stevie reached for her hand, eyebrows lifted as his lips parted softly, waiting for her reply.

But Amanda wasn't looking at him. She was staring at the fireplace. From behind the fieldstone chimney breast came a scrabbling noise—the frantic scratching of nails or claws, followed by a clatter like gravel falling from a great height. Stevie jumped to his feet as cinders exploded out onto the grate. The scrabbling grew louder and more frenzied. Stevie swayed as though drunk, his hands clawing at his ears. I tried to stand too but my legs wouldn't move.

The damper, I thought, *it can't get past the damper.*

But Melissa had opened the damper.

With a mewling shriek, a dark mass tumbled onto the hearth, a shape with too many legs and too many eyes. A charred log spun out onto the floor next to it and Stevie barely managed to kick it back toward the fireplace. The writhing shape emitted a high-pitched squeal, revealing its long legs and equally long ears, sparks that I had mistaken for eyes. Its lips peeled back in blackened petals. Nisa screamed as it leapt from the hearth, bumping into her chair. Stevie grabbed a fireplace poker.

"Don't hurt it!" shrieked Nisa.

The black hare darted from the room. I stared after it, feeling like I had after listening to Macy-Lee's story: horrified and drunk, almost drugged.

"Holly!"

Someone grabbed my hand—Nisa. I lurched at last to my feet and ran into the main hall. The window beside the door had been left open. Without hesitating, the hare leapt through the gap to land on the veranda outside.

I flung the door open. The hare still crouched on the topmost step, long ears flattened against its skull. Mist clung to its black fur. Not mist, I realized. *Smoke.*

Was it hurt? I thought wildly, *I can't let it be hurt.* Why did it keep coming here? I shook my head, coughing as though I were the one who'd been inhaling smoke.

"Come here," I croaked, reaching for the shivering black form. I pulled off my sweater, thinking I could wrap it around the animal, keep it safe. I heard the others running up behind me.

"Is it okay?" Nisa cried.

"Oh god, I don't know." I groaned and took a step toward the hare. It sprang away, landed in the driveway, and bounded again, this time to disappear into the ferns at the edge of the lawn.

CHAPTER 47

What the hell was that?" Cursing loudly, Stevie ran down the veranda steps. Nisa followed him into the underbrush, sweeping aside dead ferns and weeds.

"Her rabbit," Nisa said breathlessly, slowing down at last, "the crazy lady in the mobile home."

"Evadne," I snapped. "And she's not crazy, so stop saying that."

Nisa shook her head. "It's her familiar. Like in the play, only it's a black hare, not a black dog."

"It's not her familiar." Stevie returned to the driveway, brandishing a stick. "A familiar stays with whoever summons it—it's a servant, or someone enslaved, like Caliban."

"An animal can't be enslaved," said Amanda.

"A demon can," retorted Stevie.

"Let's not conflate theater and real life, Stephen."

"Don't call me Stephen!" Stevie's hand curled tighter around the stick.

Again I groaned and ran my hands through my hair. "Everybody, please stop. It's just a rabbit. Well, a hare. That's all."

Nisa stared at me, incredulous. "A hare that came down the *chimney*?"

The four of us stood and gazed into the woods. Finally, Nisa said, "Maybe Hill House really is haunted."

"That wasn't a ghost," I insisted.

"Only a demon," said Stevie.

"No, it wasn't." Amanda straightened, turning to stare at the house. "I was staying with friends in Maine once—they had a cabin on Little Sebago. We started a fire in the fireplace and a burning duck flapped down onto the hearth. A mallard. Of course the poor thing died, but..." She shrugged. "Things like this do happen."

Nisa scowled. "Ducks *fly*. And we saw that rabbit before. Remember, I took a picture of it in front of the trailer?" she went on, excited. "And then we didn't see the black rabbit or whatever it is—we saw her. Evadne."

I started to retort but stopped. She was right.

"But how the hell did it get up there?" Stevie pointed at the chimneys atop Hill House, and everyone looked at me.

"Listen to me." I used the tone for wrangling unruly students back into their seats. "No one was hurt, right?"

"Except the hare," Stevie said.

"It was able to run off, I'm sure it's fine." I squinted into the trees, praying I was right. "And I know that was weird—okay, more than weird—but Ainsley said that animals get inside the house all the time."

Both Nisa and Stevie looked like they were about to argue, when Amanda broke in. "Can we go back in? I'm freezing. Also," she added as she tromped up the steps to the door, "maybe we could do what we're ostensibly here to do?"

"And ignore what just happened?" demanded Nisa.

I shot Amanda a warning look—Nisa is of the *Don't go to bed mad, stay up and fight* school.

But Amanda just lifted her chin and smiled condescendingly. "Don't ignore it, dear Nisa. Use it."

We trudged back into the house one by one, glancing around, and at each other, with disquiet. Yet Amanda was right. This was energy we all could work with. A black hare on fire, fleeing through the living room...

Immediately I began planning how to write it into the play. I was so absorbed I took a wrong turn, and wandered down an unfamiliar corridor.

"Over here, Holly."

"Oops, sorry!"

I turned and walked back to where Stevie waited for me, just outside the passage. The others had gone to the living room—I heard Nisa's fractious tone and Amanda's aggressively calm one, guaranteed to wind up Nisa even more. Stevie and I looked at each other, and he smiled weakly.

"Amanda's doing it on purpose," I said. "To piss her off."

"It's better than being scared."

"I'm not scared, not really. It just startled me. Are you?"

"Yeah," he said, beginning to pace nervously. "I mean, what the hell, Holly—a rabbit comes down the chimney? How'd it get up there? This house is three stories tall. So yeah, I'm freaking scared."

My momentary calm vanished as my entire body went cold—really cold, like I'd plunged through the deceptively solid surface of one world into the frigid depths of another. *It's just a rabbit...well, a hare.*

I drew a deep breath and took his hand. It, too, was ice cold, and I rubbed it between my own hands. "Stevie, listen to me. You're a pagan, or Wiccan, or whatever. What do you think it is? If it's not a hare." I hesitated. "If it is connected to her. Evadne."

"I'm more neo-pagan adjacent. I know about this stuff, but I don't necessarily believe it. But I know a lot of people who do, so..."

He thought for a moment, calming down. "It could be connected to her," he said at last. "But not necessarily her familiar. I mean, she'd have to be pretty powerful to have a familiar, right? One like Tomasin, anyway." He smiled, trying to make a joke. "But it could be a fetch. That's when you summon something that looks like a person but is really just an empty vessel. Usually it takes the form of a human, but it could be an animal."

"An empty vessel?" I let go of his hand and pushed him away. "Jesus, Stevie—that seems a lot worse than a familiar."

"I know. But that makes as much sense as anything, right? Hares were once associated with witches, the same way cats are now."

"Yeah, but a fetch sounds like *Re-Animator* or something." I shuddered, feeling as though the corridor was closing in on us, tightening like a fist. "And who would even want to fetch anything from this place?"

"There's definitely something strange about Hill House," Stevie continued. His eyes glinted in the dim light. "It's not what I thought it would be like. It knows we're here. You feel it, right?"

"No!" I replied, angrily. Because I *did* feel it—a sick, disorienting sensation, the space around us at once claustrophobically small and limitless, a narrow mouth opening onto an abyss. "It's a big empty house and everyone is imagining things. Projecting things, like Ainsley said."

I didn't buy into what he'd said about the fetch—I *couldn't* buy into it. That was much, much more than I was willing to take on. I lived in the real world, of mobile phones and rent payments and truculent teenagers, even if I had written a play that was ostensibly about a witch. I had to maintain control of my project—my cast, my friends, my partner. The money and time I'd invested. My career.

I looked at Stevie. He'd hunched into himself, the way he used to when he spiraled after a night of heavy drinking, trying to hide inside the child he'd been long ago. Usually this would trigger me to hug him, to protect him. Now all I could see was someone indulging his private terrors, when I couldn't afford to acknowledge my own. The last thing I needed was him having a panic attack.

"Stevie! Listen to me." I rapped my knuckles hard on the wall's wood paneling. I expected an echo but there was only silence. I might have knocked on a blanket. Stevie's eyes widened, but I continued quickly. "If you're scared, channel that into Tomasin."

"He's a demon. He doesn't get scared."

"So tap into that. You're a demon in a big spooky house—you should feel right at home."

"I do." He glanced around: a wild thing released from its cage, measuring the threat and opportunities of its new surroundings. He turned back to me and nodded. "That's what scares me."

CHAPTER 48

The first part of the read-through had gone surprisingly well, Amanda thought, until the flaming rabbit interrupted. At least the rabbit—hare—seemed to have survived. Certainly it had high-tailed it out of there like a bat out of hell. A hare out of hell. This place must be infested with pests.

"There's an explanation for everything," she reassured the others when they all reconvened in the living room. Amanda had swiftly taken the comfortable wing chair before Nisa could reach it.

"We should move to the parlor." Nisa gave Amanda a nasty look. "It's smaller and cozier. This room gives me the creeps."

Privately, Amanda agreed. But Holly had insisted they remain, at least for now. "Let's keep the continuity going in this room. We can try the parlor later, how's that?"

And so they began once more to go through the script.

"We'll skip Nisa's song," Holly added, which earned her a nasty look, too.

"Good idea." Amanda smiled. "Maybe Nisa summoned that thing? Not intentionally, of course," she purred.

They made slow progress. Amanda read through each of her lines with care, trying to determine where the beats were, shifting emphasis from one word or phrase to another.

"'Reverence once waited on old age. But now an old woman, poor and losing her looks, is called a witch.'"

"'Oh, but I love a witch!'" cried Stevie as Tomasin. "'I've loved a witch since I was playing at fetch in the garden.'"

"She's like Medea, isn't she?" Amanda asked, cutting away to look at Holly. She'd decided to take the bull by the horns: if Stevie had been thinking of the incident with Jason Pratt, the others might well be, too. "I assume you had that in mind when you wrote Elizabeth?"

"No." Holly looked surprised. "I mean, maybe unconsciously, but not as regards you."

"Let's be honest here: as regards me, *everyone* thinks of Medea." Amanda fixed each one of them with her cold gaze, letting it linger on Stevie until he blushed. "I was heartbroken I never got to play the part. Not that I didn't grasp why they had to cancel the run. Elizabeth feels a bit like a second chance at that kind of character."

Holly seemed to weigh her words before replying. "Of course. Two women who were badly treated, getting away with murder—yes, I can see that."

Amanda let her icy stare melt. "Thank you."

They returned to the read-through. Much of what Holly had adapted was supplemented by Nisa's songs. Too much, Amanda thought. Tomasin had two. Amanda only had a few short verses but she'd done them well. She'd half hoped Stevie's voice had suffered over the years; she'd heard about his drug problems. She'd thought he'd be a tenor, but his voice had deepened to a rich baritone.

He read his lines well, too. She'd have to watch him, if this project ever got off the ground.

She started as Stevie let go a sinister laugh, staring at her with his huge lunar eyes. Really, he was too much. "'Let not the world witches or devils condemn—they follow us, and we follow them.'"

"'I would never—'" Amanda declaimed, embarking upon one of her better speeches when Holly cut her off.

"Let's stop there." Holly closed her laptop, beaming at Stevie. "That was excellent. You too, Amanda and Nisa. "

"I'm starving," Nisa announced. "And freezing—I'm going to grab a sweater."

"Melissa said she left some soup for us. Let's meet in the kitchen?" Holly rose to her feet as Nisa made a beeline for the hall. Amanda heard her run upstairs, with Stevie close behind. Holly paused at the door, like she didn't notice Amanda, still poised as Elizabeth Sawyer with her shoulders raised and fingers curled as if to rake the air.

"That's an interesting interpretation," Holly observed. "It did make sense, after what you said about Medea. Let's discuss it with the others later."

Amanda gave her a brittle smile, and Holly left.

Really? Amanda thought, furious. Did this girl truly think Amanda was lazy enough to rely on her Medea for this character, without developing a new one? For a first read-through anyone might do that, no shame, no blame. All actors call on sense memory, that combination of bones and breath that could carry you through a performance even if you were sick, or so hungover your dresser noticed.

For several minutes, she sat alone in the big empty room, waiting for her rage to fade. Goddamned Holly. Nisa, too, grandstanding with her secondhand songs. And Stevie's insecurity, teetering on the edge of acute anxiety—never a good look for an actor. She'd come here expecting professionals but found herself among children.

She sighed. At least the old wing chair was really astonishingly comfortable. A relic of the original furniture: it was a shame they'd gotten rid of the rest. She ran her fingers across the fabric, velvet worn to a smooth nap, like skin. The upholstery had a faint smell, smoke and rust and something sweet. It made her mouth water; what an odd thing for a chair to do.

It was good to sit and let herself breathe, to feel the room breathe around her. As though she sat alone onstage, familiarizing herself with the light, the distance between the set and the flies high above. She thought of the unsettling way the traveler curtains sometimes moved when no one was there.

Right now, the window curtains in this room were doing the same thing. Outside, the wind tossed the trees, so it wasn't that surprising that the curtains had caught a draft.

Yet the way they moved was strange. They didn't billow whenever a gust shook the house. Instead, ripples slid across the gauzy fabric, as though someone were running a hand beneath. She watched, fascinated. The movement was so gentle, almost loving. She imagined those hands stroking her back, and her eyes closed. Fingers along her spine, her neck, lingering at the base of her skull, allowing her to sink deeper, the house no longer breathing around her but breathing for her...

"Amanda! Amanda, can you hear me? Amanda!"

Her head struck the chair as she fell backward. Air filled her lungs and she gasped, trying to remember where she was. With Jason on the catwalk? But no, she'd been onstage with someone else, someone who truly cared for her...

"She's awake," a voice said.

Amanda turned her head. She wasn't onstage but some other place. *Hill House,* that was it. In her mind's eye she saw its facade, those crazed staring eyes, heard that malevolent whisper borne on a foul wind.

I see you too.

CHAPTER 49

She blinked, and the person who'd spoken came clearly into view. Nisa. They were all arranged in front of her, Holly kneeling at her feet. Stevie looked alarmed, but Nisa eyed her almost suspiciously.

"You weren't breathing," she said.

"What?" Amanda rasped. Her throat hurt, as though she'd been shouting.

"I came in to get you for lunch and you weren't breathing," Nisa continued.

"Nisa yelled and we ran in and—you weren't breathing." Stevie hugged himself. He looked anxiously over his shoulder, then back at her. "I shook you and you wouldn't wake up. Not until Holly started shaking you."

Amanda touched the side of her head. *Ouch.*

"Sorry." Holly ventured a smile, although it didn't reach her eyes. "You were like a rag doll, your head just bashed against the chair. But that's what brought you back, I think."

"Back?" Amanda winced. "I was just sitting here."

"I know, but you weren't—" Nisa began, but Stevie grasped her shoulder and she shut up.

Amanda gave him a grateful look. She got unsteadily to her feet, brushing Holly aside.

"I'm okay," she said. Just what she needed, everyone thinking she'd had a stroke. "That happens sometimes, it was just a nap."

"Really?" Nisa's eyes narrowed. *Little bitch.* "I thought you were dead. We should call 911."

"Stop it," Holly snapped at her, and turned to Amanda. "Come into the kitchen, we have lunch set up. Blood sugar drop, that happens to me all the time."

She extended her hand. Amanda smiled uncertainly but took it. Always nice to be escorted, anyway. As they walked toward the kitchen, she heard Nisa speaking to Stevie in an agitated whisper.

"I'm not imagining it—she wasn't breathing. Even if Holly doesn't believe me, you do, right? She was dead!"

CHAPTER 50

Nisa was right: Amanda had stopped breathing, he didn't know for how long. A minute? Minutes? They'd been in the kitchen for at least ten before Nisa went to get her. Could you survive that long without air? Obviously you could: she was alive.

One of Stevie's lovers had had sleep apnea, and Stevie had recognized the same slack features. His face would be flaccid, not from sleep but an absence of consciousness, a corpse's vacant eyes and half-open mouth. It used to terrify Stevie; he'd shout at his lover till he woke—afraid to touch him, in case his flesh might be hard and cold.

Thank god Nisa had returned to the living room when she did.

Still, Amanda seemed fine. She didn't even seem shaken up so much as annoyed, trying not to show her embarrassment. Once they were in the kitchen, she'd quickly set about getting herself soup and some of Tru's fresh-baked bread.

"I'm going to eat this in my room, if nobody minds," she said. "I want to go over the script again, now that I've had a chance to hear you all."

Stevie saw Holly's worried face, but Amanda gave her a reassuring look. "Seriously, I'm fine. That happens sometimes when I meditate. I go into a deep trance—delta waves, they're very good for concentration."

After she'd gone, Nisa whirled to confront the others. "Those weren't delta waves. I was there: she was out like a light. *She was not breathing.*"

"Well, she's fine now. Least said, soonest mended." Holly sipped her soup. "This is really good."

Stevie joined Nisa and Holly at the kitchen table. The pea soup was smoky with ham hocks, perfect for this cold late-autumn day. He was relieved that they'd all decided to eat here rather than in the dining room, relieved that there'd been no more discussion of what had occurred there last night. The hare and Amanda's blackout were enough drama for one morning, especially among actors.

But of course, as if reading his mind, Nisa asked, "What happened with that tablecloth?" Stevie pretended to not hear the question. It freaked him out when Nisa did that, as though she could beam in on his thoughts. She nudged him under the table. "Stevie! You were up early, right?"

He swallowed his bite of bread. "Melissa took it. And her husband— he's a creep."

Holly gave him a condescending nod. "So you said."

"It's true. I think he's—"

"I'm sure Ainsley wouldn't hire him if he's abusive," Holly broke in swiftly. "We don't know anything about him or Melissa. Or anyone else."

"Whatever." Nisa returned to the stove for more soup. "He's a great cook. Probably no one else will even come up here." She ladled soup into her bowl, grabbing another slice of bread. "We're lucky to have him."

Stevie almost lost it then. Really? Lucky to have him? Holly gave him a warning glare. *Don't blow it for me, Stevie.* He scowled and mentally amended this for her: *Don't blow it for all of us.*

He pushed aside his bowl and stood. His appetite had vanished, but if he left now, one of them would make a scene. He pulled out his vape pen, stepped through the kitchen door onto the veranda, and took a hit.

It was already two o'clock. Holly hadn't mentioned anything about another read-through. Probably she wouldn't bother—better for them all to pace themselves. She'd taken a ton of notes. The way this sort of thing usually worked was, the playwright stayed up all night, rewriting, while the actors retired to the bar. He knew that Holly liked to let her thoughts settle in before sharing them. This evening, maybe they could relax with a bottle. For now, he relaxed as the cannabis oozed into his lungs, into his bloodstream, into the lightning storm that was his brain.

He gazed out at the bleak landscape. Leafless trees and weed-grown lawn, the far-off hills black and gray and ash-white. Could that be snow? He ran his tongue over his chapped lips, tasting salt from the soup, the taint of cannabis resin. He'd brought his tarot cards, thinking it might be a hoot to get stoned and do a reading here. After a day and a night at Hill House, that no longer seemed like such a fun prospect.

He did another hit and then slipped the vape pen back into his pocket, shaking out his arms and hands, like he was readying himself to go onstage. The knot in his chest had loosened. He felt energized—weed made him hyperaware, not sleepy. So, no tarot cards, but he thought he might take a walk.

He lifted his head and saw a black wedge of cloud directly overhead. Where had that come from?

The wind gusted and rain spattered onto the veranda roof, followed by a sudden, loud rattling, like someone had released a box of marbles and sent them rolling down from the dormer. He wished he had his recording equipment with him—the rattling was becoming a sort of buzzing, like a swarm of bees. Across the lawn the air grew milky, hiding the woods. He leaned over the railing, opened his palm, and flinched as something bit into his skin.

"It's hailing," he called out to the others, still in the kitchen. "Crazy. It's like…"

His voice trailed off and he watched, fascinated, as his palm filled with fragments like broken glass. He let them drop to the ground, and only then noticed that an icy splinter had stayed lodged in his palm. He tried to brush it off but it was in too deep.

And it stung, much more than he'd expected. He grasped it, the ice melting at his touch but not fast enough. He drew his hand to his mouth, tasting blood and something rancid, like water from a vase that hadn't been emptied. He spat, and the last fleck of ice dissolved into a bloody teardrop. The cut bisected his Line of Fate—his friends at the Wiccan shop would have a field day with that detail. He used the other hand to push his way back through the door.

Inside, Holly and Nisa had their heads together, whispering or kissing, he couldn't tell.

"Did you see?" He pointed outside. "It's hailing."

Nisa yawned, rising to walk to the window. "All hail. It's not even that cold. Is it?"

He filled a glass with water, rinsed his mouth to get rid of that putrid taste. There must be some bizarre atmospheric effect, sucking pollution into the clouds. "We're high up, it could be colder than in Hillsdale. Melissa said something about a storm tonight, too, a nor'easter."

Nisa rubbed her arms. "I'm still freezing—I'm going to get *another* sweater, then poke around. Holly?"

Holly was still at the table, staring absently at her bowl. "I want more of this soup. I'll find you in a bit."

"I'll come with you," Stevie offered. "I'm going to get my mic and stuff, I want to explore."

Upstairs, Nisa ducked into the Yellow Room while he waited in the hall. He looked back at the closed door of Amanda's room. Should someone check on her? He walked over and knocked softly.

"*I'm fine,*" bellowed Amanda.

He walked away briskly. Talk about a short temper.

He paused when he reached his own room. The image of the nearly hidden little door popped into his mind, along with that same sharp spur of peculiar arousal. Making sure no one saw him, he slipped inside.

He'd made the bed before he went downstairs that morning, put away his clothes as he usually did. Fight chaos with the tools at hand. It was warm in here, almost hot, though maybe that was only compared to the rest of the house. He looked at the window. It was shut.

But he'd left it open—he always left bedroom windows open an inch or two. He liked to sleep in a cold room, something his lovers complained about. He walked over and pushed at the window frame. No dice. There were no sash locks, so he pushed again, harder. Still it didn't move.

He gave up, turned and walked over to the dresser. Bluebeard's castle was as he'd left it. He adjusted the cardboard proscenium, considered setting one of the cardboard characters onto the little stage—Bluebeard, his wife, or her sister Anne. Too much chance they might blow over and get lost, he decided.

Instead he peeked behind the dresser. The tiny brass knob of the secret door winked, beckoning him. The urge overcame him to open it. Not just open it: enter. See what it revealed. Live there, like he'd sometimes longed to live inside one of his toy theaters. The idea made him giddy.

He grabbed the dresser by two corners and inched it from the wall, careful that the toy theater remained safely on top. Then he dropped to his knees in front of the little door, not allowing himself to think about what he was doing.

"Stevie?" Behind him, his bedroom door opened. Nisa stepped inside without waiting to be asked. Stevie stared up at her in confusion. "Stevie? What's wrong?"

"Nothing."

He couldn't let her see the secret door. He hopped to his feet, grabbed the pillows from the bed, tossed them onto the floor beside the dresser, then yanked a drawer open to snatch a sweater and thrust it at her. "Here, you can borrow this."

"But I already—"

"Mine is warmer." He pushed her into the hall, darted back inside to pick up his mic and recorder, and joined her again. "Sorry, but it's such a mess in there."

Nisa pulled on his sweater, which nearly reached her knees. "Looks like a dress on me," she complained. "But thanks, it is warmer."

Stevie clipped his recording unit to his belt, switched on the mic, and adjusted the levels. He cocked a thumb toward the far end of the corridor. "Want to explore?"

Nisa grinned. "Oh yeah."

CHAPTER 51

A desolate odor of disinfectant and wood polish hung over the dark hallway. All the doors were shut, and there were no windows. Old-fashioned light sconces emitted a sepia glow that only heightened the gloom. Stevie shivered—he'd forgotten to get a sweater for himself. His palm felt numb where the hailstone had cut him, like he'd been pricked with lidocaine.

"Are you ghost hunting?" Nisa pointed at the microphone in his hand, then let her fingers slide over his own.

Stevie laughed. Now that they were alone, no longer in his room, he felt that frisson of desire Nisa always awakened in him. She'd taken time to put on eyeliner and lipstick this morning, a darker shade of lipstick than she usually wore. It looked good on her—vampy, like a silent movie star with her cap of black curls. Nisa reminded Stevie of the fox in *Pinocchio*—one of those sly companions he should know better than to follow. Usually, he did.

Now, however, he felt a bit vulpine himself. No, not foxlike; more like Tomasin, with an undercurrent of cunning and provocation that he must have absorbed from his character. Not Stevie's normal way of behaving, certainly not sober. He looked down at Nisa and gave her a slow smile. She looked delicious, her mouth a ripe plum there for the taking. Where was Holly? he wondered.

"Ghost hunting?" He shook his head. He was accustomed to being easily distracted, but being in this strange house had amped that to a whole new level. "No. I want to record the ambient sounds here," he said, and let himself lean into her. "It's such a strange place, and old houses are noisy—even if you don't consciously register the sounds, they're always settling. Wood contracts and expands, there are critters in the walls. Deathwatch beetles..."

"Get out." Nisa let go of his hand to smack his arm. "Stop, that's scaring me."

"They're just beetles. They feed on old wood and make a ticking sound. When people used to keep watch on a dying person, the room would be so silent you could hear the beetles in the walls."

"*Stop.*"

"It's not really scary. I've heard them sometimes, staying with friends upstate. Like this."

He paused to tap his fingernail on the wall. Unlike when Holly had rapped the wall downstairs, he was rewarded with a faint echo. "Like that. It's not a loud sound, you can't even hear it unless—"

Nisa hit him again, harder this time.

"Ow! Jesus, Nisa, that hurt!"

"I said *stop.*"

He started to snap at her, but caught himself and nodded indulgently. There was no point. Nisa was a little terrier: as quickly as she'd pursue some new enthusiasm, she'd hang on to a grudge, usually for some non-existent slight, and not let go until you really *did* get pissed off at her. He'd lost his temper with her more than once and always regretted it, in part because he honestly hated hurting people's feelings, and because he knew that he'd played right into Nisa's hands. Like when she'd come on to him that first night after a party, with Holly asleep in the next room, and they'd fucked on the couch.

Stevie sometimes regretted that night, and all the other nights and occasional afternoons that followed. Nisa might be irresistible, but Holly was his closest friend. He'd never confessed to Holly and never would, but he wondered sometimes if Nisa might tell her. Not out of guilt but just to stir up shit. Well, until then, Nisa would likely keep that secret close to her chest, a trump card that only Stevie knew she held, a card she might play at any time, for no reason other than that she was bored or irritated.

So many beautiful, talented people were like that. They wielded their glamor like a weapon, usually aiming at the people closest to them. But getting mad at Nisa was as fruitless as getting mad at a sparrow hawk, a creature he'd once seen attack and tear apart a bluebird in a tumult of sky-colored feathers and blood. The best thing to do was remember their beauty, and try to forget the mess they left behind.

He glanced back over at Nisa, who had paused to stare at him, head cocked. She seemed to be waiting for him to make some kind of move: to push her against the wall and kiss her, or storm off in annoyance at her quicksilver moods.

Uh-uh, not playing, he thought. Not right now, anyway.

He turned his attention back to his mic, checking the sound levels as he walked slowly down the hall. After a moment, Nisa followed, not talking, their footsteps muffled by the carpet. He was grateful for the silence—he was more stoned than he'd thought. He liked close spaces, closets and small rooms, even caves, places where nothing could surprise you, but the combination of the walls pressing in and the seemingly endless corridor unsettled him.

The lack of windows frightened him, too. It reminded him of when he'd briefly been in a hospital on suicide watch, a long time ago but he could still picture his room: windowless, its walls a smeary yolk-yellow. The sickly light here was like that. Jaundiced.

This is a lost place, he thought, and felt a growing, profound unease. Despair lapped at the walls and floors of Hill House like fetid, rising water: anyone who stayed here might drown. The others might not feel how it fed off their rancor and petty resentments, like a battery being recharged, but he did.

Though he might also just be really, really high.

Stevie exhaled, pushing his long hair from his face. He looked over at Nisa, who'd paused to open a door. She smiled at him, reaching to stroke his arm. Not seductively, more soothingly. A peace offering.

"What do you think—Narnia?" She cocked an eyebrow, switched on her phone's light, and peered into a large space, dark and empty and reeking of mothballs. "Nope."

She closed the door and walked to the next one. It revealed a linen closet, its shelves lined with brittle paper that turned to dust when Stevie touched it, releasing a sad whiff of lavender. Stacks of linens sat on the shelves above. Stevie pulled back a corner of neatly folded fabric to display elaborately embroidered letters: *HC*.

Stevie frowned. "That looks like the other tablecloth."

"Was it monogrammed?" He nodded. "We could bring this one down?"

Stevie glanced at his palm. A drop of blood welled anew from the cut. Flustered, he wiped it onto his jeans. "I don't want another tablecloth on my conscience."

Nisa laughed, too loudly. Stevie fought the urge to tell her to shut up. If he did that, she'd just start to sing. She was like a graffiti artist who always has to tag a blank wall.

Stevie was the opposite. "You could play Hamlet and disappear," Holly'd once told him.

"Hamlet wants to disappear," he retorted.

"Be careful what you wish for."

Now he ignored Nisa and replaced the tablecloth. As he did, he felt something between the layers of cloth—a plastic Ziploc bag. He pulled it out.

"What is that?" asked Nisa.

He slid open the bag, grimacing at an earthy, foul odor. A tiny handful of withered gray stems clung to the bag. Dried mushrooms. "Ugh," he said, hastily resealing the bag and shoving it back. "You don't want to know."

Nisa made a face, covering her mouth and nose. "That's disgusting!"

He felt around beneath the stack of tablecloths and found something else. Not fabric, something flat and slick. A magazine? He slid it out, careful not to tear it.

"Look at this."

He swiped at his phone light to see a copy of *Rolling Stone,* January 1985, with Billy Idol on the cover. But the musician's photo had been cut out. The only reason Stevie knew it was Billy Idol was that the cover showcased his name in big white letters above the words *Sneer of the Year.*

"That's too bad." Nisa pressed close to him to see. "You could have sold it on eBay."

He flipped through, looking for the cover story. But there, too, the head had been cut out. He began to turn the pages, more slowly.

All the heads had been cut out. Not just the heads of stars, but those of people in advertisements, figures in the background of group shots, even the head of a Labrador retriever in an ad for scotch. The owner's head was missing, and so was the dog's.

But they hadn't been cut with scissors. If someone had used scissors, you'd see where they'd cut in, from the side of the pages, or where the scissor's point had first broken through. *Right?* These had been cut with laser precision, even those heads so small you'd need a magnifying glass to remove them.

"What the actual fuck," breathed Stevie.

"Just some kid." Nisa shrugged. "Someone with a lot of time on his hands. Someone who really didn't like—who is that? The guy from *Buffy?*"

"Billy Idol."

"Billy Idol. Or anyone else. Jeez." Nisa craned her neck, staring at the defaced pages. "Let me see that."

She grabbed at the magazine but Stevie held it above his head, out of reach. "No."

"Are you kidding?" exclaimed Nisa. "That's so messed up—let me see it."

"We'll get it on the way back." Stevie's voice was steady, but the sight of the headless bodies made him feel sick. Worse, like there was something important he was missing, beyond those cutout faces. "C'mon."

He pushed her back into the hallway and, in the moments her back was turned, stood on tiptoe to shove the magazine beneath a stack of linens on the top shelf.

He turned and shut the closet door behind him. "Let's go find some deathwatch beetles."

CHAPTER 52

I finished my soup and sat for some time alone in the kitchen. I'd done my best to stay calm while the others were around. But now that I finally was alone, I kept replaying that horrible moment when the hare had fallen out of the chimney, trailing smoke and the stink of charred fur.

There had to be a rational explanation, but what? I gazed outside at sleet slashing down from the darkening sky, and thought of the boy Nisa said she'd seen that morning. Could the rabbit belong to him? But wouldn't he have come to the house, looking for it? The kids I taught were obsessed with their pets.

Evadne, I thought. Given the sightings from the road, the black hare must belong to her. If it wasn't a pet, it could be a wild animal that hung around her trailer? Or there might be an entire colony of black hares up here, the way you'd sometimes see black squirrels in the city. One might conceivably have gotten upstairs and into an attic or crawl space that led to the chimney.

I could walk down and ask Evadne if the hare was hers, tell her what had happened. Ainsley knew her, and Melissa Libby was her niece. So even if eccentric and maybe antisocial, the worst Evadne could do would be to slam a door in my face.

I stood and put my bowl in the sink. I'd left my coat on a chair in the main hall, so I didn't have to go upstairs and risk running into any of the others.

Better for just one of us to pay Evadne an unexpected visit, I thought, and again set out from the house.

CHAPTER 53

Stevie was such a beautiful freak, mused Nisa. You could see why that guy preyed on him when he was a kid. Horrible, and she was glad the guy had died. But you couldn't be that vulnerable, especially not as an adult. How did he do it? Holly once said that if the two of them didn't watch out for him, they'd be reading about him in the NYC crime stats.

Now here he was, playing Scooby-Doo with his sound equipment, like they were on *Unsolved Mysteries,* or wandering around Pan's Labyrinth. It was one of the things she loved about him, in addition to his strange pale eyes, his long fingers and the long hair falling into his face, his fits of inappropriate laughter that drove Holly nuts. The way he could make Nisa feel like they were in high school—sneaking around, getting away with something.

Like that magazine. Did he actually think she hadn't seen him stick it back on a shelf? She'd come up later with a chair and retrieve it. Whoever had doctored it was genuinely messed up. For a second she flashed back to the boy she'd seen that morning. She slowed to glance at the wall. But there were no windows in the upstairs hallway.

Besides, that magazine was from the 1980s, right? It couldn't belong to the boy she'd seen. Whatever faces had been cut from it, they belonged to people Nisa had never heard of. Probably half of them were dead now.

Yet what was it Ainsley had said—something about a family?

Downstairs, she could pretend Hill House was a normal place: a kitchen, living room, library, billiards room, conservatory...So okay, a normal place if you lived in Boddy Manor in Clue.

Upstairs was different. The Yellow Room felt sick, like an invalid wasting away. And that cheap new furniture—why had they even bothered? Amanda's pink room was a bit nicer, though not Stevie's. Everything that disgusting purple.

This hall was even worse. As soon as Nisa'd stepped into it, she felt that everything was out of plumb; not just physically but in a deeper sense. Holly went on and on about how Stevie was intuitive, but Nisa knew it was to avoid admitting that it was true for her, too. She wasn't just empathic. She was a sensitive.

It was why she sang, to reach people on a level they didn't truly notice until much later. It might be the next day or even longer before they realized that something had changed inside them, forever. Her song became part of them, in a way that only music can. Like a scar. Holly made fun of her when she'd say that, but it was true.

The upper hall at Hill House felt like that. Scarred. Nisa couldn't see where or what the deeper damage was, but she knew it was there, behind the oak wall panels lavishly carved with leaves and grapes, vines and faces, or within the alcoves that had once held statues, now only filmed with cobwebs. Her arms broke out in gooseflesh, and she had that fizzy feeling in her head that accompanied a fever. But her forehead felt cold and her hands were colder, like she'd stuck them in a snowbank.

She tugged at the sleeves of Stevie's too-large sweater until they covered her fingertips. She didn't often miss the West Coast, but at this moment she longed to be back there, with heat radiating from the sidewalks and midday sun scorching clouds from the sky. Stevie paced beside her, holding up his microphone even though there was nothing to record except their footsteps. She couldn't even hear the rain or wind here.

How many years had that magazine been hidden there? Almost forty, she bet. And then Stevie just happened to reach up and find it. So, okay, she'd give him that: he really was a sensitive, too. But that could be dangerous, she thought. Maybe especially so, here. The hallway felt contagious—if she touched the walls the sickness would get into her. Stevie might already have caught it. He walked so purposefully, almost as though he were sleepwalking.

She edged away from him, careful not to get too close to the wall herself. With no windows, it was impossible to tell if it was day or night. Her phone said it was early afternoon, but it felt much later. Sometimes, on getaways, she'd felt like she was in a place that kept its own time. Ibiza was like that, and Sedona.

Here it felt like it was always the middle of the night, and not in a good way. Shadows groped at the ceiling high above them. And where did those shadows come from, if there were no windows? The lights were barely bright enough to see by. And while she felt cold and clammy, the air was unpleasantly warm and close, breathing down her neck.

"Whoever designed this place must have been drunk," she said, breaking the silence at last.

"Or maybe the contractors were," said Stevie. "Or both. No wonder Ainsley can't sell it."

"I know. But someone spent a lot of money. All this…"

She gestured at the worn but still impressive Persian carpet that covered the hardwood floor. On the walls, ghostly rectangles indicated where paintings had previously hung. She stopped at a lone oval mirror. It was so black with tarnish, her face seemed to stare back from a murky pond, her rounded cheeks now skull-like.

She quickly lowered her gaze to where a scene had been carved into the wood panel below. An animal fled through trees bent double by the wind. Its pursuers had been left out of the frame. The wood itself appeared warped. Maybe it had suffered water damage.

When she stooped to get a better look, she saw that the warped effect was intentional. Whoever had carved it had deliberately made a beautiful piece of quarter-sawn oak look buckled and misshapen. She felt squeamish, yet she couldn't look away.

As her eyes adjusted she realized it wasn't an animal but a woman. Her long hair was fanning out around her head, her arms extended as they reached for someone, or something. Her dress appeared torn, though that might be imperfections in the wood grain. Vines encircled her bare feet. The entire image wasn't more than twelve inches long and half again as high.

It looks like me, she thought. A ridiculous idea—her hair was short, for one—yet in the same way the door knocker held a passing resemblance to Stevie, this seemed to reflect something of her posture, her hair, even her face. She could hear Holly's mocking laughter in her head—*It's always about you!*

But she couldn't shake that terrible sense of recognition. As if her fever was progressing, now her stomach began to hurt. She tore her gaze from the panel's fleeing woman, realizing there were other animals hidden in the vines around her. Nisa thought they were deer but they were so small. Hares, maybe? Like the woman, they were all fleeing from something, or trying to. Nisa shook her head, deeply unsettled.

"Hey," she called to Stevie, who'd wandered ahead. "Check this out."

He looked back, distracted, but joined her, crouching to stare at the panel. "What am I looking at?"

"The carving. Don't you think it's strange?"

"It looks like all the others. Or, wait, there's nothing carved on it, it's just warped." He gave her a puzzled look. "Is that what you mean?"

"No." She stabbed at the panel with a forefinger. "There!"

"You mean the whorls in the wood?" Stevie squinted. "I guess it maybe looks like a tree."

"That is not a tree."

"Okay, then what am I looking at?"

"That woman. She's being hunted."

"What woman?"

"Her!" She jabbed at the panel again. "In the carving."

"What carving? It's just a panel." Glancing at her, he frowned in concern. "Hey, Nis, it's okay——" He touched her face, his long slender fingers still so cold, why did he feel so cold? "When I was a kid, my room was like that—knotty pine paneling, I used to see faces in the wood."

"No! It's right there—I'm looking right at it!"

Stevie stared at her. "Sorry, I don't see it, Nis. Is this like a Rorschach?"

"No! Are you blind?" She traced the outlines of the woman's body and glared at him. "Seriously, maybe there's something wrong with your vision."

He stood, and she saw a trace of fear in his eyes. "I doubt that. But I bet the wiring is a hundred years old."

He looked toward the stairway, as though contemplating whether they should return to the first floor. But then he squared his shoulders and shook his head. "I'm surprised squirrels haven't chewed through everything and burned the whole place down."

"Jesus, Stevie, can you just stop?"

"Look, I'm sorry." He reached for her shoulder. She recognized the hurt in his eyes, like a dog accustomed to being shoved aside, but also apprehension. "What do you see, Nisa?"

"Forget it." She shot a glance at the carving again, just to make sure she hadn't imagined it. The fleeing woman was still there, grasping for something just out of reach. "It doesn't matter."

Again he looked at the stairs, and for a moment she hoped he'd suggest they leave. At last he nodded to himself, as though having made a difficult decision. He tightened his grip on the mic, gesturing at the door at the end of the hallway. "Look, I want to check that out. I'd really like to record some background sound for the show, and downstairs it's too noisy. You don't have to come if you don't feel like it."

She didn't say anything as he began to walk, holding up his mic like a torch. She closed her eyes, willing him to stop, to turn back and take her hand and lead her downstairs, or perhaps to his room, to his bed.

It worked. She didn't hear him pause, but his footsteps echoed softly through the hall, no longer walking away from her but toward her, slowly. She remained where she was, eyes shut, savoring the moment: he'd listened to her, he believed her, and somehow those two things would make it all right, erase the memory of that terrible carved image, all the inexplicable events and emotions that had torn through her since they tumbled from Holly's car the day before.

The footsteps grew louder, more forceful, moving more quickly as they drew near. Nisa kept her eyes closed tight, playing a game now, heart fluttering in her breast. *What are you doing, Stevie?* She forced a smile, forced herself not to move even though he was so close now, she could stretch her arm out to stop him, why was he walking so fast, what was he——

Gasping, she opened her eyes a fraction of a second before he collided with her. A blast of icy air struck her cheeks, flattened her curls against her skull as she saw Stevie at the end of the hall, his back to her. She couldn't breathe; something squeezed her chest like a bellows as she fought to cry out.

Then it was gone. She doubled over like she'd been punched, caught her breath, and whirled to see only the empty corridor, the sound of footsteps faint as a sigh that died in the shadows around her.

CHAPTER 54

I walked away from Hill House without looking back. I had an uneasy sensation that if I did, I'd feel compelled to return. It was still cold, but the rain had stopped, although the dark clouds massed overhead suggested it would start again before too long. So I went quickly, my hands in my pockets to stay warm.

As I passed the huge stump on the curve, my anxiety dissolved. I experienced a palpable relief, knowing the mansion was now out of sight, and reassured myself: this was only our first day here. The reading had gone really well, right up until it was disrupted. Amanda had brought a dimension to Elizabeth Sawyer I hadn't thought possible, and Nisa's songs added more atmosphere than I'd realized.

I should tell her that, I thought. I was losing my focus, my passion for *Witching Night,* in the pressure cooker atmosphere of Hill House, distracted by the impossible burden I'd put on myself and the others, to get everything perfect.

I should call Giorgio and Theresa, I thought. I'd been so caught up in making arrangements over the last month, I'd never even told them about renting Hill House. That would give me the rare opportunity to show off professionally. If we made good progress and the others agreed,

I might even ask them to visit over the weekend. The idea excited me: all the strange things that had happened here would simply become part of the bigger story of my play's success, something we could laugh at over champagne and candlelight. Theresa's acerbic wit would make short work of any concerns about black hares and strange figures spinning in the woods.

I was only getting intermittent service, but it was better down here, closer to town. I tapped at Giorgio's number. He picked up immediately.

"Holly! How are you?"

I told him what had happened since we'd last seen him—that I'd found a cast for my play, which I'd mentioned on our night out last month.

"Amanda Greer?" he asked after I'd explained the rest of the show. "Isn't she the one who pushed Jason Pratt off a twenty-foot stage?"

"No! That was her, but she didn't push him, it was an accident."

I kept walking, as Giorgio fell silent. "How's Stevie Liddell?" he asked awkwardly. "I know he was having a rough time for a while."

"He's doing great."

"And Nisa?"

"Also great. Everything's going really well, I found this amazing house to rent in Hillsdale. Not a house, a mansion called Hill House."

I could hear his sharp intake of breath. "Hill House? Really?"

"Really."

"Wow. I'm surprised it's for rent, after what happened."

I slowed my pace. "What was that?"

"Some family bought it in the eighties, and after they moved in, their teenage son apparently flipped out. I don't know all the details, but there was some story about a couple of his friends visiting for the weekend? One of them was poisoned."

"Poisoned?"

"Yeah. Mushrooms, I think, like they were supposed to be magic mushrooms but they were poisonous. The friend died. No, wait—it wasn't the friend who died"—she could hear the rising excitement in Giorgio's voice as he went on—"it was the boy's sister. He took off into the woods and they never saw him again. One of the other kids who survived thought he did it on purpose—the boy had told them some disturbing things. The parents sold Hill House back to the original owner and hightailed it out of there."

"I never heard about that," I said slowly. "Ainsley mentioned a family living there in the eighties, but nothing about this. And Stevie saw some Reddit post, but..."

"Listen, it's probably just gossip."

"Did they ever find him?"

"The boy? If so, I haven't heard. And none of it may even be true. Hillsdale is sort of the last redoubt for the rebel forces holding back flatlanders like us. The locals are pretty closemouthed, but they definitely encourage people to believe that some bad shit has gone down at Hill House over the years."

"I've never heard about anything like that," I repeated, keeping my tone upbeat as I continued to walk. "We only got here yesterday. So far, so good."

"I'm glad to hear it."

I could hear Theresa's voice in the background, and Giorgio laughed. "Right? Look, I have to go, Holly, but it's great to hear from you. Let me know if you want to meet for lunch or dinner while you're up here, we could meet in Ashton. Give my best to Nisa and Stevie, okay?"

He disconnected, and I shoved the phone back in my pocket. The road was deserted, the trees still wind-tossed, but there was no sign of the bad weather Melissa had mentioned, other than thickening dark clouds. Still, I found myself walking more quickly, scanning the woods to either side.

I thought about the teenage boy Nisa claimed to have seen that morning. Where had he come from? Impossible he could be the same person Giorgio had mentioned—he'd be an adult by now, or dead. More likely it was just some kid who'd wanted to escape from his parents, or school. *Teenagers go walkabout all the time,* I told myself. As for violence and teenage boys, as a teacher I'd undergone a depressing amount of training over the last few years. If Giorgio's account wasn't a rumor, it was a random tragedy, that's all. And there was no reason Ainsley should have gone into any specifics—it had happened so long ago. Any house will have its share of deaths and accidents over a century or more.

I refused to let gossip derail my good mood.

Almost-good mood. Ahead of me, I saw Evadne's trailer, with her car parked in front. I had deliberately not thought about what I might say to her. *Hey, did you lose a flaming rabbit?*

I'd also avoided envisioning how she might react. Would she brandish a knife at me again? A shotgun?

I could always just keep walking. Or turn back now.

But I still wanted to find out what she knew.

I continued toward the mobile home, slowing as I drew near the gazing ball. I had a flash of the strange photo that Nisa had captured.

It's called a witch ball...They use them for scrying, Stevie had said. *And protection...She's a witch...*

I was writing a play about a witch, but I'd never met someone who truly believed in witchcraft. Other than Stevie, who didn't really count. Did Evadne believe? It made sense, as much as anything else did.

I left the road and walked the few yards to the gazing ball. Something stirred at my feet and I stopped, holding my breath. But it was just a small bird that arrowed off into the woods. I reached the pedestal, hesitating before I leaned over to peer at the ball on top of it.

Yesterday, its mirrored curves had captured the colors of autumn leaves and blue sky. Now the ball held ominous clouds and a shifting pattern like broken glass, jet black and dull pewter. I watched, fascinated by how different they appeared from the sky overhead, their dance hypnotic and constantly changing. I glanced up at the sky, and when I looked down again, the miniature panorama of gray and black clouds had disappeared. In its place was a watery smear of pus-green and yellow, crosshatched with staticky black and white lines. *What the fuck?* As I stared the lines moved and swiftly formed a blurred but unmistakable image: Hill House.

"What are you doing?"

I stumbled back. Evadne Morris was standing on the steps to her home.

CHAPTER 55

In an eyeblink, Evadne ran across the lawn to grab my shoulder. "What are you doing here? Who are you?"

"Holly," I stammered. "Holly Sherwin—we're Ainsley Rowan's tenants. At Hill House?"

"Ainsley's renting it out?" Evadne's outrage became astonishment. "Has she lost her mind?"

I tried to wrench away from her but she was too strong. "Yes! And no—I signed a contract, we have it for two weeks."

"Two weeks?" She sounded incredulous, also furious. "When did you get there?"

"Yesterday."

"Yesterday. Right, I saw you drive past." She let go of my arm but appeared poised to tackle me if I made an attempt to bolt. "So you slept there last night?"

I nodded.

"How many of you are there?"

"Four, counting me."

"What about Melissa?"

"She's been dropping off food and doing some cleanup."

"Did she stay over?"

"No." I remembered then what Stevie had told me——*Melissa said that she and Evadne keep an eye on Hill House.* "Why would she?"

Evadne's face, still rigid with anger, relaxed slightly. "What about the others with you—are they still up there?"

"They were when I left. That was only about half an hour ago."

I glanced down warily, saw Evadne's gnarled hands poking from the sleeves of her hooded sweatshirt. On the ring finger of her right hand was a ring with a thick silver band, set with a chunk of amber. It caught the dim light and I saw flecks of gold and scarlet in the resin, surrounding a minute black star that might have been a spider.

When I looked up, Evadne was watching me.

"That's a beautiful ring," I said, hoping to defuse the situation. "I've never seen anything like it."

"Probably you have. Ainsley Rowan has one. And Melissa Libby."

She'd caught me in a lie. I flinched as her arm moved, then saw she was extending the hand with the ring on it, so I could get a better look. I clearly saw the fragment trapped inside the amber. Not a spider but what appeared to be a skeletal embryo, with infinitesimally tiny ribs, too many legs, an extra skull. My stomach turned.

It's a test, I thought, though I couldn't imagine what for, or why. "That's—that's extraordinary," I said.

Evadne shrugged, then fished in her hoodie pocket to withdraw a hand-rolled cigarette. She lit up, took a long drag, and exhaled a plume of white smoke. Not tobacco or cannabis, more like sage, only acrid and strong enough to make my eyes water. She drew again on her cigarette, pinched it out, and dropped it back into her pocket.

I had begun to shiver, though Evadne in her hoodie seemed unconcerned. The wind now smelled like coming snow, like iron. She looked again at her gazing ball and asked, "What the hell are you doing here, Holly Sherwin?"

"Rehearsing a play I've written, I—"

"What are you doing *here*?" She jabbed me with a finger. "Right now, at my house?"

"I..." I tried to come up with a convincing lie, but her gaze never left me, and I knew she'd see through it.

"Those black hares," I said. "I saw them a couple of times, here and up at Hill House. This morning when we had a fire going, one came down the chimney."

"That was dangerous." I was unsure if she referred to the hare. "Didn't Ainsley tell you what happened in the nursery?"

"The nursery? No. She didn't really tell us anything."

"Leave," Evadne said abruptly. "Go while it's still light."

"I can't go." I shook my head. "I can't get my money back. We need to rehearse—I'm contracted to do a showcase in a month. I'm sorry I bothered you," I said, and turned quickly back to the road.

"Listen to me." Evadne's tone was more threat than warning. "I worked with victims of domestic violence for thirty-seven years. They stay with the devil they know, and the devil they know kills them. Hill House is like that. Most people realize in a few days and get out."

"What happens to the ones who don't?"

"They all leave, one way or another."

"How do you know?"

She licked her lips. Something was caught between her crooked front teeth, a pink shred. Her tongue darted out to flick away the shred. I recoiled as her gaze shifted from me to the road.

"Hill House—how do you think it survives?" she asked.

"Ainsley said—"

"Ainsley's done virtually nothing to maintain it. No one has. Hill House looks almost the same today as when it was built a hundred and forty years ago. Why do you think that is?"

I looked into her pale eyes, the pupils so small they were almost invisible. "She must do something," I stammered.

"She doesn't. She plays with fire every time she lets someone in there. She thinks she's stronger."

Stronger than who? I wondered. Instead I asked: "Is that why you live here? To keep an eye on Ainsley?"

"I've known Ainsley my entire life. Hill House, too."

"If it's so dangerous, why does she rent it? Can't you and Melissa stop her?"

"And what would happen then, do you think?" She started for her trailer. "She's the devil we know. Forget about the money. Leave now," she said, and left me standing in the cold.

CHAPTER 56

A nice young man, Stevie, Amanda thought after he'd left her alone again in her bedroom. High-strung and no doubt high maintenance, but easy on the eyes. It seemed clear that he and Nisa had some history, and might even still be involved. Did Holly know? Amanda would bet not. Holly was one of those people so practiced at self-delusion that it had become as natural as smiling. A lot of theater people were like that, and nearly all of the successful ones.

Amanda perched on the edge of her bed. Usually she liked a bit of drama and did her share to contribute. It livened things up.

At the moment, however, she felt that she could do without any more Sturm und Drang. The tablecloth and that flaming rabbit had been enough, and now she had to contend with everyone's worries about her health, too. Her health was fine!

This was all she needed, more people thinking she was too old to work. She was barely past Medicare age, for Christ's sake. Six months ago, she'd nabbed a small part in a crime drama, playing the mother of a homicide victim. Okay, the grandmother. The series hadn't streamed yet but she'd seen an early trailer. She only appeared for forty-seven seconds (she'd timed it) but she looked good. Makeup even had to spend a bit of time making her look older.

They hadn't asked what Amanda's age was, though. No one ever did, because basically, no one wanted to know. Not in the performing arts; not anywhere, unless it was the doctor's office. No one wanted to know because nobody cared. For some reason, she'd always thought she'd be the exception to the rule, attracting male (and female) attention as the years passed. Wrong!

It sucked, especially in this business. That was why she'd been thrilled to read Holly Sherwin's script. It wasn't a work of genius, but it was very good. Elizabeth Sawyer was a role any older actor would relish: sharp-tongued, even downright nasty. Unrepentant and in the end triumphant, like Medea flying off in her dragon chariot, leaving corpses in her wake. It was too bad she shared so much stage time with the devil dog and the one-person chorus, but that might change, if Amanda could get some time alone with Holly to share her suggestions.

She stood and walked to the window. Fine rain fell, more of a mist, veiling the trees and tower so that she couldn't see what lay beyond. A chill crept over her and she stepped away. For an instant she felt dizzy. She steadied herself by grasping the side of the bureau, then took a deep breath.

The dizziness passed. She was fine. That happened to her if she stood up or moved too quickly. It was nothing new, she'd experienced it for decades. She took out her phone and checked again for service. It read three bars, but when she tried to bring up her social media feed it wouldn't load. She'd taken all kinds of photos, too, very atmospheric—shadows on the stairway, the way the light fell on that door knocker with the face. Even the fireplace in the living room. She sighed. It was too bad, but she'd just post them next time she got into town.

She opened the photo of the fireplace. Not very interesting. Too bad she hadn't caught the rabbit—*that* would have been a great post. She scrolled through the other pictures, recalling Stevie's smile as he looked at his laptop; Nisa gazing at the fireplace; Holly transported by her script.

Amanda paused on one shot. Here, Nisa wasn't smiling. She was looking at Amanda's camera, her expression disdainful, even disgusted. Amanda blinked, enlarging the photo. Nisa's disgust was even more obvious.

And, behind her, so was Holly's. Amanda had remembered Holly bent over her notes, but here she gazed directly at Amanda, seemingly repelled.

And Stevie's smile was, in fact, pitying. Also amused, as though Amanda was doing something both mortifying and ridiculous.

She closed the phone abruptly, set it facedown on the bureau, and sat on the bed, sickened.

Had she made the actor's fatal mistake? Confusing their derision with genuine laughter? No doubt they were talking about her even now.

Like Elizabeth Sawyer, was she an object of contempt?

She looked at the door to the hall. It was shut, but as she listened, she could hear them. Low voices, one quite deep—it didn't sound like Stevie but it had to be him. The other was sniggering, murmuring, then erupting in soft plosive laughter. Like cruel children, she thought, mocking her.

She released her breath and rubbed her eyes. She refused to cry: she sat and did one of her centering exercises instead. *Use it,* she thought. *Channel this rage and humiliation into Elizabeth.* As she sat, the voices receded, though she didn't hear footsteps. They must have crept away like mice. Good riddance.

How sharper than a serpent's tooth, she thought. She smoothed her hair to cover her forehead, avoiding her reflection in the far wall's mirror. But a great performance is the best revenge. She'd die before she let them know she'd heard them.

CHAPTER 57

I trudged back up the road to Hill House, the cold gnawing at my too-thin coat. I'd dressed for autumn, not early winter. I was equally disturbed and irritated by my brief exchange with Evadne. She'd ignored my question about the hares, and I hadn't even had a chance to bring up the bizarre spinning shape in the woods.

Or the rumors that Giorgio had mentioned, if they were in fact rumors. Whatever was going on, there was definitely bad blood between Ainsley and Evadne, and perhaps Melissa, too. In spite of that, they seemed bound together—by isolation, by precarious finances, by the fact that they were women.

And also, I thought, by Hill House itself. Its face appeared through the trees in front of me: upstairs windows catching the late-afternoon light so they appeared to wink, the big front door a mouth eager to open and welcome me. There was something about this place, something that recognized me, *knew* me. I began to walk faster, my fear dissolving as I broke into a sprint.

The more I considered it, the more I realized that our first read-through really had been brilliant. Some alchemy of language and music and innate skill had drawn something deep and almost primal from my three performers. Even from me, I thought, recalling how I'd taken on the few other supporting roles and read their lines—not like a director or AD casually filling in, but as though I truly knew those characters.

A sharp ebullience filled me as I ran up the steps to the veranda, the same feeling I'd had when I first drove up to Hill House. The sense that I belonged here, that we all belonged here, but me most of all. It was finally coming together, my play; I'd only needed time, and the right space, to animate it. Evadne's warning faded, replaced by the memory of Amanda and Stevie and Nisa in the living room, Stevie leaning forward in his chair to extend a hand as he smiled at Amanda.

"Your dear Tomasin is here, so now for a morning's quick mischief!
I've put my mind to it and with a single touch, our bodies will fall in
line..."

I pushed open the heavy door. Of course we wouldn't leave yet. We would all return to work.

CHAPTER 58

S tevie!"

Stevie paused as Nisa raced up to him, panicked. He looked past her worriedly, but the upstairs hall was empty. "What's wrong?"

"I—I thought you were—"

She grabbed his hand, looked down at it, and immediately dropped it with a small gasp. Stevie waited for her to explain, but she just shook her head.

"Oh god, never mind," she said at last. "I just—I thought you were right next to me, that's all."

He looked at her, bewildered, then continued walking. A few yards ahead of them, at the end of the hall, a half-opened door beckoned: bigger than the tiny secret door in his room but charged with a similar feeling of anticipation, and also a fluttery sense of déjà vu.

"What is this?" asked Nisa. "An attic?"

"No, the attic would be up there." He pointed at the ceiling, then at the top of the doorframe. "Wow—check those out."

Stevie nudged the door with his foot, so it opened the rest of the way. Light spilled from the room beyond, illuminating a carved face mounted on each side of the door, like the masks of comedy and tragedy, only both of these were grinning—lipless smiles distorted by time or shadow into leers.

"Jesus, they're horrible," Stevie marveled, rocking back on his heels. "Is that like what you saw back there? The carving? If it was, I don't blame you for being freaked out."

"No. That was horrible in a different way." As though desperate to escape their eyes, Nisa took a step into the room. But just inside she stopped and cried out, turning to Stevie. "Do you feel that?"

He followed her, holding tight to his microphone after a check to make sure the recorder was on. "Holy cow. It's like walking into a freezer."

"But once you're in the room it's different, right?" She shook her head. "I mean, it's *warm*. Only the doorway is cold."

Stevie agreed. The large room wasn't just warm—it was hot. He rolled up his sleeves, then took a look around.

The room extended almost the entire width of the house, occupying most of this end of the second floor. It was empty, which made it seem even larger, but which also seemed strange—there'd been some attempt, no matter how ineffectual, to furnish most of the other rooms in the house.

His gaze snagged on a small object on the floor beside the wall. He walked over and crouched to examine it. A broken jumble of black plastic, wires, and bits of plexiglass, tangled up in what he realized was snarled tape from an old cassette.

"What is it?" asked Nisa, coming up behind him.

"An old Walkman. Really old." He picked it up curiously, turning it in his fingers. "Like first generation, the kind that played cassettes, not CDs."

"Really? Can you tell what it was? The tape, I mean?"

Stevie shook his head. "No. It's just trash."

He set it back on the floor and stood, taking in the rest of the room. A frieze ran along the upper part of the walls, a sad procession of painted animals. Zebras, elephants, rabbits, lions and tigers, a crocodile. The images were blotched and faded, the animals crudely drawn. The sight filled him with a deep melancholy, bordering on dread.

Above the frieze, the ceiling was webbed with cracks where beams had been removed. "There were other rooms here," he said slowly to Nisa. "One more, anyway—they took down the walls."

"It's so empty." His oversized sweater made her look as though she'd been swallowed by a giant sock puppet. "You'd think they'd use it for storage. Or something. What do you think it was?"

He gazed up at the sad zoo parade. "A kid's room."

"A bedroom?" Nisa shuddered. "More like a prison."

"A nursery," said Stevie. "Big old houses like this, they stuck all the kids away with a nanny or governess. That's why it's so hot—they'd have kept it warm for the children."

Nisa shuddered again. "Can you picture being a kid and trying to sleep up here? You wouldn't. *I* wouldn't."

"No, me neither," Stevie admitted.

"Plus it must be ninety degrees—but right by the door, it's freezing."

He tore his gaze from the painted animals and returned to the doorway. He hesitated, then stepped back over the threshold into the hall.

He hadn't imagined it. Frigid air surrounded him—it felt almost solid, a wall of ice. Then, in the hall, it immediately dissolved. He stood, breathing hard, glanced at the levels on his recorder but saw nothing unusual.

"Don't you think that's weird?" Nisa prodded him again from inside the room. "Can you measure the temperature with that?"

"It's a microphone, Nis, not a thermometer. There must be some anomaly in how the house is designed." He made an effort to sound unfazed—Nisa looked like she was ready to take off running. "That, or it just feels cooler, relative to how warm the nursery is."

But he didn't believe that. Once, working on an old downtown stage, he'd touched a live section of the outdated lighting system and been thrown to the ground. It hadn't felt like an electrical shock, more like he'd punched a slab of concrete. His hand and forearm had been numb for hours.

Passing through the nursery doorway felt similar: like a physical assault. He leaned forward, and the chill grew stronger. He looked up at the two grinning faces.

"I think the cold comes from there," he called to Nisa, pointing at the masks. *Not there,* he corrected himself: *them.* He glanced again at the recorder. It had registered only his voice.

"We should go," said Nisa. She'd started to shiver, barely keeping her shit together.

"I will—I promise, I just need to see what's going on with those masks. One more minute..."

He stepped back into the nursery, slowly, holding up one hand. This time he noted a distinct difference, like wading into a spring-fed pond where the water can feel icy in one spot and much warmer just inches away.

"It's them for sure," he said, gesturing at the carvings.

As he spoke, a sharp dread lodged in his chest—a foreboding so palpable, he might reach inside his rib cage and grasp it, razor-edged like an arrowhead.

Someone touched his arm and he yelped.

"Stevie! Hey, I was looking for you! Where is everyone?" Holly stood just outside the door, staring in at him. "Stevie? What's the matter?"

He looked at her, confused. "Holly? Where'd you come from?"

"I went for a walk, down to Evadne's place. Listen, I'd like to do another read-through. Now, while there's still daylight."

"Evadne?" Stevie repeated in disbelief. "What—"

"Holly!" Nisa's voice echoed from inside the nursery. "We found the haunted room."

"What room?"

"The nursery!" answered Nisa.

Holly's face grew pale, her expression shifting from excitement to concern to outright fear. She pushed past him into the nursery, and Stevie saw how she immediately stiffened.

"Get out," she ordered, taking Nisa's arm and pushing at Stevie. "We have to get out."

"What?" Stevie gaped at her. "Why?"

"Just go!"

Bang.

Stevie clapped his hands over his ears and shut his eyes. When he opened them seconds later, Holly and Nisa were huddled together.

"Was that thunder?" Nisa whispered in the sudden silence.

Stevie tucked the mic into his waistband, then hurried to the nursery's back wall to stare outside. Beneath a threatening sky, trees bowed to the wind. Yet he'd seen no lightning flash. "I don't know."

Nisa said, "It felt like it came from inside this—"

Bang.

This one rang out like an explosion. Nisa shrieked, although Stevie couldn't hear her over the noise, just saw her open mouth and frightened eyes. For a second he thought his eardrums had been damaged, but then he heard Holly shouting.

"Get out! We need to leave *now*!"

Disoriented, he grabbed Holly's hand, dragging her across the nursery with Nisa racing after them. As they reached the doorway, it seemed to waver, its stiles moving inward so that the space between them narrowed. The air grew darker and also somehow thicker, as though he fought against an oncoming wave, its force pressing against his mouth and nostrils so he couldn't breathe, crushing his eyes like two thumbs seeking to blind him.

Somehow, he staggered through with the others, stumbling back into the hall. He made it halfway to the stairs before he stopped. Nisa and Holly were leaning against the opposite wall. Holly fought to catch her breath while Nisa stared at Stevie, trying vainly to form words.

A door opened and slammed. Blearily, Stevie looked up to see Amanda hurrying toward them from her bedroom. She halted beside him.

"What the hell is going on?" she demanded.

CHAPTER 59

Downstairs. Now." Holly just managed to gasp the words as Nisa saw Stevie hurry down the hall, appearing desperate to get away.

But when he reached the door to his bedroom, he paused to peer inside. A look of intense yearning overtook him, as though he gazed at an unseen lover on the bed. He closed the door quickly, and Nisa looked down before he could catch her watching him. She heard him hightail it for the steps, taking them two at a time until he reached the bottom.

What was in his room? Nisa started to take a step toward it, stopped. Better to do that when she was on her own. She turned to Holly. "You all right?"

"I'm fine," Holly replied, even though she didn't seem fine. "I just think it would be better if we went back downstairs." She looked at Amanda. "You heard those noises, right?"

Amanda regarded the two of them with mistrust, and nodded. "I thought you were lighting firecrackers in the house."

Nisa burst into indignant laughter. "Why would we do that?"

"That's what I wondered," Amanda retorted. "I thought you were trying to scare me."

"What?" Nisa looked at her, astonished. "Why?"

Amanda said nothing. Her gaze flickered past Nisa to land on Holly. "No play can succeed without trust," she said imperiously. "I'll see you downstairs."

She spun on her heel and followed Stevie down the steps. Nisa turned back to Holly. "What the hell is going on?"

Holly didn't answer, still staring down the long hallway to the nursery. A strange reddish light leaked from the room, though the windows had grown dark. Nisa watched as Holly walked quickly back to slam the nursery door shut. Retracing her steps, she passed Nisa and paused at the head of the stairs. "You coming?"

"Yeah, just a sec."

She waited until she heard Holly's footsteps reach the hall below, and gave a low whistle.

What the hell was happening? Stevie was obviously fucking with her, but why? And why here?

She shivered, forcing herself to stay in the moment, stay calm. She looked to make sure no one could see her, pulled out her phone, and darted back in the direction of the nursery, slowing as she approached the spot where the tarnished oval mirror hung. She opened her camera app and bent down to take a picture of the carving, to show Stevie again when they'd all gathered.

It was gone. She ran her fingers across the wood but felt only its fine grain. Fighting a wave of nausea, she straightened.

There were no mirrors other than this one. The carving had disappeared.

Unless, as Stevie had said, it had never been there at all.

CHAPTER 60

I waited impatiently for Nisa to join me in the main hall. Stevie and Amanda had wandered off, still arguing about the noises upstairs. I'd nabbed my copy of the script from where I'd left it in the living room earlier. I opened it to where we'd stopped, right before Elizabeth first unintentionally summons the demonic Tomasin.

> *Oh, grant me power for good or ill!*
> *Show me how to avenge myself upon these men,*
> *Teach me to invite rage into my body*
> *And let it burst from this ruined house of bone...*

So, so good! I thought, exhaling. I couldn't even remember typing those lines; it had been like when I first wrote down Macy-Lee's story: like someone whispered to me as I slept, and I merely transcribed the words once I woke.

Out of nowhere, more words crashed into my mind now, so quickly that I couldn't make sense of them—but that would come later, I told myself, jubilant, after the others went to sleep. I envisioned myself staying up through the night, writing and rewriting, emailing the new pages to Nisa and Amanda and Stevie, their delight when they read what I'd done.

But for now, we needed to sit down again, scripts in hand, and resume where we'd left off. We were creating an enchantment here, we'd all felt it. Yet every time I regained my balance, ready to jump back into the play, something knocked me down again.

Almost literally—those explosions, or whatever they were, felt like a car had crashed into the house. Was it structurally unsound? Was that the big takeaway from Evadne's alarm?

Ainsley's done nothing to maintain it...She plays with fire, every time she lets someone in there...Didn't Ainsley tell you what happened in the nursery?

I walked to the front door. Rain streaked the windowpanes and veranda, but the wall felt solid. I knocked on it, heard a reassuring *thunk*. Stomped once on the floor, hard. It, too, seemed solid enough.

Leave, Evadne had said bluntly. *Go while it's still light.*

Yet where would we go? Giorgio and Theresa were an hour and a half away, and I couldn't bear the thought of what they'd say if we showed up. *Some bad shit has gone down at Hill House over the years.* They'd make a meal of this whole experience, my pathetic attempt to bring my career back from the dead. They'd never let me forget about it.

Really, Nisa and Stevie had just been ghost hunting, I thought, and my fear finally gave way to annoyance. Stevie had his microphone and recorder with him. He might even have played those sounds to scare Nisa. Though he hadn't looked like he was having fun. He'd looked scared shitless. They both had.

I needed to break the spell, find a room that was neutral and press the reset button. I recalled seeing a small parlor on the first floor, perfect for another read-through—Ainsley had blown past it when she gave Nisa and me our first tour.

It took me a few minutes to locate it, stumbling down one dim passage after another, into yet another narrow corridor. I ran my hands across the wall until I found a light switch. A ragged line of small, flame-shaped bulbs came to life, each set high up in a sconce. Old incandescent bulbs, not more than fifteen watts, and most had burned out.

I switched on my phone. For some reason the battery was low, even though I'd just charged it that morning. I swore under my breath, wishing I'd gotten a flashlight from the kitchen.

I kept going. The feeble lights made the darkness seem like something tangible. I remembered Stevie's fingers on my neck the day before, playing with my hair. But Stevie had denied doing that. *"Maybe it was Nisa? I didn't touch your hair."*

The passage was freezing, a penetrating cold like nothing I'd felt before. *It's because there's never been any sunlight here,* I thought. No sun, no windows, no central heating...

I considered turning back. But when I looked over my shoulder, the dark tunnel behind me seemed endless. The flame-shaped bulbs flickered like real flames. I became aware of a roaring sound, low yet insistent; like a bonfire when someone tosses a Christmas tree on it.

The wind, I realized. The storm that Melissa had warned us about was gathering force. Even this deep within Hill House, I could hear it.

I jumped as one of the remaining bulbs went out with a *pop*. I spun around and lost my bearings. Was I going the right way? What *was* the right way?

"Hey," I called out. "Nisa? Stevie?"

Silence.

Pop. Another bulb died. I yelled again, louder, the sound swallowed by the darkness.

Pop.

I ran a hand across my eyes, desperately looking for the outlines of a door or opening somewhere. I saw nothing. Darkness swaddled me, soft and somehow greasy, seeping into my nose and throat until I choked, filling my ears like warm oil. The light dissolved. *I* dissolved, feeling myself floating apart, face and limbs and vertebrae liquefying, to be absorbed like a stain by the walls around me.

"Holly?" Nisa's voice echoed from far away. "Holly! Where are you?"

I tried to reply. Fleshy fingers thrust into my mouth, and I gagged. Nisa called out again and this time I grunted a reply. *"Here."*

Through the darkness I glimpsed a door, only inches away. I fell on it, twisted the knob, and almost tumbled inside.

Here it was, the small parlor. I stood, breathing heavily, and felt my horror recede. The parlor had no overhead light, but two old-fashioned lamps with beaded shades sat on side tables, and I switched them on immediately. Even then, the light didn't do much to brighten the space, which I could cross in six steps.

But there was a fireplace with a tile surround, and beside it a large basket of firewood, a brass bucket of kindling and old newspapers, with a box of matches. I felt inside the fireplace for the damper and opened it, settling back on my haunches to build a fire. Crumpled newspaper, splinters of wood, a few birch logs. I lit the match and within minutes had a blaze going.

"Holly!" Nisa practically leapt through the doorway, followed by Stevie and Amanda. "Where were you?"

I settled onto the floor in front of the fireplace, nearly overwhelmed by exhaustion. "I got lost. But this was where I wanted to be, so..."

I sighed in relief at having escaped the passage, also to see I'd managed to hang on to my script pages. I held them up, determined. "You guys ready?"

The others nodded. Nisa claimed a posh-looking leather armchair, leaving Stevie and Amanda the other two. These sported worn purple upholstery, shiny with age. I stayed where I was on the floor, holding my hands up to the flames. They didn't generate much heat—I could feel the draft as warmer air got sucked up the flue—but the blaze made me feel pleasantly muzzy, as though I'd just awakened from a long nap.

"Let's all move in here," said Nisa, pulling the armchair closer to me.

Stevie exhaled loudly, extending his long legs until they reached the fireplace tiles. He seemed tired, as though, like me, he was grateful to have found a refuge. But Amanda perched on the edge of her chair, looking wary, and my fleeting sense of relief crumbled. For a minute or so we sat in silence, watching the fire, until Nisa swiveled in her armchair. "Can we please talk about how messed up this place is? I feel like we're suppressing it, or ignoring it."

She raised a warning hand when I tried to break in. "No, Holly. This isn't helping us. I'll start."

I sighed, and set the script on the small table beside me. I had to choose my battles: I'd let everyone air their concerns. Then I'd reassure them, tell them how far we'd already come, in such a short time. We needed to get back to work. "Yeah. You're right. Go ahead."

Nisa recounted what had happened upstairs—the inexplicable booms, the penetrating cold in the nursery doorway. Amanda listened, brow furrowed. Now and then she seemed on the verge of sharing something, but mostly she remained quiet.

"There was also this strange carving in the hall," Nisa said. "I saw it when we were walking toward the nursery, but when I tried to show it to Stevie, he couldn't see it. When we came back down, the carving wasn't there."

Amanda turned to her, speaking at last. "What was it a carving of?"

"A woman running through the forest. Like she was being hunted..."

At first we all spoke in turn, but soon everyone started interrupting each other with conflicting accounts of what they'd seen or heard or been told by someone else. I chimed in about the voices I'd heard in the night, the smothering weight on my chest, the foul odors.

Yet I held back from mentioning whatever had toyed with my hair yesterday, that gentle pressure on my neck, words I couldn't quite hear. Everything else could be explained, kind of—bad dreams, creaky old house, overactive imaginations—but I felt a strong reluctance to admit to anything that might be construed as assuredly inexplicable.

As I listened to the others, I could tell they were doing the same thing. Hiding something. Making excuses, looking for a reasonable explanation for what they did decide to share. Even Nisa had her own answers—*the lighting here is terrible, my eyes were tired.*

I looked closer: Amanda continued to watch us all warily. Suspiciously, even.

As for Nisa—her face and body were almost as familiar to me as my own. Curled in her comfortable leather chair, she still radiated that cat-like self-possession, yet I saw how her eyes shifted. She listened intently to whatever was said, including—especially—by me, and calibrated her reactions accordingly. Nisa could never admit to being wrong. It was a central fact of how she moved through the world.

Stevie had leaned forward, knees drawn up so he could clasp them with his big hands. Unlike the rest of us, he'd said little. His mind seemed to be elsewhere. I pulled my attention back to the room as Amanda was asking, "Was there anything else you two saw upstairs?"

Nisa and Stevie exchanged a glance. "Just some mothballs in a linen closet," he said finally.

Stevie's face was as transparent as a glass of water: a single drop of doubt or fear or desire or joy, no matter how small, colored it for all to see. He was lying.

But I was growing impatient to resume rehearsal, so I didn't prod him. He did have his own theory once we came back around to the black hare.

"That fireplace is huge. It might have been hiding where we couldn't see it, and run out once we got the fire going."

This seemed vaguely plausible, and everyone nodded, comforted. The only other thing we had all witnessed together was the sounds in the nursery. But there was a nor'easter heading our way, after all.

Stevie still had his mic and recorder clipped to his belt, and he fidgeted with them nervously. He didn't look shifty or furtive, but increasingly disturbed. The firelight played over his delicate features so that he seemed to age even as I watched him, from his still-handsome youth to a very old man sinking into despair.

"Maybe we should just leave," said Nisa, seeming the least convinced. "Before the storm hits. I'm getting creeped out."

"No!" I protested. "We only got here yesterday. We've barely started on the play."

"I think leaving would be premature," agreed Amanda, and I shot her a look of gratitude.

"We could rehearse in the city." Nisa toyed with her hair, thinking. "Regroup. I can probably find a space we could use on the weekends—"

"There's no reason to leave," I said, fighting to remain calm. Even if I sucked up the lost rent, I knew that, once we were back in the city, the stale rhythm of our ordinary lives would resume. "You all heard how beautifully that went this morning, right? When we read in the living room? It gave me goose bumps—all of you..."

I turned to point to each of them. "Amanda, that bit when you cover your eye and deliver the line about looking daggers—only it's your good eye, not your blind eye—it made my hair stand on end. And Stevie's line about unappeased hunger and swallowing the night? And Nisa—I swear to god, babe, if your music doesn't get an Obie nomination, I'll take out a full-page ad somewhere. This play is going to be extraordinary. It already *is* extraordinary. Don't you feel it?"

I rattled my sheaf of pages. "I have all these notes for tomorrow, but let's do another run-through now. We'll all feel better. It's so cozy with the fire."

"Is it?" Nisa stretched like a cat, then stared at the ceiling, its plaster medallions blackened by cobwebs.

"We could run our lines anywhere," Amanda said evenly. "The kitchen. Even my room, it's quite pleasant."

"Wait!" We all jumped as Stevie hopped up from his chair. "Hang on, I'll be right back—"

He raced from the parlor. Nisa avoided my eyes, but Amanda leaned over and touched my knee.

"It will all be fine, Holly. There's nothing wrong with this place. I mean, there might be plenty wrong with it," she corrected herself. "Like the color schemes and the fact that no one has consulted an interior designer since 1901. But it's just an ugly old house. We should keep working."

Nisa didn't bother to hide her scowl as Amanda went on. "Do you know why certain houses make people feel uneasy?"

Nisa rolled her eyes and cut in. "Because they're obviously haunted?"

"No. It's because we can't tell whether they're actually a threat. I heard it on a podcast. If you were to open the door to Hill House and see a dead body, or a collapsed ceiling, you'd refuse to enter. But nothing here is *obviously* wrong. It's just all slightly wrong. Which makes it harder for us to know if it's safe." She settled back into her chair, pleased with herself.

"What about a rabbit coming down the chimney?"

"That is a very good question, Nisa. Holly, what did Evadne say?"

I hesitated, wary of upsetting the fragile balance I was desperately trying to maintain. "She's seen a black hare. She thinks it might be someone's pet that got loose. Maybe that boy this morning was looking for it, Nis?"

Nisa seemed to consider this, even as her fingers tugged, again and again, at her close-cropped curls. Amanda, however, was staring at me keenly.

She knows I'm lying, I thought. *God damn it, she knows.*

CHAPTER 61

We all looked up as Stevie ran back into the room, grim-faced and carrying his laptop.

"Give me a minute." He pulled a small table in front of his chair and set his computer on it, along with his phone and the recording equipment he'd been carrying around earlier. We waited as he fiddled with cords and spent several minutes transferring files. Satisfied, he leaned back and said, "Okay, listen to this."

"What is it?" I wondered, annoyed at this new disruption.

"The whole time Nisa and I were upstairs, I was recording. I just now did a quick edit in my room—I cut a few spots where Nisa and I were talking and you couldn't really hear anything else, but otherwise it's intact. We can listen to whatever we all heard up there, and maybe figure out what it was."

"You *were* ghost hunting!" Amanda said accusingly.

"No, I wasn't," Stevie retorted angrily. "I was recording ambient noises to use as sound design—I do it all the time. It's cool because there are all these noises that are constantly going on around us but we just don't notice them. Like when you're in bed at night and all of a sudden you can't fall asleep because you hear your heartbeat? It's not that your heart has suddenly started beating—you're just lying down with nothing else going on in your mind. I've done this at other places and it's amazing what you hear—the wind, mice and beetles in the walls—"

"Stop." Nisa held up her hand. "I don't want to hear about the death beetles."

"Okay, no deathwatch beetles. Like I said, I haven't played this back yet, so I might have to adjust the levels. But here goes..."

He tapped his laptop. Peering at the screen, I saw only bar graphs and squiggles, those moving lines that indicate varying sounds and frequencies. After a moment, footsteps echoed from the computer's speaker, then Stevie's and Nisa's recorded voices.

"Want to explore?"

"Oh yeah...Are you ghost hunting?"

Amanda gave him another glare but said nothing. There were more footsteps, then Stevie's laughter followed by his explanation of the deathwatch beetles, which I found interesting but which made Nisa scrunch into her chair and cover her ears. A short while later, she gave him an odd look as the sound cut out for a microsecond.

"You cut—" she began, but at Stevie's sharp look she slipped back down into her chair.

The recording continued, most of it banter.

"Whoever designed this place must have been drunk."

"Or maybe the contractors were. Or both. No wonder Ainsley can't sell it."

Now and then Stevie tapped at the screen, adjusting frequency levels so that their voices and footsteps faded out.

And yes, now I could hear other sounds. Nothing strange or creepy, just ordinary noises. A creaking door, the whistle of wind outside. Stevie and Nisa arguing about the carving, their voices subdued and faint, like whining insects. Then more footsteps, the ambient sound levels dialed back so the footsteps sounded like echoes of his fingers on the keyboard. Then Nisa's gasp.

"Do you feel that?"

A soft thump. I could see Stevie tense. "That's me," he said. "This is when we first entered the nursery. This is what we want to listen to."

"Can you picture being a kid and trying to sleep up here? You wouldn't. I wouldn't."

"No, me neither."

"Plus it must be ninety degrees—but right by the door, it's freezing."

Their recorded back-and-forth continued, and then I heard my own voice.

"Stevie! Hey, I was looking for you!"

Another minute of chatter followed.

"Holly! We found the haunted room."

"What room?"

"The nursery!"

"Get out. We have to get out."

"What? Why?"

"Just go!"

Stevie held up a warning finger, and we listened for the thunderclap.

Only there was no thunderclap. No boom, no explosive sound of any sort. Stevie stared intently at his laptop as the recording played, until we heard my voice again, and Nisa's.

"Was that thunder?"

"It felt like it came from inside this——"

I held my breath, waiting for the next explosion—but again, nothing. I looked around and saw Nisa burrowed deeply into her chair, like a child scared by a bedtime story. Amanda sat with her head tilted, intent but calm. Stevie pulled the laptop closer, putting in his headphones as he tapped at the keyboard. Onscreen, hair-thin lines rose and fell in a strange silent dance. After a minute, he looked at me.

"I'm trying to clean it up," he explained. "There's something there..."

The fine jagged lines grew thicker, as though drawn by Magic Marker. Their dance slowed, the loping rise and fall now a steady motion. It was like watching someone draw on an old-fashioned Etch A Sketch. Stevie's mouth grew tight as his finger scrolled across the track pad. He no longer looked puzzled, but afraid.

"Listen," he said, and removed his headphones.

CHAPTER 62

We all stared raptly at the screen, like it was an EKG reader in a hospital and not an audio app. "I've edited out our voices," Stevie whispered. "This is what I got..."

I held my breath, listening. Static, then a soft whirring sound—wind, I thought in relief—followed by footsteps. Then more static, followed by an unknown man's voice.

"*Could there be a draft across that doorway?*"

"*A draft? In Hill House?*" A young woman laughed, but not any of the three of us. "*Not unless you could manage to make one of those doors stay open.*"

"What the fuck—" murmured Nisa.

I grabbed her hand. "Shut up."

"*The very essence of the tomb.*" Static momentarily drowned the man's voice. "*...the heart of the house.*"

More static, a sound like heavy breathing and a different man's voice, younger than the first. "*When you stand where they can look at you, they freeze you.*"

"*Don't leave us alone in here,*" the woman said. "*A fine place—*"

The audio cut out. The four of us looked at each other.

"Play it again," Amanda urged.

"Don't!" cried Nisa. "Stevie, stop—"

"Shh," I said, and joined her in the oversized armchair. "It's okay, baby, it's just—"

"Just what?" She looked at me wildly. "That's *not us.*"

"It's some glitch with the software, that's all. Right, Stevie?"

I turned to Stevie, who'd already started to replay the recording.

"Could there be a draft across that doorway?"

"A draft? In Hill House?"

Nisa started to bolt from the chair, but I held on to her.

"Nisa, dear, calm down," said Amanda. "It's just voices on a laptop."

"No, it's not!"

"Well, whatever it is, you don't want to be running around on your own in the dark." Amanda's tone grew brisk. "Stevie, what have you got there?"

"I don't know." He stuck the headphones back over his ears, tapping the trackpad as he listened intently. I scrutinized his face, trying to read his thoughts, but sensed only increasing dismay.

At last he removed the headphones, set them on the table, and closed his laptop. Nisa nestled deeper into my arms, and Amanda moved her chair until it was touching mine. "Well?" she said.

"I don't know what it is," Stevie admitted. "But it's something. I thought maybe I'd inadvertently recorded over an existing file, or that this file somehow got corrupted. But it's fine. I can restore everything else—our voices, me and Nisa walking down the hall and talking, both of you coming upstairs. I can hear all that. And when I edit that out, I hear those other voices. What I still can't hear are those booms."

He hesitated, gnawing on his finger. "The booms—I think they occurred at the same time as the voices. I mean, the voices come in at the moment when we heard the booms. See?"

He opened the laptop and pointed at a frozen sound wave. "Based on our reactions, that's when we heard the first boom. It's like it left a hole for the voices to enter, or..."

He raised his hands helplessly.

"Ghosts," Nisa whispered, frightened. "Jesus—you've actually made a paranormal recording."

"They're not ghosts." Stevie's eyes gleamed oddly crimson in the firelight.

"Then what are they?" I looked at him, praying he had a reasonable explanation—any explanation for what we'd just heard.

"Jesus, Holly, how do I know?" He raked his hands through his hair. "Nisa and I didn't hear them, or see them, when we were up there, and neither did you. Or Amanda."

"But we all felt how cold it was in the nursery." I felt Nisa shivering, and held her to me more tightly. "They were there, we just didn't see them."

"I don't think so," Stevie said, thinking it through. "Those other voices—I think those people were like us. They'd just entered the nursery, they felt the cold, they noticed that it came from the faces above the door. *'When you stand where they can look at you, they freeze you.'* That's exactly what I thought, too."

He seemed to shrink into his seat—really shrink, the shadows engulfing him, an amoeba devouring an inconsequential microbe. "Those voices—I think they were more like echoes, or an auditory imprint. Have you ever seen the shadow print left by a leaf on a beach house deck? The leaf is gone, but the bright light makes a kind of photo of it—a sun print. I think these voices are like that."

I shook my head, and Stevie smiled wryly. "What can I say? I'm a font of useless knowledge."

He pointed at the laptop. "I don't think these are ghosts. A ghost has some kind of agency, right? Usually they're seeking retribution, or trying to tell you something about what happened to them. They interact with people on some level. I think these voices are echoes from a long time ago."

"How can you know that?" demanded Nisa.

Stevie looked beseechingly at Amanda.

"I only heard the bangs," she confessed. "I thought it sounded like firecrackers. Or a car accident, but inside the house."

Stevie took a deep breath. "I think they were more like a recording," he said. "I've been thinking, this place, it absorbs our energy. Like a battery, only it gets its charge from us. What if those people were here, too, at some point? Maybe the previous tenants?"

"That's worse than ghosts." Nisa sat up, wild-eyed. "God, doesn't anyone else feel how messed up this is? If they were tenants, they were like *us*. But what if they're still *here*?"

She turned to me, obviously hoping I'd refute this.

I avoided her gaze. I desperately wanted to pretend I hadn't heard those voices, desperately wanted—needed—to bring our attention back to the script on the table beside me. But Stevie jumped back in before I could say a word.

"It's the house." He slammed his laptop closed, as though something might emerge from it. "Can't you feel it? It hates us but it also wants us here. It wants us here because it——"

"That's enough." Amanda got to her feet. She pushed past Stevie's chair to stand in front of the fireplace, blotting out the flames. "We can argue about this all day—you can, anyway. I'll be back in a bit."

I watched her in alarm. "Where are you going?"

"I want to talk to Evadne Morris about this house."

"She had nothing to say!"

"She obviously had nothing to say to *you*."

I bridled. "So why would she talk to you?"

"Did you see her house? The stone circle and the animal bones? I'll tell Evadne I'm researching my part."

"She won't let you in," I said. "She's not friendly."

"I have my little ways." Amanda drew herself up and swept us all with a commanding look as she strode to the door. "I'll be back."

CHAPTER 63

Amanda drove down the hill, unnerved—she'd left quickly, so that the others couldn't register her disquiet. Like Holly, she didn't want to lose what they'd begun to accomplish.

And after listening to Stevie's recording, she wondered if the sniggering whispers she'd heard in her bedroom *had* in fact been him and Holly and Nisa. What if there really was another force at play?

She recalled that first time she'd seen Holly in the audience during her performance of *The Stronger,* decades ago, and Holly's frightened reaction when Amanda broke the fourth wall. The temporary sanctuary of the performance had been destroyed, breaking the implicit promise between actor and viewer: that none of this was real, that there was a boundary between the two that could not, would not, be breached.

That was what was happening at Hill House, she thought. A protective threshold had been breached, some kind of psychic fourth wall broken. Others disparaged Amanda for her belief in the ritual power of theater, but she knew she was onto something.

Holly was right—their reading this morning had been extraordinary. Amanda was accustomed to hyperbole from directors and playwrights, along with their criticism and rafts of notes—you needed that unbridled, occasionally delusional, belief to carry you through opening night.

But Holly's excitement hadn't been misplaced. Amanda had felt it too, and the others as well—she'd seen their faces in the minutes before that damn hare arrived. They couldn't leave now. If there was even the smallest chance that Evadne Morris could provide a rational explanation for what was going on at Hill House, Amanda was willing to take whatever came with it.

And even an irrational explanation might do, Amanda thought broodingly as she drove on. Holly either had lied about talking to Evadne or chosen not to share what Evadne had said. And the others were lying, too. At the least, they weren't being totally honest. Neither was she, Amanda admitted to herself. She'd said nothing about the horrible voices. She hadn't imagined them, she was sure of that. But the others already thought she was in her dotage—spilling wine, dozing off. She didn't need to add any fuel to that fire.

She drove down the hill with care. She knew her Morris Minor wasn't the best car for northern winters, but it was one of her few remaining vanities. She'd be damned if she'd replace it with a Subaru. Amazing to think that the day before, there had been blue October skies and golden leaves.

Now it felt like winter. Or, if not winter, its sullen and tantrum-prone younger sibling. The wind had torn the last leaves from the trees and sent them whirling back into the air, making it difficult to see. Very large drops splattered against the windshield, grayish-white and viscous. Snow? It couldn't be snow, it wasn't yet Halloween.

Evadne's car was in front of her home. Amanda parked and sat for a minute, composing herself. She hadn't rehearsed what she was going to say—sometimes it was better just to improvise. In any case, she suspected that Evadne was far too canny to be taken in by politesse or dissembling. She stepped out into the rain and marched through sodden leaves to the front door.

It opened before she could knock. A woman about her own age, with long graying hair and a face that looked like it had never seen the working end of sunscreen or concealer. She stared at Amanda, though not with suspicion. More resignation, perhaps, like she'd been expecting her.

"I apologize for coming here like this," Amanda said. "I'm—"

Evadne peered past her to the Morris Minor sitting in a deepening puddle. She brought her attention back to her uninvited guest. "I know who you are. Amanda Greer."

"Oh. Well, thank you." Amanda smiled. Always nice to be recognized.

"You were in that awful movie about the talking clam. But you better come in. Give me your coat."

Amanda stepped inside, shaking rain from her hair as she peeled off her cashmere Prada, secondhand but no one knew that but her. She waited as Evadne shoved aside old barn jackets and an ancient yellow sou'wester to make room for her coat in an alcove beside the door.

While she was busy, Amanda took a few quick steps into the kitchen to get a look at the living room beyond. Beard the lioness in her den, she thought. Evadne's home was extremely tidy. Braided rugs on the floor, original artwork on the walls, a sleek small woodstove that glowed cheerfully. A short hallway that must lead to the bedrooms and bathroom. A low table held a number of candles carefully arranged around piles of stone, along with a statue of a bare-breasted woman in ancient attire—conical cap, elaborately patterned skirt. In each hand she grasped something that might have been a small crescent moon, or maybe a snake.

"What do you want, Amanda?"

She turned to see Evadne, arms crossed and head cocked, regarding her coldly.

"Hill House." If Evadne wasn't going to mince words, neither would she. "I have some questions."

Evadne remained where she was. She wore a sweater that looked hand-knit, not a frumpy pattern but bright zigzags of indigo and violet, the kind of sweater Amanda saw on young actresses on Instagram, with their blown-up lips and buccal fat removal. When Evadne said nothing, Amanda volunteered, "That's a beautiful sweater. Did you make it?"

A long silence. "I did. Sit."

She pointed at the couch. Amanda sat. Evadne continued to fix her with that Medusa's stare, then settled in the armchair across from Amanda. "Why are you at Hill House?"

"I'm part of a group of actors who've rented it. I think you met one of us this afternoon? Holly Sherwin? I'm sure she told you—"

Evadne's mouth tightened. "I asked you."

Amanda nodded and gave her the short version. Amazingly talented playwright, wonderful small group of performers, including an incredible singer, a terrific opportunity for all concerned...

"Why are you here now at my house?"

"Well..." Amanda chose her next words with care. "The play is based on an actual event, the burning of an old woman accused of witchcraft in 1621. Elizabeth Sawyer. That's my role. I thought you might share some insight into the character."

"Because I'm old and poor and alone?" For the first time, Evadne smiled slightly.

"No, of course not!" Amanda shook her head, horrified by her gaffe. "But—I saw your garden, the standing stones and the mirror ball. I have a friend who's a Wiccan, and I thought you might—"

"Why didn't you ask your friend, then, instead of barging in on someone you don't know?"

Amanda stared at her helplessly. Evadne's pale blue eyes appeared almost white: her fury had sucked away whatever color they once held. Amanda swallowed. When all else fails, tell the truth.

"Hill House—I thought you might know something about it."

"Why?"

"You live nearby."

"No! Why do you want to know about Hill House?"

"Because..."

Amanda lowered her gaze, trying to figure out how to respond, and noticed Evadne's ring. Heavy silver, with a large piece of amber in it. Like Melissa Libby's. Like Ainsley Rowan's. She looked up again. "Because some things have happened there."

"What kind of things?"

"A rabbit came down the chimney. A black rabbit. Holly said she'd seen it by your house, so we thought it might be yours."

She stopped, thinking how ridiculous this would all sound to a disinterested observer. "We wondered if it was all right. If it was yours, I mean."

"He wasn't a rabbit."

"Right, sorry—your hare."

"He wasn't that either."

Amanda licked her lips. "Oh. Well. I hope he wasn't hurt."

"He'll recover." Without looking at it, Evadne tapped her ring. Tap. Tap. Tap.

"How did he—how did he get into the chimney?"

"How would you get into a chimney?"

Amanda laughed, but Evadne wasn't smiling. She tapped her ring again, twice this time. Tap. Tap. "Just tell me what else happened at Hill House."

Shit. Amanda had seriously misjudged this woman. Evadne was friends with Ainsley—Holly had said that. Melissa too. They all had matching rings. If Amanda told Evadne what they'd seen or heard at Hill House, she would no doubt pass it on to Ainsley. Who might take offense and boot them out.

And Amanda didn't want to leave.

Evadne's eyes had narrowed, her finger poised above the amber stone on her ring. Tap. Tap. Tap. Tap.

Amanda's heart fluttered. *It's a code,* she thought. *She's signaling them—* Ainsley and Melissa. *She actually is a witch.*

She raised her eyes and saw Evadne staring at her. Very slowly, Evadne began to smile.

CHAPTER 64

After Amanda left, Stevie remained in the parlor with Holly and Nisa, watching the flames leap and gutter and rise again. The chimney drew poorly. Several times it belched a cloud of acrid smoke that sent them all coughing and wiping their eyes. Their conversation lagged, despite Holly's best efforts.

"We could run lines for just five minutes," she suggested again. "Just until Amanda comes back, and then we can do another full read-through."

Stevie said nothing. He couldn't understand how Holly continued to willfully ignore how fucked up things had become.

Oh, he got it: the show must go on! But it was clearly an effort for Holly to keep her own fears under wraps.

Poor Nisa looked awful—dark circles under her eyes, her curls a mess because she couldn't stop raking her hands through them. He knew a cure for that—gently kiss her temples until she groaned and melted into him. He couldn't do that now, for obvious reasons.

Anyway, Nisa herself would surely prefer her own form of self-care: singing. Though at the moment, Stevie would rather not have that added to the mix. He knew how Nisa's otherworldly voice

242

could cast its spell, even, especially, among those who'd heard it many times. He couldn't shake the feeling that here, it might wake something none of them would want to acknowledge.

He started as Holly prodded him gently. "Stevie, I know you're almost off-book. Nisa, you could read Elizabeth Sawyer, if you wanted."

Reluctantly, Stevie turned his head from the blaze. "'Bow wow wow.' How's that."

Nisa, to his surprise, perked up. "Tomasin has some of the best lines, Stevie, you know that. Okay, I'll read. I need to shake this funk."

Holly looked at her gratefully. "Thanks, babe."

The two women leaned into each other. As they kissed, Stevie felt a shaft of intense arousal pierce him: desire, and jealousy, unusual for him. Also, hunger. His mouth watered—how long since they'd eaten? Only a few hours, but he felt ravenous, and unmoored.

Get a grip. Safe, you need to feel safe, he thought, remembering what a beloved acting coach had told him. *You may not feel safe in your real life, but inside a character you can disappear, you can have control.*

With care, he unfolded his legs, stretched his long arms toward the fireplace. He shook his head vigorously, lank hair flying about his face, and let it fall where it might. He flexed his hands, curled them into paws as he ran his tongue across his teeth. Tomasin really did have the best lines in the play; for sure the best character arc. It would be good to disappear into him, slough off this exhausted, human form and sink into another, stronger one.

He glanced at Nisa, how beautiful she was, despite her own exhaustion and fear. With Amanda as Elizabeth, he'd had to command the energy to seduce her, gazing at the older woman through slitted eyes as he imagined how Tomasin would view her—a mass of energy and need to be manipulated.

With Nisa, he didn't need to summon that energy. It spilled from him like a liquid, almost like he could see it, a golden stream flowing between the two of them. He felt the firelight in his eyes, saw it wash over Holly's and Nisa's faces: their rapt gazes as they watched him slide from his chair to crouch on the floor, then swiftly rise to his full height, a towering black figure silhouetted against the flames.

"I'm Tomasin, dear Elizabeth, but call me Tom. Dogs love where they are beloved: cherish me, and I'll do anything for you. Anything. Fear neither my presence nor my absence—I have so much work to do tonight! Until now I have served only one master, but I will serve you, Elizabeth, sweet Elizabeth..."

Stevie drew his hands to his chest, crossing them there. He lifted his head to stare directly at Nisa. He smiled, a long slow smile that bared his teeth, holding Nisa's gaze so long he felt Holly begin to shift uncomfortably beside her.

As Nisa stared back, he saw the effort it took for her not to look away. Something woke and moved behind her eyes, something Stevie was more accustomed to seeing when he looked at himself in the mirror. Something he'd never in all these years seen in Nisa: raw terror.

Almost he pitied her. He felt another self uncoil within this one, a thread that rippled inside him, slipping from his groin through his heart until it reached his throat, where he felt it tighten. The face in front of him blurred. He ignored the impulse to stop talking, to push his hair from his eyes and let that other Stevie-self emerge and say something comforting, to whoever she was, whoever these people were.

He whispered, "See?"

He reached to take the person's face in his hand—it was a person, he remembered that, how soft they were and warm and pliant. He moved closer to her eyes, his mouth filling with saliva. He swallowed, tasting something foul yet also sweet. Her eyes. He opened his mouth, murmuring.

"Those who are denied joy must take delight
In death and darkness—the Devil's right."

He saw his own mouth reflected in her eyes, his teeth, his tongue, heard a low buzzing. Like a wasp was trapped in his ear canal, beating its wings as it struggled to reach his skull.

"*Stevie! Stop!*"

He fell backward and hit something, hard, toppling over a chair onto the floor. Blinking, he looked up and saw Nisa staring at him in horror, her hand raised as though to strike him.

Holly hopped from the chair, ebullient, as Stevie pushed himself groggily back to his feet. "Oh my god—that was amazing, Stevie! Where did you—"

"He was going to bite my eyes!" Nisa turned furiously from Holly to Stevie. "What the fuck is wrong with you?"

He shook his head, covering his ears. The firelight burned his eyes, too bright. He tried to distinguish between the two figures in front of him, tried to remember not just who but what they were.

"Holly." His mouth felt like he'd been chewing on cinders. "Nisa. I—"

"Are you tripping?"

"What? No—"

"Are you sure?" Nisa stared at him, her terror fading but anger intact. "Because you sure as hell look like you're on something."

"Stop it, Nisa." Holly took his hand. "Stevie, that was incredible— *exactly* what we want for Tomasin. I wish Amanda had been here! But you can do it next time together. Maybe tonight."

"Of course." Stevie tried to remember who Amanda was. His ears rang, these voices were all too loud. "Yeah. I—I think I'm going to walk around and clear my head." He looked at Nisa. "I'm sorry I scared you. I was just—"

"Whatever. I'm fine. Only don't bite me, you freak. Especially in front of my girlfriend." She turned, picked up another log, and threw it forcefully onto the fire. "I'm going to hang here and stay warm. I want to hear what Amanda has to say about the Witch of Hillsdale before I do anything else."

Stevie smiled weakly. "Me too."

CHAPTER 65

"Did you see that?" Nisa demanded after Stevie was gone.

"Wasn't it amazing?" Holly grinned ecstatically, hugging herself as she sank into an armchair. "People are going to be blown away by him—by all of it. Stevie is incredible, freaking incredible."

"Stevie is a freaking lunatic! He was *this* close to me—"

Nisa grabbed the arms of Holly's chair, leaning over until their faces were inches apart. Holly's eyes glittered in a way she'd never seen before. Nisa knew her girlfriend wasn't drunk, but Holly—sober, hardworking, reliable Holly—appeared almost manic with pleasure.

"Holly!" She snapped her fingers in Holly's face. "Listen to me. I swear to god, he was going to bite me. He was going for my eyes."

Holly's delight curdled into an expression Nisa had never glimpsed before. "He was acting, Nis. You should try it sometime."

Nisa sucked in her breath. "What the fuck, Holly." She stepped away, shaking her head. "He's a loose cannon, he—"

"Like who here isn't? So maybe he got carried away. My play's supposed to be edgy—"

"That section of dialogue isn't edgy!"

"I know, which is why it's been so hard for him to own it. And he finally came up with a truly scary bit of business—you can see that, right?"

"I saw that he looked like he was losing his shit. Honestly? You look like that, too. I think we should leave, Holly."

"Are you kidding? We've had one run-through—"

"One run-through and a boatload of genuinely bad stuff. The nursery, Amanda's fugue state, that carving I saw upstairs—"

Holly sighed. "Baby, no one else saw that. I didn't, Stevie didn't—"

"I don't care if you saw it. I know that I did. Like we all heard those sounds in the nursery, like we all saw Amanda's eyes rolled back in her head. Stevie's acting weird—"

"Stevie always acts weird."

"This is different. He's trying to hide something—in his room, he acts like there's something there he doesn't want anyone to see."

"How do you know? Have you been in his room? You have, haven't you?"

Nisa had been expecting this question ever since she and Stevie first hooked up. Holly always bristled whenever the conversation turned to Nisa's former lovers, jealous of Nisa's past as well as her voice. Yet now Holly sounded utterly blasé.

Nisa shrugged, disoriented. "Yeah, sure. He always wants me to hang out, when he's couch-surfing, or whatever..."

She let her words trail off suggestively, but Holly didn't take the bait. "But he pushed me out today. That's not normal."

"He's working on his lines, Nisa. And the sound design. He's so embedded in this project, and it's paying off." She looked up at Nisa, eyes glowing as though someone were shining a flashlight into them. "It's so fabulous."

She doesn't see me, Nisa thought, with sharp unease. She said, "You're wrong, Holly. Just once, I'd love you to admit that you're wrong."

"What am I wrong about? The fact that Stevie wants some space and you're not giving it to him? Listen to yourself, Nisa." Holly reached for her hand, but Nisa didn't take it. "What are we even arguing about?"

"Last night you were talking in your sleep."

"Really?" Holly appeared taken aback. "What did I say?"

"I'm not sure. I can't remember now. But it was...messed up. It sounded like you were talking to yourself. I mean, you *were* talking to yourself, but you were using two different voices."

Holly shook her head. "Are you sure you don't remember what I said?"

"I wish I did. Or no, I'm glad I don't—it sounded horrible." She stared at Holly, her eyes no longer bright but sunk in shadow. "Holly, it didn't sound like you—neither of the voices did. It freaked me out."

Holly was silent. Finally she admitted, "I heard them too. When I was sleeping—or no, not when I was sleeping, they woke me up. I was lying awake in bed and I heard them, laughing and murmuring and whispering. About me." Holly ran a finger nervously across her palm.

"What did they say?"

"I don't know. I couldn't understand them, but I knew it was horrible. Whatever they said, it sounded disgusting, and...and dangerous."

"We have to leave," Nisa said.

Holly didn't budge. She stared intently at the fire, as though reading some message inscribed in the flames. After a long silence, she shrugged. "But you just said it was only me talking in my sleep."

"That doesn't make me feel better. You sounded...demented."

Holly smiled. "Cut me some slack, Nis—I was dreaming. I've been under so much pressure. But this morning, everything went great. Your songs are so beautiful and spooky and—just unearthly. I've always thought that, but here—"

Nisa followed her gaze as Holly glanced around the room, the firelight drawing patterns on the paneled walls like faces and long-fingered hands. "It feels like this is where they truly belong. I mean that, Nis," she went on, and touched her hand. "You've brought so much to this play. Amanda is a consummate pro—"

"'Consummate'?" Nisa snorted. But she let her fingers close around

Holly's, accepting her peace offering. "More like 'conspicuous,' as in 'conspicuously a total flake.'"

"Maybe, but that's why she's so brilliant as Elizabeth—she doesn't have to fake it. And Stevie. . ." She shook her head. "I'm sorry he upset you, Nisa—I really am. But if you could have seen him the way I did—well, Stevie nailed it. He was so scary and seductive. I had no idea what he was going to do next."

"I did," Nisa said darkly. "He was going to bite my eyes out."

Holly pulled her toward her. "I will not let Stevie bite your eyes out. I won't let anyone bite your eyes out," she murmured, and kissed her neck.

Nisa sighed, relenting. "Promise?"

"Promise. Look, you and I knew this was going to be a pressure cooker before we got here, and that was before we even met Amanda. But I really do think the play will be amazing—it already is. All the odd things about being here, we can *use* that."

Nisa nodded. She kissed Holly's soft mouth, the memory of Stevie's twisted face receding as Holly kissed her. When she at last drew away from Holly, she asked, "How about we all just step away from the play for a little while and come back tomorrow, or later tonight? Why don't we open one of those bottles of Rhône I brought?"

"It's still early. I really wanted to go for another read-through."

Nisa glanced at her phone. "It's almost five."

"That's impossible. When we came in here, it was just after two." Holly pulled out her own phone and stared at the screen. "What the hell?"

"Time flies when you're having fun." She waited to see if Holly would change her mind about another run-through, take some time alone with Nisa with a bottle of wine and their shared bed.

But Holly's gaze had returned to the hearth, once again watching some imagined scene unfold within. After a minute, she stood and started for the door, without waiting to see if Nisa followed.

CHAPTER 66

The sky had deepened to a bruised purplish-gray when Amanda turned to glance out the window behind her. Gray shapes rose from the yellowing grass—the circle of standing stones, which from here resembled tombstones. Rain beat against the panes, big drops that splattered like insects striking a windshield. *Snow,* Amanda thought. *It's turning to snow.*

"We always get a bad storm this time of year," Evadne said thoughtfully. "Once we got twelve inches the day after Halloween. The trees still had their leaves, so a lot of them came down. The whole valley lost power for a week. I didn't get mine back for another ten days. That's when I got my generator…"

She pointed to a metal box in the backyard, the size of a dog crate. "When we lose power up here, they don't fix it for weeks. Not worth the trouble for just one older woman. They think it's my own fault for living here."

"Why do you live here?"

"To keep an eye on it."

"Hill House?"

Amanda didn't think she'd answer, but Evadne gave a small

nod. Emboldened, Amanda continued. "The others, too? Ainsley and Melissa?"

"Ainsley is one of my oldest friends. Melissa is my niece."

Amanda waited a moment before asking, "Why do you need to watch Hill House?"

"Because no one else will. Ainsley rents it out despite Melissa and me warning her how dangerous it is. Not just dangerous—fatal. Nothing good has ever happened there, ever, ever, ever."

She stood and walked to the window, looked out at the black woods, the standing stones laced with snow.

"There's a kind of wasp that lays its eggs inside insect larvae," she said. "When the egg hatches, a baby wasp grows, just as the insect grows around it. Over time, the wasp eats the insect from the inside. Eventually the insect dies, and the adult wasp finds another host to lay its own eggs in."

"Stop it," said Amanda. "Stop it, that's horrible."

Evadne turned to her. "No, it's not. That wasp is part of the natural world. Hill House isn't. You and your friends need to leave. Now, before it's full dark."

Amanda glanced outside. She'd lost track of the time—the sun must be close to setting, not that she could see it through the clouds and sleet. "Holly's not going to want to leave. *I* don't want to leave. We're here to work, and we'll work. And who wants to drive in this?"

"It's only going to get worse. There's a storm warning."

Evadne pulled out her phone, tapped it, and held the screen up to Amanda.

Winter storm warning for Tanarak County and the following towns: Hillsdale, Ashton, Mill River...8–12 inches of snow expected. Expect power outages and downed trees. Avoid driving and stay off the roads...

"Twelve inches?" She looked at Evadne. "But it's not even Halloween."

Evadne shrugged. "Trick or treat."

She pocketed her phone and walked to the door, halting to wait for Amanda. "You came to me for answers. So I am telling you the truth. Or were you hoping I'd say there's nothing to worry about—stay and work on your little play?"

Amanda grew hot: that was exactly what she'd been hoping. "This is not a little play—"

"I don't care. Neither does Hill House. Tell your friends you have to go now." Evadne stared at her: not with disdain but appraisal, and an unexpected hint of recognition. "You and I, we're old enough to know better. They won't see reason, but you will. Tell them you're having a medical emergency."

"I am absolutely fine," Amanda said coldly.

"You're an actor. Convince them otherwise."

Her pale gaze grew even more intent, until Amanda had to look away. She straightened, her head held high, and went to the door that Evadne now held open for her. She waited for Evadne to give her some sort of farewell, or another warning. But she merely watched in silence as Amanda made her way to her car and got inside. Evadne was standing in the doorway, stone-still except for her finger, tapping again at her amber ring. As Amanda drove off, she looked in the rearview mirror and saw a black shape flow through the early dusk. It stopped to rear up on its hind legs in front of Evadne, who let her hands fall to her side, the amber ring glinting, before Amanda rounded a curve in the road, and they were lost among the trees.

CHAPTER 67

H e had to clear his head. Or no, not clear it but fill it with something other than the memory of Nisa's terrified face. And there was something else, something that scratched at the border of his consciousness, trying to get in. The same sensation as when he was on the verge of falling asleep, trying to hold on to a thought that dissolved before he could grab it. Only he wasn't in bed, he was wide awake and walking quickly along one of Hill House's inner hallways, away from Nisa and Holly and the bright glow of the fireplace.

The lighting back here was terrible, little flame-shaped lightbulbs, most of them burned out. He bet the wiring was ancient, definitely not up to code. Probably installed before there even was a code.

He took out his phone and turned on the flashlight. Immediately he felt better, not because it illuminated much—he could still see only a few feet ahead of him—but because it gave him an illusion of control. He knew that was what it was—an illusion—but for decades his therapists had told him how important it was for him to feel in control, even if he wasn't.

Like now. He actually had no idea where he was. He stopped, looked over his shoulder to see if he could spot the parlor's telltale gleam of firelight. But the door had shut behind him and was now indistinguishable from myriad other doors, themselves almost indistinguishable from the oak-paneled walls. The air felt close and reeked of mildew. He didn't see any air vents. Or heating registers or radiators or any other kind of house infrastructure. It was like whoever had designed and built the place had then abandoned it to fend for itself.

He continued for a few more steps, then paused to open a door at random. A rush of cold air carried the scent of moldering leaves and crushed acorns. He peered inside what appeared to be a very large room. He could just make out drifts of dead leaves on the floor. Someone must have left a window open.

But he couldn't see any windows, just a faint orange blur, as if his eyes were closed against the sun. From somewhere came the soft buzzing of an insect, something crawling among the dead leaves.

With a jolt he recalled what he'd heard while running lines with Nisa: a buzzing in his ears, not tinnitus but something alive, beating its wings against his skull.

> *Those who are denied joy must take delight*
> *In death and darkness…*

He slammed the door shut, running back down the corridor until he reached a blank wall—a dead end.

Terror overcame him. He needed a way out, he needed to find Nisa and Holly and Amanda. He pounded the wall with his open hands, looked down and saw a rim of light encircling something. A knob. It wasn't a dead end, but another door. How had he missed that?

Shoving it open, he stumbled into the main hall, with its familiar stained carpet and massive stairway, the padlocked door to the tower and tall front windows letting in the wintry light. His terror dissipated. He drew several deep breaths, the way his therapist had taught him, let his autonomic nervous system take over.

Why had he been so frightened in the passage? He loved small spaces, felt safe in them. It was a delayed response to Nisa's anger, he thought. He'd never been able to deal with her drama queen tendencies.

He turned and walked past the cloakroom where they'd left their coats and empty suitcases, past the first entrance to the dining room. He checked his phone for the time. Much too early for dinner, only three thirty, and he wasn't hungry, anyway; that soup had been fantastic. Tru Libby really was a great cook.

But then he recalled Melissa's bruised face—why was he the only one who worried about her? It seemed so callous of the others, especially Holly. She seemed so caught up in the play, but how could nothing else matter? Though Stevie himself had felt it, too, in the parlor, that primal thrill as he felt himself fold into someone else. Something else.

He peeked through the dining room's second doorway, just in case someone was there. But Holly and Nisa must still be in the parlor. He wondered if Amanda really had gone to see Evadne Morris. He glanced again at his phone to see if she, anyone, had texted him, but he had no service. That didn't bother him; it was one of the things he'd most been looking forward to, coming here. Escaping from that world. Escaping from everything.

And it seemed to be working. The fear he'd felt just minutes ago drained away and a deep sense of comfort enveloped him as he walked the halls.

He knew from Holly's expression that his performance had already surpassed whatever she'd hoped for. He still felt it, a flash of the intense charge he got when he'd nailed a part, a shivery current that ran through his entire body, everything seeming to tremble, on the verge of coming apart. The others had laughed when Amanda talked about actors being possessed, but he knew that she was right.

It had been years since he'd felt it, like a drug he'd forsaken. Only this wasn't bad for him, like drugs. This was what he'd needed, all along. This was what he'd been secretly praying for, the chance to give himself over to something more powerful than himself. The muse, an old acting teacher had called it. The other students laughed, but Stevie was thrilled, that someone else—a teacher!—had openly acknowledged what Stevie had always hoped might be true. *There are more things in heaven and earth, Horatio, than are dreamt of in your philosophy.*

He looked up. Without realizing it, he'd wandered into the conservatory. Heavy rain drummed at the glass roof, countless unseen hands tapping at the panes. The soaring ceiling was too far away; he felt unnerved to see all that air above him, the watery green glow stinging his eyes. He headed toward the far door, avoiding the toad-shaped ottoman and couch, arrows of sprung wicker protruding through rotted cushions.

As he approached the door, he heard another sound. A sharp *clack* followed by a series of bumps. He glanced up, thinking that it was more hail. But the noise didn't come from the ceiling, or outside. A sound he recognized, though he hadn't heard it for a long time.

Clack!

There it came again. He tracked it through the abandoned living room, with its sad shadows on the walls where paintings had once hung, the fireplace that exuded a cold smell of ashes and singed fur.

Clack!

The noise sounded loud as a gunshot. The thuds were followed by the sound of an object rolling down an incline. The sounds came from the next room—the game room. Holly had told him about it when they first arrived. There'd been a billiards table, but hadn't Ainsley sold it?

Clack!

The door to the game room was closed. Had Amanda returned? Was she in there shooting pool? Or had Holly and Nisa slipped by without him seeing them?

He paused as he reached the door, straining to catch conversation or footsteps. He heard only the bounce and bump of ivory balls, the soft drop of one into a pocket. Holly was wrong. Ainsley hadn't sold it. Maybe she'd lied, because she didn't want a bunch of amateurs ripping the expensive felt.

He opened the door.

The room was empty. Ragged curtains hung from the windows, their heavy dark-green velvet faded to a lichen-gray. A stale smell of cigarette smoke and booze permeated the air, and the wood floor underfoot felt slightly sticky.

He looked around. Where was the pool table? The room was big, but not that big. He saw only a cabinet bolted to the far wall. Its open shelves held pool racks, a small felt pocket full of squares of blue chalk. He crossed the floor to the cabinet, his steps softened by whatever clung to the floorboards, picked up a chalk square, and rubbed it between his fingers, inhaling its dusty mineral smell. He retrieved a wooden cue that had tumbled to the floor—too small for his height, too light—and returned it to the rack. A long rolled-up carpet lay on the floor beneath it. He bent to touch it, and the rug's backing crumbled beneath his fingertips, yellowish dust and the chemical odor of cleaning fluid.

He straightened and again looked around. Other than the ceaseless drumming of sleet, the room was silent. Could he have imagined those noises? It seemed impossible. Yet he was certain the sounds had come from here. He rubbed his eyes, confused, and noticed something he hadn't seen before. A small white ball, sitting on the floor beneath one of the high windows. A cue ball.

Where had that come from? He blinked: it was still there, not really white but a mottled shade, like curdled cream. Even from here he could see the crazing on it, fine lines that made it look like an eye with no pupil. It would be real ivory, and valuable. Ainsley must have overlooked it when she sold off the rest of the set. He'd return it to her. Or he might keep it for himself, he thought, and took a step toward it.

As he did, the ball began to move. With excruciating slowness, it rolled in a straight line toward him, not deviating even for a broken floorboard, simply rolling over its groove and continuing on.

Stevie stared in disbelief, frozen in place. Outside the sleet grew louder. A shadow passed across the room, but he couldn't tear his gaze from the white ball. It continued toward him, slow as a faltering heartbeat, until he could have crouched to grasp it. The realization filled him with horror.

How was it moving?

He heard again that buzzing in his skull. Before he could blink, the ball leapt into the air and flew straight at his face.

He flung himself to the floor, covering his head with his arms. The cue ball smashed into the wall behind him. He lay there, panting, until he could finally ease his hands from his head and look around.

He was still alone.

He got to his feet. There was no sign of the ball, or that anyone had been in the room with him. Nothing but a dent in the wall: head-high, green paint flaking from its edges and flecks of plaster drifting to the floor beneath. The plaster seemed to form some kind of wobbly pattern on the worn floorboards, but it wasn't until he stooped that he could make out the words.

COME IN

CHAPTER 68

She'd be damned if she went running after Holly after all that. Stevie attacking her and Holly behaving like it was just all some Method actor bullshit, when it was so obvious Stevie was losing his shit. Pretending she appreciated everything Nisa brought to this play, when she was really just thinking about herself, as always. They could have used this time without Amanda to rehearse some of Nisa's songs. Instead, she'd been used as a punching bag by someone who hadn't had an Equity role in ten years.

She slumped in the leather chair, watching the fire dwindle to a heap of black and glowing red. She felt the heat ebb from the room as the flames flickered out, but she was too pissed off to set another log on the embers. Let them die, let them all die.

She could hear Holly chiding her during a long-ago argument: *You wouldn't just cut off your nose to spite your face, you'd cut off your whole face.*

Holly was right—Nisa knew she could hold a grudge.

Let it go, she thought. *Get back to your own work.* At least Holly had admitted how great her songs were, how much they were bringing to the show. Nisa could feel it; this was going to be her break. And she remembered how fabulous the acoustics had been, on that first house tour with Ainsley. Nisa had barely had a chance to play with them yet.

The tower, for instance—if only she could get in there. Ainsley said it wasn't safe, but the rest of Hill House seemed like it could survive into the next century with barely a new coat of paint. She bet Ainsley had been feeding them a load of crap all along, about the house and its history. Riling up the flatlanders so they'd leave early—less wear and tear—and Ainsley could keep Holly's money.

Nisa softened at the thought of Holly. This all meant so, so much to her. Nisa had seen the effort it took, Holly returning home, day after day, from her students, to hunch on the street-salvaged couch in their cramped apartment, wearing earbuds to keep out the wail of sirens from the fire station across the street as she wrote—and rewrote, endlessly—the play that would become *Witching Night*. Nisa deserved her star turn, and Holly did, too.

Yet Holly was wrong about Stevie. He really had been on the verge of losing it earlier. Nisa had never seen him look like that—she'd never seen anyone look like that. As though someone else had slid inside him, to stare out from Stevie's eyes.

Shivering, she hopped to her feet, grabbed another log, and set it on the pile of ashes. But the fire was dead. She gazed at the hearth and thought about the hare. And then about Amanda's dead face, her empty eyes. Holly, talking in her sleep. Stevie, again…

She turned and walked resolutely from the parlor. Maybe she'd join Holly, after all. She could drive herself crazy brooding about all this shit. Her friends, the house, Amanda and those other crazy women. Ainsley, Evadne. The three of them were like the Weird Sisters. Nisa almost wished Holly had written another part for someone closer to her own age. But then, all eyes might not be on Nisa whenever she made an entrance.

The parlor lamps cast enough light into the hall that she didn't need to use her phone. A good thing, since the charge was way down again. She'd have to remember to plug it in when she got back to the room later.

No one was in the main hall when she got there.

"Holly?" she called. No answer, so she texted, pleased to see a flickering bar of service for once.

Where are you?

> In the room. Decided to shower.
> I'll meet you down there w the
> wine in a bit love you xoxo

Nisa smiled. Love you too

She'd wait to bring up the whole Stevie thing again, she decided. She didn't want to get into it with Holly, not so soon, not here. She needed to save her own energy for singing. She walked to the front door and looked out through one of the side windows. It was sleeting heavily now, the goldenrod beaten down, the fallen leaves a brown pulp. There was no sign of Amanda's car. At least she hadn't walked to Evadne's. If Nisa had been Amanda, she'd have just driven to town in search of a bar.

But Melissa was right: bad weather was coming, and the roads likely wouldn't be safe. And since they were stuck here, Nisa hoped it would turn to snow. She'd always loved snow days, and there were fewer of them every year. In fact, she decided, this would be a perfect place to be stuck. They had enough food, plenty of wine, plenty of candles. Firewood, too. Her younger self would have killed for the chance to have a sleepover with her friends in a spooky mansion during a storm.

Maybe they could all sleep downstairs tonight, in front of the living room fireplace? Drag the couch over, pile up blankets and bedding. Amanda might not be up for it, but she could be convinced. She wouldn't want to be the only one sleeping alone upstairs. It felt safer down here.

Nisa hummed softly to herself, a melancholy, slightly threatening tune that was the perfect counterpoint to the bleak weather. She turned to gaze at the door to the tower.

The heavy padlock bolted to the wood frame hung loose. Not broken but unlocked. Frowning, she walked over to examine it. She was pretty sure it'd been secured when they arrived. But since it wasn't...she slid it from the hasp and set it on the floor, creaking open the door to enter the tower.

"Oh!" she exclaimed softly. Struck by how her breath echoed in the air, almost as though expecting an answer. Such a beautiful space, why had they closed it off? A round room, its lower walls paneled with wooden bookshelves, only broken by windows that looked out onto the front drive and side lawn. A library, with an iron spiral staircase rising from its center to the stone turret.

The spiral stairway had a queasy tilt, like a carnival ride that had frozen in place. But otherwise the tower seemed safe enough. Stabilized by those gigantic rebars, Nisa thought, noting where they protruded like ribs through the lower section of the wall. From the upper windows, you would have a commanding view of the distant mountains.

Books still lined the shelves, mostly moldering Victorian-era texts on spiritual living and the horrors of sexual congress out of wedlock, or maybe even in it. Nisa made her way over and flipped through a volume titled *Rewards of Chastity, or, The Golden Life after Marriage*. It reeked of mildew, and as she turned its damp pages, silverfish wriggled out. With a yelp, she dropped the volume, heard a satisfying crack as it struck the stone floor and split apart.

As she walked on, she saw other books, too, waterlogged paperbacks and *Old Farmer's Almanacs*, some hardcover bestsellers from the 1980s. An old cassette tape. She picked this last up and opened it, disappointed to see that the case was empty. She pried the paper sleeve from the once-clear plastic, now fogged with age. The Psychedelic Furs. The cover art was plain, a black-and-white photo of six young guys.

Thoughtfully, she turned the paper in her hands, recalling the broken Walkman in the nursery, with its tangled wad of magnetic tape. It might have come from this, she thought, rubbing a thumb along the plastic case. She had a vague memory of her mother liking this band, the two of them watching some old movie with a song of theirs. But also listening to a CD of their music, maybe even this one. A song that her mother had played over and over when she was high.

"Your father always said this was about me," she'd told Nisa, more than once. "When we first met in London."

What was that song? Nisa could almost remember it. Ominous drumbeats and a man's voice, a repetitive chorus like an incantation. The song had spooked Nisa back then, especially after what her mother told her. She squinted at the label, struggling to read the list of songs in the afternoon's dying light.

And there it was—"Sister Europe." All at once the words came back to her, along with a rush of yearning she'd been too young to comprehend when she'd first heard it: yearning and threat.

She imagined the teenage boy or girl who'd owned the Walkman, rewinding the cassette to listen to that same song again and again, until the Walkman devoured it. A boy, she thought, remembering the figure she'd seen staring at her window that morning. The connection made her skin crawl. She stuffed the slip of cover art back into the cassette case and replaced it on the shelf, setting a heavy book on top of it, as if to keep it from escaping, and turned back to survey the tower.

Why was it off-limits? The room had more light than the rest of the house, its high windows that would keep it bright even in winter. The spiral staircase was obviously a liability, but why not simply remove it? You'd have no way of accessing the uppermost shelves, but they were empty anyway.

Though there was a door up there, at the top. She hadn't noticed it at first—a dark rectangle set into the gray stone. Once it must have opened onto the top of the spiral stairs, but now they leaned a good ten feet away from it. *That* was the door that needed to be padlocked, otherwise you'd take a step to nowhere fast. If you could even reach it, of course.

She rested a hand on the stairway's curving rail. She expected the iron to be cold, but it was warm. The entire room was warm, which was odd. If anything, the granite walls should make it feel colder. Like the rest of Hill House, the tower seemed to generate its own weather.

She grabbed the rail with both hands, testing it, and let herself slide beneath it, still holding tightly, before she straightened. Like playing in the outdoor jungle gym near their home when she was a girl. The spiral stairway was solid, much too heavy to be moved by someone as slight as she was—it was bolted into the stone floor. It felt enticing, the way the jungle gym had, with its struts and spires reaching to the sky. She took a step up, then another, until she was about a dozen feet above where she'd started. With each riser she felt the staircase shift ever so slightly.

When she looked down, she was overcome not by fear but a giddy joy, as when she'd reached the top of the jungle gym and could look out over their neighborhood, glimpsing her own home a block away. Now, though, her joy was undercut by fear that she might fall; she clutched the rails, her hands slick with sweat. She lifted one foot and stomped hard on the step.

She was rewarded by a bright ringing note, as though a bell had been struck. The sound echoed in the circular chamber and she listened, enchanted, her foot poised to do the same thing again.

But then she thought of the others hearing it, and rushing to find the source of the ghostly carillon. Holly would yell at her for entering the tower. And everyone else would know about it. She liked that, for a few minutes, she had a secret. Maybe she'd wait and just tell Holly. The two of them could slip down here after the others fell asleep and make love on the warm stone floor. She began to sing, softly, testing the room's acoustics.

"Dead girl, dead girl, won't you come to me?
O, where did you lie last night?
In the earth, in the earth, where my soul found its worth
And I waited but no morning came..."

She'd rewritten one of her favorite songs, the one she'd had the most trouble convincing Holly to use in the show.

"It's too well known," Holly said dismissively.

It was—originally recorded by Bill Monroe and then Lead Belly in the 1940s, long before it became notorious after Kurt Cobain sang it in his final performance before his death, broadcast on MTV thirty-odd years ago. Nisa had watched the clip on YouTube when she was a girl. It had terrified her. Not the words, which went over her head, but the way Cobain sang them. The verses an incantation until the end, when his voice rose to a scream then dropped to a hoarse whisper.

Her own voice echoed against the stone walls, soaring like a hawk released from a cage. She forgot to worry about the others hearing her as she flung her head back, her voice rising to a pitch that made her entire body shake. It was the most extraordinary feeling she'd ever had: as if she and her voice had merged with the tower itself, bringing everything around her, stone, stairs, even the old books, into being. She drew a deep breath, clinging to the rails, staring up into the turret above her, dark like the inside of a witch's hat, perched upon Hill House.

"Nisa?"

Nisa's breath faltered. She looked down to see Amanda Greer at the foot of the staircase.

"Nisa! What the hell are you doing?"

Nisa stared at her, confused. "I'm singing. The acoustics here, they're amazing."

"Get the hell down, it's not safe!"

"It's fine!" Nisa gestured at her feet, stable on the step.

Amanda grabbed the rails and shook them, hard. The staircase swayed sickeningly as Nisa yelped in alarm.

"Stop that!" she shouted at Amanda. "Why the fuck would you do that?"

"You get down here!"

Amanda stormed up the lower steps, the extra weight causing the entire structure to shimmy.

"Stop it!" Nisa yelled. "I'm coming, you're going to make me fall—"

She remembered then what had happened to that actor, what was his name? The one Amanda Greer had played against, years ago? Nisa had been too young then, but when Holly'd cast Amanda, Nisa had googled *Amanda Greer.*

Amanda stared up at her, hair wild and eyes wide, her mouth yawning open like a gorgon's. "*Get down!*" she howled.

She's losing it, Nisa thought in sudden panic. *Like Stevie in the parlor...*

"I'm coming! Jesus!" Nisa clutched the rails, walking down as quickly as she dared. The staircase vibrated with every step, threatening her balance.

And yet, Amanda continued to climb. What the fuck was she doing? She was still wearing her rain-soaked coat, wet hair clinging to her face.

"Go back down, damn it!" Nisa screamed at her.

They met eight feet above the floor. Amanda blocked her way, still angry. "What were you thinking? That door is locked for a reason!"

"It wasn't locked," Nisa snapped. "Why the hell are you up here? Move!"

Amanda didn't budge. Was she drunk? Amanda wasn't a big woman but she was taller and stronger than Nisa, and right now she looked like she was ready to throttle her.

"I thought you were in danger," Amanda said at last, biting off each word. "Will you please just get off the stairs?"

Nisa gritted her teeth. She slung one leg over the rail, then the other, took a deep breath, and dropped to the floor. She fell on the balls of her feet, caught her balance, and waited as Amanda huffed back down. The woman looked enraged, way out of proportion to the situation. Nisa was fine! She hadn't even climbed to the top of the stairway—she wasn't crazy.

While Amanda looked like someone who could have pushed a man to his death.

The two of them stared at each other, until Amanda broke the silence.

"What the hell were you thinking, breaking in here?" she demanded, and peeled off her wet coat. "You scared the shit out of me."

"I told you, the door wasn't locked. I wanted to hear what it sounded like. I felt like...singing."

A wave of loss overcame her. To have heard her own voice echoing within this glorious space, carving another room from the air. It was a place where they might all have gathered and been safe, protected by Nisa and her songs: an ancient chain that uncoiled through the centuries, Nisa the most recent link holding them all in place.

And then Amanda had broken the chain.

"You could have killed yourself," fumed Amanda.

"I wasn't going there," Nisa said, with a nod to that upper door. "I'm not stupid."

"I could hear you from outside. It sounded like someone screaming!"

Screaming? Really? Nisa clenched her hands, afraid she might strike this hag who'd insulted her. "Where were you?"

"I went to see Evadne."

"And?"

Amanda said nothing, her face obdurate.

Nisa pushed past her and out into the hall. Amanda followed, stooping to pick up the padlock.

"Leave it," Nisa ordered. "Maybe someone wants it open."

"'Someone'?"

Amanda jammed the padlock back into place and locked it, giving it a tug to make sure the hasp was securely bolted to the door.

"I didn't mean to offend you," she said, more calmly now that she was in control, "but whatever you were singing—it scared me. What was that song?"

"Something I'm working on. Old melody, new lyrics. *My* lyrics."

Amanda sighed. "You do have a beautiful voice. It must have been the acoustics in the tower. Or the weather. The storm is picking up."

"Thank you." Somewhat mollified, Nisa glanced out the window. "It looks nasty out."

"Evadne said it's going to change to snow," Amanda replied dully. "There's a winter storm warning for the whole valley. Up here we could get a foot. Maybe more."

Nisa looked back at her, surprised by the shift in the older woman's tone.

Amanda appeared subdued, shaken, even. By the weather? But Amanda lived upstate and seemed to pride herself on her toughness. Nisa would have thought her a good match for Evadne Morris, another shrewd old bird. She cocked her head, deciding to move past the argument in the tower.

"Amanda, what's wrong? Did she say something?"

Amanda hesitated. "She said we could lose power for days. She seemed to think it was a really bad idea for us to stay here..."

Amanda looked like she was going to continue. But then she glanced past Nisa, who turned to see what had caught her attention.

"Who said that? Evadne?" Holly ambled toward them from the central stairway, her hair damp and face dewy from her shower. "Hey, baby," she murmured, slipping alongside Nisa.

"She talked to Evadne," said Nisa, watching for Amanda's reaction.

Holly glanced at Amanda. "And...?"

Amanda repeated what she'd just told Nisa. Holly shrugged. "I think we'll be okay," she said. "We've got food and plenty of firewood and candles and stuff."

"Maybe we need some garlic," Nisa said sarcastically. How could Holly not see that Amanda was holding something back? "And wolfsbane—I mean, dogbane," she added, as Holly gave her a dirty look.

"Look, we're basically on our own anyway," Holly retorted. "We'll just hunker down. I'd love to have another read-through after dinner. If we lose power, we'll read by candlelight—that's how Elizabeth Sawyer would have done it, anyway."

"So flattering to older complexions," sniped Nisa.

Amanda made a show of ignoring her as she turned to Holly. "Have you seen Stevie?"

"He's probably upstairs," said Nisa. "Sharpening his teeth."

"Look." Amanda pointed to a window. White flakes the size of nickels whirled in the wind, already cloaking the driveway in white. "'It will be rain tonight,'" she said in a sepulchral tone, waiting to see if the others would recognize the line that presaged Banquo's death in the Scottish play.

Holly nodded, then slowly smiled. "'Let it come down.'"

CHAPTER 69

Stevie had fled to his room. With the door firmly shut, he now sat on the edge of his bed, staring at his reflection in the mirror on the opposite wall. He looked haggard, his high cheekbones and deep-set eyes making him appear gaunt and older than he was. *It's this damn play.* Why had he ever agreed to play a demon, especially a dog demon?

And then that cue ball had moved across the billiards room floor. He'd seen it as clearly as he now saw his own face in the mirror. If it had been an eight ball, he'd at least know that the ghost, or whatever it was, had a sense of humor. But no, instead it'd tried to brain him.

He needed to keep his shit together, do whatever he could to kill the burgeoning panic attack he could feel inside him, the electrical current beneath his skin, a taste like old pennies in his mouth.

Yet all he could think of was the message he'd seen.

Come in.

He hugged himself and rocked back and forth on the bed. He couldn't tell anyone about what he'd witnessed. They'd think he was crazy. Maybe he *was* crazy. He practiced his mindful breathing, tried to clear his head of dark thoughts and bring up memories of tranquil blue water, green trees, birdsong. All the shit he'd been taught.

None of it helped. He felt the same horrible sense that an immense black wave was hanging just above his head, poised to drown him, if he let it.

Stop, he thought, rocking faster as he tried to outrace the wave. *Stop stop stop stop...*

He mustered all his strength, slumping across the bed to reach for his duffel on the floor. He found the bottle with his antianxiety meds, removed one of the little blue pills, and split it, using his fingernail to break off a tiny piece. He swallowed it dry, then grabbed his water bottle from the nightstand and tried to wash away the bitter taste.

The medication wouldn't take long to work. Knowing that calmed him. He closed his eyes.

Where did he go from here? That's right, Holly had mentioned another read-through tonight. A short while ago the thought would have filled him with dread, but now he realized it could be a good thing. A chance for him to make amends with Nisa and try another interpretation for his final speech, his favorite lines in the show.

I'll stretch myself, make my body small as a silver wire
And enter the next soul through a breath of tobacco smoke——
They will never know I'm there,
Nestled between heart and ribs, a mote of darkness
Smaller still than air...

He didn't know when he changed from thinking the words to murmuring them aloud, only that his eyes were wide open and he was staring at the wall where the dresser was. The pillows he'd tossed on the floor to hide the little door from Nisa had moved. He must have kicked them aside when he stumbled in. He saw the door clearly, its tiny brass knob sun-bright against the dark-green paint.

He slid from the bed and knelt in front of it.

Come in

What if the flying cue ball hadn't been a threat but an invitation, a means of getting his attention?

Come in

For a long time he stayed where he was, thinking. Was the message still there, on the floor, where he could find it again?

What if it wasn't?

Or what if it was, but someone else—Nisa, no doubt—saw it? What if it somehow led her here, to his little door?

He regarded the door with yearning and trepidation. As though it were a beautifully wrapped present: what if the gift itself was a disappointment? The door was far too small to open onto anything other than a cubbyhole.

Most likely outcome: the door would open onto the nursery. The original owner might have been a perv, though in that case he'd expect the peephole to be set higher up on the wall.

And there was no one in the nursery to be offended if he took a look. He grasped the little knob between his fingers and pulled the door open.

CHAPTER 70

As soon as I walked in, it was clear that Nisa and Amanda had been involved in some kind of argument. Amanda's face was red, and Nisa's gold-brown eyes had gone black, a sure sign she'd lost her temper or was on the verge of doing so.

But then Amanda's news about the storm appeared to shift their moods. Nisa was channeling her earlier fury at Stevie into sarcasm, a good sign. And Amanda seemed to have reverted to playing the Theater Elder, quoting from *Macbeth* as she struck a pose, her dripping coat over one arm.

I glanced at Nisa to see if she'd caught Amanda's reference. She had: she gazed at Amanda in mock horror, holding up one hand as she cried, "'O, treachery! Fly, good Fleance, fly, fly, fly!'"

"Well played, Banquo," said Amanda. "Who's up for a drink?"

Before either of us could reply, the low whoosh of a car came from the driveway. I looked out the window to see Melissa's pickup at the foot of the veranda steps. The passenger door opened and she stepped out into the whirling snow, wearing a hooded parka. I opened the front door, confused, and she hurried into the main entry in a rush of frigid air. "Melissa, hello."

"I'm not staying," she announced, peeling her gloves from cold-reddened hands. "Ainsley says you should leave. So do I. And so does Evadne. For once we all agree on something."

As she mentioned Evadne, she gave Amanda a knowing glance. Amanda's brow furrowed, and Melissa turned to me.

"Once you get down to Hillsdale, the weather isn't so bad. Route 9K is clear, they've put down salt and sand. You should be able to make it to Ashton without any trouble, there's a couple of motels there."

I listened to her politely, then glanced at Nisa, who was watching me carefully. She caught my eye and shrugged. "What do you think, Holly? Your call."

Both Amanda and Melissa began to protest this, but I cut them off.

"Look—like I said, we've got plenty of food and firewood. Candles if we lose power. If it's such a bad storm, who's to say it won't be worse trying to drive through it?"

"Didn't you hear me?" Melissa's voice rose in anger. "The main road is clear, you could—"

"I want to stay." I gave Melissa a tight smile. "I appreciate your concern—thank you. But we're all adults here, with a job to do. And we don't need lights to rehearse," I continued, seeing in my mind's eye how the others would look in the glow of candles, Nisa's voice circling us, a silver bird on the wing. The experience would draw us even closer, bind us so that we could carry it back to the city, into our showcase.

I looked again at Melissa. "We've paid to stay here. I signed that lease in good faith, and Ainsley had no problem with cashing my check. I don't want to drive around looking for some crappy motel that's open in the off-season. I don't even think we could find one this far north."

"Don't you have rich friends outside of Ashton?" Melissa's expression clearly signaled she thought I was not just foolish but out of my mind. Impatiently, she tugged back her parka's hood. "You could stay with them. It's not safe for you here, Holly. For any of you. Some bad shit has gone down at Hill House over the years."

I began to reply, and stopped. She'd parroted Giorgio's exact words to me. I stared at Melissa's red hands, clasped so that her amber ring caught the light from one of the wall sconces, its stone shining like a lit match. When I lifted my gaze to her face, she gave me a nearly imperceptible nod.

"Thank you, Melissa." Nisa stepped beside me and linked her arm through mine. "We really do appreciate how concerned you all are. But we'll be fine."

Melissa looked from Nisa to me to Amanda. Without a word, she hurried past us to the door that led to the kitchen. I started after her, but she'd already rushed back into the main hall.

"We have plenty of food," I said, assuming she'd checked the fridge.

"And we'll fill the tubs with water," chimed in Amanda. "Where I live, we lose power for a day or two every winter."

"If you stay here, you're on your own." Melissa scanned the entrance hall, her gaze lingering on the main staircase. "Where's your friend Stevie?"

"He needed a time-out," said Nisa. "In his room, probably."

"You should all stay together. Try to keep a fire going."

Amanda mimed rabbit ears. "That didn't work out so well this morning."

"Keep a fire going," Melissa repeated as she pulled her hood up. "If something happens, calling 911 won't help you—if you can even get a signal. We only have state police, and they're dispatched from county headquarters. It would take them at least an hour to get here. That's a best-case scenario, in good weather. This isn't a town road, and Tru won't come out to plow till the storm's over. You could be up here for days. A week, even."

"We're all good." I smiled, ablaze with that certainty. We really were.

Nisa's hand tightened on my arm. I looked over to see her smile reassuringly at Melissa. "Thank you again. Be careful out there."

Melissa raised a finger, silencing us. She tipped back her head as though listening, and gazed up at the ceiling. Her eyelids fluttered shut, and when she opened them wide, I saw her anger give way to something like despair.

"It's too late, then," she murmured, and walked to the front door.

I watched her, surprised and unnerved—I thought she might put up more of a fight. Having glimpsed her distress, I almost hoped she would.

Instead Melissa opened the door and only briefly hesitated, her hand resting on the heavy knob. Again the light struck her amber ring. Would it burn you, if you touched it? She stared at the ring, too, before lifting her head to look directly at me. Her lips didn't move, but I clearly heard her words again, as if they were coming in through earbuds.

Too late.

She hurried down the steps, through the blowing snow and into her truck, and drove away, fishtailing around the curve in the road until lost to sight.

CHAPTER 71

He'd expected to uncover a small, dark space. Not a crawl space: maybe a boarded-up doorway, or an opening that held ductwork. That, or he should be gazing into the nursery.

Instead, the little green door opened onto what appeared to be a long, straight, narrow tunnel, blindingly bright. He covered his eyes with his hand. Waited for the brilliant light to disappear, for everything to dim to a pleasing shadowy darkness.

That didn't happen. Smears of light moved across his eyelids as his heart beat faster and faster. When he couldn't stand it anymore, he dropped his hand, blinking painfully.

The tunnel was still there, a brilliant rectangle framed by torn bits of purple wallpaper. The passage couldn't possibly extend more than a few inches from where he crouched, at most a foot, before it opened onto the nursery.

But it did. It stretched an impossible distance, to a far-off point where it pulsed with an intoxicating swirl of color, like a cartoon vision of a black hole. Bleached copper shot through with veinous green and blue-black, a lurid red that reminded him of the wine-stained tablecloth. The play of colors seemed oddly solid, as though objects moved deep within, like the bits of colored glass or shell inside a kaleidoscope.

Squinting, he saw them, then, within the whorl: tiny human shapes—children, and larger figures in navy blue and white. A reddish slash that was a tablecloth on a patch of emerald-green lawn freckled with daffodil yellow, tiger lily orange. He drew closer to the doorway, pressing his face into it, longing to be closer to them, until he felt a warmth like the summer sun.

He wasn't imagining it. The tiny figures were real, they were alive—he saw them as through the wrong end of a telescope. One child wore red. The other was too faint for him to make out. A yellow shirt? A lively speck raced between them. Another child? But a child that small wouldn't be able to move that fast. A dog, he thought. It was like one of his paper theaters come to life.

An irresistible urge overwhelmed him, to grasp the magical panorama and hold it.

He moved his face away from the opening and rolled up one sleeve. Then he angled himself so one shoulder butted against the wall, and reached inside. He had long arms and big hands, with very long fingers; yet still he couldn't reach, pushing himself harder against the wall, extending his arm until it felt like it might pop from the shoulder socket.

Then, incredibly, his shoulder passed through the little doorway, into the tunnel. He expected his skin to scrape against the wooden doorframe but felt only a delicious heat, and a loose bit of wallpaper brushing his cheek, like a kiss. But with his face pressed against the wall, he could no longer see the bright figures. He'd have to get his neck and head in there, too.

Abruptly he felt exhausted. Also sore, the way he felt after a heavy yoga session. He lay there with a crick in his neck, staring at the hideous violet-patterned wallpaper. Some remote part of his brain whispered to him that this was wrong, that he must be hallucinating; yet the reality he'd entered shouted otherwise. And why would he—why would anyone—choose to remain here, in this world, rather than in the shimmering landscape he'd glimpsed, just out of reach?

He listened for sounds from the hallway but it was silent. The others must be downstairs, or napping. He was safe.

He caught his breath, and pressed on.

CHAPTER 72

As the door closed after Melissa, Amanda said, "My, that wasn't upsetting at all."

Nisa laughed shakily as I walked to the window and stared out. The sense of triumph I'd felt at standing up to Melissa slid away from me, replaced by unease.

Too late.

Had she been threatening me? I remembered how I'd felt after Macy-Lee's accusations, that sense of her trying to wrest away something that was mine by rights.

Ours, this time, I reminded myself. My play's success depended on the others, too. I needed to remain calm, keep them on the rails.

"It's cold enough that we can just put all the food outside if we lose power," I said, pushing away my disquiet. I walked to the front door and bolted it. "There're plenty of flashlights. And candles, and matches."

"I saw some water jugs in the pantry," Nisa piped up.

"And we have lots of wine," added Amanda. "All the major food groups."

"So we won't end up like the Donner Party," said Nisa.

"More the Dishonor Party," said Amanda.

I turned toward them, smiling, and froze.

A huge black hare stood upright in the kitchen doorway—far bigger than the ones I'd seen before. Its front legs were crooked like those of a praying mantis, its lips drawn back to reveal long white teeth and a red tongue. It stared at me fixedly, its coppery eyes twin suns in eclipse.

"Holly?" Nisa asked in a small voice.

Before I could say anything, she too turned, then screamed.

"What is it?" cried Amanda. Whirling, she clapped her hand to her mouth. "Oh my god."

Nisa ran to the stairway as Amanda dashed in the other direction. I remained where I was, too dumbfounded to move. The hare leaned back slightly, as if considering, then sprang toward me.

It struck my chest, knocking me down, and I cried out as my head hit the floor. Yet when I tried to push it from me, I couldn't get hold of its fur—my hands ripped through it like wet newsprint. No matter how I fought, there was only moist warmth, something gelatinous smearing my cheek as I rolled onto my stomach and covered my head with my hands, its weight pressing me down. It grew heavier, far more so than a creature that size should be, and I felt something else moving inside it, something—

A blast of cold air hit me, nearly as shocking as the hare.

"Get out!" Amanda shouted. *"Get out!"*

The weight pressing into my back lifted as the hare bounded from me to the floor, landing with a loud thump and scurrying off. I pushed myself up to see Amanda brandishing a broom. She must have also flung the front door open. Snow gusted in. Within the blue-white doorway, the hare paused to stare at me, its silhouette as precise as though cut from black paper, before it turned and vaulted into the night.

"Holly! Are you all right?"

I saw Amanda standing above me, her hair wild, still clutching the broom.

"I think so," I replied, shaken, my elbows aching as I got to my feet. Amanda closed the front door and took my arm as Nisa rushed to join us.

"Holly! Holly, are you——"

I stumbled past her to sit on the bottom step of the central stairway. I wiped my hands on my jeans, shuddering as I thought of the hare's horrible moist touch. I drew a hand to my cheek, expecting to find some slimy residue. But my skin felt dry, cool from the blast of cold outside air. When I looked at my hands, and where I'd rubbed them on my jeans, I saw nothing.

Stevie's fetch, I thought, sickened.

Nisa sank onto the step next to me and took my hand in both of hers. "Are you sure you're all right? Holy fuck. How the hell did it get in?"

"The kitchen." Amanda used the broom to point across the hall. "When I ran in there to get this, the back door was open. She opened it—Melissa."

Nisa looked up. "I wondered what the hell she was doing."

"Letting the hare in." Amanda strode to the front door, closed and locked it.

"But why?"

"Because she's a witch," said Amanda. "They all are. Inside Evadne's house, she had some kind of altar. She told me we need to leave Hill House. Ordered me, actually. She and Ainsley and Melissa, they're up to something. Those rings…"

She looked at me, as realization dawned. "You were there, Holly. You talked to her. What if Hill House is their coven house, or whatever it is witches have? That's why they don't want us here. They're trying to scare us off."

"Well, it's working," said Nisa, stroking my hair.

"No." I forced a smile. The simple act of sitting here, feeling the sturdy steps beneath and behind me, strengthened my will. I was damned if I was going to let Evadne and her creatures—hare, fetch, whatever they were—keep me from the play. "I'm okay—it just knocked the breath out of me. But Amanda, I think you're right. Evadne, Ainsley, I guess Melissa, too—they have been trying to scare us."

"But that doesn't make sense," said Nisa. "Ainsley rented Hill House to you."

"Because she really needs the money." I stared at the front door, glad that Amanda had turned the deadbolt.

"It could be a scam," Nisa said thoughtfully. "It's not like this place has any online reviews. No one ever stays here long. So she just takes their money and banks it?"

Amanda thumped the broom on the floor, calling us to attention. She waited for Nisa and me to look up before she continued, in the powerful voice I recalled from *The Stronger,* her eyes flashing as though she stood on a stage and not in the hallway, hair and makeup in disarray from the storm.

"Didn't you hear me? They're witches—*real* witches. Like I said, this is where they meet, their coven or whatever. And yes, Ainsley needs the money, but the others don't like that she rents it out. It's dangerous, that's what Evadne told me. That's why Melissa keeps an eye on us while we're here, as Evadne tries to scare us off.

"You can't deny it," she said curtly when I opened my mouth to argue. "Every single one of us has witnessed something strange, even supernatural. What if it has all been *real*? The three of them are in some ongoing power struggle, and we're simply collateral."

Amanda fell silent, head thrown back like she was waiting for applause. After a moment, she looked down at us where we sat. "Well?"

"Okay," I said, "but still—what do we do? I'm not leaving."

"Me neither." I turned in surprise at Nisa's decisive tone. "This place—it does bring something out in us. Even Stevie in the parlor—that was weird, but you were right, Holly. He finally came up with a really scary bit of business for the play. For *us*.

"You'll see, Amanda," she went on. "That scene with Tomasin and Elizabeth? I read for you while you were out. And Stevie nailed it. Almost nailed me," she added. "And okay, it was scary. But this is like one of those spaces Stevie always talks about with his pagan friends—a thin place, where you can access things you can't, normally. I think that's what inspired Stevie. And me. That's why Evadne and the others don't want us at Hill House—they don't want to share it, and they're trying to frighten us so we leave." She tightened her hold on my hand. "But I'm not going. My voice sounds better here than it ever has."

Nisa's face had gone pale, but her eyes gleamed as she lifted her head and sang.

"If all those old women were like hares on the mountain
Then all us young maids would get scythes and go hunting..."

My neck prickled: she'd changed the words. Her voice, too, sounded altered—much deeper, almost like it had been looped through Stevie's music software.

Her expression was one I'd never seen before.

I whispered, "Stop, Nisa."

"It's just a song," Nisa murmured as the words died in the soaring shadows above us. She withdrew her hand from mine.

"It sounds more like a spell," said Amanda. "Which I'm all for, by the way." Still holding the broom, she looked like a witch herself. "Fight fire with fire. We're here to workshop Holly's play—a play *about a witch,*" she went on. "It's like rehearsing *Hamlet* in an actual castle. The publicity will be fabulous. Tell me I'm wrong."

"I don't think you're wrong." I chose my words carefully. Nisa's singing, the shock of the hare, Amanda's admission that she thought witches were real—I was starting to feel like I'd been drugged. Like I could no longer trust my own senses.

But this thought receded quickly, drowned out by another. Louder, stronger. Insisting that nothing was more important than being here, now, with my friends and this play. The two warring sensations ricocheted inside me, sickening me.

I took a long breath and pushed myself up from the step, taking in the hall around us. The outside light had leaked away from the windows. The dark, empty room seemed cavernous. Streaks of black seeped from beneath countless closed doors, and the side halls looked like train tunnels, impossibly long and leading only into an even greater darkness. The casements rattled as the wind whined outside, snow and sleet pattering against the glass.

I walked to a window and gazed out. Several inches of snow already covered the veranda. My car and Amanda's resembled large white animals crouched in the driveway. I peered past them to the woods, stiffened.

A silvery, shifting column of light moved within the trees, rotating, a great spindle being turned by huge invisible hands. The same spinning apparition I'd watched earlier.

I started to cry out, pointing for the others to see. But as I raised my hand, the column shattered into myriad flecks of light, which dissolved like sparks into the darkness, indistinguishable now from the storm.

CHAPTER 73

H as anyone seen Stevie?"

I jumped as Nisa came up behind me. Did she know what I'd been watching? "No."

I walked quickly from the window, noting the faint glow that clung to the second-floor landing. Stevie must have left his bedroom door ajar.

"I'll go find him." Nisa accompanied me, leaning forward to whisper in my ear. "You're brilliant, baby—don't you ever forget it. I'm so glad we're here."

She moved away, her lips brushing my cheek, and headed for the stairs. I smiled after her. She understood what I was doing here, after all. The dark spell of whatever I'd seen outside was broken.

Amanda still stood in the middle of the hall, broom in hand, mouth pursed as though questioning how she'd come to hold it. She shook herself and looked at me. "We should get dinner going, right? While we still have power."

I heard Nisa's footsteps on the second floor, the creak of a door opening. "Good idea," I agreed, and together we started for the kitchen.

CHAPTER 74

Nisa took the first few steps of the wide stairway quickly, but slowed as she approached the landing. The memory of the carving returned—that woman being hunted like an animal—and she tightened her hold on the handrail. And then those terrible explosions, like a car crash. For a moment she paused, halfway up the stairs. Below, milky light from the snow outside dissolved the shapes of furniture, doors, walls, until they all disappeared into a blue-gray haze. A cold draft snaked along the staircase, sliding up the sleeves of Stevie's too-big sweater, so that she shivered. She'd give it back to him, he might want it for himself, skinny wraith that he was.

She recalled the times they'd lain in bed together, skin to skin, Stevie luxuriating in the warmth of her body, his hands tangled in her curls. That was over, she thought, certainly while they were all here together, working. She'd forsake Stevie and anything else, to have the chance to hear herself sing again, as she had in the tower.

As quickly as they'd come, her fears melted away. The house was so beautiful, even now as night filled it. Especially now. What was that line Stevie used to quote to her, whenever she told him his pagan friends were irrational? Something about the mark of true intelligence being the ability to keep two opposed ideas in your head at the same time.

That was what she was doing now. What they were all doing.

She began once more to walk, until she reached the landing. Despite the lack of windows, somehow the same eerie light spilled into the corridor, but gentler now, moonlight on a dark pond. She paced carefully past the doors to Amanda's room and the one she shared with Holly, the carpet muffling her footsteps as she drew near to Stevie's room.

Like theirs, the door to his room was shut. Again she halted, listening for any sound inside. Not a peep. He might have his headphones on, listening to a playback of his recording. Or he might be napping. She raised her hand to knock, thought better of it as she glanced down at his baggy sweater, the frayed hem of her short skirt. She'd change first, into something nice. Remind him of what he was missing, even if she had no intention of falling into bed with him again.

She drew her arm to her face. The sweater's soft wool still held a trace of Stevie's scent, his acrid sweat and the warmer smells of bay rum mingled with cannabis. *Oh, Stevie,* she thought, and let her arm drop. Holly smelled sweeter, of musk and salt and burnt sugar. Holly's mouth would taste of wine and her skin would burn from Nisa's own heat.

A sound came from somewhere down the hall. A click, followed by a low whir and a voice singing. It was the same song she'd been thinking of earlier, from the empty cassette tape she'd found in the tower. "Sister Europe."

Nisa yanked her head around and stared at the end of the corridor, where a seam of gray light emanated from beneath the far door. She'd seen Holly close the nursery door that afternoon, heard the latch click with relief.

Now she felt a sharp, electrical urge to walk there, open it and fling herself inside. Like the way she felt sometimes when she was onstage, gazing down at the upraised faces: at the longing and ecstasy they held, rapture or desire that Nisa herself had ignited, that she wanted to leap into, to let herself be swallowed by that sea of yearning. She'd never leapt, of course—folk singers don't have mosh pits.

And there'd be nowhere to fly inside the nursery.

The singing stopped. Or perhaps she'd just imagined it? Frightened, she backed away from Stevie's door and quickly walked to her own room. Inside, she turned on the lights, reassured by the ugly, too-bright glow of the incandescent bulbs behind their cheap shades, the scents of shampoo and Holly's Jasmin et Tabac. She remembered her earlier resolve to dress up before she got Stevie. She'd brought her favorite vintage tunic, purple velvet with silver embroidery and tassels on each sleeve. She tugged off Stevie's sweater and let it flop onto the floor, pulled on her tunic, black leggings, and purple pleather ankle boots.

She inspected herself in the mirror, swiped on some blusher and touched up her lips with her own rose-pink lip gloss. She couldn't remember why she'd used Amanda's earlier. No one had even noticed, except, perhaps, the house itself. Maybe that was reason enough? She brushed her hair, the black curls springing up even as she patted them down, dabbed her throat with her lilac and freesia perfume.

Turning from the mirror, she paused, then stepped to the window to look outside. Snow caked the glass. The cold draft moved the curtain, and she watched how the paper birches tossed in the wind, white gouts falling to the ground beneath them. Something moved among the trees. The boy? The hare? But this was only a hemlock branch, whipping upward as it dislodged its load of snow. Nisa pressed her face to the window, so cold that ice sheathed the glass. She scanned the ground below, but all had grown still, only her breath fogging the pane into ghostly shapes.

Satisfied, she moved away, picked up Stevie's sweater from where she'd dropped it, and, leaving the light on behind her, returned to his room.

She still didn't hear anything from inside. Usually, when Stevie played back and edited his recordings, he didn't wear headphones. Sometimes it sounded like he had an entire party going on behind his door, and occasionally he really did.

But not now. He really must be hard at work, or asleep.

"Stevie?" she called out softly. He didn't answer. "Dinner's ready, you want to come down?"

Still no reply. She rapped at the wood, raising her voice. "Hey, Liddell—it's wine o'clock! Everyone's downstairs!"

Glancing down, she noticed bright light now glowing from beneath his door, and flickering hints of color. Was he watching a movie? Something he'd downloaded before they left the city?

She cracked the door and peeked inside. Clothes were strewn across his bed, amid rumpled blankets, his empty duffel. His closed laptop sat on top of a pillow. The bedside lamp was off.

But on the far side of the room, beyond the bed, a carnival swirl of light and shadow jumped and receded, like a lava lamp. It seemed to be coming from the floor, its source hidden by the bed. His phone? Some app he was playing? Maybe he did have his headphones on back there.

She knocked again, yelling his name as she pushed the door open and walked inside.

"Stevie! C'mon, we're—"

It took her a few seconds to find him, once she'd rounded the bed—lying on the floor beside a bureau he'd shoved out of the way. His head was twisted, so she couldn't see him clearly. Had he fallen, or hurt himself?

"Stevie?" she called, frightened. The sweater slid from her hands to the floor.

He noticed her then, and shouted something unintelligible, contorting himself as he moved away from the wall.

What the hell was he doing?

She felt hot, then cold, mortified: she'd caught him jerking off. She backed toward the door as he lurched to his feet, grabbed his duffel, and threw it against the wall right behind him.

It fell beside the bureau and the room dimmed. But not before Nisa saw the source of the carnival colors: a small gap in the wall, just above the floor. Stevie kicked at the duffel until it slumped firmly against the wall, and the light went out.

He raised his head to stare at Nisa. She couldn't read his face clearly. Not embarrassment or shame. He looked more angry, and also furtive. High, maybe? His pupils shrunken, dark circles around his eyes.

She pointed to where the light had flickered moments ago.

"What—what was that?"

"Nothing!" He stumbled across the room and pushed her through the doorway, hard. She cried out, his fingernails biting into her arm as he held on to her. "Let's go."

She tried to escape but he was too strong. "But what was that?" she demanded, as he dragged her down the hall. "That light? Is something on fire?"

"Nothing is on fire!" His face contorted the way it had when they'd read the scene between Tomasin and Elizabeth. He wasn't Stevie but some in-between thing. Like the hare, she thought in growing horror. "What the hell is wrong with you, barging in?"

"I knocked! I was shouting at you, you—"

"I was doing yoga."

"Yoga?" she repeated in disbelief.

"Shut up. Let's just go."

They'd reached the top of the steps. Stevie held on to the newel cap, blocking her way so she couldn't get past him to return to his room. "Let's just go," he said again, calmer now.

She waited for him to explain or apologize or laugh it off. But he only remained where he was, breathing hard. Staring at her yet somehow not seeing her. She bit her lip. Stevie was so sensitive, you never knew what might set him off. He might have smoked something stronger than weed or, god knows, taken some psychedelic, thinking it would improve his performance. Such a fucking Stevie thing to do.

She glanced down the hall again to his room. Out of nowhere, she felt that same urgent electricity, a low-level shock pulsing just beneath her skin. Her worry over Stevie's odd behavior was replaced by an avid curiosity, powerful as the need for a drink or cigarettes.

"I'm sorry I barged in, okay?" She plucked at his sleeve. "I brought your sweater, I thought you might be cold. But I dropped it..."

She smiled at him in apology, pretending that she was looking at the wall, the floor, anything other than what she was intent on: the door to Stevie's room. She knew him too well—he was hiding something. What?

What does he have in there?

"Don't worry about it," Stevie said after a moment. Only it didn't sound like Stevie, but someone pretending to be him. *Like an actor playing Stevie,* she thought, even though that was crazy. An actor playing himself.

"Yeah, okay." She looked at him and smiled, an actor playing Nisa. "We should go downstairs, they're waiting for us to start dinner. Melissa came by a little while ago and told us about the big storm. Everyone thinks we should leave."

"I'm not leaving."

His voice was the same, almost robotic, though now he stared at her with an implied threat. Like he'd hurt her if she tried to make him go. *Really?*

"Nobody's leaving, Stevie," she reassured him, and pushed past him to head downstairs. "We all agree. We're all finally having breakthroughs here. Maybe we started something this afternoon in the parlor, you and me."

"That's good," he said. "I'd like to think that." He walked beside her, clinging to the handrail like he might lose his balance as he ushered her down. He took a deep breath, then released it. "Wow. I really am hungry."

Abruptly he sounded like himself again. Nisa took a few more steps, keeping her face composed and voice steady as she asked, "What was that light in your room? By the floor?"

"Just an app on my phone. I was meditating."

"I thought you were doing yoga."

"Same thing."

She nodded, trying to feel relieved. She'd have to ask him if he'd taken something, once he'd had a couple of drinks. Maybe he'd share with her, later. In his room, where they could watch the light show.

They'd reached the bottom of the steps. Stevie appeared distracted. He looked in the direction of the kitchen, its blade of cheerful yellow light slicing through the darkness, and turned the other way.

"I'll be right back," he said, peeling off toward the other wing, where only the blue gleam of the snow filled the dark windows. "Meet you in the kitchen."

Nisa watched him go.

He was lying.

As he walked away, she'd seen his phone in his back jeans pocket. He hadn't picked it up from the floor. It had been there all along. That light had come from somewhere else. A crawl space behind the wall?

She dug her nails into her palms in mounting anger. Why had he lied, what was he hiding from her? Something special: something beautiful. They'd always shared with each other, always had so much in common. She and Holly were so different: Holly down-to-earth and ambitious, if often dogged. Whereas Nisa and Stevie were mercurial, their moods prone to change with the light.

Especially here.

And they'd never kept secrets. Not from each other. So why was he doing it now?

She'd see for herself, later. She deserved to have a secret, too.

CHAPTER 75

He ran to the billiards room, nearly tripping over the rolled-up carpet just inside the door. There was barely enough light for him to see by, so he used his phone's flashlight, feeling along the wall until he found the rough depression left by the cue ball's impact. He flicked plaster dust from his fingers, swept the phone's light across the floor. There it was, the message, white as frost against the hardwood boards.

COME IN

It was real. Just as the door was real, and the numinous colors that had bloomed inside it.

COME IN

A message meant for only him. Not Holly, not Amanda, certainly not Nisa.

He checked that he was still alone, then used his foot to erase the words, stooped to run his shirtsleeve across the pale smudge that remained. What a freaking bitch Nisa was, storming into his space like that! She knew what he'd found, he could tell from the way her bratty little eyes had scanned the bedroom.

At least the message was gone now. He couldn't do anything about the dent in the wall, but he bet the others wouldn't even notice it. If they did, he'd just play dumb. This place was like a funhouse; everyone was constantly stumbling over some new pocket of weirdness.

Yet he was the only one who'd found something beautiful. He yearned to be back in his room, to reach into the tunnel and hold his hand out toward those tiny enchanted figures, watch them drop into his cupped palm. He would never hurt them. He'd protect them—or, better still, he'd squeeze into the passage and join them, shrinking until he, too, was a glittering spark, safe.

He had never been anywhere before that made him feel so safe.

Tonight he'd lock his door, push the night table against it so Nisa wouldn't be able to sneak in again. For now, though, he needed to keep her, or anyone else, from suspecting what he'd found.

He turned and went to join the others.

CHAPTER 76

I'll set the table," Amanda announced, alone with Holly in the kitchen. She'd put away her wet coat in the downstairs closet, set the broom back where she'd found it. Glancing in the dining room mirror, she briefly weighed going upstairs to change, decided against it. She smoothed down her hair and adjusted her sweater. She looked fine, dignified even, despite her disturbing run-in with Evadne.

Or perhaps because of it. Now that she was safely back at Hill House, she felt a peculiar solidarity with Evadne, whose warnings demonstrated that she took Amanda seriously, maybe even trusted her. If Evadne and her cronies were, in fact, witches—and Amanda was willing to believe they were—so what? Evadne had made clear how she felt about Ainsley's irresponsibility in renting out Hill House. Amanda would keep that in mind, moving forward.

But she wasn't scared. She couldn't imagine Evadne gossiping and whispering about her with Ainsley and Melissa, the way these children had. Evadne's iron-rod demeanor reminded her of Elizabeth Sawyer's, once the witch had acknowledged her own power.

I can tap into that, too. Literally, she thought, recalling Evadne's finger tapping her amber ring. That would be a nice bit of business to bring to her performance.

The memory of the others' whispers still disturbed her, but she forced herself not to think of it. These people were young enough to be her children. She wasn't inclined to forgive them their youth—she wished she could seize it for herself—but she knew that sabotaging another's performance could easily backfire. Stevie might steal the show, and perhaps Nisa, too; but only if Amanda let them. Her years of experience overshadowed theirs by decades. Give her a stage, even a makeshift one in a rickety old house, and she knew what to do.

Acting demanded a safe space, a fine and private place within the larger world: Amanda knew that Hill House was fulfilling that role.

She knew Holly felt the same way. So much was riding on these precious few days and the showcase that would follow. It was good for them both to indulge in something mindless for a few minutes—warm up food for dinner, light candles—reset after the shock of that animal attacking Holly. Though right now, Holly herself seemed mostly fine. Did rabbits—hares—carry rabies?

But it hadn't bitten her, just knocked her down.

Still: who expects something like *that* to happen in their short-term rental? Amanda paused as she opened a cabinet. "Are you all right, Holly? That hare..."

"I'm okay. Thanks." She mustered a smile, peeling foil from the tray of lasagna that Melissa and Tru had left the day before.

She's putting a brave face on it, thought Amanda. *Good girl.* They understood one another and the need to keep going, then. She smiled back and rummaged through the cabinet, rooting through piles of white napkins and tablecloths, until she found some brightly colored vinyl placemats. She pulled them out, wrinkling her nose at their musty smell, and examined them.

Clean, just unused for a very long time. She held one up: a familiar, bright floral pattern, popular in the 1980s—Marimekko. Vibrant poppies, red and black and yellow. Vinyl meant they wouldn't stain. She searched until she found four matching cloth napkins and put them on the dining room table, along with plates and silverware and flashlights. Outside, the wind battered the walls and windows, and snow was piling up on the veranda. Still, the lights hadn't flickered yet, and Tru Libby's lasagna smelled delicious as Holly heated it in the oven.

But beyond the brightly lit kitchen loomed the rest of the house. If Amanda let her gaze extend past this room, she could sense it, crouching like a trapdoor spider, waiting to spring. *Light,* she thought, *we need more light.*

She stepped past Holly and into the pantry, where she found a box of beeswax candles and some matches. She set the candles into a heavy crystal candelabra and placed it on the dining room table, lit the candles and inhaled their honeyed fragrance. Even with the lamps turned on, the room remained dim, though the candles danced bravely. Amanda regarded them for a minute, wishing there were more.

Not even a row of follow spots could dispel the gloom here, she thought grimly. But she wasn't going to let it get the better of her. What would Elizabeth Sawyer do? Make her alliances. Fight back.

She returned to the kitchen, where Holly had removed the lasagna and garlic bread from the oven.

"That smells divine!" Amanda exclaimed, opening a bottle of wine. She poured two glasses, handed one to Holly. "'Give them great meals of beef and iron and steel, they will eat like wolves and fight like devils.'"

Holly laughed. She wiped her hands on her jeans and took the proffered glass. "How about vegetarian lasagna, and we eat like actors, then play devils after we're finished?"

"Works for me," Amanda replied, and clinked her glass against Holly's. "I'm just having a titch," she assured her, indicating her glass. Which held more than a titch, she admitted to herself, but it had been a very long day. "I would love to do another read-through after dinner."

"Great minds think alike. Oh, I think I hear Nisa." Holly poured another glass and walked into the dining room. "Nisa, there you are! I was going to send a search party."

Amanda followed, carrying the lasagna to the table and watching as Nisa hurried to join them. "Where's Stevie?" she asked.

"He'll be right here." Nisa's expression clouded, though she immediately took the wineglass and smiled at her girlfriend. "It smells amazing, Hols."

Holly dished food onto the plates, and Amanda carried in the garlic bread. Nisa stood by the door, staring intently into the darkened hall as she sipped her wine. She looked different than she had an hour or so ago—she'd dressed for dinner, which made Amanda regret not doing the same.

Holly seemed not to have even noticed Nisa's efforts. Had the vintage purple tunic and stylish ankle boots been meant for Stevie? Hmmm. But the shift in Nisa extended past her wardrobe. She seemed to be measuring how best to draw, or perhaps deflect, attention, posed on the threshold between the dining room's candlelit glow and the deepening shadows of the hall. Less the engaging, capricious, young artiste; more conniving diva. *Takes one to know one,* Amanda thought, and set an empty wineglass at Stevie's place.

He appeared moments later, pale and disheveled. Amanda felt an uncharitable frisson of schadenfreude. The others had remarked on how wonderful Stevie had been, rehearsing one of their biggest scenes *sans* Amanda. If he was so drained now, perhaps he'd give a lackluster performance when they rehearsed later.

"Sorry," he said, running a hand through his long hair. "I lost track of time."

He blew right past Nisa—if she'd dressed up for him, he took no more notice than Holly had—and went directly to the table, slipping into his chair and reaching for the wine to fill his glass. He took a gulp, caught Amanda's disapproving look as she settled beside him.

"Sorry," he said again. He set down his glass and waited until Holly and Nisa had joined them, like dutiful children who've been scolded.

"To the Devil's dog," Amanda said, raising her glass to his wan face. She'd take the high road, or pretend to. Stevie eyed her warily, his own glass still on the table as Holly and Nisa toasted him, too.

"The Devil's dog!"

Amanda finished her wine. When Stevie remained silent, she refilled her glass and raised it once more. "'The dog, to gain some private ends, went mad and bit the man,'" she recited. "'The man recovered of the bite, the dog it was that died.'"

Nisa laughed, but Stevie regarded her coolly. Amanda shrugged. "A mote of levity, Stevie, to relieve the dark."

She reached across the table for the casserole dish. "More lasagna, Stevie?" she asked, though he hadn't yet touched his. Still, he nodded, and Amanda spooned some onto his plate.

"I heard you were fantastic this afternoon," she continued, her tone confiding, though she made sure he took note of her sharp gaze. "Really immersing yourself in the part. I gather Nisa was a bit surprised? That made me rethink certain elements in the script, things I hadn't really thought about before."

Holly raised an eyebrow. "Like what?"

"Like the real danger that Tomasin poses to Elizabeth. In the original, the dog's sometimes comic relief. But people really did believe in witches back then, and devils, too. That's why the real Elizabeth was executed. Shakespeare had only died a few years before. Probably he wrote the Scottish play as a believer."

"I doubt that's true." Stevie dug into his lasagna. "Seriously, what kind of idiot believes in witches?"

"You, for one," said Nisa, with an edge of hostility.

"That doesn't mean Shakespeare did."

"You're just being contrary."

Amanda broke in before their tiff could escalate. "Here, I'm willing to give them the benefit of the doubt." She lowered her voice to Elizabeth's gravelly tone. "'And so in this twilight and midnight of the world, when sin flourishes everywhere, when charity has grown cold, the evil of witches and their companions surrounds us.'"

"That's not from my play," said Holly.

"No. It's from *The Malleus Maleficarum, the Hammer of Witches*," said

Stevie. He turned to Amanda, a glint of admiration in his eyes at last. "'And it is a fact that some definite agreement is formed between witches and devils whereby some shall be able to hurt and others to heal, that so they may more easily ensnare the minds of the simple and recruit the ranks of their abandoned and hateful society.'"

"Hear, hear." Amanda lifted her glass. She had him now. "To an agreement between witches and devils."

They all drank, and the mood improved. Outside, the wind howled, gusting so that the windows shook. Heavy snow obscured the world beyond Hill House, trees and road hidden behind a scrim of leaden gray.

Here, however, they were safe, and Amanda let herself bask in the candlelight and camaraderie that she'd conjured. Like Elizabeth, she thought, and smiled to herself. She held court, regaling them with stories, making sure everyone's wineglass was charged.

Holly opened a second bottle, then a third. Everyone drank copiously, so Amanda didn't worry that she was the only one cutting loose. They needed the release, for god's sake! The chance to let down their guard and relax. They'd earned it.

She had, anyway. Amanda refilled her glass.

After an hour or so, they segued again into the day's unsettling events, agreeing this time that they'd become part of a story they'd tell each other for decades, after the triumphant opening night of Holly's play, after their own individual successes during its run, and in all the years to follow. The wine made it easier to believe.

"To *Witching Night*," said Amanda, standing to make a toast.

"And to Holly," said Nisa.

Stevie lurched to his feet. "To Amanda."

"To Amanda," they chimed, and Amanda beamed, knowing that whatever the future brought for Holly's play, tonight she was its star.

"We need to keep our heads clear enough for another read-through," she said modestly. "Right, Holly?"

"Wait." Nisa hopped up, steadying herself before she wove into the kitchen. She returned with a bottle of single malt and four small tumblers. She poured an inch into each glass and passed them around, held hers up to the candlelight, the tumbler glowing like Evadne's and Ainsley's and Melissa's amber rings.

"Who fears a painted devil?" She gazed pointedly at Stevie. "Not me."

She knocked back her whiskey, face flushed, lifted her head, and began to sing.

> *"Said the lord to his mistress*
> *As he rode away*
> *Beware of dark Lamkin*
> *Who comes up this way…"*

Stevie's eyes narrowed. Amanda's, too. Only Holly smiled as her lover's soaring voice filled the room.

> *"Why should I fear Lamkin*
> *Or any of his men*
> *When my doors are all bolted*
> *And my windows shut in?"*

Nisa stared at the ceiling. She seemed to be watching the wisps of rising candle smoke as they faded into the shadows. Her voice hitched and her eyes widened, but then she caught herself.

> *"There was blood in the nursery*
> *And blood in the hall*
> *And blood on the stairs*
> *Her heart's blood was all…"*

"Stop." Holly grabbed Nisa's hand. "Do you hear that?"

Everyone turned to where she pointed, into the main hall. A series of low, insistent knocks echoed through the dining room.

"Someone's at the front door," Holly whispered. She let go of Nisa and stumbled to her feet, hurried to the entrance to the hall where she stood, listening. The knocks continued, louder and more urgent. Her eyes caught the flicker of candlelight to gleam eerily from the shadows. She glanced nervously back at the others. "Make sure the kitchen doors are locked."

Stevie looked confused, but Amanda sprang up and went into the kitchen. "They're locked," she called back, and strode into the main hallway herself.

The space was now fully dark, with not even a trace of light seeping through the snow-coated windowpanes. The others joined Amanda. They gathered by a window, trying to peer out.

Snow had buried the veranda, at least six inches, and it was still coming down. There was no sign of anyone she could see—no headlights, no footprints, nada. She looked at Holly. "Is there an outdoor light?"

"I couldn't find one."

Thump.

Everyone jumped. Nisa let out a cry as someone knocked softly from the veranda, outside one of the other rooms. The sound was followed by a series of sharper raps. On the wall? A window? They remained motionless, listening as the rapping sound began to travel along the veranda, racing from room to room, quicker and quicker, circling the house.

Amanda saw Holly's mouth fall open, mirroring her own terror as they both realized—as they all realized—that there was no way a person could move that quickly.

CHAPTER 77

Stevie swore under his breath as Holly gestured frantically for him, for everyone, to back away from the front door. "We should hide," whispered Nisa, her voice barely audible.

Holly shook her head. "They can't get in, not unless they break a window," she said confidently, but Amanda heard the effort it took for her to remain calm. "Or the door. And there's four of us."

"Maybe," said Amanda. "We should get away from the windows. Slowly. Get out of the hall. And stay low."

They did as she commanded. Holly slipped into the dining room and stood beside the entry. Amanda darted past her into the kitchen, Stevie at her heels. Nisa slid into the shadows on the far side of the grand stairway.

The rapping continued in its circuit of the house. To Amanda, each knock seemed to echo not just through the rooms but inside her, as though she'd become a bell being struck. When the sound reached the conservatory, it echoed like a thunderclap. Amanda waited for the glass to shatter but the sound had already moved on. Now it was nearing the kitchen, outpacing the wind and drowning out its howls, a ghastly clattering, drawing closer and closer. Beside her she could hear

Stevie murmur wordlessly. His voice rose shrilly, like a child's trapped by a bad dream, and she covered his mouth with her hand.

"*Stay still,*" she hissed.

She closed her eyes and held her breath as Stevie pulled away. It would see him first, it would take him. *Please take him,* she thought, tears welling behind her closed eyelids. *It can't see me, it doesn't know I'm here...*

Abruptly the rapping stopped. In the silence Amanda gasped, afraid to inhale. After a few seconds, she saw Holly peek out into the hallway. Amanda waited, fighting panic as she looked at Stevie for reassurance.

"Do you think they're gone?" he whispered, still trembling.

No one moved. The house remained silent. After several more minutes, Holly gave a nod, and the three of them tiptoed to the long dining table, where all but one of the candles had burned out. A rancid smell crept through the scents of beeswax, wine, and whiskey, as though a drain had backed up.

"It's gone," Holly said.

Stevie stared at her. "*What's* gone? What the fuck was that?"

"I don't know. The wind or—"

"That wasn't the wind."

At that moment the wind gusted, shrieking in the eaves. Everyone started, and Amanda grabbed Stevie's hand. Holly looked around, squinting into the shadows.

"Nis?" she called out. "You all right? Nisa?"

Holly walked into the dark hallway, the others behind her. "Nis?" Holly repeated, her voice cracking. "Nisa? We're all here, where are you?"

But Nisa was gone.

CHAPTER 78

Nisa had seen the black shape outside one of the windows from where she crouched beside the staircase: a sinuous shadow that slid across the veranda and then flung itself against the glass. As she watched in horror, two other shapes had joined it, all three leaping repeatedly at first the windows, then the doors, striving to get in.

The hares, she thought, giddy with terror. *They've come to kill us.*

But then the rapping stopped, and the black shapes disappeared, winking out like matches pinched between two fingers.

A deep silence blanketed her, and darkness. For a few seconds she stayed where she was, her heart pounding so hard she thought she might pass out. But then her terror receded. A strange warmth filled her limbs, almost liquid. She blinked, staring out into the hall but not seeing anything. The front door, the windows and walls, even the floor had melted into the same fluid shadows that now flowed inside her.

Instead of fear, she felt calm. Protected. Safe.

Like Stevie hiding in his room, keeping his secrets.

Just the memory of what she'd glimpsed there filled her with a mysterious, violent yearning. It was how she'd felt the night she met

Holly, singing "Hares on the Mountain" at that open mic. It was how she'd felt this afternoon in the tower. Those minutes when her voice and body and the space around them all seemed to cohere, to create some new, more powerful entity, vaster than Nisa herself. A kind of ecstasy, like an orgasm, only both inside and outside her body. She would give anything to feel that again now. The darkness knew that; it understood. She waited till Holly and Stevie and Amanda had scattered to hide, then rose to run silently up the main stairway.

It was dark up here, too, but the gloom felt more familiar, gentler. All the lights were off, save a fuzzy gray glow from the open doorway of the nursery, like a frozen computer screen. The wind must have caused the door to open.

She walked on tiptoe until she reached Stevie's room, hesitating at the door. She knew he wasn't inside, but she still felt a pang of guilt at what she was about to do. Yet he was the one who'd betrayed her. He was the one who was hiding something.

Now she grew angry. They were supposed to all be in this together, with the same goal: the play. Yet there was Stevie, upstaging her in the parlor, pulling out all the stops as that damned dog. Her voice and her songs were what knit the entire story together, even Holly had admitted that.

And where was her reward? Nisa had brought beauty and a sense of ancient mystery to Holly's words. She'd infused them with a power and terror that echoed down through centuries until Nisa held them, protected them, *shared* them with those she thought she could trust with something so precious.

But all they could see and hear were their own voices. *Petty. Selfish. Greedy.* Deaf to beauty when it rang out.

She realized then what those black shapes were—not the hares but Stevie, Holly, and Amanda. Manifesting themselves as they truly were: abominable creatures intent on stealing her voice, her power. Destroying her.

In the play, Elizabeth Sawyer cursed Tomasin. As her fingers closed on the doorknob, Nisa did the same, only she cursed Stevie, and Holly, and Amanda.

"Would I had a devil now to tear you all to pieces."

Her voice echoed in the empty hall. She hadn't realized she'd spoken aloud. Nervously she glanced at the top of the stairway. She was still alone. She opened Stevie's door and slipped inside, locking it behind her.

She used her phone's light to find the way, in case Stevie raced back upstairs to stop her. She stubbed her toe against the bed as she walked to where she'd seen him lying on the floor. His duffel bag still slumped against the wall. Hiding something, what was he trying to hide, *you goddamn sneak?* She kicked aside the duffel and trained the phone's light on the wall, where a baseboard might have been.

Oh, Stevie, she thought, and sank to her knees, *oh, Stevie, what did you find?*

A little door had been set into the wall, like something from a dollhouse. Bright green, the green of sunlight on summer grass, with a doll-sized brass doorknob. The door was waiting for her, she felt it, it might have been waiting for her since she was a girl, since that first time she opened her mouth and sang along to the radio in her father's car. Since the first time she'd seen his reaction to her voice: the power it held, even when she was a child, a power that had grown stronger in all the years since, until she arrived here and at last found the one place that could do her voice justice, a space she could fill until it shattered. She glanced over her shoulder again, grabbed the tiny doorknob, pulled it open, and gasped.

Radiant light spilled into the room, almost blinding her, the most beautiful light she'd ever seen. It didn't even register as light; it was more like an emotion, like meeting someone you immediately love. But it hadn't felt like this with Holly, not with anyone, only when she sang. She wiped tears from her eyes, hearing her heart inside her chest, its steady *thump, thump.*

Though perhaps that sound came from behind the door, as well. She bellied onto the floor and peered inside, blinking.

Shapes moved within a long tunnel, their colors luminous and shifting, colors on a butterfly's wings as it fluttered past. She cried out softly, in amazement and delight. What would it be like to touch those colors, hold them? She thrust her hand inside the tunnel, but the brilliant shapes remained just out of reach.

She took a deep breath and pressed herself against the wall, sliding her arm into the passage until it could go no farther. Grunting, she twisted, pressing harder, until she felt her shoulder slip inside the narrow space. The tunnel must have been larger than it appeared; that or the doorway was expanding. She didn't think about how strange that was, not merely strange but preposterous, only continued to push until not just her shoulder but her head and neck were inside, and then her other shoulder, her other arm. Impossible as it was, she was here, she was doing it!

She snaked into the passage, its sides scraping against her hips, until her legs were inside, too, and she could pull herself forward. Her fingers dug into the warm floor as she crawled, and all the while those dazzling shapes flickered and danced in front of her, just out of reach.

Gradually, the tunnel grew colder. Her face felt numb, and her hands. The passage must have led to an attic or an outside space—the eaves? One of the abandoned dormers she'd seen from the driveway?

But she'd gotten closer to the dancing shapes, she was sure. They'd grown slowly larger; now they loomed, immense.

She paused, for the first time unsure of herself, of what she was doing and why. The huge shapes were no longer doll sized. And they no longer shone. Their brightness dimmed, the colors bled from them until they no longer resembled toys or butterflies but something else, something from another kind of dream, a dream she'd had long ago and forgotten and now desperately didn't want to remember.

Gasping, she began to push herself backward but barely budged. The tunnel pressed against her, squeezing the air from her chest. She tried again to move but couldn't. She felt a weight against her chest and spine, massive hands cupping her, as if she were the thing to be captured and held.

Why was she here? she thought wildly. Where was Holly? *I love it when you sing.* Wait—was Holly there? She tried to turn but couldn't. "Holly?" Holly loved her, loved Nisa's voice, her songs. *Everything you do just makes what I've done so much better. I'm so lucky. We're so lucky.*

Holly had said that, right? Nisa wasn't just imagining it, she'd really said it, and meant it. Holly loved her, she'd always loved her, how could she have forgotten that? Nisa swallowed a sob. She needed to save her breath: like readying herself for a crescendo. She felt her vocal cords strain, felt the muscles quiver and vibrate, near a breaking point. But she wasn't singing, she was barely even breathing.

It wants my voice, she realized.

She flailed in the darkness, struggling to shout. *It wants my voice,* she thought again frantically. *It doesn't care about me at all only my voice it wants my voice...*

She tried once more to cry out to Holly—who was surely just there, behind her, eager to hold Nisa and feel her warmth, to press her mouth against hers. Holly was with her, she would always be with her. *Holly Holly Holly I'm so sorry Holly Holly Hol*

The air rushed from Nisa's lungs as something clasped her wrists and roared.

CHAPTER 79

Stevie stared in horror at the stairway where, minutes before, he'd seen Nisa in the shadows. The terror he'd felt at the rapping noise gave way to a greater fear: the realization that she'd seen what he had in his room and crept up there, alone, to steal it from him.

He pounded up the stairs without waiting for Holly or Amanda. "Nisa!" he shouted. "Nisa, stay out of my room!"

His door was locked. "God damn it, Nisa, let me in!" he yelled, and yanked fruitlessly at the knob. Finally he stepped back and kicked as hard as he could. The door gave way, and he fell onto the floor inside. Staggering to his feet, he switched on the overhead light and lunged across the room.

"Nisa!"

Her name died in his throat. The little door was gone. He stared, stupefied, then knelt to run his hands across the wall. The hideous wallpaper came away as he tore at it, until he was surrounded by curls of sickly violet.

But the plaster wall itself was undamaged, the surface smooth save where flecks of glue and paper clung to it. He dug his nails into the plaster but barely made a dent. He pulled at the dresser to look behind it, saw the same thing: no door, nothing but stained wallpaper and crushed silverfish.

"Nisa. Oh, Nisa..."

The door's spell was broken. He stood alone and bereft in an ugly, desolate room. Gazing at the unbroken wall where the door had been, he felt the house's gleeful spite. It had taken her, Nisa, beautiful quicksilver Nisa, and left him here, alone.

He collapsed onto the floor, weeping, where Holly and Amanda found him moments later. "Is she here?" demanded Holly. "Stevie, where is she? What did you do to her?"

"Nothing!" He looked up at her white face. "It's this room, this house—I tried to find her but it was too late..."

He stared at Holly, then Amanda.

"We have to get out of here." He stood, steadying himself against the dresser, sick with dread. "We have to leave now."

"*Where is she?*" Holly punched his arm. "Stevie, *tell me.*"

"Holly, don't," said Amanda. She looked at Stevie with concern, and also fear. "Stevie, please listen. Do you know where—"

The three of them jumped as a scream ripped through the house.

Nisa.

Holly cried out and ran into the hall. Stevie started after her and Amanda grabbed him. "Stevie! It's not safe—"

He shook her off, racing after Holly. *Hill House,* he thought in a panic, the words circling his mind, probing for a way in, like that diabolical knocking. *It hates us.*

Holly screamed again. *"Nisa—"*

"Holly, wait!" he yelled.

He saw her running from one door to the next, flinging each open to look inside before she staggered back into the hall. On the wall beside him, a tarnished mirror held a blotch of grayish white, a deformed face reflected from somewhere across the hall. *Nisa,* he thought, reeling, but then it shifted from Nisa's face to that of a teenage boy, his long hair combed back so Stevie clearly saw his deep-set, hostile glare, the frayed collar of a denim jacket. An earthy taste filled Stevie's mouth, grit and a spongy substance clinging to his tongue.

Mushrooms, he thought, trying not to gag. Bad mushrooms. He ran his hands through his own hair and glanced again at the mirror. The face was his own. Quickly he looked down, to the wood panel beneath the mirror.

"Oh god, no. Nisa..."

He bent to trace the carving there. A young woman fleeing some unseen pursuer, her arms outstretched, her mouth a perfect O of terror within the nimbus of her wildly curling hair.

CHAPTER 80

S tevie!" Amanda grabbed his shoulder, pulling him upright.
"Come on!"

Stevie looked at her, dazed. She pointed to where Holly stood, just outside the nursery. When he didn't react, Amanda snapped her fingers in his face. "Stevie! Wake up! We have to get Holly. We all have to leave, *now.*"

But Amanda, too, was staring past Holly, into the nursery. Things were moving inside the room, glittering shapes that emerged slowly from the shadows. They rolled across the room like fog, black and oily, accompanied by a low hum like an electrical current; she felt its charge all the way out here. A putrid smell filled the hall as grainy figures appeared in the haze, flickering in and out of view. A skinny teenage boy? A woman, dress flowing out around her as she danced. Even more ghastly, inching grublike across the floor—an infant.

And another young woman, whose fractured silhouette Amanda knew was Nisa's. Her form roiled in the fog, turning to the open doorway, lifting her hands in supplication. Stevie watched her, helpless and aghast, until Holly's voice rang through the hall.

"Nisa!" she screamed, and started for the door.

"Holly!" Amanda shouted. She began to run after her. "Holly, don't—!"

Holly flinched as though she'd heard Amanda but didn't look back. Instead, she stepped over the threshold, into the nursery.

An earsplitting boom rattled the hall. Stevie lurched to one side, striking the wall as Amanda fell beside him. He righted himself and pulled her to her feet. The two of them turned to see Holly framed just inside the nursery door.

Another boom, as though a jet had exploded overhead. Again Amanda fell, but this time she scrambled back up on her own, pushing Stevie away roughly. Ahead of them, Holly's form was disintegrating into the shadows.

Amanda drew her arm up in front of her face and strode resolutely toward the nursery.

"Amanda, no!" Stevie yelled again, and grabbed her.

CHAPTER 81

Amanda tried to shake him off, but Stevie was strong for such a scrawny guy, his fingers digging into her arms. The two of them wrestled until they were inches from the doorway, a charged pulse like static electricity shimmering in the room beyond. Inside, Holly turned in a slow circle, staring at the walls. Amanda could barely see, but something was dripping down them in heavy streaks, black runnels that shone in the glittery light.

Blood, thought Amanda. *It's blood.* A rusty scent flooded her mouth, carrion and copper, and she fought the urge to gag. Inside, things were being carried along by the dark flow, like leaves in a stream. Scraps of purple velvet, a twist of silver thread. Part of a shoe. An ankle boot? Amanda stumbled forward, nauseated, and nearly fell.

"Hold my hand," Stevie ordered, tightening his grip. "Don't look at the wall—don't look at anything but her. Holly!"

This time, he called out in a deliberately casual tone, a man trying to calm a spooked horse. "Holly, come here."

His grasp grew even tighter as he nudged Amanda forward. "I have you," he whispered. "Grab her hand. I'll pull you both back out. Don't let go of me, whatever you do. We have to make a circuit." He glanced up at the carved faces, their malign gazes meeting just above his head. "I'll stay out here; that way I'll ground you. All of us."

The entire house shook as another boom ripped through it. Behind them, doors slammed open and shut. Amanda swallowed, tasting bile. She nodded and, keeping her gaze fixed on Holly, stepped into the nursery.

Frigid air poured over her. She felt her hair crisp and her skin tighten.

"Holly," she called. Could Holly even hear her? Amanda's own ears rang like she'd been struck. "Holly, take my hand."

Holly gazed only at the wall, her face blank in the shimmering gray light. Amanda lifted her own head to stare up at the ceiling. There was a crack she hadn't noticed before, spreading quickly, scattering tiny chunks of plaster across the floor, like shattered teeth.

The house was breaking apart.

As she stared, something else emerged from the crack, glistening white and streaked with red. *Oh my god, please no...* Amanda squeezed her eyes shut and strained forward, until her fingers grazed Holly's arm. Despite the freezing cold, her other palm was slick with sweat where Stevie clasped it, and she felt her fingers sliding from his, little by little. A smell filled her nostrils, rotting meat and putrid water, but also the hint of something sweet and fragrant, narcissus just starting to bloom, or lilacs, or freesia. She couldn't look, yet she could sense it in the room above them, its steady heartbeat as it pushed down against the ceiling, until it had nearly broken through...

For a second she hesitated. But then, behind her, she felt Stevie tighten his grip. She opened her eyes, grabbed Holly's arm, and yanked her backward with all her strength.

An infernal crash resounded as plaster exploded into the air. Amanda screamed as she fell toward the threshold, but she managed to keep hold of Holly. Stevie let go of the doorframe to grab them both, and all three tumbled out, onto the floor of the hall.

"Go go go go go," Stevie chanted, staggering to his feet. Amanda frantically ran her hands over her face, her hair, but there was no plaster dust, no blood, only her own skin. *Thank god.* Next to her, Holly swayed, half standing, her eyes unfocused. He and Amanda hoisted her between them and stumbled toward the stairs. Behind them the roaring continued, the walls beginning to move in and out like a bellows, like the rise and fall of a chest as someone breathes. A closet door flew open, nearly knocking Stevie over and releasing a cloud of rancid air. Amanda choked but kept going, slowing only when she approached her bedroom.

"No!" Stevie shouted, seeing her longing glance. "We'll have to come back—"

At the top of the steps, Stevie took Holly's chin in his hand. "Holly. Your keys—do you have your car keys?"

She stared at him without comprehension, and he patted her down, dug his hand into her front pocket to withdraw the keys.

"Go," he directed Amanda.

They half ran, half fell downstairs, still carrying Holly between them. Amanda didn't look back. She didn't need to. She felt the house bearing down on them, saw blood trickling from the walls, a clotted shape clutching a ribbon of wallpaper, peeling it from the wall.

When they reached the main floor, Holly was only a limp mannequin, her head lolling. But the floor beneath them was stable, until they neared the front door, where Amanda slipped on something wet. She looked down.

"Amanda, hold her," Stevie yelled as Amanda, too, began to crumple.

It took all her effort but she straightened, keeping her gaze from the floor. She clung to Holly's dead weight as Stevie grabbed the doorknob, turned it, and pushed. The door didn't move. He tried again, then leaned over to look out the window.

"The snow's blocking it," he said. "It's drifted onto the porch."

Amanda shouldered alongside him at the door, trying not to drop Holly. Together they pushed until the door moved, first an inch, then another. Snow fell into the house, like crumbs of white cake. When the door had opened about eight inches, Stevie motioned for Amanda to go through first.

She squeezed out into a wall of snow, thigh deep. Holly emerged next, as Amanda tried to keep her from sprawling facedown into the drifts. The cold seemed to wake her from her stupor, and she clutched at Amanda.

"Did you hear her?" she whispered, eyes wild.

"Amanda!"

Amanda looked back to see Stevie standing half-in, half-out of the door with its cast-iron knocker, its leering face a mocking mirror of Stevie's terror. As she stared, the door began to close on him, slowly but inexorably, trapping him inside.

"Holly, don't move," Amanda commanded.

She swiped snow from her eyes and fought her way back through the drift to the door. Fury surged through her, the same fury that had fueled Elizabeth Sawyer in Holly's play, the fury that kept Amanda alive. *Not here, not like this.*

"Let go of him!" she yelled, and thrust her arm through the gap to grasp at Stevie's shoulder. Bracing herself, she gritted her teeth and pulled.

With a cry, he fell forward. Amanda caught him as the door's jaws snapped angrily shut, the sound reverberating through the house behind him, its echo roaring like flames, like a refrain in her head, words she couldn't understand but whose hateful meaning was clear.

"Keys," Stevie murmured weakly, his face white, and he opened his hand.

Amanda took them. "Ready?" she shouted above the wind. Holly, still standing dazed where Amanda had left her, nodded slowly.

They made their way through the snow, sliding down the steps to the drive, arms intertwined, and on toward Holly's half-buried car. Behind them, deafening hammering echoed from Hill House, some vast trapped thing trying to fight its way out.

When they reached the car, Holly turned to stare at the upper story, her eyes wild with anguish.

"I heard her," she sobbed. "I heard her..."

Amanda drew Holly into her arms as Stevie furiously swiped snow from the windshield with his shirtsleeves.

"It's okay," Amanda whispered to Holly, though of course it wasn't, nothing was. She felt Holly shudder in her arms.

"She was singing," Holly went on through chattering teeth. "That song, her favorite. When I was in the nursery, I could hear her."

Amanda shivered, remembering Nisa in the tower. How, from outside, her song had sounded like a scream. She could never tell Holly. "I don't think so, Holly." *That thing in the ceiling.* "I didn't hear anything."

Slowly, Holly turned her ruined gaze from Hill House to Amanda.

"That's because she wasn't singing to you."

EPILOGUE

For a long time, over a year, Stevie and I avoided each other. Nisa's disappearance cast ripples into our small circle, ripples that, as the months passed, extended out, into the realm of podcasts and Reddit and arcane websites.

I extended my leave of absence from teaching. Nisa was officially a missing person. But only a cursory investigation took place, and her body was never found. Even the state police were reluctant to probe too deeply into whatever might have occurred at Hill House.

Ainsley had refunded the money I'd given her, with a terse note appended to her email, signed not just by herself, but by Melissa and Evadne as well.

We warned you.

She had—but she had also allowed us in Hill House. Why? Perhaps Ainsley, in a way, was as much its victim as Nisa.

Giorgio had gone back, with Ainsley, to get our things. When I asked him if Hill House appeared badly damaged, he looked confused.

"No. It seemed fine. Like no one had ever been there."

I gave up the apartment I'd shared with Nisa and moved into Giorgio and Theresa's two-bedroom in Sunnyside. The whole time, I felt insulated by shock. The police told me Nisa had simply run away. Stevie, Amanda, and I knew that wasn't true.

Still, the year did pass. I'd offered to return my grant money, but the arts director had gently refused. "Take some time, Holly," she said on the phone. "You may yet be able to make something of your play. Or write a new one. Right now, you need to grieve, and not worry about the money."

Slowly, as another year wound down, I started writing again. About the same time, Stevie appeared at my door one night, unannounced.

"Here," he said, pushing past me as he held up his laptop bag. His unwashed hair hung below his shoulders, and he hadn't shaved for weeks. "I want you to listen to these."

It was a stash of recordings he'd made of Nisa singing—old open mic performances, recordings of when she was working out early versions of the ballads for the play. Even the voices he'd discovered on his laptop on that fateful day when he'd explored the nursery. I almost couldn't bear to listen to them, but as Stevie sat beside me and held me, I began to sob uncontrollably, thinking of Nisa and also of Macy-Lee, and how their voices had been silenced, except for these eerie traces that Stevie had managed to retain.

"This is what we have, Holly," he said when the recording at last ended, and I could finally breathe again. "We should use it. You should use it."

I did, hours spent at my laptop, writing new material and revising what I'd already done. *Witching Night* became a palimpsest—Elizabeth Sawyer's story, Macy-Lee's, Nisa's, my own, shuffled and reshuffled like a deck of tarot cards. The Witch. The Muse. The Singer. The Ghost Child. The Lover. The Balladeer. The Dog.

Death.

Now when I cried, I felt like different nerves were firing in my head.

Stevie joined me in working feverishly on the project. He tracked down demos that Nisa had made, from clubs and friends, and added them to what we already had.

Amanda had kept her distance from us, but she'd never stopped working. One morning, I called her to ask if she'd consider getting on board with the revamped play. I gave her the details and projected dates, holding my breath when she said nothing.

"You're too busy," I finally said, not bothering to hide my distress. "I'll see if I can find someone else."

"Do that and I'll sabotage your opening," she retorted.

Another year passed. As October approached, we finally had the downtown showcase ready, reframed as a two-hander for Stevie and Amanda Greer, with Nisa's ethereal voice echoing through the shoebox theater. Within days, I had an offer to bring the show to a prestigious experimental venue in DUMBO.

The unsolved disappearance of a beautiful young person always makes good box office.

None of us ever told anyone else what happened at Hill House. Sometimes—often—I dream of it, and of Nisa. Not as I'd last seen her, trapped within the nursery, but singing "Hares on the Mountain" in a forest clearing. Three fluid black shapes circle her, their dark forms gradually shimmering into columns of light, figures that rise into the night sky, silver rings bright as stars.

Stevie had the same dream, he told me once, and Amanda, too.

Only Hill House neither sleeps nor dreams. Shrouded within its overgrown lawns and sprawling woodlands, the long shadows of mountains and ancient oaks, Hill House only watches. Hill House waits.

ACKNOWLEDGMENTS

Writing this novel was a dream come true for someone steeped in Shirley Jackson's work from a very young age. I can't offer enough gratitude to Laurence Jackson Hyman, Jackson's son and literary executor, who entrusted me with this project and offered his suggestions and encouragement throughout the years it took to bring it to life.

Heartfelt thanks to my agent, Danielle Bukowski, for all her advice and support, and to everyone else at Sterling Lord Literistic, as well as to Murray Weiss, representative for the Shirley Jackson estate. Their combined efforts made this book possible.

Helen O'Hare, my editor at Mulholland Books, as ever did an exceptional job of reading, rereading, editing, and re-editing my work. Thanks, too, to my wonderful publicist, Alyssa Persons, and marketing director Bryan Christian for all their help, as well as to copyediting chief Betsy Uhrig. A big shout-out as well to Rosanna Forte, my UK editor at Sphere, who shares my love of ghost stories, haunted houses, and, of course, Shirley Jackson.

My Stonecoast colleague and friend Tom Coash offered insights and suggestions based on his long and successful career as a playwright (unlike Holly's).

ACKNOWLEDGMENTS

My daughter, Callie Hand, read an early draft and shared her comments, especially as regards who should and shouldn't die at the end.

While writing this novel, I discovered the music of the extraordinary singer/songwriter Fern Maddie, whose rendition of "Hares on the Mountain" haunts Nisa's own. (Longtime readers may recognize this as the same song I used as an epigraph for *Waking the Moon* many years ago, under the title "Maying Song.") Check out Maddie's work at fernmaddiemusic .com and https://fernmaddie.bandcamp.com.

Finally, my love to my partner, John Clute, as always my literary and emotional true north.

ABOUT THE AUTHOR

ELIZABETH HAND is the author of more than nineteen cross-genre novels and collections of short fiction, including *Hokuloa Road, The Book of Lamps and Banners,* and *Curious Toys.* Her work has received the Shirley Jackson Award (three times), the World Fantasy Award (four times), and the Nebula Award (twice), as well as the James M. Tiptree Jr. and Mythopoeic Society Awards. She's a longtime critic and contributor of essays for the *Washington Post,* the *Los Angeles Times, Salon, Boston Review,* and the *Village Voice,* among many others. She divides her time between the Maine coast and North London.